OTHER BOOKS BY THIS AUTHOR:

Out of the Storm

The Bridge Series

Deception Bridge
Broken Contracts
Premonition Bridge

The Whispering Art Series

Watercolor Whispers
Whispered Warnings

GLORIA BOSTIC

Year of the Book
135 Glen Avenue
Glen Rock, PA 17327

Print ISBN: 978-1-64649-128-5
eBook ISBN: 978-1-64649-129-2

Library of Congress Control Number: 2020923568

Dedication

To some of the most important people in our lives:

- Our military who leave their families and friends to protect our country and our freedom knowing they could pay the ultimate price
- Our police officers and firefighters who leave home and family to protect us here at home knowing they may not return to their own
- Our medical professionals who work tirelessly to care for us when we are most vulnerable
- Our teachers who, at every level, help us to continue to learn and grow to our full potential
- Our mental health workers who are there to guide us and help us become our best selves
- Our support groups who encourage us, let us know we are not alone, and keep us moving forward
- Our friends and families who bring joy into our lives and make life worth living

Thank you.

ACKNOWLEDGMENTS

I would like to acknowledge all those in Ramona's Sprint Club for being there each morning and providing a place for accountability and mutual encouragement to write every day. Special thanks to Ramona herself who founded the group and helped so many writers along the way, and Wende who has kept it going since Ramona's passing.

I would like to thank Year of the Book Press and Demi Stevens for the constant love, support, and encouragement that make me believe I can do this.

I would like to thank my family and friends, especially my husband, for their patience as I hammer away at the keyboard day after day in pursuit of my goals.

And finally, I would like to thank my readers. Without you I fear I would feel like a crazy person talking endlessly to myself.

CHAPTER ONE

It was a stroke—not of luck, but of a brain blockage—that was about to change Mia Reed's life and take her away from Pittsburgh and everything familiar and comfortable in her new life as an art therapist.

Stunned, she clutched her phone, barely noticing when Simeon jumped in her lap to comfort her. She stared out the window, absently stroking the cat's silver-gray fur with her free hand.

"I'd better get going before..." Morgan took one look at her roommate and put on the brakes before reaching the door. "What's wrong?"

"My mom called. It... it's my grandpa." Mia lowered her head, letting her light brown hair hide the tears. "He... he had a stroke."

"Oh Mia, I'm so sorry. What can I do? Is he..." Morgan didn't finish her sentence, but Mia knew what she was asking.

"No. No, Grandma was there when it happened and called 9-1-1. He's in the emergency room, and she's there with him. They're all at the hospital..." The words trailed off as Mia stared out the window. "I should be there."

Mia crumpled into the chair, and her roommate quickly crouched next to her and took her hand. "Can I get you some water or something? Maybe tea?" Mia appreciated that, even though she was only four years younger than her roommate, Morgan had a tendency to look after her. Mia assumed it was because she looked much younger than her twenty-three years, and perhaps, as she'd often been told, because she was somewhat naïve.

"No, no, I'm okay. I mean, I don't need anything. But..." When the tears Mia had been holding back started rushing down her cheeks, Morgan ran for the tissues. "Aren't you going to be late?" Mia managed to ask between sobs.

"Don't be silly. Lunch with the girls on our floor is no big deal," Morgan said pulling out her phone and texting a quick message. "I know I'm the comic relief, but they can manage one lunch without me."

Mia attempted to smile, but there was no sign of her usual dimple as she gave it up and blew her nose. "I want to go home," she said still stroking Simeon who, determined to help, nuzzled under her chin.

"Of course you do, and you won't have any trouble getting time off."

"No, Morgan. I mean yes, I need to get some time off right away, but I need more than that. I don't want to be this far away from my family every time something happens." Mia stared out the window of their small southside Pittsburgh apartment that she and Morgan had shared for the last few years. She had created a comfortable life here, as comfortable as the oversized brown chair they called the big brown beast... the only thing holding her up at the moment. But there was another place calling her away. Calling her home. "I should be there when they need me."

"I get that, and I know it must feel that way now, but you couldn't have done anything if you'd been there. I'm sure everything's going to be okay."

"You don't understand, Morgan. This isn't the first time I've thought about it. I know it may sound crazy—I'm not a child—but I miss my family. I miss being near them and seeing them whenever I want." Mia looked up at her roommate. "I don't want to desert you and leave you stuck with no one to share expenses, but I've been considering it for a while, and I think I want to move somewhere closer to my hometown. Closer to my family."

Morgan's face lost all its usual animation. With her eyes cast down, she nodded. "I can't say I'm shocked," she said. "I know how you feel about your family, and honestly, if I had a family like yours, I guess I'd want to spend more time with them too." Morgan patted Mia's hand. "Don't worry. With my winning personality, I'll find another roommate in no time. But where will you live, and where will you work? And what about Ron?"

Yeah, what about Ron? Mia's relationship with Detective Ronald Bishop was still new and she wondered if it could survive the distance. "I know. I've got a lot to figure out," she said, getting up slowly and moving toward her bedroom, "but right now I've got to make a few phone calls and pack. I want to get to Madison by early evening."

***

The trip home began smoothly on that sunny, summer afternoon, but two hours into the drive Mia hit a gray wall of torrential rain. Bolts of lightning cut through the purple sky ahead, joined almost immediately by thunder like a drummer gone mad. She wasn't shocked by the downpour since this August had been filled with hot humid days, many of which turned into angry afternoon storms followed by calm and beautiful rainbows. *But this is ridiculous!* With the windshield wipers working frantically to give her a tiny bit of visibility, Mia squinted to keep the taillights of the car in front of her within sight while she searched for another rest area to pull off the turnpike. She didn't see anywhere to exit the highspeed highway until she was passing the off-ramps and too late to make the turn.

Luckily, before long she'd driven through the storm and could lower her shoulders from her ears. Mia turned off the windshield wipers, gave thanks for the bright sunshine, and searched the sky for one of those rainbows.

But the lovely respite was not to last. Long before she reached her exit, Mia could see the next storm front, and passing through this curtain of rain was like rushing headlong from daylight into a dangerous dungeon of darkness.

Mia leaned forward. She turned the radio way down so she could see better. Fingers clenched in a death grip on the steering wheel, her nerves were raw. Then the cell phone shrieked. Mia jumped at the sound. She fumbled to grab the device and read the screen: *Tornado warning!* Having passed the last rest-stop on this part of the turnpike, there was no escape… nowhere to go to get out of the storm. Beyond panic, she thought, *Why did I say no?*

When she'd called Ron to tell him what was going on, he had offered to drive her home, but Mia thought that was ridiculous. Since starting at Seton Hill University, she had made the drive from Pittsburgh to her hometown enough times to almost do it in her sleep. And though he said it would be a good excuse to spend more time with her, Mia was sure the man she was falling in love with was actually worried about her driving while upset over her grandfather.

"I am not a child," she had argued. *"And I'm totally capable of keeping my emotions under control while I drive."* It was their first disagreement—if you could even call it that—since Mia and Detective Ronald Bishop had started seeing each other. Ever since that terrifying night at the Alessi house when she'd thought a suspected murderer might end her life, she and Ron had been spending as much time together as their schedules allowed, and as soon as they said their goodbyes, Mia would look forward to the next time she'd see him.

But now she had to find a way to tell him she was leaving Pittsburgh permanently. *Am I crazy?*

Another crack of thunder called her attention back to the task before her—getting to Madison, Pennsylvania, and not Oz. *God, please keep me safe.* And from within she heard the familiar *"Trust in the Lord."*

Though the storm didn't let up until Mia was nearly home, she saw no sign of a tornado—the only whirlwind was in her mind which calmed when she reached Madison General and the arms of her family.

She soon learned Grandpa Reed would probably have a long recovery, but with time and therapy, he should fully regain the use of his left side. And Mia knew somehow everything else would be okay too. She had many decisions to make—questions for which she must find answers—but the important thing right now was being with family. As for the rest, she decided, like Scarlett O'Hara, *I'll think about that tomorrow.*

And Mia knew, somehow, she must find a way for her tomorrows to include Ron Bishop.

CHAPTER TWO

When she got to the hospital, Mia dashed through the rain and spotted her sister Julie rushing across the hospital lobby to meet her. "I love my sister!" Lacking the joy and giggles that usually accompanied this phrase, the two girls murmured the familiar words in unison as they embraced. Then stepping back Julie said, "I thought you'd never get here. They said the storms were wicked. Are you all right?"

"Yes, I'm fine, but how is Grandpa? Is he still in the ER?" Heading for the elevator, Mia shoved her keys in the side pocket of the small backpack she'd thrown over her shoulder.

"No, they finally got him settled in a private room a couple hours ago. It was a long night for Grandma and Dad, and a long day for all of us." Julie's long, thick mop of dark brown hair was pulled back into a hasty ponytail, and Mia noticed she hadn't even bothered with any makeup. Just a little lip gloss.

"Is he really going to be okay?" Mia asked.

"Yes, eventually, but don't be surprised when you see him. He looks pretty rough... older, yanno?" Julie pushed the button for the third floor. "And his speech is slurred—kind of sounds like he's had too much to drink." Julie laughed but Mia could see the fear in her eyes.

"Don't worry, Jules," she said with a sudden need to comfort her sister. "From what Mom said, Grandma got him help right away. He should have a good chance of a full recovery. Speech therapists are great with stroke victims." Mia wished she was as confident as she tried to sound.

A nurse Julie recognized from earlier when they were getting Dr. Reed settled was coming out of their grandfather's room. She motioned for them to stop before they could go rushing in. "I'm sorry, but he should only have two visitors at a time, and his wife is with him now."

"No worries, you go ahead, Mia. I'll be in the visitor's waiting room. It's right across the hall down there," she said pointing to the sign and backing away.

When Mia finally entered his room, after the shock of the phone call, hours driving through a crazy storm, and scary conversations in her head, she still wasn't prepared for seeing both her grandparents looking so much older than when she'd visited over the Christmas holiday.

Mia gave her grandma a tight squeeze and whispered, "Is he sleeping?" Valerie Reed shrugged so Mia quietly approached the bed and placed her hand on his. Dr. Andy Reed's eyes snapped open and he gave her a slow lopsided smile.

"I'm sho glad you came, but you... didn't have..."

"Shh, don't be silly, Grandpa. Of course, I'm here." Feeling his gentle squeeze, Mia thought at least it was fortunate that it was his left side experiencing the paralysis. Temporary paralysis, she hoped. "You just rest."

"But you drove—"

"Now Andy, don't argue with your granddaughter," Grandma Val interrupted. "She's right, and besides," she said turning to face Mia, "she must be tired after that long drive. Aren't you, dear?"

Mia nodded and saw her grandfather's resignation. He rolled his eyes, then allowed his heavy eyelids to close. "Grandma, are you okay?" she asked softly.

"Your grandpa gave me quite a scare, but I know he's going to be okay. He's a fighter," she said nodding in his direction. "Where's your sister?"

"She's waiting for me down in the visitor's waiting room. Since she came with Mom earlier, she's going to ride back with me."

Sudden heightened awareness of her grandparents' aging became the deciding factor. Mia made up her mind then and there. It was definitely time to come home to be near her family and spend time with them while she still could. After all, everyone she loved was here.

Well... almost everyone. Everyone but Ron...

On their ride back to the family home Julie was checking emails on her phone when Mia shared her decision, and she was surprised by her sister's reaction.

Julie abruptly stopped looking at her phone and gave Mia her full attention. "It's about time," she said. "I knew you couldn't stay away forever. You're such a home-body. One question, though—what about your new beau?"

Mia took her eyes off the road long enough to glance over. "I... well, I don't know exactly. And who even says *beau* anymore anyway?" She grinned, loving how Julie used language. "But I'll just have to figure out this whole *beau* situation somehow. I think Ron will understand. It will either work out between us or it won't. Regardless, like I said, my mind is made up."

There was a long pause before Julie said, "Well, if you're sure—absolutely sure—then I have an idea." Her smile grew wider and her eyes crinkled. "Turn here," she said pointing to the next intersection.

"What? Why?" Mia asked.

"I have something I want to show you."

After fifteen minutes and several more turns Mia asked, "Isn't Mom going to wonder where we are?"

"You're right. I'll text her. Oh, there, turn right at the corner onto Glen View Court."

Mia gave Julie another sidelong glance, curiosity piqued, and made the turn onto a quiet, tree-lined street. It was a dead-end, and Julie told her to pull up to the little cottage with a For Sale sign at the end of the cul-de-sac.

"Well... what do you think?"

"About what?" Mia asked.

"About this, this splendid little cottage." Julie had already opened her door and hopped out. "Do you love it?"

Mia looked at the two-story cottage with its yellow siding, white trim, and big front porch. It even had a little white picket fence that made it storybook perfect. "It's adorable, Jules, but who lives here? I mean, what are we doing here anyway?" Even in the fading daylight, Mia could see the charm of this place and understood her sister's enthusiasm. What she didn't understand was why Julie had brought her here, and why she had such a big grin and twinkle in her eyes.

"I think we should buy it," Julie said pointing to the For Sale sign.

"What?"

"I think we should buy it. You and me. Think about it." Julie headed up the path toward the front porch then cut over to stand in front of the two-car garage. "You're going to need a place to live. And listen, I've been saving my pennies while I lived at home, and even this past year in my tiny apartment. I'm finally ready to move on... I want a house, more space, a yard. You know, like a grown-up." Julie's childlike joy was contagious and Mia began to imagine it. "And heaven knows we've had our whole lives to test our compatibility in living together. C'mon," Julie said taking the path around the house. "Come look at the back."

Mia followed, her mind spinning. "Aren't we trespassing?" She glanced up at the windows to see if they were being watched, and jumped as raindrops fell down her neck from the young silver maple in the front yard.

"No. The owners have already moved out—something about the guy being transferred—so it's priced to sell. I'm telling you, this is perfect!"

"But, but how did you know it? I mean, I didn't even know until this afternoon that I was moving back. How could you—"

"I didn't know you were coming back now, but I've been looking for a place, and even though it would really be stretching my budget, I knew I wanted this one." Julie extended her arms and turned in circles across the pavers and onto the wet grass. "Look at it, Mia! And wait 'til you see the inside. There's even a stream beyond that tree line." Her words bubbled out with her enthusiasm as she twirled back to face Mia. "So, what do you think, sis? Wanna be roomies?"

"I think I need to sit down," Mia said reeling from all the events of the day. "Let's head back now, okay? I'm exhausted." She also needed time to think. Everything was moving so fast. Could she really live with Julie again? Yes, she loved her, but their personality styles were so different, and though she would never tell her, Julie's laid-back attitude, her habit of procrastinating, and her tendency to presume things without asking, could all be rather annoying.

"Oh Mia, I'm sorry. Of course you are. And I'm rambling on and on. I didn't mean to overwhelm you." Once back in the car she added, "I got so darned excited thinking we could afford this together, and I'd have the best roommate ever."

"Yeah, right," Mia said pulling the seatbelt across and fastening it. "Until Mr. Right comes along and you kick me out."

"That's not going to happen. At least not for quite a while. Since Travis, I haven't even started seeing anybody. Anyhow, we'll cross that bridge when we come to it."

Mia looked at her sister. *She really is the sweetest.* And then she saw it. "Look Julie, there's a rainbow." It was one of those special ones she could see from one end to the other, and it ended right behind the charming little cottage. She wondered if it was a sign.

On the drive back to the Reed family home, the conversation drifted back to Grandpa Andy's condition and other family matters, but somewhere in the back of her mind, the idea of living in Sweet Glen with her sister—despite their differences—began to take root. Mia didn't want to make such a big decision—such a drastic change—on a whim, but the idea certainly had its appeal.

***

The next morning, sitting around the breakfast table with Julie, her dad, and her step-mother, Mia poured herself a second cup of tea and refilled her step-mother's cup. Mia's biological mother had died in a tragic accident when Mia was five years old, and her father had eventually married Sarah Reed, creating a blended family that worked. Sarah had always been a coffee drinker until she began trying the wonderfully home-brewed teas introduced to her by Mia.

"Where is everybody this morning?" Julie said reaching for the bacon.

"Destiny had her junior golf tournament so she won't be home for hours, and Cody got in late last night, about 2:30. I'm glad he's sleeping in," Sarah said.

"Is Bobby going to be here?" Mia asked, looking around the big eat-in kitchen. The blue banquette in front of the bowed window was so much cozier than the dining room which, though beautiful with its long table and gorgeous chandelier, was better suited for their big family gatherings.

"No, I convinced your little brother he really didn't need to come home. We know your grandfather is going to be all right." Sarah met her husband's eyes. "Honestly, between his summer job and this latest girlfriend, I think Bobby was relieved to be able to stay in West Chester. Craig, did you want more coffee?"

"No, I'm good." Mia's father leaned back in his chair and smiled at her. "It's good to have two of my favorite girls here although you really needn't have come, Mia. Grandpa is going to be okay." Craig Reed had been shaken by his father's stroke, and the realization he could have lost him. Mia had heard it in the short prayer he'd uttered when she arrived the night before.

"I know, Dad, but I had to come home and see for myself. Besides, I missed you guys. As a matter of fact—"

"She's coming home!" Julie interrupted.

Sarah and Craig looked from her to Mia, seeming bewildered. "What are you talking about?" Sarah grinned. "She is home."

"What she means is, I'm *thinking about* moving back to the area." Mia could have strangled her sister for making the announcement before she was certain. Instead she sipped her tea and saw how delighted her parents were by the possibility. Their reaction pushed her even closer to making a final decision.

Now, as she listened to and joined in the chatter, it was like she'd never left—well almost. This was the familiar, comfortable life she missed. This was what she wanted... to spend time with her family.

And someday she wanted a family of her own, but she wanted it with Ron. Mia could envision sitting around a table—something more modest would be fine—with Ron seated across from her and maybe a highchair next to her. Perhaps there would be Sunday dinners with lots of family enjoying a beautiful ham and pineapples... But Ron was back in Pittsburgh, and she didn't know if he would ever be willing to move to a small town like this. If he would ever be willing to leave that area until he found his missing twin sister, Robin.

"Have you thought about where you'll work?" Her father's question quickly brought Mia back to her present-day reality.

"No," she admitted, "and that could put a screeching halt to all my plans." She took another sip of tea and turned to Sarah. "You wouldn't happen to need an art therapist in the Reed Practice, would you?"

Sarah's answered surprised her. "As a matter of fact, yes. First of all, your grandpa will be off until he is fully recovered—that is if he doesn't retire altogether—and besides that, we were already short-handed since we lost Nancy."

"What? You mean Nancy isn't at the Center anymore?" Nancy Owens had joined the practice about two years earlier.

"Oh, that's right, I didn't tell you..." Sarah's eyes filled with tears, and she seemed unable to go on.

Mia turned to her father for help understanding. He explained that the young therapist had apparently jumped to her death exactly one week before. Mia gasped, and her jaw dropped.

"No!" Sarah said. "I'll never believe that. Nan had everything to live for and no reason to end her life. We saw her fiancé, Garrett, at the funeral, and he seems devastated—"

"But maybe they were having problems you didn't know about," Julie said.

"Maybe, but still..." Sarah went on to explain that she and Dr. Reed were certain someone had pushed her to her death. "As you can imagine, Mia, we were struggling to meet the needs of all our clients between the four of us. Now—at least for a while—there will only be Gabby, Dr. Block, and me trying to see everyone. We were already looking for someone to take Nan's place, and having an art therapist on staff would be wonderful. Seriously, you joining the practice would be a real godsend."

Mia no longer needed to think about it. "It kind of looks like it's meant to be. I guess I'm in." She smiled as her mother reached across and took her hand. She was coming home.

Chapter Three

Fifteen years earlier

Dazed and confused, Robin Bishop stared at the gray cinderblock walls. There was nothing else to look at. Nothing but damp, blank walls and a doorway into the bathroom—if you could even call it a bathroom—where she knew there was nothing but a toilet and sink—not even a light—and barely room to turn around. No mirror. No tub or shower. Not even a door. Certainly nothing like her bathroom at home with its soaker tub and separate shower. She tried to remember the warm water and the scent of lavender as she lingered in the bubble bath, but the dampness and odor of must and mildew invaded her senses.

Pushing herself to a sitting position, she stared up at the bit of light coming through the single, tiny window near the ceiling. She could tell there were some kind of overgrown shrubs blocking it because of the small amount of light coming in, and even that little bit was fading. Soon she would be in total darkness again.

Robin tried to focus, tried to remember, but she was losing the battle against something—the will to fight—what? What was it that kept stealing her reality? And what was her new reality? She reached for the paper plate on the floor. Maybe if she ate a little more... no. She had to lie down again. She was spiraling down, down, down...

Robin woke to total darkness and the absolute need to use the bathroom, but she couldn't begin to see how to get there. She vaguely remembered that if she got up from the side of the bed, it should be straight ahead, so she slowly moved in that direction, arms extended, until she felt the block wall. She reached her hands out to either side and found the opening with her right hand.

Feeling her way to the toilet, she was able to relieve herself. Then out the door... straight ahead... "Ow!" She fell onto the bed and grabbed her shin, crying out. She realized she would have to count the steps, learn how not to crack her shin on the damn metal bedframe.

Lying in the darkness, the fifteen-year-old dragged her fingers through stringy blonde hair that hadn't seen a comb or brush in days—she didn't know how many—and thought of all the mornings she'd sat at her dressing table brushing her silky golden locks, admiring herself, especially her blue eyes that everyone said looked so much like her brother's. Thinking of Ronnie brought a new wave of despair rolling over her. She drew the flimsy cover under her chin trying to stave off the cold dampness, trying to flee the discomfort, trying to erase the memory of seeing her parents' bodies and being told her brother was dead upstairs, by going back to sleep. But sleep eluded her. Wide awake but still in a nightmare.

Only this nightmare was real, and she saw no escape. Even if she could get out of this hell-hole, she knew she would never get her old life back. She could still see her parents' bodies—and all that blood—so much blood—and remembered the scream that wouldn't come out. And the faces of the monsters who killed them. The monsters who took her from her home and locked her in this place.

How long ago was it—three days, four, a week—since she'd celebrated her fifteenth birthday with her twin brother, Ronnie? She'd been so happy, so excited when her parents said their birthday present was going to be a trip to Disney. Now, instead of Disney World, she was here and they were gone. All of them gone. Though she never saw Ronnie's body, she knew he was dead too. The monsters told her so when they locked her in. And it had all happened so fast. Why?

Though she thought she had none left, her tears fell again until she was completely drained. She couldn't believe she would never see her parents or her brother again. Couldn't believe they were dead, yet knew it was true.

But she was alive, and she meant to stay that way.

Robin didn't know if she'd dozed or was simply lost in thought, but her eyes flew open at the sound of footsteps on the stairs. Daylight had crept in. The outline of the locked door near the foot of her bed appeared. When it burst open, she saw the silhouette of one of the monsters—the young one. He was meaner than the old one.

"Well, look at you. Ya finally woke up, huh?" he said. Robin hated the cocky smile on his face, and his mocking tone matched the derisiveness of his grin. "So, is the poor little rich girl hungry this morning?"

"Why are you doing this?" Robin hated the sound of her whimpering voice almost as much as she hated the monsters, but she was helpless and couldn't stop herself from begging. "Please let me go. I won't tell anyone, I promise." They both knew she was lying. "What, what are you going to do to me?"

"Oh, don't you worry, kid. We've got plans for you... big plans." He laughed an ugly laugh, then put a plastic bowl of lumpy oatmeal on the foot of her bed, tossed her a spoon and grabbed the paper plate from the floor and turned to leave.

"Wait! Can I have something to drink? My, my mouth is so dry."

"There's a water faucet in the bathroom, and you've got two hands. Maybe I'll bring some paper cups next time I come down."

He disappeared without another word, and Robin stared at the door in the darkened room. Without the light from the other side, she could barely see the mushy mess in the bowl. Hunger drove her to down most of it before gagging and running for the bathroom. She scraped the remains into the toilet, rinsed the bowl with water, then used it as a vessel to quench her thirst.

With nothing to see, nothing to do, Robin escaped the only way she could. She let her imagination carry her to another place. She went into a world of fantasy.

In her mind, she ran and ran until she found the police and led them back to the monsters. She imagined the police shooting and killing the senior monster, but the younger fiend was handcuffed and shoved into the back of the police car. She watched, and when he looked out the window, she grinned her most evil grin.

"What are you smiling about?"

Lying there, eyes closed, Robin had been so lost in her imagined escape, she hadn't heard his footfalls or the door opening. There was suddenly nothing to smile about. It was the ominous senior brute standing over her, and she clutched the thin blanket to cover her vulnerability.

"The kid said you been asking for something to do... something to read. We're not big readers, but I scrounged these up." Robin could hardly believe her eyes when he dropped some books on the floor with a loud thud. "And here's a cup. You can get water in the bathroom." She thought he was leaving her alone again, but he turned back. "You been doin' better—not yellin' anymore—so maybe I can get ya some soda or something."

"Thank you," she whispered as he turned to leave. "Wait!"

He spun back around with a puzzled look.

She was almost afraid to ask, but pushed the words out. "I, I can't really see well enough to read. Do you think, I mean, could you get me a lamp or something?" She saw him look up at the ceiling before he answered.

"Yeah, okay. I mean, no. I don't have a lamp, but I guess I can put a new bulb in." Before she could thank him again, he was gone, the door was closed, and she was left alone in the silence.

Squinting at the books in semi-darkness, she discovered there was a dictionary, what looked like a paperback of jokes for the john, a Bible, and a Louis L'Amour western. Robin thought about all the books at her house. What she wouldn't give for one of her Harry Potter hardbacks. *Better yet,* she thought, *some of Harry's magic to get me out of here.*

CHAPTER FOUR

The cottage turned out to be all Julie had said it would be and more. From its charming curb appeal with the beautiful red maple tree and colorful perennials, to the spacious open-concept interior, Mia fell under its spell. There was so much more space than she had thought from the exterior, yet it felt warm and cozy.

Julie, of course, called dibs on the master bedroom which had a sitting area large enough for her to use as an office for her writing. Mia wasn't at all surprised Julie claimed it like it was her right, but the other two bedrooms upstairs were decent sized as well. Mia decided the larger of the two would work for her, and the third bedroom would work for guests—like perhaps a certain blue-eyed beau.

"What about the sunroom for your studio?" Julie asked on their first walk through with the realtor. "Or the basement family room?"

Mia could already see herself sitting in front of an easel with the light pouring in through the big ground floor windows and sliding doors that opened out on the perfect backyard and garden. "Are you sure you won't want to use the basement for entertaining, Jules?"

"Absolutely. We have plenty of room upstairs, plus we can make the other little room down there into a cozy 'get-away' if one of us wants a little privacy."

"I love it," Mia said. "Can we do this, really?"

"I've crunched the numbers, sis, and with the two of us sharing expenses, we definitely can."

The realtor had been standing quietly by the kitchen island wearing a smile, and Mia was certain the older woman was already planning how she would spend her commission. After a long pause, Mia said in barely more than a whisper, "Let's do it."

Julie squealed with delight, and gave the realtor the go-ahead to write up the offer. By the end of the week it had been accepted with closing just one week later. The weeks that followed were a whirlwind of busy-ness for Mia.

***

Fortunately, now that Mia had completed her internship, they had a new intern ready to take over the patients she'd been seeing in her old position in Pittsburgh. She made sure all her files were completely up to date and said her goodbyes to staff and patients alike. But there were three farewells that were especially difficult.

Saying goodbye to Lillian Perry, who'd been her favorite Alzheimer's patient, tore at her heart. She knew the elderly lady probably wouldn't remember or think of her when Mia moved away—or perhaps even five minutes after she left her—but she couldn't help wondering if the new intern would understand and give her the same loving care.

When she said goodbye to her roommate, Morgan, Mia made her vow to come visit, and Mia talked so much about Sweet Glen, Morgan agreed she would definitely have to come see it for herself. "I'm going to miss you, girl, and you'd better come visit me too!" she cried. Mia promised she would.

But the most difficult moments came on her last evening with Ron Bishop.

"When will I see you again?" Ron asked. Mia swallowed the lump in her throat and could think of nothing to say. Ron pulled her close and whispered, "This isn't fair, you know?"

Still at a loss for words, Mia looked into his blue eyes and felt the sting of fresh tears. "It's not that far, really," she said at last. "Once I get settled, you'll have to come visit. You can come for the weekend. That is, if you don't mind the futon we brought from my sister's apartment. Julie and I have both tried it, and it really is rather comfortable." She quickly added, "And we plan to get something better in there soon—"

"I'm sure it will be fine, but I might have to get a vehicle that's not such a gas guzzler," Ron said wrapping her in his arms. At 5'11" he was half a foot taller than Mia and rested his chin on the top of her head. "I have a feeling I'm going to be putting a lot of miles on it." He pulled back enough so she could see his grin and the wink that said everything was going to be okay. Mia hoped he was right. These last few weeks being apart had shown her how difficult this separation was going to be.

***

Mia breathed in slowly, then out, then in again, and out. Feeling more relaxed, she looked around at her new surroundings. Once the office of Nancy Owens, this would now be her office in the Reed Mental Health Center. All of the other woman's personal things had been removed and replaced with Mia's pictures, mementos, and paraphernalia she'd accumulated while going to school and working in Pittsburgh. She was surprised at all the space she had, and sitting behind the desk, looking at framed photos of her family and Ron, Mia felt like she had arrived. Everything leading up to this had been preparation. Now, with her name on the door, it had suddenly become real.

I am a professional... and a homeowner. Mia had a sudden urge to call Julie before seeing her first client. "Hey, Jules," she said to her sister, "I just realized something. I think we've become grown-ups." After the sisters shared the moment of laughter together, Mia opened the file in front of her, and a little of that grown-up, professional feeling slipped away. Knowing she no longer had a supervisor to turn to whenever she faced something troubling, she prayed she was really ready.

Sarah Reed had promised to be her mentor as needed, but did Mia really want to go to her mother with professional problems? Probably not. And of course, there was Grandpa. Dr. Andrew Reed was making remarkable progress since his stroke and vowed he would be back to seeing clients within the next few months. In the meantime, he also assured Mia he would be there for her should any questions arise.

But it was Gabriella Ortiz, another therapist in the practice, who showed Mia around that first day and familiarized her with the few cases she would be starting. Two of them were Nancy Owens's clients, and three others were Dr. Reed's. Mia expected she would most likely only see her grandpa's clients until he returned to the practice, but Owens's clients would now depend on her for the help they needed. And she was about to meet one of them—a young man named Adam Grant who she would learn had witnessed the death of his therapist.

Fifteen minutes into their session, Mia was startled by Adam's declaration that he knew Nancy didn't commit suicide.

"What makes you think that?"

"I don't think it, I know it!" he said. "She wouldn't!"

"It's hard for us to understand how someone we know could take their own life, but—"

"No, you don't understand." Adam squeezed his lips into a thin line and shut his eyes tight. When he opened them again, the tears he was trying to hold back, slid down his cheeks. He swiped them away with one hand, accepting the tissue offered by Mia with the other.

Mia waited. *Give him time. Don't push him or rush to console.*

"I saw it, you know." It was more of a statement than a question. "I didn't know it was her, but I saw her... saw her hit the ground." Head bent and hands over his face, he sobbed. "It was horrible."

Mia was shocked. Her first day, her first client, and he drops a bomb like that. Mia could feel her self-confidence slipping away.

But then she stopped thinking about herself and focused on Adam's needs. She pulled her rolling office chair closer and put her hand on his forearm. "It's okay. Let it out. Anyone would be shocked and horrified to witness such a thing." She waited, and when he had pulled himself together and blown his nose, she asked, "Do you want to talk about it? Can you?" *Are these the right questions to ask him now?*

"Yeah, like I said, I didn't know it was her... not until the next night when they finally identified her on the news. I couldn't believe it. I don't believe it!"

"I'm sure it's difficult—"

"No, damn it!" Adam paused and looked up apologetically. "I'm sorry, but did you know Nancy?"

"No, Adam. I'm sorry, but I never met her."

"See, maybe that's why you don't get it. But I did know her, and I know how she felt about suicide."

Mia had gone over Adam's file carefully and knew he was a recovering alcoholic and suffered from a major depressive disorder. He had contemplated suicide himself scarcely six months earlier, so possibly his former counselor had shared her views.

"Nancy said there is always hope for the future," Adam said, "unless you remove it by ending your life. She told me, 'Suicide is the thief of all hope.' I'll never forget those words." He locked eyes with Mia, and added, "I think someone pushed her off that rooftop. I think she was murdered."

Chapter Five

At the end of her first stress-filled day at the Reed Mental Health Center, Mia needed the soothing comfort she always got from Simeon, and he did not disappoint. Like most Persian cats, he was quiet and affectionate, and he always seemed to sense when Mia needed his love and attention.

"Oh, sweet Simmie, you are such a lover." He purred back his agreement. "What a day I've had. No, what a month is more like it. Yes, I love you too," she said in answer to his slow blinks.

Mia had worried how he might adjust to his new surroundings, but she needn't have. He had his Mia, and he was already used to Julie from her many visits to Pittsburgh. Even Julie's cat, William Shakespeare (Willie for short) hadn't turned out to be a problem. The two felines basically ignored each other—at least most of the time.

"Well, let's get you some dinner before I go for my walk."

Once she'd taken care of Simmie's needs, Mia changed into her New Balance running shoes, shorts and top, brushed her light brown hair back behind her ears, and threw on a sweat band. Then, after bidding Simeon a quick goodbye, she headed through the tree line at the back of their property where she'd discovered the perfect trail for her daily exercise. It was so completely different and much more serene than her route back in Pittsburgh. Here she could focus on the beauty of her surroundings and let go of the day's stress.

Much of this new route was along the lake with several wooded areas where she could stop, get relief from the heat, and simply stand among the trees and watch the busy squirrels scampering about. Beyond that, the trail broke back out along the water's edge where there were benches. People often sat and watched the two swans who had taken up residence there. Another part of the trail went along behind homes with lovely plantings, children's play areas, and the occasional picket fence. Mia delighted in all of it.

She had walked or jogged this trail every day since she and Julie took possession of their cottage—sometimes twice—with a short walk in the morning and a longer one with intermittent jogging in the evening, and she was beginning to recognize the familiar faces of some of the others who were on the same schedule.

There was Miss Perky in pink—so far she'd been wearing some shade of pink every time Mia saw her—jogging with her earbuds and oblivious to anything but whatever was coming through them. Then there was the man who looked like a professor walking his miniature poodle, the jock who was obviously in training for something or other, the young and handsome Mr. Hot Stuff who smiled and nodded to everyone he passed, and the elderly grandma who toddled along, stopping often to rest and soak in her surroundings. She had a sweet smile that immediately reminded Mia of her Grandma Val's best friend, Bonnie. When Mia passed the little grandma today, she reminded herself she should pay a visit to Aunt Bonnie, as she'd called her since she was old enough to talk.

Today Mia promptly broke into a sweat and slowed her pace with only brief jogs between her walking. As she approached the entrance to the wooded area, she began her cooldown. She looked forward to reaching the shade and standing among the trees. But when she neared that area, she saw Mr. Hot Stuff approaching from the other direction. He didn't even seem to have broken a sweat!

"How do, Miss?" he said with a smile and a nod.

Sounds like a Brit. "Hi, how's it going?" she returned his greeting and continued on, not waiting for an answer, but noticing he plopped down on one of the black iron benches. It was in the direct sunlight, and Mia thought it must be hot, but he didn't react. *Strange.* "Have a good one!" she called over her shoulder.

**

"How do, Miss?" Harold Muncy Tate had leapt out of the bushes and onto the trail right before Mia took the last turn. Since he'd been watching her every day—just like he used to watch the Owens woman—his timing was no accident. He knew she would have slowed for her cool down with only a quarter-mile to go, and he knew she'd give him her usual greeting.

"Hi," Mia said showing her dimple. "How's it going?"

"Hot," he answered dropping onto the black iron bench and realizing immediately he hadn't thought that move through. The sun had been cooking it for the past hour, but he wasn't about to let this little Trixie know he was burning his ass off. He rubbed his finger under his nose as she strode on by with her usual, "Have a good one." But Harry knew she didn't mean it, knew she wouldn't look back, so he popped back up rubbing his burning behind, then scratched his nose again.

He strode the quarter-mile back to where he'd left his Jeep, hopped in and pulled the visor down to check his appearance. Harold, his former self, wouldn't have even bothered looking. He had never wanted to see the geeky Pillsbury Doughboy looking back at him. But the new and improved Harry liked checking himself out. He'd worked damn hard to become the hunk he saw looking back at him now. Sixty-five pounds lighter and in the best shape of his life, females didn't ignore him anymore. They wanted him, and he knew he could get any one of them he wanted. For as long as he wanted.

CHAPTER SIX

August 12, eleven years ago

"All right. Let's go, girl. You're comin' with us this time." Robin grabbed the raggedy hand towel and dried her hands even though she hadn't yet finished washing the dishes. She knew better than to keep him waiting. She remembered the time she'd said, *"Just a minute, I'm almost done here,"* and Buddy had backhanded her so hard she fell and cracked the back of her head on the kitchen wall. If it hadn't been for his father, Charlie, he would've hit her again. The older man was kinder—if you could call it that—and almost never hit her. He did other things, mostly at night, and she hated him for that, but during the day she felt safer if he was around.

Robin couldn't guess Charlie's age but had a feeling he probably wasn't as old as he looked. He had alcohol eyes and an ever-unshaven whiskered face. Well, he did apparently shave about once a week, on Fridays, but by the end of the day, there was already enough stubble to hurt if he visited her room that night. All of his clothes hung on his bony body making him look like a scarecrow, and it was no wonder with his diet of meat and potatoes, hardly any vegetables, ice cream, and beer. But at least the scarecrow was kinder than his son.

Buddy was the truly dangerous one, full of animosity and hate toward her and everyone else. Robin often wondered what had made him so mean, but the one thing she knew was that the only one who could rein him in was Charlie. He was definitely afraid of his father even though he was half a foot taller and had him by at least fifty pounds.

Buddy never shaved at all but kept his beard neat and his mustache trimmed. He reminded Robin of a young Alan Rickman

29

in *Die Hard*—some might consider him good looking—but she saw the evil and found him repulsive. Buddy's jeans fit, and he obviously featured himself a bit of a lady's man. Better dressed than his old man, he still never left the house without his jean-jacket or a leather vest long enough to conceal the gun he kept tucked in his waistband in the back.

So today, she obediently followed them out the side door to avoid the abuse. Besides, they didn't often take her along, so any time she could get outside was precious to Robin. She breathed in the warm air, savoring the scent of summer—the freshly mown grass from the neighbor's yard. Their own yard was overgrown, as usual, but Robin didn't care. It was green.

There was someone hanging clothes in the distant yard, and Robin wished the houses were closer together so she could see the woman better. Maybe the lady would see her and somehow know she needed help. But the reality of Robin's world, of her life, she knew was this endless captivity.

"Get in," Buddy snapped, and she jumped in the car. There was danger in those cold green eyes.

Robin looked to Charlie as she climbed in, but he was already behind the wheel of the old pickup starting the engine. So she sat back and stared out the window at a world she no longer felt a part of, imagining what might be going on behind those closed doors. She imagined normal families sitting around their tables talking and laughing and living a life like the one she should be living. Like the one she'd had with Mom and Dad and Ronnie... until these two took it all away.

When they reached the grocery store, Charlie handed her a list and enough money to cover everything on it. Then he ordered Buddy to go along in. "And keep your eyes open," he said. "I don't want any trouble." Buddy didn't bother answering. Just slammed the car door and gave Robin a shove.

She had everything on the list but the ice cream when she saw him. A uniformed police officer—probably off-duty and on his way home—was coming down the aisle toward them. Robin looked pleadingly in his direction before she felt Buddy put his hand on her shoulder.

"What kind of ice cream do you want, *dear*?" he asked. And the moment was gone. The officer had moved on. Buddy's vice-like grip on her shoulder loosened, and she wanted to scream. She wanted to run and grab the policeman, cry for help... but she knew better. She had seen the gun Buddy had tucked in the back of his jeans, and she knew he'd use it. The memory of her dead parents was proof of that.

"Any trouble in there?" Charlie asked when they got back to the truck. "I saw that cop and almost followed him in—just in case."

"Nope. But the girl might'a caused a problem if she didn't know better. Get in!"

Robin searched the parking lot and saw the officer exiting the store as they pulled out. *If only...*

They made one more stop before heading back to the house. This time she was left to wait in the car with Charlie while Buddy ran in for another couple cases of beer. Neither of the men ever went a day without drinking about half a dozen unless they switched to the hard stuff. And the more they drank, the more likely they would come down to visit Robin in her bedroom. Sometimes one of them. Sometimes both. Sometimes they even invited their friend, Yancy, to partake. He was about 6'4", weighed at least three hundred pounds, and when he was done with her, Robin hurt even more than she did with the others. Those were the nights she imagined—longed for—death. Mostly theirs. Sometimes her own... just to escape the pain, shame, and hopelessness.

But Buddy was the most brutal and punishing. Because of his sadistic treatment, Robin held him in the utmost contempt, and for the first time in her life, recognized that she might be capable of murder... if only she had the means. Though she hadn't witnessed the murder of her parents—she only saw the aftermath—Robin was almost certain Buddy did the actual killing.

All Charlie seemed to care about was the next place they'd hit to get enough money to pay for all their drugs and alcohol. Buddy exuded hatred and cruelty.

Robin prayed he would pass out before he decided to come down the steps that night, unlock the door, and repeat the nightmare. And she thanked God for the miscarriages she'd had last year and again three months ago. She couldn't have a child by any one of these beasts... *and I wouldn't even know who the father was.* Robin grieved for the child she'd never have but knew she was better off in the hands of the angels than being born into this miserable world.

After preparing a dinner of hamburgers, beans, and applesauce, Robin ate quickly, cleaned up all their dishes, then quietly sat down at the kitchen table. She hoped one night they might both pass out before they locked her in the basement room. She hoped that one night she might find a way to escape. But it wouldn't be tonight.

"Time for bed, girl," Charlie said with a bit of a slur.

As much as she resented being called girl—they had stolen her "girlhood" from her four years ago—Robin meekly descended the steps praying for a peaceful night. Sometimes he stayed. Sometimes the other one came down right behind him. But tonight, without another word, the old man locked the door behind her, and she listened as he stomped back up and across the floor above her. She could hear the sound of the TV, but there were no more footfalls.

Moments went by, and as the silence continued, Robin began to relax. She knew one of them, most likely the younger, might still come down later, but for now she could breathe. Looking around at her surroundings, Robin appreciated the gradual improvements Charlie had made to her space. It was still a prison, but over the last few years he had granted her more books—she didn't know or care where he got them—an old wooden table with a lamp and a clock on it, and a decent pillow and blanket for her bed. Charlie had even brought her an ugly old brown rope rug to put by the bed when she said how cold the floor was on those first winter mornings of her captivity.

Her latest gift was a whole ream of printer paper he'd gotten her. Robin thought back to the previous December 25th. When they'd let her upstairs to fix their breakfast, there were no signs of Christmas. No tree. No decorations. No sugar cookies.

"Merry Christmas," she said barely above a whisper.

"What? Oh yeah," Charlie said. He looked around, then the chair scraped the old tile floor as he pushed away from the Formica-topped table, disappeared into the dark sitting room where they spent all their time drinking, smoking dope, and watching TV. When he reappeared, he had a bag from Staples. "Here, Merry Christmas," he grumbled, dropping the bag on the table in front of her.

Robin reached in and pulled out the pack of white paper, a pack of Bic pens, and a pack of yellow pencils. He had even remembered to get a little plastic pencil sharpener. Her face lit up and she grinned like a child who'd gotten exactly what she wanted from Santa. "Thank you, Charlie!"

Buddy had been sitting bent over his coffee mug and now looked up at Robin. "Well, would ya look at that. The girl can smile." His snarky comment was accompanied by an evil grin. "I gotta present for ya too, girl. C'mon downstairs and I'll show it to ya."

"Knock it off, Buddy," Charlie said, staring him down with cold, gunmetal blue eyes. "It's a holiday."

"Oh sure, that's right. So where's my present?"

Charlie grabbed a bottle of Jack Daniels and a two-liter bottle of Coke and slammed it down in front of his son. "See, I didn't forget you, ya little dick."

Robin watched the whole scene in horror. She knew this day probably wouldn't end well with Buddy drinking the hard stuff, so she hurried back downstairs as soon as she had the kitchen cleaned up to enjoy some time writing and drawing while she could.

Just as she had last Christmas day, Robin picked up a pencil, a sheet of paper, and the old phonebook she used as a desk, and began drawing a picture of a bird. She loved birds, and though she knew she was no artist, she was teaching herself how to draw simply by practicing, simply by doing it. She had plenty of time to practice, and she could see the progress when she compared the latest drawings to her older ones.

This one was taking shape and could soon be recognized as an eagle soaring into the sky, flying free. When it was completed, Robin ran her fingers over the wings and dreamed of the day she might fly away... fly away to freedom...

But where would I go? Robin thought about her last day of freedom—her fifteenth birthday—sitting with her parents and twin brother, blowing out the candles together, planning their trip to Disney that would never happen...

There would be no birthday cake for her nineteenth birthday tomorrow, just as there'd been no sweet sixteen and getting her driver's license, no celebration of turning eighteen and becoming an adult. She imagined what it would have been like, how she and Ronnie would have toasted to their adulthood, and what a wonderful day it could have been.

But she knew her brother didn't live to see his next birthday. He would forever be fifteen in her mind. She could see his beautiful face grinning after they blew out the candles together, and she was glad she'd never seen his dead body like she'd seen her parents.

Tomorrow, she would wish him a happy birthday in heaven while she *celebrated* hers in her personal hell.

CHAPTER SEVEN

August 13

    Ron slid into the booth across from Mia and couldn't help laughing at her expression.

"It's not funny, Ron," Mia said.

"I'm sorry, sweetie, I'm not laughing at you." He saw the disbelief in her eyes and added, "But it's not my fault you look so cute with that pouty face."

"Well, don't you think I have a right to pout?" she asked.

"Hey, c'mon. I'm the one with the birthday, and I don't mind eating at the Sweet Glen Diner. It's no big deal to me, so don't worry about it," he said looking back at the laminated menu.

"But you drove all the way out here, and I wanted to make you the perfect birthday dinner with your favorite chili-mac casserole. I can't believe I burned it. Stop it!" Mia grumbled. "It's not funny."

"Listen love, any dinner I have with you is perfect. Yeah, I know it sounds cheesy, but I mean it. There is no one I'd rather spend my birthday with than you." Ron meant what he said, but he knew there was one other person he wished could be there to celebrate with him.

"What's wrong, Ron?"

"What do you mean?"

"I don't know, but you had such a far-away look in your eyes just now."

"I'm sorry. Birthdays are kind of hard, you know? I can't help thinking of Robin and wondering where she is... or if she's even alive to celebrate our thirtieth birthday." He saw the pity in Mia's eyes and wished he hadn't said anything. "Yikes, I'm thirty!" He feigned shock and dismay. "Are you sure you should be seeing an old man like me?" Ron was relieved by the look on Mia's face and the way she reached across and put her hand on his.

"I am absolutely positive." When she grudgingly released his hand, she picked up the menu and looked around for a waitress. "Is it me, or is it taking an awfully long time to get service?"

Ron had been wondering the same thing, but didn't want to make Mia feel more miserable about coming here. "I don't mind. That gives me more time to gaze into your eyes."

Mia rolled those very same hazel eyes. "Laying it on pretty thick there, aren't cha?"

Ron saw the waitress hurrying toward their booth and just winked.

"I'm sorry for the wait, folks, We're a little short-handed today. Can I get you something to drink?"

Ron noticed the woman's puffy red eyes and wondered if there were problems in the kitchen. Everything seemed quiet out here, and none of the other diners seemed particularly annoyed or rude. "No worries," he said. "Iced tea for you, Mia? Two iced teas, thanks."

"Poor girl. She looks upset," Mia said.

"Yeah, she does, and as a matter of fact, so does the rest of the staff." He looked around. "Something's sure wrong."

Once they finally got to order and had their meals, the food turned out to be quite good. It wasn't until they finished eating and were paying the check at the register that the mystery was solved. The cashier apologized, "I'm sorry if your service was slow today. I hope you'll come back and give us another chance when we're not so short-handed."

"Don't worry about it," Ron said. "We all know what it's like when somebody calls in sick."

"Yeah, but this was worse. One of our girls didn't show up this morning, and I was really ticked until we found out why." The cashier's eyes filled. "She won't be coming back because she... she died last night."

Ron and Mia said how sorry they were and promised to return sometime soon. Though their mood was dampened by what the cashier told them, it brightened—especially for Ron—when they got back to the cottage and found Julie waiting with a birthday cake.

"Mia told me you liked carrot cake so I ordered one from Bunny's Bake Shop," Julie said. "Her stuff is so good. Now, I'll leave you two lovebirds alone."

"Don't leave without having some of my birthday cake," Ron said, and he enjoyed the relaxed dessert time with the three of them. But he was also glad half an hour later when Julie insisted she had a deadline to meet and headed up to her bedroom-office to work.

Ron was relieved Mia had listened to his plea for a quiet evening rather than a big hoopla for his birthday, and sitting on the couch with his arm around the woman he loved, he felt more at peace than he had since the last time they'd parted. This was what he wanted... needed... and he didn't want it for a couple of days each time with too many days or weeks in between. He wanted to see her every day.

Keeping his right arm securely around his girl, Ron stuck his left hand in the bowl they shared and grabbed a handful of popcorn. He smelled the sweet scent of her hair and thought, *Why did you have to move?*

"Hey, what are you thinking about?" Mia asked.

"Why you had to go and move away from Pittsburgh... and me." Mia's head bent, and he saw her smile fade and wished he hadn't said it. Lifting her chin with his forefinger, Ron looked into those hazel eyes and knew what he had to do. "Don't worry, love. Nothing's going to keep me away from you."

"I'm sorry I've made it so difficult." She rested her head on his chest.

"I said, don't worry about it. Besides, Sweet Glen is starting to grow on me. And it's not so far from the city that a person couldn't drive in whenever they wanted to see a game." Ron rarely missed a Steelers game.

"Ron, are you serious?" Mia asked jerking her head up and looking at him with a face full of hope. "I mean would you consider moving closer?"

"Let's just say I haven't ruled it out."

All in all, it was the best birthday Ron could remember since he lost his family fifteen years earlier. Yet sleep did not come easily that night, and when it finally did, he tossed and turned with unpleasant dreams and memories. At 5:30 A.M., he couldn't stand another moment of the fitful sleep... or the futon. The promised bed would be a great relief, and though he'd rather be sharing a bed with the woman he loved and wished he could go down the hall and crawl in beside her, he had to respect her faith and her choices for now.

He pulled his iPad out of his overnighter, and using its flashlight he headed down to the kitchen. Glad there were no squeaky boards along the way, Ron went straight to the Keurig and took one of Julie's K-cups from the assortment in the basket. They were mostly flavored coffees but he managed to find a medium roast breakfast blend which he decided was better than nothing, though he could really use one of his bolder cups of joe after the night he'd had.

Thirty's feeling a little rough.

He filled one of the big mugs and was startled when he heard Mia's voice behind him. "It's awfully early. Did you sleep okay?"

"Yeah," he lied. "I'm an early riser. Sorry if I woke you though."

Mia said he hadn't, and Ron was pretty sure she was lying too. He watched as she went about brewing her morning tea in her sleep clothes and little ballet slippers with no makeup, and he loved seeing her that way.

She laughed when she caught him staring. "I guess I look a sight, but this is what you get when you wake a girl up this early."

"Aha, you lied! I did wake you."

Mia raised one eyebrow. "Yeah, and you slept well. Right!" She promised there would be a more comfortable bed by his next visit. She saw he'd been checking the news on his iPad and asked if there was anything new or exciting.

"Yeah, you know that waitress from the diner, the one they said died? They identified her and it sounds like her death was suspicious."

"All right, Mr. Detective. What makes you say that?"

"Well, for one thing, it says this Dana Dawton was engaged— supposed to get married in a couple weeks, had everything to live for. Ron looked up from his tablet and read shock on Mia's face. "What's wrong?"

"I think I knew her. Is there a picture?"

"Yeah, it's her engagement picture." Ron turned the screen toward her and recognized the look on Mia's face. He'd seen it on the faces of so many survivors when he showed them pictures to ID someone they loved. At least this time it wasn't a gruesome crime scene shot.

"That's her... they have the last name wrong. It's Dana Dawson. We went to high school together." Mia shook her head in disbelief. "How did she die?"

"I'm sorry, Mia. It says she jumped to her death."

CHAPTER EIGHT

My name is Harold Muncy Tate. All through school I went by that name, Harold, because that's what my mother always called me. She didn't care much for nicknames. But Harold—especially chunky Harold—is, or was a geek. Kids like to make fun of chubby kids named Harold. So that's not my name anymore.

I figured once I got out of school, things would be different, but they weren't. At least not with the girls. They still ignored me. Even when I got up the nerve to talk to one of them that worked at the diner where I was bussing tables, she just rolled her eyes and walked away. She didn't even recognize me from school. Didn't know I'd had a crush on her all through high school. Yeah, her name was Dana. A real bitch. That's when I decided to change.

I'm Harry now, and I'm not that geek. I'm not the guy all the boys made fun of and all the girls totally ignored. I've made some changes... now I'm in charge. First, I lost sixty-five pounds. It wasn't easy, but I did it. And it wasn't just giving up all my favorite foods—damn, I miss pizza—but it was running and working out at the gym. Seven days a week I stayed focused, I sweated, I starved. And I got rid of fat Harold.

I even got rid of his whiny voice. Yeah, the whiny kid my dad always made fun of is gone. He said I whined like a baby—that is until he *accidentally* fell off the roof. Too bad I wasn't close enough to save him. Ha! And now, even if he was alive, he couldn't call me whiny. Not anymore. It took a lot of time and practice, but now I have a British accent. And guess what. All those idiot broads eat that stuff up. They buy it hook, line, and sinker. And Harry is a hit. But they don't know me. They don't know me at all. They just like the packaging.

It's only been five years since Dana snubbed me. I guess she didn't even really look at me so why would she remember?

Besides, like I said, that guy is gone. This guy doesn't get ignored. Not anymore. I've made something of myself, and she's still working at that stupid diner. But she noticed me when I saw her last week, and she liked what she saw. I could tell.

I knew if I asked her out—which I did when I was good and ready—she'd say yes.

Shallow bitches... I hate 'em all.

I went to the diner last week, and little Miss Fancy Pants noticed me this time all right. I saw her flirty little smile when she came over to take my order. She never looked at chubby Harold that way, that's for sure. So, I stared at the menu, not willing to give her more than a glance, then told her I'd have the mushroom and cheese omelet. It wouldn't be a problem. I'd just skip lunch and have a piece of fish and some broccoli for dinner.

I remember all the times Harold the geek sat looking into an empty cup, waiting for a refill on coffee, but Harry didn't have to wait. She was right there, topping off my cup before it was half gone. Yeah, I had her—didn't even have to try. Then I made my move.

I was ready for her when she brought the check. With my best British on, I met her gaze and showed her the smile she was waiting for. She was hooked.

I kept going back every day, and, in spite of the little diamond on her left hand, by the fifth morning I knew she was ripe for the pickin'. By then we were on a first name basis—Harry and Dana— yeah, and all I'd have to do was crook my finger, and she'd come runnin'.

"Thanks, Dana," I said when she brought the check, and when she turned to walk away, I added, "You've been taking such good care of me all week, I wondered if I can buy you dinner tonight... I mean, if you're not busy."

She looked around, and with no hesitation said, "I'm kind of engaged, but he's away on a fishing trip with his buddies, so I don't think he'd mind. Sure, Harry. Sounds like fun."

I didn't correct her, and I figured she would like it at first. And she did. She ordered a big meal—the seafood platter—and appeared to enjoy every bite, which was only fitting for her last meal. I didn't even have to worry about carrying the conversation. She was plenty gabby. I threw in an occasional "bloody" this or that in my best British accent, and she was putty in my hands. When I asked her back to my place, she didn't hesitate. Stupid Trixie.

After a couple drinks and a quick roll in the hay, she was ready to sleep, but that wasn't the plan. It took a bit of persuasion, but I finally convinced her the night was too beautiful not to take advantage of the rooftop view. She wasn't real steady on her feet— a real lightweight—but I took the bottle along up with us. One more drink oughta do it.

I refilled her glass, she drank, we walked to the edge, and with just a little help, she was flying.

The next morning, I skipped the diner, but the following day I ordered my omelet and asked the waitress if it was Dana's day off. The poor girl apologized when she saw how shocked I was to hear of her demise.

Guess I'll just have to find a new waitress.

CHAPTER NINE

"Oh my! What did you draw, Alice?" Mia asked her five-year-old client. This was only her second session with the child, and she knew she couldn't take all the credit, but she loved the little girl's progress.

Pulling the grape lollypop out of her mouth, Alice nearly shouted with excitement, "It's a spider!"

"Wow, he's a big one, isn't he?" The child nodded with a wide toothless grin and purple tinted lips. "Oh, and how many legs does he have?"

The precocious little blonde counted out loud, and when she got to seven, grabbed the marker, added one more, then proudly announced, "Eight legs!"

"That's right! Spiders have eight legs... good counting, Alice. So, what are we going to do now? Are we going to run away?"

"No!"

"Are we going to cry?" Mia put on a pouty face but couldn't hold it long as the five-year-old shook her head and giggled. "Well then, shall we just ignore it?"

"No, I'm going to smoosh it!" Alice popped the lollypop back into her mouth, picked up the little plastic mallet, and killed that paper spider, then doubled the paper into a ball and tossed it in the trash. She wiped her hands of it and with a most serious Shirley Temple look said, "I wasn't afraid."

"I'm so proud of you, Alice." Mia let the little one run into her arms. She was always amazed at how quickly the bond formed between her and her youngest clients—the youngest and the oldest seemed to know that they could trust her—and how much more easily the little ones could communicate their feelings through art.

Alice's fear of bugs, according to the patient notes, had bordered on incapacitating. As she grew more and more fearful, she had lost all interest in going out to play in her backyard, and her parents were terribly concerned. But the child had grown comfortable with looking at, and now drawing, pictures of bugs. Definite progress.

Mia quickly jotted her notes in Alice's chart after the girl left, then reviewed her schedule for the next morning before calling it a day. This had been a short workday, with only three clients before lunch and two after, so Mia said goodbye to Ann, their receptionist, and looked forward to going home to her little art studio and some relaxation. She had a peculiar itch that could only be scratched by putting pencil to paper, or charcoal to canvas. "Oops, I almost forgot something. Is Gabby in a session?"

Ann took a look at the schedule. "No, her next client is in about ten minutes if he shows up."

Before leaving for the day, Mia had nearly forgotten she needed to stop by her colleague's office. "Hi, Gabby. Mom, I mean Sarah, said you wanted to talk to me about something."

"Oh, yes. It is about my little Maria... you know the child I mean?"

"Yes, I think so. She's only five or six, right?"

"*Si*, yes. And her verbal skills are limited even in Spanish. I am wondering if I can get your help."

"My help? Are you kidding?" Gabby had joined the Reed Counseling Practice five years ago as their only bilingual therapist, and Mia couldn't believe she was asking for help from a newbie like her.

Gabby smiled at that. "Yes, beautiful. I do need your help. I do not have your skills in doing art therapy, but I think it is a good thing to help Maria," she said. "I spoke to the little one and her mama already. They said it would be okay if you would join us to do some art. What do you think?"

"I'd be happy to do that." Mia felt both honored and anxious. Before finally leaving, she told Gabby she was happy to be increasing her caseload and promised to look over Maria's chart the next day and see her early the following week.

Leaving early, Mia beat the rush-hour traffic, so her drive from Reed Mental Health Center, a few miles south of Madison, back to Sweet Glen only took twenty minutes. Even at its busiest, traffic here wasn't near the nightmare she'd had in Pittsburgh, and turning right onto Glen View Court put a smile on Mia's face. She loved the familiar small-town setting and still couldn't believe she was a homeowner there.

As she pulled into the driveway, Mia wasn't at all surprised to see Julie's little white Ford Escape in the garage since her sister did most of her freelance writing at home. But she was more than a little surprised when she saw Julie perched on a small riding mower grinning and waving.

"How do you like my new toy?" Julie asked after turning off the mower.

"What the heck? Where did you get it?"

"I bought it," Julie said. "Everybody in the neighborhood has one."

"Mmm, smells so good." Mia sucked in the scent of freshly mown grass. "You know we could pay someone to do this for us, right?"

"Nope, our house, our yard, our job."

"Well, I hope you're not expecting me to ride that thing," Mia said arms akimbo.

Julie laughed. "Nope. You've got a *real job*, but I'm here all day and it's a nice break from the computer screen. It gets me out of the house," she said with a wink. "Now, enough chit-chat." She looked at her Fitbit. "I've just got to finish up this little section and I should have time to get my shower and maybe do a little editing before dinner."

"All right, Farmer Jane. I'm going down to my studio for a bit. Are you still going to have enough energy to fix dinner after all this? It's your night, but if you're too tired—"

"Nope. It's already cooking in the crockpot." Julie started up the mower and rode off with her baseball cap pulled low, shading her eyes and wearing a very self-satisfied smile.

The aroma coming from the crockpot got Mia's attention as soon as she walked in the kitchen. She couldn't resist lifting the lid enough to peek. *Boy, she has been busy. Yum, pulled pork.* Opening the fridge to grab a water, she saw Julie even had a big salad already prepared. "Looks like somebody was putting off doing her editing," she said to Simeon who had wandered in to greet her. Yet she knew her sister, and she knew it would get done on time... but just barely.

"C'mon Simmie, let's go," she said scooping him up and carrying her purring bundle down to her studio. With her coarse white paper on the tabletop easel, Mia took a charcoal pencil and began to outline. She started with a simple rectangle, then adding lines and angles, it began to take form. A building... with broader strokes she filled in its sides, creating depth and shadows with her blending stump and white chalk.

Stepping outside to spray her finished charcoal with a workable fixative—in case she wanted to make any minor changes—she wondered why this drawing had itched to come out. Normally that familiar itch resulted in one of her "special" art pieces inspired from a source outside of herself. A source Mia believed might be the Holy Spirit. But this was a simple building.

Back inside, holding her finished piece at arm's length, she said, "It looks like a diner." Then it struck her. "Oh my gosh, Simmie, it's the Sweet Glen Diner." Just to be sure, she carried it upstairs and propped it up for Julie to see. Her timing was perfect because she had no sooner set the drawing up, than Julie came bounding down the steps from her bedroom office.

"Done!" Julie said. "I'll give it another read through after dinner, but I think I'm finished with that article at last." Julie stopped in her tracks in front of the charcoal drawing. "Oh, I like it." The crease between her brows deepened as she studied it for several seconds. "Holy macaroni, that's so good, sis. You should take it over there and show it to them."

"Over where?"

"The diner, of course," Julie said, then paused. She looked at the picture again and then back at her sister. "That is the Sweet Glen Diner, isn't it?"

"Yes," Mia said. "I suppose it is."

CHAPTER TEN

Nine years ago

R obin didn't remember exactly when her fear and anger had turned to rage, but fury now burned like a fire in her gut. The flame grew greater every day until she feared she might spontaneously combust. She imagined bursting into flames, rising above the inferno, and watching this old house and the two animals upstairs turning to ashes in the hellhole they'd created.

After six years as their prisoner, Robin had given up hope of ever being free. Now Charlie had developed a terrible and very concerning cough, and it sounded worse all the time. Yet he still chain-smoked, often lighting the next cigarette off the one he'd just finished. About the only time he didn't have a Marlboro hanging out of his mouth was when he was smoking weed.

Robin didn't see that too often—she was usually locked in the basement by the time father and son got high—but last night they'd gotten an early start, lighting up right after dinner and blowing the fowl smelling smoke in her face. Then Buddy took a big hit and tried to blow it right in her mouth and nose. Robin choked, sending both men into gales of laughter, but Charlie's laughter ended in a cough that sounded like he was headed to the grave.

He could be dying. Though she had no love for the older man—quite the opposite actually—the idea of him dying and leaving her alone with the younger was utterly terrifying. As disgusting as Charlie was, he acted as a buffer between her and Buddy who was much more physically abusive when left to his own devices.

The two men had continued to blow their smoke at Robin until it had an unexpected effect. Though it was no more than 7:30, she was so sleepy she couldn't keep her eyes open. She felt like she was drifting away and had only the vaguest memory of being led downstairs and going to that faraway place in her mind where she escaped the reality of what was happening to her. She retreated to the world of her childhood and danced among the coneflowers. It wasn't until the next morning, fully awake with a familiar pain between her legs, that she knew the abuse of the night before. And she knew it was over. Someway, somehow, she would end it.

Robin figured it would be a while before the jokers upstairs dragged themselves out of bed, but when they did, she planned to be ready. Buddy had reminded her at dinner the night before they'd be going to pick up some stuff at the grocers. *"Don't forget, tomorrow's Thursday. We wanna get there early, so you need to get your ass ready... and put on something clean. I don't like the way some a' those assholes were lookin' at you last time. You don't need to be drawin' attention to yourself, ya hear?"*

Robin had tried too often to be noticed, to have someone—anyone—see her and know she needed their help, but she'd long since given up hope of that happening. Even though she knew she looked like a ragamuffin in the cheap, ill-fitting clothes Charlie got for her, no one seemed to take notice. If anything, they'd take one look at her then quickly look away. People either didn't see her... or didn't care. *"Will you be coming, too, Charlie?"* she'd asked cautiously.

"Sure, darlin'." He'd snickered then added, *"I know you'd miss me too much if I didn't."* He seemed to find his own words hilarious in his mellow mood. That's when he'd decided to *share* his smoke with her. How often had they drugged her for their own amusement?

But today, Robin affirmed, it would end. She had been warned repeatedly that if she tried anything funny, she could wind up as dead as the rest of her family, and that had kept her too afraid to try to escape. Dredging up that cruel reminder of how they destroyed her life that day so long ago and how they tormented her all these years, today she made a decision. Death would be better than her current existence.

Today I will be free. I will get away, or I will die. Either way, I will be free.

***

Charlie parked the beat-up white pickup, slid down in the seat, and pulled his baseball cap over his eyes. "Don't take all day," he said. Robin knew he would probably be napping by the time they came back and wondered why they needed to hurry. But it didn't matter. She didn't plan on coming back.

"Buddy, I... I have to use the bathroom."

"What the hell? Why didn't you go before we left? Just hold it," he snapped.

"But I think I started my period," she said timidly.

"Damn it! Well, hurry up! Gimme that list so I can get started." Buddy snatched the paper from her hand and headed inside while she went around the side of the building toward the restroom.

Frantically she searched for the best escape route. If she tried to run across the highway, she took the chance of being seen by Charlie or getting hit by the fast-moving traffic. Behind the store there was a tree line that seemed to go nowhere. There was a gas station on one side and a furniture store on the other. The empty parking lot told her the furniture store wasn't open at 8:00 A.M. so there'd be no help there.

Knowing she couldn't stand there much longer before Buddy would come looking for her, Robin considered making the dash for the highway until she saw another option. Parked on the side of the building was a Ford 150 with a blue tarp loosely covering its contents. Without even thinking it through, Robin went for it. She put her foot on the rear bumper, hoisted herself up, and climbed into the back. She lifted the corner of the tarp and found she could squeeze in under it next to the scraps of wood it covered.

It was hot and dirty and she discovered there were nails when she felt one tear at her upper arm. She put her hand over the

53

scrape and felt the blood, but there was nothing she could do about it right now. Every time she made the slightest movement the plastic tarp rustled loudly, so no matter how cramped and uncomfortable, she had to be perfectly still.

How long would she have to wait?

Time crawled on. She heard footsteps. Then someone pounded on a door.

"You still in there?" Buddy called. After a short pause, he shouted, "I'm comin' in." Seconds later he passed close to the pickup muttering, "Little bitch..."

With her knees pulled up close to her chest, and her arm crooked under her head as a makeshift pillow, Robin prayed Buddy wouldn't find her there. *If he finds me, I'll scream. I'll scream and scream until he has to let me go or kill me. I won't go back. I won't.*

She heard his footsteps retreating and let out her breath. She wanted desperately to get out from under the tarp and wished the vehicle had been parked further down in the shade. Still, she didn't dare move. She imagined Buddy and Charlie searching. Were they back in the store checking the aisles? Were they looking between the rows of cars? Looking in the cars?

Footsteps sounded again... coming closer. Robin felt her heart pounding in her chest and throat. The steps were close now. Robin couldn't breathe. But Buddy didn't climb into the back of the truck and yank the tarp over her. The pickup rocked slightly and a door slammed. The motor started, and she felt the truck moving.

Oh my God. Parked where it was, Robin had thought it probably belonged to an employee. Her plan to wait until her captors left then get out and find help suddenly changed. The owner of the vehicle was leaving. *Where is he going? And what will happen when he finds me?*

Once on the highway, Robin breathed easier. When the driver got to his house, maybe he'd go inside without looking in the back of the truck. Maybe they'd get there soon, and she could get out of there. But they rode on and on.

Robin carefully stretched her legs out as far as she could and inched away from the sharp-edged lumber scraps. She had no idea which direction they'd taken when leaving the store's parking lot. Did they turn left or right? She tried to remember. It was useless. She'd been so shocked by the sudden turn of events and worried about Buddy and Charlie seeing her, she hadn't thought about it. What if they were going right back to the area where she'd been held captive for the past six years?

Robin realized they were slowing down, then the pickup turned off the main road, slowed, and came to a sudden stop, jolting her body and mind. Before she could even think about trying to somehow pull the tarp back over her, she heard the driver open the door, hop out, and slam it. She held her breath and waited.

Chapter Eleven

"I should be there by about seven o'clock, okay?"

"Perfect." Mia knew she'd have time to get Simeon to his appointment with the veterinarian and get back home and change before Ron arrived. She also knew she'd be counting the minutes. "Love you," she said casually before ending the call. It still amazed her how easily that rolled off her tongue now. She'd been so afraid to utter those words the first time. Afraid he wouldn't say them back, but that's not how it went. He said them first!

It was when he was saying goodbye before her final move to Sweet Glen. *"You know I've fallen head over heels in love with you, right?"* he'd said. It was a wonderfully terrible moment. His words both made her heart soar and filled her with guilt for moving away. It was hard to believe he had only come into her life a few months before and now she couldn't imagine her life without him.

"Hey Jules, are you almost ready?" she called upstairs. Her sister had highly recommended Dr. Curtain, the vet where she took her own cat, William Shakespeare, and was going along for Simmie's first visit to introduce them. Although, by the way Julie described him, Mia had an inkling her sister might be more interested in seeing Dr. Curtain.

When Mia met the young vet, she could see why. He was the very image of the age-old description "tall, dark, and handsome," plus he had smiling eyes and an obvious adoration of felines.

Julie stood off to the side to make room when the doctor's assistant entered. He was quite good-looking too, and Mia noticed a look being exchanged between him and her sister. *Interesting.*

There was also something awfully familiar about the assistant. The way he looked at her and smiled made her somewhat uncomfortable. Mia was certain she knew him from somewhere, but couldn't quite place it until Dr. Curtain said, "Did we receive all the handsome little Mr. Simeon's records, Harry?"

"We've just got them. Shall I bring them up?"

That accent, yes, it's him— Mr. Hot Stuff from the trail!

Julie went out to start the car while Mia stayed to take care of the bill for the day's appointment and schedule her feline's next wellness check. She was waiting for her receipt when Harry came out of one of the exam rooms and casually leaned on the counter next to her.

"Did you need something, Harry?" Treva, the receptionist, asked.

"Not unless this lovely young lady would like to have coffee with me some time," he said making Mia quite uncomfortable, and removing Treva's smile.

Mia gave a little laugh as she accepted her receipt. "Sorry, I'm a tea drinker." Then she hurried out the front door.

"So, what did you think of Dr. Curtain?" Julie asked as soon as Mia put Simmie's carrier in the back and hopped in the passenger seat.

"You were right about how he takes as much time as you need. And Simeon liked him too. But he didn't seem too crazy about Dr. Curtain's assistant, Harry."

"Yeah, I noticed that tell-tale tail of his. I don't get it though. Harry's a really nice guy, and that British accent is so sexy."

"Yeah, I do love a British accent, but I don't know... Do you have something going on with him?"

"No! At least not yet, but he really is a hunk, don't you think?"

"Sure, I guess. I mean if I didn't already have my own hunk, I might think so." They both laughed at that, but Mia's intuition— along with Simeon's—made her wonder. "I think Dr. Curtain's receptionist has her eye on him."

"Oh yeah," Julie said. "It's so obvious. But I don't know if he's interested in her."

"So, what about Dr. Curtain? What do you think of him, Jules?"

"I recommended him to you, didn't I?" Julie said with a sidelong glance.

"Yes, as a vet for Simmie... but that's not what I'm talking about, and you know it. So, are you attracted to him?"

"Is the Pope Catholic?" Julie asked taking her eyes off the road long enough to give her sister a wink. "Speaking of attractions, what time is Detective Charming gonna get here?"

"About seven-ish. And this time I don't plan on burning his chili-mac casserole."

Mia didn't burn the casserole that evening, and not long after Ron arrived, the two of them were sitting at the little table filling their bellies with the delicious concoction while catching up on each other's week.

It was when Mia was serving Ron a piece of her homemade peach pie that he asked about Dana Dawson. "Has there been any more in the news about what happened to her? Is there an ongoing investigation?"

"No, not that I know of. It was probably ruled a suicide."

"I'm not buying it. I mean sure, it's possible, but two suicides... two women jumping to their deaths... and both of them engaged to be married?"

"Well, I know it sounds like a horrible kind of coincidence, but I guess it's possible."

"Sure, anything's possible. But Mia, is it probable?"

Mia saw the crease between Ron's eyes deepen and knew he was in detective mode. A greedy part of her wanted his attention to be on her—on them—tonight. Not on police work.

"How was the pie?" she asked trying to change the subject.

"Huh? Oh, delicious! Best peach pie I've ever had," he said earnestly. Then after a brief pause, "Now what was the other woman's name? The one that worked in your Mom's agency... Nancy something?"

"Nancy Owens." Realizing Ron's investigative mind was not going to be able to let this go, she made a suggestion she hoped could assuage it for now. "Tell you what, tomorrow morning why don't we look into it?"

"Seriously?"

"Yes, seriously. Remember I told you about that Sgt. Evans our family knows from when I was kidnapped?" Mia rarely thought about the time she'd been held captive as a teenager, but she remembered how caring Evans had been when they rescued her all those years ago. "We can run over to Madison, and I can introduce you to him if he's there—or find out when he will be—but on one condition. Tonight, we just concentrate on each other."

"It's a deal."

Ron was true to his word as they spent the next couple of hours walking along Mia's familiar trail, then sitting on the back deck sipping iced tea and talking until the mosquitoes sent them inside. It was after midnight when they decided they must tear themselves away from each other and retire to their separate bedrooms.

"I hope you'll get a better night's rest on the new bed," Mia said when they reached the top of the stairs.

"I'm sure I will, but I bet I'd sleep even better with you by my side." Ron immediately added, "Just kidding, love. I mean it's true, but I can be patient."

Mia loved him so much more for that.

"So, what time do you think we should head over to Madison police station?"

"Oh my goodness, probably not until after nine o'clock, *Detective.*" Mia hoped he wouldn't lie awake wondering about the two women's deaths. She was exhausted and knew she would sleep well, especially after Ron's warm embrace and a kiss that would hold her 'til morning.

Mia read one of her short devotions, said her prayers, then lay in the darkness imagining the day she and Ron would not have to say goodnight and head to separate beds. She dreamed of him lying beside her until her thoughts were interrupted by the memory of a British accent... *"Unless this lovely young lady would like to have coffee with me..."*

CHAPTER TWELVE

Nine years ago

Robin held her breath. She felt a slight rocking as the driver got out of his pickup, praying he wouldn't come to get the junk out of the back. His steps moved away from the truck, and she heard a door close nearby. Then silence. The only sound Robin heard was the pounding of her heart. Finally, the sound of a bird. And then another. Robin listened to them talking to each other for a few more minutes before slowly lifting the tarp and pushing up to a sitting position.

Getting to her knees and craning her neck, she brushed her sweaty hair off her face and looked around the side of the truck. There was no sign of anyone outside the modest home. Robin considered her options.

Should I knock on the door and ask for help? But what if they know the monsters? What if they take me back? Or worse? No, I've got to get farther away. I have to get somewhere more familiar... back to the city maybe. But how? Unable to think clearly, there was only one thing Robin knew. She had to get as far away from Charlie and Buddy as she could, and the first step was to get out of this truck and away from its filthy contents.

Robin climbed over the back and jumped down to the gravel driveway. She was surveying her surroundings when she heard a noise from behind.

"Hey, what are you doing back there?" a man's voice called.

Struck by panic, Robin ran into the wooded area off to the right of the little house.

"Hey!" the voice called again.

Robin ducked behind the trunk of a large oak and froze. She wasn't going to let another man hurt her.

"What's wrong?" she heard a woman ask.

"Somebody was hangin' around the back of the truck, but I guess I scared 'em off."

"Are you sure?" she asked.

"Yeah, I think so, but lock the door just in case. I should be back from the dump in twenty minutes or so," the man said. "And call 9-1-1 if you see anybody."

Robin didn't move until several minutes after she'd heard the front door slam and the truck pull out of the driveway and speed off. When she finally believed it was safe to move, she didn't dare go back out in front of that house and risk being seen.

Dodging puddles left from the previous night's heavy rain, she moved deeper into the woods until she felt her chest tightening from the smell of damp leaves and mold. Though it was mid-summer, with no sunlight coming through the dense trees to warm her, Robin shivered. She trudged through the forest headed in the direction she thought would get her out of the woods until she finally saw a break in the trees ahead.

When she broke out into the sunlight, Robin found herself on a two-lane road and decided to take a chance. She stepped onto the shoulder and put out her thumb to catch a ride.

The first few cars flew by without so much as a glance in her direction. Looking down at her once clean clothes, she saw they hadn't fared well in the dirty truck or her stint in the woods. She brushed as much dirt off as she could, pulled her fingers through her hair, and prayed as she watched a silver sedan approaching.

"Thank you, Lord," she said, seeing that the driver was a woman. The car slowed and pulled off about twenty yards beyond where she stood. Robin had almost given up praying as the days, months, and years had gone on with no chance of escape, but now...

Surprised at how young the driver of the sedan was, she was relieved. The girl asked very few questions and apparently believed Robin's story that she'd had a fight with her boyfriend and had to get away. Robin figured the girl probably wasn't much more than sixteen and a new driver by the way she held onto the wheel and kept her eyes on the road. *Probably just got her license... like I was going to when I turned sixteen...*

It was long after they passed the "Welcome to Pennsylvania" sign that they came to a small town. "Well, this is about as far as I can get you," the young girl said pulling into a gas station.

Robin thanked her and added a warning about picking up strangers along the side of the road. "I really, really appreciate your help, but there are some very bad people out there, believe me."

Alone with only the six twenty-dollar bills Charlie had handed her for groceries and in an unfamiliar town, Robin felt lost and alone. But she strolled Main Street looking in the shop windows and savoring her freedom. Seeing a family restaurant about a block down seemed to cue her stomach to growl furiously. She made a beeline straight to it, then went directly to the bathroom to freshen up as best she could, and pulled one of the twenties out of her bra where she'd stashed them.

Once seated and sipping coffee the waitress brought right away, Robin smelled French fries, and her mouth watered. She looked over the menu and finally settled on a Reuben and fries. Thanks to her disheveled appearance she knew she was getting some inquisitive looks from the staff as well as the few other diners enjoying a late lunch, but she didn't care. She wolfed down her meal then ordered a slice of the lemon meringue pie she'd been eyeing in the glass case up near the register.

Grateful to the waitress who refilled her coffee cup, Robin took a little longer to enjoy it. But when a guy in jeans wearing a neatly trimmed beard walked in the front door, she nearly jumped out of her skin, quickly paid her bill, and left. The stranger had reminded her so much of Buddy. What if they were looking for her? What if she hadn't gone far enough away? She knew they'd gone several hours after crossing from Ohio back into Pennsylvania, but how far in Pennsylvania she wasn't sure. Robin considered the idea of hitting the road again—maybe traveling farther east. But she was exhausted, and getting in the car with another stranger, she might not be so lucky.

At least her stomach was full, so she dragged herself down Main St. until she saw a welcoming sight. A library. Robin hadn't been in a library in more than six years, and its doors seemed to welcome her with open arms. Once inside, she looked at the rows and rows of books, touched them, smelled that familiar smell, and finally selected a copy of *To Kill a Mockingbird* and a local newspaper, The *Martin Star*. She passed the children's section and paused to watch the librarian read to five preschoolers listening with rapt attention, and thought about the child she never had.

Stop it, Robin! Shaking off the wretched memory of her loss, she moved to a quiet area where a studious looking young woman appeared totally engrossed—Robin presumed in some kind of research or homework. She settled in one of the two comfortable brown upholstered chairs in the corner by a window, and curled up in it knowing a comfort she'd forgotten existed.

She watched the other young woman, guessing she was probably a college student—or at least a senior in high school—and felt a sudden jealousy. She envied the normal life this girl must have and wondered why God had let her own life go so terribly wrong. Fighting her internal battle between sorrow, anger, and hatred, she determined to find some way to live and be free from now on.

The exhaustion of the day and her dangerous ordeal finally caught up with her, and Robin fell sound asleep. She woke much later with a start and was totally embarrassed when she noticed the eerie quiet. The preschoolers were gone, as was the young woman with all her notebooks and markers. Robin looked around for a clock, and was stunned to see how much time had passed. She timidly went to the desk and asked how long the library was open.

The librarian behind the main desk gave her a reassuring smile. "We close at 8:00, dear."

It was already 6:30, and Robin knew she had to move on. She had to find a place to stay for the night.

"Can I help you with anything, dear?" the librarian asked.

Robin hesitated, uncomfortably aware of how she must look to this well put together woman, but she swallowed her pride. "I'm new in town, and I'm looking for a place to stay for a while. Someplace inexpensive?"

"Well, let's see. I guess your best bet would be the YWCA at the other end of town... or there's the motel down on Duke St. It's a little closer, and they have weekly rates."

"Yeah, okay, that sounds good. Is it easy to find?"

"Oh sure. You go out here and to your right. In about half a mile you'll come to Duke St. Just turn left, and you'll see it almost right away." The woman quickly added, "Are you sure you're okay?"

Robin assured her she was fine, thanked her for her kindness, and said no, she wouldn't be checking out any books today, but yes, she would probably get a library card next time.

She passed the restaurant again on her way to finding the motel and noticed something that hadn't caught her eye earlier. A help wanted sign. It was worth asking, so she stopped in to inquire and learned they needed a waitress, but when asked if she had any experience, she had to admit to none.

"Well, we also need someone to bus tables," the woman at the register said.

"I can do that," Robin said enthusiastically and was told she could start Thursday.

It's Tuesday. I have tomorrow to explore. Robin hoped to find a Thrift Shop the next day. She couldn't live in what she was wearing, and all she had were the clothes on her back plus those now five twenties and the little stack of ones from any time Charlie had forgotten to ask for his change.

When she got to the motel, Robin was relieved to see the vacancy sign out front. She hadn't thought about it until the desk clerk asked her name, but his question put her in a panic. What if they were still searching? What if they heard there was a Robin Bishop staying in town?

For whatever reason, she thought of Miss Rachel Haverford, the neighbor in *To Kill a Mockingbird*, and said, "Rachel... Rachel Cooper." The clerk didn't look much older than her.

"Do you need help with your luggage?" he asked, and she didn't miss the strange look he gave her when he saw she had none.

To escape further inquiry, she quickly went down the hall to her first-floor room, locked the door behind her, and leaned against it. Looking around at her new surroundings, she saw what to many would look like a rather drab bedroom with its stained and threadbare carpet and the smell of stale cigarette smoke. But after the barren basement she'd had to endure for years, to Robin this was sheer luxury. There was even a TV with a remote control.

She tried out the bed and reveled in the comfort of its mattress and pillows—two pillows! Though tempted to continue to lie there, her stomach grumbling reminded her she hadn't had anything to eat. Unlatching the door, she peeked down the hall and spotted a vending machine. That would have to do.

Hunger satisfied, she checked out the bathroom—her own private bathroom—with a tub. This greater temptation told her the bed could wait. She filled the tub, and enjoyed the first hot bath she'd had in six years, then washed out her underwear, hung it over the shower rod to dry, double checked that the bolt was on the door, and crawled between the sheets.

The people in the next room must have been watching an action movie on TV, and thanks to the thin walls, Robin expected it would keep her awake... yet she was almost immediately fast asleep.

It was near morning when she dreamed of her shopping trip, starting her new job at Danny's Family Restaurant, and then dropping a whole tub of the restaurant's empty dishes and silverware with a crash. Apparently, the crash was actually nothing more than someone in the motel making a loud noise, but it was enough to startle Robin into her new reality.

Rachel... I must remember my name is Rachel Cooper now. She knew she had done nothing wrong and railed at the need to take such measures.

It doesn't matter. I have a place to stay. I have a job. And I'm free.

CHAPTER THIRTEEN

I can't believe that Mia chick. I give her the opportunity to go out with me, to get some coffee, and she says, *"I drink tea."* And here I am British. A tea drinker should go for that, right? But no, Miss Nose-in-the-Air says, *"I drink tea,"* and just leaves me standing there like a schmuck. I'm Harry Tate! I'm not that schmuck Harold anymore. And she doesn't know I'm not really from England so she should'a been impressed as all get out. I guess little miss Myopic Mia is too stuck on herself.

Let it go, Harry! You don't need her!

I don't. Nope, there's plenty of women I can get. Like that little slut, Treva. She's been practically beggin' for it. So maybe I'll just give her what she's lookin' for. Maybe. But not yet, Harry. Let's put her on the back burner because you can have her anytime you want.

No, I'm not giving up on this one. Not yet. And now I've got her address. I knew about where she lived from where she cut off the trail, but now I know exactly where to find her *and* her sister. That sister, Julie, is more of a looker anyway. Plus I've seen her checkin' me out. Yeah, I just might have to turn on the charm with that little Trixie. Maybe I'll take both of 'em. The Reed sisters.

I haven't tried that yet... Yeah, I like it. That might be all kinds of fun. I will be their king and subjugate them both. Like the kings of jolly old England. Have a little drink. Have a little fun. Then one by one, teach 'em to fly!

CHAPTER FOURTEEN

Mia lingered over her second cup of tea and smiled at Ron rinsing the breakfast dishes and putting them in the dishwasher. "I like this side of you, but I can't help but wonder where this sudden helpfulness is coming from."

"Aw, c'mon. I've helped out before, haven't I?"

"Yes, you have, but you've got to admit that's usually after I've started cleanup and you jump in—not that I don't appreciate that because I totally do—but you jumping up and doing it all while I sit and watch? You can't deny, that's new." Mia couldn't resist teasing him though she was certain she understood his motivation.

With the few dishes cleaned up, Ron went behind her, put his hands on her shoulders, and kissed her on the cheek. Mia delighted in moments like these. It felt so comfortable... so right. "I'd think you were trying to win my affection, but since you already have that, I must ask, what's spurring you on this morning?"

"Nothing, my dear. It's simply in my nature." He had taken the seat next to her and now took her hand. "But you did say we'd head over to Madison around nine, right?"

There it was. "Yes, Detective Bishop, and don't worry. Give me five or ten minutes, and I'll be ready."

"Okay. Mind if I go down to your studio and enjoy your work while I wait?"

"Be my guest," Mia said already hurrying upstairs.

True to her word, she quickly brushed her teeth, combed her hair, freshened up and went down to the basement studio where Ron was meandering around looking at the peaceful landscapes, the several portraits of Simeon, and stopping to examine one of

73

her most recent works. "Is this the diner where we ate on my birthday?" he asked.

"Yes. I think I'm going to give it to them, like Julie suggested, if they want it. What do you think?"

"That's a good idea, and it's a great rendering. Isn't that why you did it?"

"No, I hadn't planned it. But I had an itch to do a charcoal, and that's what developed." Mia didn't miss Ron's doubletake. Since he'd come to understand and accept her gift for creating pieces with special meaning when she got that itch, she knew he'd be wondering why this. But then, so did she.

"Do you think you were *inspired* to draw this because of that waitress's death?" Ron gazed at the painting on the easel. "I mean maybe you don't think it was a suicide either."

"Maybe. I don't know. But speaking of that, don't you want to get going?"

"Absolutely."

They waved to Julie who was already riding around on her toy. "I offered to do the mowing for her," Ron said, "but she insisted she likes doing it."

"I know. The grass hardly has time to grow before she's out here mowing again. I think she's just found a new way to procrastinate her writing deadlines. How 'bout I drive?"

"Sure, you know where we're going, and instead of watching the road, I can chill and look at my favorite view." He jumped in the passenger side of Mia's Civic, fastened his seatbelt and turned at an angle from which he could stare at her.

Mia giggled nervously and quickly tried to distract him by bringing up the reason for their trip. "I was talking to Gabby from the office about Nancy Owens, the first suicide, and Gabby said the other counselor had confided in her that although she was engaged, she was having some doubts because she was attracted to someone else. She was even thinking about going out with this other guy."

"I wonder if the local police know that?"

"If she did, maybe she felt guilty. That might explain it, right?"

"Possibly. Did this Gabby know who the other guy was?"

"No, she said Nancy never told her his name."

When they arrived at the police station, Mia checked in and asked to see Sgt. Evans. They were told to have a seat, and expected to wait a few minutes.

Twenty minutes later, watching Ron's knee bouncing up and down, Mia wanted to ask if they'd been forgotten. Although it wasn't in her nature to be assertive, she got to her feet and said, "Let me see what I can find out."

"Is that really Mia Reed?" a voice called from a doorway down the hall. Evans, looking much like he had the last time she saw him, came bounding out wearing a grin. "How the heck are you?"

Mia gave him a quick thumbnail sketch of what she'd been up to then introduced him to Ron. "Detective Bishop is with the Pittsburgh Police Department."

"Nice to meet you, and really sorry I kept you waiting. We're a little short-handed at the moment and I was knee-deep in paperwork. That's actually the only reason you caught me here today. So, come on back." Evans led them to a small office where stacks of files told Mia he wasn't kidding about the paperwork.

She sat quietly listening to the detectives share information, and it was soon evident the local police had been looking at the two suicides. They had a lot of the same questions Ron did, but they weren't aware of the information Mia had gotten from Gabby.

"That's interesting, Ron. And what may be even more noteworthy is the Owens woman wasn't wearing an engagement ring when we got to the scene."

"So I guess maybe she'd broken the engagement after all. She must not have been in a good place... maybe suicide is a possibility, Sgt. Evans."

"You can call me Jason, and let me give you another bit of information that wasn't in the news. The Dawson woman's fiancé told us she'd been acting kind of weird—his words—but she hadn't broken their engagement, and guess what... we didn't find a ring on her finger either."

Even Mia thought that might be too much of a coincidence.

Sgt. Evans checked the time. "If there's nothing else, I really do need to check in with my captain. You remember my old partner, Jack Webb, Mia?"

"Yes. Isn't he your partner anymore?"

"No. It's Captain Webb now. Our old captain retired a month ago, and Webb got his position. And we haven't found a replacement... so if you want to get away from big city life, Bishop..."

CHAPTER FIFTEEN

Seven years ago

Brushing her long, brown hair Robin marveled at how much her life and her appearance had changed. Her hair color was only one of the many changes she had made since arriving in Martin Township two years earlier.

When she caught her reflection in the mirror, she could barely recognize the healthy, somewhat overweight brunette looking back at her or reconcile it with the image of that skinny, frightened looking child-like young woman with stringy blonde hair who had first come to this little town. She had no longer been a child either chronologically or in the theft of her innocence, but she most certainly had lacked the real-life experiences of the average twenty-one-year-old woman.

And those first few months had continued her nightmare of fear—fear that somehow the two animals who had held her captive would find her. She knew they would never hold her prisoner in that basement again—she wouldn't let that happen—but they might carry out their threat of killing her if she ever tried to escape. The only time she'd felt relatively safe had been from the time she locked her door and threw the bolt each night until she ventured out the next morning.

But slowly, gradually, as the months went by uneventfully, Robin had begun to relax, and her time bussing tables only lasted six weeks before the owner recognized her reliability and suggested she train as a waitress. Robin's quiet, pleasant manner made her great in the new position, and the improved pay—especially with the generous tips of *most* of the customers—had enabled her to gradually add to her thrift shop wardrobe. Within the first three or four months, she put on a little weight, and by saving every penny, it wasn't too long before she was able to get out of the motel and rent a studio apartment. She remembered how nervously she'd signed the lease as Rachel Cooper, her new name.

"Rachel," Danny called her out of her reverie. "Are you about ready to go?" Dan Hummel, owner of Danny's Family Restaurant, had been charmed by the young waitress and taken her under his wing. After nearly a year, Robin had learned to trust him and finally succumbed to his desire to be with her. His gentle touch and tender kisses warmed her and made her feel less alone. It was only when he went further that she turned cold.

"Ready." *Rachel* came out of the bathroom of her small apartment and joined Danny for the short ride to the restaurant. "Thanks for the ride, but I really could have walked and you could've gone home later," she said fastening her seatbelt.

"You know I like to make sure everybody shows up and there aren't any problems in the morning. However," he said reaching over and taking her hand, "we could save the drive if you'd move in with me." After divorcing his wife, Dan had moved into the large, spacious upstairs apartment of the big old building that housed his business.

Robin smiled demurely. "I know, but... I'm sorry, I'm just not there yet." Robin appreciated Danny's kindness and patience, and she certainly felt safer from harm when he was with her, yet each night that he stayed over, as he crawled into her bed, her muscles tightened. She could never truly relax until she heard his deep breathing and knew he was asleep.

And then there was the big question... did she love him? She didn't think so. She allowed him to make love to her, and when he did, it was nothing like the cruel torture she'd endured with Buddy and Charlie, but all the same, it was something to be borne not enjoyed. Not at all what it looked like in the movies or the way it was described in her library books.

Danny parked in his reserved parking space, and they went in the brick building's private side entrance where, after a quick embrace, Danny headed up the steps to his apartment and Robin went down the hall to a door leading into the restaurant's kitchen.

Jackie, who was in charge of the kitchen, was already prepping and called a quick, "Good morning," barely pausing from her task.

Robin turned on the rest of the lights and was checking the booths and tables to be sure everything was in order as the rest of the staff filed in. Before long the closed sign was turned around to open, and the first few diners arrived. Then, as though the chow bell had been rung, the morning rush began.

Robin had become quite used to the hectic pace, and these first couple hours always flew by. "Thanks, Rachel. See you tomorrow," was repeated many times by their morning regulars, and when they reached the typical lull between breakfast and lunch hours, Robin reached for a piece of lemon meringue pie—her favorite—and a cup of coffee.

"Hey Rache, there's a couple guys at table eight," Jackie said looking out the pass-through.

"Don't worry, I'll take it," Flo said. "You enjoy your pie." Her fellow waitress, Florence, had become her one close friend since she came to Martin. The only person she let get close to knowing the truth of her past.

"Thanks, Flo!" She was indeed enjoying her pie, savoring every bite, when a sound caused her to choke.

"Are you all right?" Jackie asked.

Robin nodded and took several small sips of water to clear her throat. But the sound reverberated in her ears. *It can't be.* She was afraid to turn around. Afraid to look. Afraid to discover that the person behind that laugh was one of the men from her nightmare.

Without looking, she picked up her plate and cup and quickly went to the kitchen.

"Is something wrong with it?"

"What?" Robin didn't understand Jackie's question.

"The pie... I've never seen you not finish a piece of lemon meringue. Is it okay?"

"Yes, yes, it's good. I just need to go to the bathroom," Robin said dashing off. She closed the bathroom door and leaned against it trying to stop the sudden shaking that had taken over her body. The room tilted, and she sank to the floor to keep from falling.

That laugh. She'd heard it too many times to have any doubt. But how? Why? How did they find her? She didn't know how much time had passed when the knock on the door startled her back to the present.

"Are you all right? Rachel?" It was Flo, and Robin heard the alarm in her voice.

"Yes, I'll be right out," Robin called. Clambering to her feet, she rushed to the sink and ran the cold water, splashing some on her face to take out the burning stress. When she emerged, Flo was still standing near the door.

"What is it? You look awfully pale. Are you sick?"

"No, I, I just... well maybe. I mean, I might have wolfed that pie down a little too fast."

"Okay, well take your time. The guys at table eight just had coffee, and looks like they're about ready to leave—didn't want refills. We should still have a while before the lunch bunch comes in, so relax."

"Thanks, I think maybe I'll get some air."

Struggling to breathe evenly, Robin wasn't likely to relax, but she made it to the back door, cracked it open, and scanned the back lot. The only car she saw was Danny's so she ventured out cautiously. Part of her wanted to run upstairs and hide under Danny's protection, but another part of her was driven to find out—to know for sure—if Charlie and Buddy had found her.

She crept along the side of the building and guardedly looked around the corner to Main Street just in time to hear the truck's engine start up. It pulled out from the curb half a block down. It was them. Robin knew that pickup too well to have doubts. If there had been any, it vanished as they drove by and she saw who was sitting in the passenger seat. It was Buddy.

Robin stumbled through the rest of her shift, keeping vigilant watch on customers coming in the door, especially the men, but when Danny drove her home and expected to stay, she disappointed him. "I'm just really tired, and I believe I'm getting a migraine. I think I want to go to bed early... and alone."

When he was gone though, Robin didn't lie down. Instead, after a good cry, she made a plan. She wasn't going to hang around and risk having those two thugs grab her again. Unlike when she escaped two years earlier, this time she had money. Danny had taught her to drive, and now she could afford to buy a klunker and drive herself. A quick check on the internet and Robin chose her destination and started packing. It was time to move on. Tomorrow she would call in sick, leave a note for Danny, walk to the used car lot at the end of town, then come back for her belongings, and simply disappear.

CHAPTER SIXTEEN

L ooking at her schedule for Monday, Mia saw it was going to be a long and arduous day. She was still amazed at how quickly her caseload had grown. Even though Sarah and Gabby had each taken on many of her grandfather's patients, a few remained for Mia, and she was seeing the majority of Nancy Owens's clients too. However, she knew she wasn't alone. Everyone was working long hours and would continue to do so until her grandfather returned to work or—in the event of his retirement—another therapist was hired to take his place.

As a young man Dr. Andrew Reed, founder of the Reed Mental Health Center, had joined two other psychologists in a small practice, but after the first ten years, the owner of that agency had decided to retire and sell his practice. Grandpa Andy and his wife, Val, had taken a giant leap of faith and a second mortgage on their home to buy the practice, and within a few years it had grown to the need to hire additional staff and eventually find a larger building to house them. Now, even if Andy returned fulltime, Mia imagined they would need a larger staff.

Mia's attention was brought back to her current situation as everyone got to their feet to sing the next hymn. It was one of Mia's favorites, but she was embarrassed at the chorus. She sang, "And He walks with me, and He talks with me, and He tells me I am His own..." She felt it happening. It was beyond her power to stop it. Her chin quivered, her eyes filled, and the lump in her throat kept the rest of the words from coming out aloud. It happened every time. Mia was always overpowered by the words, by the message, by the truth of it.

She could feel Ron looking down at her, and she took a deep controlling breath, swallowed and continued to sing. But when they came around to the chorus again, she took a safer route and lip-synced. Not until they sat back down in the pew, did she realize Ron wasn't laughing at her. When she glanced up at him, she saw nothing but adoration in his eyes.

Knowing the man she loved didn't have the same religious conviction as her, had been a concern for Mia until she learned he respected her beliefs. She could understand his anger with God and even why he might doubt His very existence after He had *allowed* Ron's parents to be killed and his sister taken from his life.

Of course, she had her own opinions and had once tried to explain that God wasn't a puppet master pulling the strings. He didn't make these things happen; but He gave the strength to get through them. When their disagreement on the topic nearly developed into an argument, they had agreed to simply respect each other's views and beliefs. Besides, she had to admit she too grappled with understanding why God seemed to help them sometimes and leave them floundering at others. Yet she held onto her beliefs through faith, and she needed the man in her life to respect that, and maybe someday Ron would share her beliefs. So, having him standing next to her taking part in her church service gave her hope.

"I love you," Ron whispered as they slid out of the pew to leave after the final hymn. She gave his hand a squeeze in response, loving the warmth of his hand in hers.

"Are you ready for this?" Mia asked once back in her Civic. She laughed at her boyfriend's sudden look of fear and anguish.

"Oh no, meeting the whole family!" His feigned horror was quickly replaced with a look of amusement, but Mia believed he was hiding a bit of anxiety. "They don't bite, do they?" he asked wide-eyed.

It was Mia's turn to be amused. "No... well at least I don't think so. You might have to watch out for Cody though. He kind of sees himself as my protector. No, seriously, he'll love you—they all will—but for some reason, ever since our mother died when we were kids, we kind of looked out for each other, and then when we hit our teens, he got the idea he had to look out for me." Though she didn't mention it, she knew it had all started after she'd been kidnapped. Cody wasn't ever going to let anything happen to his sister again.

"Okay, I'll watch out for him."

As it turned out, Ron needn't have been afraid. Before they'd even made it to the Reed dinner table, he and Cody were bonding over their mutual love of Penn State football. With Cody as a recent Penn State grad and Ron a long-time fan, they had lots of stories to share and even made plans for the future.

"Yeah, we can go to the games, and I'll take you to The Creamery—best ice cream ever!" Cody said.

"Okay guys, enough football talk," Mia said. "Dinner's on the table, and Mom said come and get it."

Once seated around the table, and as Ron was reaching for his fork, Craig said, "Shall I say grace?" Mia saw Ron yank both hands into his lap. As her father said the short blessing for them and their food, she slid her hand over Ron's and he peeked with one eye and gave her a slight smile of appreciation.

"Let's eat," Craig said immediately after his amen. "Ron, dig in... don't be bashful." Mia's father helped himself to a couple slices of baked ham, passed the platter to Ron, and reached for the scalloped potatoes. "I'm almost glad the weather forecast changed our plans. A cookout would've been fun, but this is one of my favorite meals."

"And there's plenty of summer left for cookouts," Sarah added. "Maybe we can do that next weekend."

Mia appreciated her parents' casual acceptance of the man she loved, and she could tell by the way Ron's shoulders relaxed that he did as well.

"I think a cookout is a good idea for next week if the weather's good, but not here," Julie looked across the table at her sister. "At *our* house," she said.

Mia could have hugged her. She wasn't sure their little house could handle a sit-down dinner for her whole family, but their backyard was perfect for a cookout. Now all they had to do was get an outdoor grill. "Do you think Bobby might want to drive back for it?"

"Don't count on it, sis," Cody said. "I'm going out there Tuesday so I'll ask him if you want, but I don't know if he could separate himself from Megan that long." He rolled his eyes and described his brother as madly in love.

"Well, tell him to bring her along, for heaven's sake. Ron needs to meet the rest of the family," Mia said.

"Should I be afraid?" Ron asked.

Cody laughed. "Yes, be afraid. Be very afraid. He's the crazy one!"

The whole family laughed at that, and it was Sarah who said, "I think you and your brother might share that trait. When we get the boys together," she said looking at Ron, "it can be a real circus."

"Not to change the subject, but how's Grandpa doing?" Mia looked to her father. "Do you think we should ask him and Grandma to join us?"

"Yes, that's a great idea, hon. You'll be surprised at the progress he's made already. Especially his speech. There's not so much as a minor slur anymore." Craig rubbed his chin with his forefinger. "I've seen him pause and get frustrated a few times searching for the right word, but I don't think anyone else would even notice."

"And guess what," Sarah chimed in looking at her husband. "Your mom said he's planning to come back to work week after next. Just a few hours a day, couple days a week at first—Mom insisted—but eventually he's thinking of seeing clients three or three and a half days a week."

"Good for him. I know he's getting restless being home all the time. PT doesn't keep him busy enough and he's starting to drive Mom crazy."

Mia was sure her father was right about the physical therapy. And she was even more certain the agency needed him back. "So

Mom," she said, "are we still going to be searching for another staff member? Grandpa coming back will certainly ease things up a bit, but we don't want to have to refer anymore clients to other agencies."

"We've been searching, and we do have a couple of candidates who seem like a good fit, but we need your grandpa's input before we make a final decision. I hope we can get somebody soon because honestly, since we lost Nancy we've been swamped."

The mention of Nancy Owens had a sobering effect on the family until Julie jumped up. "Hey, didn't I see dessert in the kitchen?" This brought a lighter, happier mood to the room.

By the time the meal was over, and the key lime pie cleared away, Mia knew Ron was a perfect fit with her family. She had given him a questioning look when they talked about plans for the following week's cookout but hadn't been able to read his expression.

About an hour after dinner Mia and Ron said their goodbyes to her parents and siblings and headed back to the cottage to have some alone time before Ron left for his drive back to Pittsburgh. "So... what do you think?" she asked.

"I think they're great. No wonder you turned out so good."

"No, I mean thanks, but that's not what I'm asking. What do you think about next week? I hate to ask you to drive out here two weeks in a row."

"Try and stop me." Ron laughed. "I can't stay away from my lady for two whole weeks. Your brother, Bobby, isn't the only one who can't handle being separated from his girl," he said with a kiss on her forehead. "Besides I told Evans I'd check back with him. I think I might use a vacation day and come out Friday if that's okay with you?"

"Okay? I'd love it! But I know I have clients booked all day so I probably won't get home 'til about four or five o'clock. Julie will probably be around though."

"I can keep myself busy. Besides, I've got some things I want to check out. I'm gonna have to get the lay of the land if this could become my home."

***

On the drive back to Pittsburgh, Ron had lots of time to think, and his brain was like a washing machine agitating his thoughts. The mention of Nancy Owens at the Reed dinner table had put the detective part of his mind in gear, and of course when he said goodbye to Mia again, the man who wanted to love, be loved, and have her as a permanent part of his life struggled with finding a solution. This long-distance thing was tiresome, and what hold did Pittsburgh really have on him?

The job. Of course, there was the job. It was a grind, but it was all he knew, and maybe, just maybe, he'd find a clue to solve the cold case that haunted him. *But why Pittsburgh? Couldn't I work on it from a small town same as I can in the city? And family— and the small-town pace—and Mia... And I know there's a homicide to be solved. Suicides? Nope, double murder—I'm sure of it.*

And could Mia and her drawings possibly hold a key to finding his long-lost sister? Ron no longer struggled with whether Robin was dead or alive. He was now convinced his sister was out there somewhere.

And Sgt. Det. Jason Evans said they were short-handed... *Why not? I want Mia in my life. I want a family with her. But I will find you, Robin!*

CHAPTER SEVENTEEN

Seven years ago

Getting out of town had been a little trickier than Robin anticipated, but she was finally on the road in her green 2001 Ford Fiesta. It had a lot of miles on it, but the body was in great shape, and the used car dealer had assured her the previous owner was fastidious. *Someday,* she thought, *I'm going to get that new car smell, but this will do for now.*

So there she was, driving down the highway with a full tank of gas, and a full belly from her quick stop for a breakfast sandwich. It was good, though she knew breakfast at Danny's restaurant would have been better. She had become attached to the place and loved that the service came with a personal small-town touch. She'd been a part of that small-town touch, getting to know all the regulars and what they liked. Many had become friends, and she would miss them. But now she had to move on, to another place, another town, and she knew exactly where she was going. Robin began to relax and think about what was next.

It was time to shake off the fear of her early morning encounter. Driving back to her apartment from the used car lot, her blood had run cold when she'd seen the familiar pickup driving toward her. As they passed, she stole a glance at the driver and saw Charlie look over in her direction and do a double take. Then she saw the pickup's brake lights in her rearview mirror. With no doubt he'd be turning around, Robin sped up and made several turns, winding around to the back of her apartment. She'd quickly grabbed her belongings, thrown them in the car, wiped the sweat from her hands and headed out of town.

When she'd finally gotten about fifteen miles out of Martin, Robin had stopped for a soda, parking behind the building and watching out the window for any sign of the pickup. Seeing none, she got back on the road thinking and hoping Charlie was still searching for her in town—or maybe he didn't really recognize her new look. With her nicely styled brown hair and the pounds she'd put on, Robin knew there wasn't much resemblance to the skinny sickly-looking girl they'd last seen. And if they asked around for Robin Bishop, they'd have no luck. No one knew her by that name.

But she wasn't taking any chances. She knew Rachel Cooper had to move on, and remembering where she was going this time, it wasn't as daunting. A special childhood memory was drawing her to the area where a relative had lived. Thinking about Aunt Patty's house by the lake made her smile, and even though the woman had lost a battle with cancer two years before the rest of her family was taken from her, Robin still cherished her memories of that peaceful place.

Her recollection of playing hide and seek and tag with Ronnie made her melancholy, but was somehow comforting at the same time. When she finally reached the area near the lake and saw bunches of coneflowers growing in front of one of the bungalows, the vision blurred through her tears. It evoked memories of Aunt Patty scolding Ronny for running through her beautiful flowerbeds...

By mid-afternoon Robin checked into a small locally owned motel—it would do until she could find a better place to stay. Then she checked the internet for places to eat nearby. Her primary goal wasn't so much the food, although it was way past lunchtime, as to find a job. At least this time she had a skill, and she knew she was damn good at it. All she had to do was find a restaurant that needed a good waitress, so two birds...

Back in the car, she drove to the first location and deciding it was too fancy, drove on. Robin thought the diner a few miles away might be a better fit, and when she parked and went inside, it felt familiar and comfortable. She slid into the red vinyl booth and checked the laminated menu.

"Hi, yes. I'd like a Diet Pepsi, and I'm ready to order if that's okay," Robin told her waitress. She took note of the girl's name tag. "Thanks, Connie. Could I have the mushroom and swiss burger and fries, please?"

She thanked Connie again when she brought her food, and not until she had relished every morsel, did she broach the subject of employment. "Thanks for the great service," she said wearing her most charming smile. "I saw there was a help wanted sign in the window, and I'd like to apply for the job. Do you know who I should talk to about it?"

"Sure, hold on and let me get her." Connie dashed off and returned moments later with the hostess.

"Hello, dear. Connie says you're interested in a job. Do you have any experience?"

Robin quickly mentioned her previous position and explained she'd left that job to move to this area. She had chosen the perfect time—the lull between lunch and dinner crowds—so after a quick interview, Robin filled out the short application and was asked how soon she could start.

Before leaving she had learned the woman doing the interview was the manager, Katie, and the owner left the hiring to her. "I'm sure you'll meet him when you start," Katie said. "I think you'll like Kevin. He's a good guy to work for. See you Thursday. That will give us time to check your references—just a formality. Oh, and did you say you've worked in the kitchen too?"

References? Robin's heart quickened. She took a breath but answered evenly. "Yes, a little. I mainly learned to help with the breakfast rush when needed. But I like cooking, and I'm a quick learner."

"Good to know. Okay, Rachel. Welcome aboard." Katie shook her hand—it was a good handshake—and Connie gave her a big smile as she was leaving.

Robin felt good about this place. She liked the setting and the vibe she got from the people. She had checked the bathroom—a good way to evaluate the cleanliness of a place—and it was immaculate. Even the name of the place was sweet... The Sweet Glen Diner. But without a good reference none of that would matter.

Back at the motel, Robin made the phone call she'd been dreading. She was ashamed of the way she'd left Danny with nothing but a note to explain, so contacting him would be tedious. She never meant to hurt him, but then she'd never made him any promises either. All the same, she knew she'd hurt him and calling to ask him to give her a good reference tugged at her conscience.

Danny kindly let her off the hook though she heard the hurt in his voice and the trace of anger when she couldn't give him an explanation that made sense. But in spite of it all, he promised to tell her new employer what a good worker she was.

"Just do me a favor, Rachel," he said.

"What's that?"

"Try to find a way to be happy."

Robin ended the call with the knowledge she would never see or speak with Danny again. That chapter of her life was over. *I've got to make a new life here. I will.*

She spent the next two days exploring her surroundings and searching for a place to live. Robin didn't require much and was delighted to find a second-floor apartment within her means. Her thriftiness over the last two years was paying off, and the lovely couple who owned the big old house and lived downstairs said it was vacant and clean so she could move in whenever she wanted. Although the apartment came furnished, it lacked any personality, so Robin moved her meager belongings in that same day, then scoured the local shops and picked up pieces of décor to help make it her own.

On the way back to her new apartment, she passed a hair salon, "Tresses by Tracy," and made a quick decision to circle back around. Three of the six chairs were empty, but Robin didn't think they would be able to give her a cut and color without an appointment. She was wrong. An attractive blonde, who turned out to be the salon owner, Tracy, said she'd had a cancellation and could do her hair then and there if they got started right away.

Less than two hours later, back in her Fiesta, Robin pulled down the visor and checked out her new look. Rachel Cooper was looking downright sassy with her chic auburn wispy-layered pixie cut. She hardly recognized herself, but she loved the look and had a feeling her new hairdresser would become a good friend.

Juggling her packages, Robin unlocked the private entrance to her apartment, then made three more trips carrying her finds up to her new home. The final trip included the *pièce de résistance*... a painting for over the sofa. She removed the one hanging there and replaced it with the picture that had stolen her heart. "Perfect," she said stepping back to admire the beautiful watercolor of three purple coneflowers.

Chapter Eighteen

"Hey, Jules. I know it's my turn to do dinner, but I had to squeeze in an extra client this afternoon." Mia placed her last patient's file in her To-File tray and picked up another. "I have one more person so I'm not going to get out of here until a little after five o'clock. Then I have to be back for two more starting at six-thirty. How about we grab something at the diner tonight... my treat."

"Sure, should I meet you there?" Julie asked. "Okay, see you at 5:15."

The sisters pulled into the diner's parking lot at the same time, and Julie led the way inside where the hostess showed them to a booth. Julie took the seat facing the entrance and sitting across from her Mia looked around at the other diners. There were mostly couples—many of them senior citizens—one three-some that looked like a special day for a grandchild, and a single sitting in the next booth with his back to Julie.

"Hi, my name is Connie, and I'll be your server today."

"Looks like you've made some upgrades since the last time I was here." Julie patted the new brown vinyl bench seat in the booth.

"Yeah, the owners have been fixing it up little by little. The old red vinyl was lookin' a little worse for the wear. Can I get you something to drink?"

"Yes, we'll both have unsweetened iced tea, and we're ready to order if that's okay."

After the waitress had taken their order, Mia said, "Looks the same here as it did when I brought Ron for his *fancy* birthday dinner."

"Really? I guess they must've done them shortly before that. Speaking of your beau, he is coming for our cookout this weekend, isn't he?"

"Definitely." Mia's cheeks warmed and she wondered if her sheer pleasure in thinking about him showed.

"Look at you beaming over there. Well, that's good. Grandma said Grandpa is going stir crazy and needs to get out of the house, so they are definitely coming too. And wait 'til you see the new gas grill I got at Home Depot."

"I hope you didn't spend too much." Mia couldn't believe the way her sister seemed to throw money around and worried she'd have to carry the burden of paying for any unexpected work needed at the house.

"No, it wasn't that bad, and I'm doing six months same as cash—I'll probably pay it off in three. It's all good. Now all we have to figure out is what we're going to cook on it," Julie said pulling a pen and tablet out of her bag.

Before they'd finished the last morsel of their dinner, the sisters had planned the menu. "We don't have to worry about dessert," Julie said. "I talked to Grandma Val today, and she said she and Mom have that covered. And speaking of dessert, did you see the strawberry cheesecake?" She eyed the assortment of glass domed desserts on the counter.

"No, and I'm not looking. I've gotta run." Mia reached into her purse. Handing her sister forty dollars she added, "That should cover it. You stay and have the cheesecake. On second thought, could you get me a piece to go? I'll have it when I get home. I'm probably going to be up late because I've got an itch."

"Uh-oh..."

Mia laughed. "Yeah, I don't know what will come of it... maybe another diner picture. That reminds me, I want to bring that other one over here this weekend."

Mia grabbed her bag and slid out of the booth, but hesitated at the sound of a familiar accented voice coming from the man in the booth behind Julie.

"What's wrong? Did you forget something?"

"No," Mia said checking the time. "I really have to get going. I'll see you in a few hours." *I know that voice,* she thought as she walked back to the car.

***

Miss Nose-in-the-Air left, and I had sister all to myself. This was the perfect opportunity to put the moves on that little Trixie. She had no idea Harry Tate was sitting behind her all through dinner, and even though I had other plans, I wasn't about to miss this chance.

I lingered over my tea—I'd rather have coffee like I do at home, but that's not British enough—and waited for Connie to bring my target her dessert.

"Would you like anything else, Harry?" Connie asked me. I figured the bimbo in the next booth would realize it was me when she heard my name, but no. She was too busy stuffing her face.

"No thanks, luv. Just the bill please," I said, and turned enough to see if Julie Reed had recognized my voice—my wonderful British accent. She had.

"Harry, hi. How are you?" she asked turning to be sure it was me.

"Why hello," I answered widening my eyes to show my surprise. "It's Julie Reed, right?" I rose to my feet and nonchalantly slid into the booth across from her. "May I join you while I wait for my bill?"

She nodded her assent, and Connie left to get the check. She would be easy game too, but two waitresses from the same diner might not be a good idea. Especially this soon after Dana. Besides, I could imagine the little lass sitting across from me in her brightly colored smock flying like a butterfly.

"I hope you won't consider me too forward, but if you have no plans for this evening, I would love to take you for a drink."

"Thanks Harry, but I really can't tonight. I have a deadline to meet."

"Oh, that's right, you're a writer, aren't you?" Of course, I already knew the answer. There wasn't much I didn't know about either her or her sister.

"Maybe another time," I said, and when she agreed, I knew I had baited the hook. I could bide my time, but then on second thought... "How about this weekend?"

"Oh, I'm sorry, but I already have plans."

I'd heard them talking about some cookout, but that wouldn't take the whole weekend. I could feel my blood begin to boil. *Who does she think she is?*

At that moment Connie gave me the check and her usual big flirty grin, so I slid out of the booth prepared to say goodbye *for now,* but as I turned, I heard, "Harry..."

"Yes, luv?"

"I don't have any plans for next weekend," Julie said.

Ha! Now I've got her. "I'll call you then."

"Um, don't you need my number?" she asked. *How naïve.*

"Oh, that's okay. Your information is on William Shakespeare's file." I winked, thinking what a stupid name for a cat, and walked away leaving her drooling, I'm sure. A week and a half to wait. Yeah, this one's gonna be fun to teach.

***

It was hours later that Mia finished her drawing, and when she put down her charcoal pencil, she sat back and looked at it in amazement. *Julie, you're beautiful, but why did I have such an itch to draw you... and where's your usual smile? You look so, so... somber.*

Chapter Nineteen

Three years ago

"Everything looks good, Connie. You can head on out and I'll close tonight," Robin said.

"Okay thanks, Rache."

Robin had long since learned to answer to her new name.

Connie threw her bag over her shoulder and headed out the door. "See you in the morning... that is if you haven't had that baby by then."

"She wasn't going to give you a chance to change your mind, was she?" Kevin said coming up behind Robin and putting his arms around her.

Kevin Long, owner of the Sweet Glen and Robin's husband, had been attracted to her from that first morning he'd seen her standing in his diner nearly four years before. She hadn't known of his attraction right away though. It wasn't until more than a year later that he finally approached her. By then she knew he'd lost his wife and daughter in a tragic accident three years after they'd married. Connie told her Kevin had been devastated, and for a while, she didn't think he would ever come out of it.

It had taken him a long time to be ready to love again, but that time had finally come, and though Robin held him at arm's length for quite a while, Kevin's persistence and his kindness eventually won her over. Though she didn't feel the romantic movie kind of love, she had learned to love the goodness in him and recognized he could give her that normal life she longed for.

Robin had insisted she didn't want a big church wedding—she couldn't imagine having such a ceremony without any family—and since Kevin had gone that route with his first wife, he agreed. Robin thought he seemed relieved.

They had married at the courthouse with only her best friend, Connie, and Kevin's brother, Guy, as their witnesses. "Rachel Cooper" had become Rachel Long, and the four of them had then enjoyed surf and turf at the best little steakhouse in the county before the newlyweds left for a week at Cape May.

"What are you thinking about, sweet cheeks?" Kevin asked spinning her around.

Robin couldn't tell him the thoughts that had run through her mind seconds before he touched her, so she lied. "I was thinking about how much our lives are going to change when this little one arrives," she said patting her baby bump. And it wasn't too much of a lie since she thought about that so often. What she couldn't tell him was that when he'd just touched her, she flashed back to another time—a horrible time—when the men who touched her caused so much pain.

Kevin knew she'd jumped, but he'd grown accustomed to that and accepted her explanation about being easily startled. Robin could never explain the real reason for her reactions without giving up her façade as Rachel Cooper Long. Sometimes she was tempted, but she'd been living the lie too long. And what would her husband think of her if he knew? Since her marriage was based on a lie, was it even real and legitimate? Besides, Robin wanted nothing more than to lock those memories up in a corner of her mind, throw away the key, and never visit them again. If only she could...

"Yes, our lives will be different, but we'll figure it out." Kevin kissed her forehead. "And this little boy is going to be blessed to have a mother like you. Don't worry, we have the nursery ready... crib's set up. We're ready."

Robin still couldn't believe she had carried this baby to full term. Because of the miscarriages she'd had when she was not much more than a child herself, she didn't think she'd ever be a mother. But would the baby be all right? And what did she know about being a mother? *Nothing,* she thought.

"Uh-oh..."

"What? What's wrong, Rache?"

"I think we're going to have a baby." She nearly doubled over with the pain. It didn't last long but it was more intense than the earlier ones had been.

"Here, sit down, sweet cheeks. Do you think you're in labor? Have you been having contractions?"

"Yes, but I wasn't sure... I mean, I thought maybe Braxton Hicks, but no, this hurts too much."

Kevin pulled the phone from his back pocket, asked how far apart they were, and called the obstetrician when she said probably about five minutes. "Okay. Just try to relax. She's going to meet us at the hospital," he said.

The drive to Madison General only took about twenty minutes, and when she admitted being scared, Kevin reassured her and squeezed her hand. It wasn't long before she was the one squeezing his hand—only harder—until another pain subsided. "I'm sorry," she said.

"No need to apologize, love. I know it's bad... it's okay. You're doing great."

Of course, he knew. He'd been through this before when his first wife had their child. Robin wondered if he was thinking about that time, but her wondering was soon interrupted. The next contraction brought her back to the present, and she saw Kevin check his watch.

"They're getting closer together," he said pulling into the emergency room entrance. "Sit tight. I'm gonna run inside and get somebody to bring you in, then I'll park." He sprinted through the doors and was back before the next contraction hit. From there everything happened so fast and, to everyone's amazement, by midnight Robin was holding her newborn son in her arms. She looked at the child in awe and said, "Hi there. I'm your mommy... oh, you're beautiful... I love you so much." Never before had she spoken those words with such utter truth. Never before had she known such love.

The nurse who had just put the newborn in her arms smiled and asked, "Have you decided on a name?"

"Not yet, Susan," Robin said.

"I guess we'd better finally decide on one, huh?" Kevin took several pictures of his wife and son.

Robin wondered what this was like for him. Was he remembering when he held another newborn child who he was destined to lose? But she wouldn't ask... wouldn't risk the pain it might cause. There were questions better not asked... at least not yet.

They had tossed around several names, and Robin knew Kevin's first choice wasn't the same as hers, but she couldn't... wouldn't concede this one. She looked at the tiny baby boy in her arms, then up at her husband, and through a blur of tears she introduced him to their son.

"His name is Ronald."

CHAPTER TWENTY

"Where's your stuff?" Mia asked Ron when he came into the house empty-handed.

"I'm not sure I'll be spending the weekend here this trip," he said trying to keep a straight face. But when he saw Mia's welcoming smile dissolve into a look he could only read as dismay, he couldn't hold back any longer. "I have a surprise for you." He took Mia into his arms and kissed her.

They were interrupted when Julie came bounding down the steps. "Oh. Hi, Ron. How's it going?"

"Good. Very good, actually." Pulling some twice-folded papers from his pocket, he handed them to Mia. He watched as the wrinkle between her brows smoothed, her eyes widened, and her jaw dropped.

"This... this is a lease... But—"

"What? Let me see that," Julie said grabbing the papers. "Holy macaroni!" Her eyes flew from the page to Ron then to Mia. "It's here! Just five miles down the road."

"Are you all right?" Ron asked seeing the tears in Mia's eyes.

"Yes, yes, but how... I mean when?"

"Well, I've been busy. First, I did some searching online, made some calls, and found a place—nothing fancy—where I can be closer to the woman I love." Ron relaxed as he watched Mia's reaction. He had been sure this would make her happy, actually seeing her joyful reaction made it a certainty. As hard as it was to leave the Pittsburgh area where he'd lived his whole life, he knew it was worth it. "And I didn't just get to town. I came here yesterday to check the place out and meet with Captain Webb."

"For real?" Julie piped in. "You got the job?"

"I knew you would." Mia took Ron's hand and led him to the couch. "They would've been crazy not to hire you." Simeon joined in the celebration, hopping onto Mia's lap but slow blinking at Ron.

"So, you approve, Simmie?" Ron had quickly fallen under the Persian's spell and had been relieved the feline accepted him. William Shakespeare was not quite as friendly and had a tendency to watch him from afar. Mr. Shakespeare meandered around the room, hopped onto Julie's lap then back down—not being much of a cuddler—and eventually settled onto his cat tree to keep an eye on everyone. Meanwhile, Simmie snuggled in and started his engine.

"My furry little purring machine seems as happy about all this as I am," Mia said. Ron scratched the pet's head between its ears and watched him close his eyes. "Keep that up and he's going to be taking another lap nap."

Ron knew she was right. "Yeah, he's a lazy little bugger."

"So, tell us about this place," Julie said waving the lease papers she still held.

"Well, there's not much to tell. It's not nearly what you have here, but it's got everything I need. You know, living room, kitchen, bedroom. It's clean, oh, and it's right on Main Street. Over a coffee shop, so that's handy."

"Oh, I think I know exactly where you mean. Look at the address, sis," Julie said holding out the lease agreement. "It's the Hav-A-Cuppa Café." Ron saw the sisters exchange a look, and when he nodded, their laughter made him wonder what must be wrong with the place.

"All right, what's so funny? Is the place haunted or something?" he asked.

"You're not going to believe this, but—"

"That's my old apartment," Julie interrupted her sister, and they both went into fits of laughter. "Can you believe this?"

"All right, you two. Cut it out, you're scaring me. Is there something wrong with the apartment? Are there bugs or rats or something? What did I miss?"

"No, I wouldn't live anywhere with varmints," Julie said indignantly, "but it's just crazy that you're going to be in my old place. I thought it was a great apartment. And when I used to get tired of my four walls, I'd often go downstairs and hang out and do my writing there. I only moved out because I wanted a house like a real grown-up."

Ron could imagine her sitting there with a pencil tucked behind her ear, just like it was now, working on her laptop. "Well then, I guess you won't have any trouble finding me. I have the keys right here, and I was going to ask if you guys want to go see the place, but I guess that won't be necessary."

"I'd like to see it, Ron," Mia said. "I was only there a few times when Julie had it, and the last time was back in December."

"I'm sure it looked better then—it's pretty empty now—but let's go take a look." Ron and Mia got to their feet, disturbing the sleeping Simeon who gave them a look of disdain. "Are you coming, Julie?"

"No, I'll pass. I know what it looks like," she said with a wink. "Plus I need to get some red-ink editing out of the way so I can relax and enjoy our cookout tomorrow."

Ron was glad she declined so he could have this time alone with his girl. He drove most of the way steering with his left hand while holding Mia's hand with his right.

The tour of Ron's new apartment didn't take long. It was only sparsely furnished. Much of what had been there when it was Julie's had gone with her to the cottage. The kitchen with its black refrigerator had a built-in microwave above the gas stove, a window over the sink, which let in plenty of sunlight, and there was a small table and four chairs by the other window. The only furniture in the carpeted living room was a green plaid sofa, an olive green over-stuffed chair, an oak side table, coffee table, and empty TV stand. The spacious bedroom was also carpeted, and there was a queen-sized bed, two nightstands, a dresser, and a big empty space where Julie's computer station had stood. A single lamp on one of the nightstands enhanced the overhead lighting.

Finally, there was the bathroom which had obviously been recently remodeled. The clean, modern gray and white bath seemed almost out of place compared to the rest of the apartment.

"This is new," Mia said. "They must've remodeled in here after Julie moved out. Nice. But we definitely need to get you some lamps, and these bare walls..." she said moving back to the living room. "We've got to do something about those."

"True, but I know an artist who I'm hoping can help me out with that."

"I'm already going through my portfolio in my mind. I think we can make this a lot cozier."

"Cozy enough that you'll want to spend lots of time here with me?"

"I'm sure of it," Mia said, and Ron knew, as difficult as it had been, he'd made the right decision in moving to Sweet Glen.

Back in the car after their tour, Mia asked, "So, when do you report for duty on your new job? And will you be doing the same thing? I mean the same rank or whatever?"

"Yes, and I have one more week to wrap things up in Pittsburgh, so I'll be starting here a week from Monday."

"Are you really okay with it? I mean the whole move away from your roots and all?"

"Yes, Mia, I am. I've been living in the past for too long. I'm ready to put down new roots." And he meant every word. Though he would never give up on that one cold case, never give up on finding Robin, he was now drawn to this new life in this new place. On a personal level he was drawn by the love of his life sitting next to him. But on a professional level, he felt compelled to solve a new case—a case of two women he was sure did not commit suicide.

CHAPTER TWENTY-ONE

I drove down to Glen View Court this afternoon, and it looked real quiet. That Trixie wasn't out mowing or anything, and that nosy neighbor next door to her house was giving me the stink-eye so I had to get outta there. Damn cul-de-sac. Can't so much drive by unnoticed like most places. So then I went back down and parked by the trail. It's only about half a mile from there to where I can cut through to the back of her house.

No luck there either today. The other one was out for her run earlier—if you can even call it a run—the wuss walks more than she runs, but not that Julie. What does she do in that house all day? Says she's a writer. I guess she's writing the world's greatest book. Yeah, right. The book that will never get an ending.

I called her yesterday, all proper and everything.

"Hello, lovely lady," I said. Told her how I'm looking forward to seeing her next week. She had no idea how much I was looking forward to it.

Then she said, *"Oh Harry, I'm so sorry. I completely forgot my kid brother is going to be home next weekend. Can we make it the following weekend?"*

She's got a helluva nerve breaking a date with me. When she has a chance to go out with me, she should be jumping at it. Ha! That's a good one, Harry. Yeah, she'll be jumping all right.

Not for another whole week though? How am I supposed to wait that long? No, I can't. I grabbed the dish towel to dry the sweat that broke out on my head then dried my hands on my pants. I was pacin' around the kitchen tryin' to wear a hole in the tile when it hit me...

Like they always say, there's plenty of fish in the sea. Or birds in the sky. Yeah, I knew where I could find me another birdie who just couldn't wait to fly.

"Hello, luv," I said when Treva answered the phone. I could hear how flustered she was by the way she stumbled through her greeting. Once she finished stammering around, I threw out the bait. "Treva dear, my weekend just opened up. Would you like to go out for a bite tomorrow?"

"Tomorrow? Oh gosh, I sort of had plans..."

She paused, and my blood began to boil. This chick has been making eyes at me for months. Now I give her a chance, and she's gonna put me off? But before I could get too pissed and say the wrong thing, she started talking again.

"You know what, Harry? I think I can make a call and change that. Yeah, sure, I'd like that. What time?"

"Tell you what, luv, I've got a lot going on in the afternoon. I heard about a great place about ten miles north of town, but I'll be coming from the other direction. Could you meet me at The Black Angus around 8:00?" There was no sense having her neighbors see me picking her up. She agreed, of course, and was there waiting when I arrived at 8:10.

She pulled the usual chick schtick, dabbling over her salad and asking for a box to take half her steak home. She giggled. Said she'd have it for lunch the next day. Ha, that's what she thought.

By the time we left there it was getting pretty dark, and she was easy.

"How about a little ride? Why don't you take your car, and follow me? I know a spot with a beautiful view."

"Why don't I just ride with you, and you can bring me back for my car after?" she asked.

"We could, my dear, but it would be out of the way for both of us. This way we can both head home from there. But don't worry, luv. I'll follow you to make sure you get home safely. And maybe you can show me your place when we get there." Though I knew I would never see her place.

She agreed, of course... putty in my hands. When we got to the destination I had in mind for her flight, I told her how much I wanted her, how I'd been dreaming of holding her in my arms. She gladly hopped in the back seat of the car with me. I guess she doesn't like it rough though, because right after, she said she wanted to go home. I let her out of the car, but she wouldn't be going home tonight.

And she wouldn't be having that steak tomorrow either. Looks like Dr. Curtain will need to find a new receptionist.

Chapter Twenty-two

"I think the gang's all here, Jules," Mia said. "All but Bobby. I'm beginning to wonder if he's ever going to come for a visit."

"Oh, I forgot to tell you. Mom said he's coming home next weekend, and guess what... we're finally going to meet his girlfriend, Megan," Julie said. "I'm anxious to check her out. I think she's a real free spirit, and a bit of a health nut. I'm pretty sure they're sharing an apartment. It sounds like it's getting serious."

"Really? You mean serious like maybe wedding bells could be in his future kind of serious?"

"Can you imagine? Wouldn't it be funny if he was the first one to get married?"

"For sure," Mia said grabbing the condiments out of the fridge. "Especially since he's the youngest, not counting Squirrel of course." The four older children considered their youngest sister as more of an only child with lots and lots of parents. When Cody and Mia's father, Craig, had married Julie and Bobby's mother, Sarah, they had become a blended family of six, and then Destiny came along years later. She was adored by all, so of course they spoiled her. It was Julie who had started calling her Squirrel when she was three years old and used to giggle and chase the bushy-tailed critters. The nickname stuck.

"Speaking of Squirrel, where is she anyway?" Mia asked.

"She was playing eighteen holes this morning, but her friend's mom is going to drop her off when they're done."

"How come you know so much more about what's going on with everybody than I do?" Mia struggled against the jealousy that sometimes snuck up on her when seeing how close Julie was to their mom. Sarah didn't feel like a stepmother to Mia since she'd been her mom for almost as long as she could remember. But what she saw when she watched Sarah and Julie together, and when she heard how much they shared, she often felt left out.

"Because when you're not working or painting, you're hanging out with your *beau*. Whereas I'm mostly home... writing."

"Yeah, or procrastinating," Mia said.

"Ha-ha. Besides, Mom doesn't go in 'til two o'clock on Thursdays, so we have lunch and catch up."

"Every week? Hmm, how come I never heard about this before? Neither of you ever mentioned it or invited me."

"That's because you go in early that day, duh."

"Yeah, okay." Mia shrugged it off. "Let's get the rest of this stuff outside." She grabbed the tray full of condiments and headed for the door out to the deck.

"Do you need help with anything?" Valerie Reed asked, popping into the kitchen.

"No, Grandma. Julie and I have this. You go relax on the deck with Grandpa. And you guys stay inside," Mia said shooing Simeon and Willie away from the door.

The next few hours were filled with the wonderful smell of hot dogs and hamburgers cooking on the grill, Craig asking who wanted cheese on their burgers, and lots of laughter and family fun. Watching Ron relax with her family, Mia envisioned a future filled with many more such gatherings.

"Does your family always eat like this?" Ron asked with a grin and a plate holding a burger, Grandma's potato salad and homemade baked beans, Mia's seven-layer-taco dip and a pile of chips, and Julie's pasta salad. "It's a good thing you got these big plates."

"Not always, but cookouts, yeah." Mia laughed at how much he'd piled on. "You'd better save a little room. We've got watermelon and Mom's brownies for dessert. Oh, and I almost forgot, Grandma made a lemon meringue pie. It's in the fridge."

Ron looked at his plate and said, "I think I'm in trouble," which brought a laugh all around. But a shadow crossed his face. Whenever he heard the words "lemon meringue pie" it evoked the memory of ones his mother made when they were growing up. It was his sister's favorite.

"Hey, speaking of trouble, there's our squirrely girl," Craig said when his youngest daughter came bounding around the side of the house. "You'd better hurry up and dig in, kid, before the food's all gone."

Destiny took him at his word and filled her plate then pulled a chair up next to her grandpa. Dr. Reed showed very little evidence of the stroke he'd suffered, but his youngest granddaughter was still shaken by the scare. She adored her Grandpa Andy.

"Hey Ron," Cody said getting to his feet and tossing his Styrofoam plate in the trash. "You wanna give me a hand with this, and we can throw some shoes?" The horseshoes were a housewarming gift from Cody, and though Mia knew he got them because throwing them was one of his favorite backyard pastimes, she was delighted with the gift.

Ron said he didn't know anything about throwing horseshoes—which drew a look of incredulity from Cody—but he would be happy to help, and it wasn't long before Cody was calling a challenge.

"Let's go, Dad. Time to wup some butt! Are you in, Ron?" He was in. "Okay, we need one more. Jules?"

"All right, me and Ron against you and Dad."

Mia laughed when she heard Ron's feeble agreement and saw his look of helplessness. She understood more when he tossed the first horseshoe about two feet beyond the stake.

"Holy crap! My partner is the Hulk," Julie said stepping up to take her turn. "You guys are toast!"

"I don't think so," Cody said. "Power ain't no good without aim."

Mia watched with delight as the four of them laughed and teased each other. It didn't take long before Ron got the feel of it, and he and Julie were giving their opponents a run for their money. Julie was good, really good, of course. Mia had gotten used to her sister being better at sports. *She's good at everything.*

"Julie tells me Ron found a place, and he's moving here," Sarah's voice interrupted her thoughts.

All eyes turned to Mia. "Seriously? When did she tell you that? We only found out yesterday."

"She called me yesterday afternoon and said you'd gone to see his new place. Oh yeah, and she said it was her old apartment that he rented."

"No shit?" This time everyone's attention jumped to Destiny as she clamped her hand over her mouth. "Sorry," she said sheepishly.

Mia saw a mix of surprise and amusement on her grandparents' faces—though her parents didn't look too amused. She rescued her little sister by bringing the attention back to the subject at hand. "Well that sister of mine spoiled the surprise, but yes! He's moving here. And yes, it's Julie's old place." She would have said more, but the hum of Ron's cell phone, which he'd left on the table, drew her attention. She glanced at the caller ID. It said *Capt. Webb.* "It's Ron's new boss. Hey Ron," she called across the yard. "You're getting a call from Captain Webb."

Ron didn't get to the phone in time to catch the call, but when he checked voicemail, all the fun and joy of the day seemed to drain from his face.

"What did he want? You didn't even start yet," Mia said.

"I know, and I don't need to go in, but he said I might want to meet him. They found the body of a young woman. Webb said it looks like she jumped off the cliff by the bridge that goes over the railroad tracks about five miles north of town. Could be suicide, but he's not thinking she jumped, and I've got to agree. More likely she was pushed. I thought it before, but now I'm convinced... we're looking for a serial killer."

CHAPTER TWENTY-THREE

"Kevin, can I leave Ronnie with you while I run these errands? Shouldn't take more than an hour."

"Sure, I think he's about ready to fall asleep anyway, and could you stop by the diner and check on things?"

"No problem... love you." Robin closed the door behind her. She didn't mind adding to the stops she needed to make, and having a break from their active little three-year-old—as much as she loved him—was nice too.

Robin loved her husband and their son and was happy and content with the life they had made together. It was more than she ever thought she'd have. She rarely even thought of herself as Robin Bishop anymore, at least during the day. In her waking hours, she was Rachel Long, and she rarely thought about those teenage years she'd spent as a prisoner, used and abused by those cruel animals disguised as human beings. She was too busy taking care of her little boy and helping out at the diner.

But at night, the monsters would come out to haunt her once again. And since it was happening more and more frequently, Kevin had become concerned. He had even recommended that she might need professional help to deal with whatever hidden issues were causing her so many nightmares. Robin tended to become defensive when he made such suggestions. *What is he insinuating? That I'm crazy?* She knew she wasn't. And the idea of bringing up the past and talking about it with a stranger tied her insides in knots.

After completing the few errands on her list, Robin pulled into the diner's parking lot just as it began to rain. Out of the corner of her eye, she noticed a man and woman jumping in the car to her left and decided she'd better hurry herself before getting caught in a downpour. She fixed the emergency brake and opened the door to get out but stopped short as the car to her left pulled away. The young woman in the passenger seat was looking at the driver, but it was the driver who caught Robin's attention. There was something so strikingly familiar about him. Her eyes filled with tears as she remembered her twin brother who had been so brutally taken from her when they were only fifteen.

The memory of that cruel night came rushing back along with the vision of her dead parents... the shock of seeing their bloodied bodies and then being grabbed by Buddy and dragged out of the house, pulled into the backseat of their old pickup while Charlie sped away. She remembered crying, begging them to let her go, and worst of all she remembered how she'd screamed for her brother and been told he was dead.

After fifteen years, the anguish returned as fresh as if it had happened only yesterday. *Stop it, Robin,* she chided as the ground seemed to tilt beneath her. *Get it together.* Wiping away the tears and blowing her nose, Robin gave her head a shake, and when she regained her equilibrium, she went inside.

All was well. The kitchen was closed and the cook was busily cleaning his grill, two of the girls were setting up for the next morning, filling salt and peppers, putting out flatware wrapped in napkins, setting coffee cups upside down, and Connie was closing the register. Satisfied, Robin was about to leave when Connie stopped her.

"Rachel, wait. Come see this." Connie led her to a booth way in the back where there was a large framed picture leaning in the seat. "One of our customers is an artist. She drew this. Isn't it amazing? She said she thought we might like to hang it here. What d'ya think?"

"Wow," Robin looked at it and smiled. "That's incredible. Of course, yes. She's good... really good." Taking out her phone she snapped a photo to show Kevin. "I think it would look great between the two windows up by the register. Do you know the woman's name? I'd like to write her a thank you note... or do you think we should offer to pay her for it?"

"Hmm, I don't know. But her name is Mia something."

Robin showed Kevin the picture when she got back, and he was likewise impressed and pleased. "Yeah, we should definitely offer her something." They decided to ask this Mia woman how much she wanted for it, and go from there, hoping she wouldn't be insulted if she'd meant it as a gift.

Even though Kevin assured her Ronnie was sound asleep, Robin had to look in on him. He had kicked off his covers, so Robin covered her little boy, then sat down on the side of his big boy bed, stroked his cheek and kissed his forehead. This was a ritual she cherished, and Ronnie was always the last image she wanted to see before going to bed each night.

Once in bed herself, Robin pleaded a headache to avoid her husband's advances. Fortunately, he was a very patient, loving husband who never pushed too hard, but his sigh told her how frustrated he was getting. *I'm not being fair.* Yet as much as she loved him, intimacy was still, at times, quite difficult and painful. And recently the flashbacks had intensified the problem. She didn't really relax until she heard the soft snoring next to her.

Lying quietly in the dark, Robin's mind wandered back to the parking lot—she couldn't believe how she'd fallen apart because she saw a man who reminded her of her brother Ronnie—and back to her long-ago ordeal... And it all followed her into her dreams and restless sleep until she sat straight up, awakening with a gasp.

"It's okay, sweet cheeks. It was only a bad dream." Kevin held her until she felt safe again in his arms. *Maybe he's right. Maybe I need help.*

CHAPTER TWENTY-FOUR

R on held Mia in his embrace, hating to say goodbye after such a fun weekend again. The last few days had flown by, but he reminded himself he'd be back in a week. Maybe less. "I really should get going," he said. "They're calling for some pretty rough weather later tonight. If I leave now, I can probably beat the storms."

"Yeah, I guess I'd better let you go." Ron noticed Mia's actions weren't matching her words. She didn't move from his embrace. And he didn't loosen his hold on her either. "Thanks for going to church with me again this morning," she said turning to face him.

"You don't need to thank me, sweetheart. Anything that important to you is important to me. Besides, I kind of like hearing you sing, and you've got a good preacher." Ron had attended church with his family growing up, but at fifteen, in his mind, God had betrayed him and left him alone. While in the depth of despair, he had tried attending his old church a few times, but he could never accept that a loving God would have done this to him, and he had carried his anger with God for all these years.

But now he smiled remembering the part of the sermon where the man in the pulpit seemed to be talking to him directly. Ron wondered how many other people had the same feeling. *At least he didn't make me want to storm out of there.* "I didn't doze off once even though you did keep me up late last night."

"Hey, that wasn't my fault. You should blame Captain Webb. If he hadn't called you away for nearly two hours, we would've gotten an earlier start on the movie."

"All right, we'll blame Webb." Several more minutes passed, and he wasn't sure how much longer they would have sat there if Julie hadn't come in the front door.

"Don't mind me, you two lovebirds," she said going straight for the kitchen. "Just grabbing a water and heading upstairs."

"You don't need to rush off on my account. I really have to get going." Ron peeled himself away from the woman he loved and got to his feet. "But I'm going to do my best to wrap things up at the Burgh by midweek so I can get back and really settle in."

Mia's face brightened. Ron didn't have the heart to tell her what was creating such urgency in his mind. Of course, he did want to be settled in one place and stop driving back and forth to the city, and there were no open cases in his old job that were keeping him awake at night. There was, however, a case here that wouldn't let him rest.

After bidding goodbye to Julie, he ambled out to the car with Mia. "Do me a favor. Be careful," he said lifting her chin and looking into her eyes. "There's somebody out there killing young women—"

"Don't worry," Mia interrupted. "I'll be fine."

"Yeah, okay, but warn Julie to watch herself too, all right?" He couldn't shake the uneasy feeling in his gut. He didn't like leaving them alone, and that only added to the pressure he felt to locate this killer.

Ron gave Mia another kiss, making it even more difficult to leave, then finally climbed in his vehicle and waved goodbye. Before he reached the end of the cul-de-sac, he placed a call.

"Yeah, Jason, it's Ron Bishop again. What did you find out?"

"We still don't have a lot, but we got an ID on the woman. Name's Treva Wolf, single, lived alone. She worked for a Dr. Curtain. I can let you know if I learn anything when I interview him in the morning."

"Yeah, I'd appreciate it. I'm hoping to get back in town by Thursday but maybe you'll have this thing solved by then, huh?"

"Your mouth to God's ear... I'll keep you posted."

"Thanks Jason, and by the way, thanks for talking to the Captain about me. I'm sure that helped me get the job."

"No problem. It was all about timing. We needed somebody, and you fit the bill. Sometimes things actually work out."

"Yeah, I guess, but thanks anyway... and we're gonna get this guy."

Ending the call, Ron tried to focus on all he had to do before leaving the Steel City for good, but his thoughts kept coming back to the killer—and if there'd ever been a doubt in his mind these were murders, not suicides, he had put it to rest—the killer who somehow lured his victims to a place where, without evidence of a struggle, he could push them to their deaths.

Before transitioning to his new job in a new town, Ron needed to complete all the paperwork in front of him. He set aside his concern about the serial killer to focus on dotting every i and crossing every t. Nothing would be left to chance with cases he'd investigated. But when Det. Jason Evans called him the next night with more information about their latest victim, his new case immediately had his full attention.

"This Dr. Curtain is a veterinarian, and he was pretty broken up about the Wolf woman's death," Jason said. "He described her as 'a sweet and kind, loving girl who got along with everybody'."

"Was she engaged?"

"No, widowed actually. Her husband died about a year ago—had an aneurism—and she hadn't been in any serious relationships since he died. At least as far as her boss was aware."

"Okay, that's not the same as the other two, but still..." Ron thought for a minute. "Say, can you text me pictures of the body?"

Within seconds of ending the call, Ron was viewing the images on his phone. He transferred them to his PC to get a better look, then got Evans back on the phone. "Jason, you said Wolf was widowed. Did the vet happen to mention if she was still wearing her wedding ring?"

"No, that didn't come up. Why?"

"Well, I'm zooming in on this picture, and I can get a pretty good look at her left hand. There's no ring on it, but it kind of looks like a tan line where one might have been."

"I'm on it, Ron. Thanks."

Two days later, Ron was back on the road looking at the City of Bridges in his rearview mirror. He headed for his new home, his girl, and the case of the ring killer. He had been so busy the last few days tying up loose ends and packing the last of his belongs into his new Land Rover, his head was spinning from all the changes. A little part of him struggled with leaving his hometown and all he'd ever known, but he determined to close the door on that chapter of his life and move forward. *Here we go. New job, new apartment, new girl... new life.*

CHAPTER TWENTY-FIVE

Mia opened the door to the waiting area, called the name of her new intake client, and scanned the room. She gazed at the redhead nervously flipping the pages of a magazine expecting the woman to react, but she didn't even look up. Out of the corner of Mia's eye, she saw another woman get to her feet and approach.

"Hi there. Do you go by Kathy or Kathleen?" Mia asked the middle-aged woman.

"Kathy."

"Nice to meet you. Come this way." Mia focused her attention on her new client and put the redhead out of her mind, at least for the time being.

It didn't take long to come up with the diagnostic code she needed for Kathy's insurance, and a treatment plan was already forming in Mia's mind. Like so many people her age, Kathy was overwhelmed by being the primary caretaker for her aging mother who was in poor health while managing the responsibilities of caring for a husband and three children. She had given up her volunteer work in the community as her mother's health had deteriorated, and as a result, she fought off moments of resentment followed by guilt for feeling that way. Mia recognized her new client's pain because she'd seen it before in other women who took care of everyone but themselves. Mia's goal now was to teach Kathy the skills she needed to reduce stress and to take care of herself, or she'd soon be trying to pour from an empty bucket.

At the end of her hour with Kathleen Hummel, Mia walked her out to the reception area, and said, "I'll see you next Thursday." She saw that look of gratitude on Kathy's face that said *thank you for hearing me and giving me hope.*

Kathy took her appointment card and exited the empty waiting room. Mia had hoped to see the woman who had caught her attention earlier but realized she was probably gone by now.

"My next client isn't until two o'clock so I'm going to grab my bag and go get some lunch," she told the receptionist, but when she turned to go back to her office, she came face to face with the woman with auburn hair. "Oh sorry," she said stopping short to avoid running into her.

The woman smiled then headed out to the parking lot. *Those eyes!* Mia rubbed the goosebumps on her arms.

"What's wrong?" Ann asked.

"Nothing... but I, I think I've seen her somewhere before. Do you know who she saw today?"

"Um, yeah, I remember Sarah took her back. Why?"

"Oh, no reason. Wait, what's my mother doing here? She doesn't come in 'til 2:00 on Thursdays."

"I know, but your mom's a peach. We needed somebody to do this intake because everybody else was booked, and this lady needed a morning appointment."

Mia looked around at the empty waiting room. "So did Mom take somebody else back or is she free?"

"Nope. We're all done until one."

Mia thanked Ann, but instead of going to her office, she made a bee-line to Sarah's. "Hey Mom, quick question. You know that intake you just had?"

"Yeah."

"By any chance was the woman's name Robin?"

"No, it wasn't. Why?" Seeing her mother's look of concern, Mia considered telling her who she'd thought it was, but even though Mia had shared how Ron lost his family, she had never mentioned a name or explained that she suspected Robin was still alive. This wasn't the time or the place to go into it.

"Not important. She just really reminded me of someone." *Especially those blue eyes.*

It was many hours later that Mia finally sat before her easel to draw the woman with the familiar blue eyes, and when the portrait was completed, she was totally drained. When she'd finished with her final client and saw that Ron had called and left a message, she'd expected him to say he was back in town and coming to see her. She was only half right. He was back in town. But he was not coming over

Normally, Mia would have been disappointed, but this time she viewed it as an opportunity to scratch an itch. Ron had to work, but so did she. The task had begun calling her from the time she saw her mother's new client, and persisted until she'd gobbled down a quick dinner, fed Simeon, and finally answered its call, no longer able to resist its pull.

Mia studied the woman's image for several minutes upon its completion and noticed a look of fear in the eyes. Swiveling around in her chair, Mia opened the folder on her PC labeled portraits, and found the one she was looking for. It was the same face. The same eyes. The same fear.

The unknown woman in the drawing she'd done months ago... the one Ron had recognized and believed to be his missing sister, Robin... had long blonde hair and blue eyes. The woman she'd drawn today had beautiful auburn hair in a pixie cut. But the eyes were the same. *She said her name was Rachel, but that has to be Robin.*

"Boo!"

Mia had been so engrossed by the two images, she didn't hear the footfalls coming down the stairs.

"Sorry, sweetheart. I didn't mean to scare you. Are you all right?"

Mia laughed at herself and assured Ron she was fine but warned him not to be sneaking up on her like that. "I didn't hear you, and besides, you said you weren't coming over tonight."

"I lied," he said with a devilish grin and a twinkle in his blue eyes. "I got done sooner than I expected and decided to stop by for a little while. That is, if it's okay with you."

"Of course. It's more than okay," Mia said finding her way into his arms.

"Julie said I should come down and surprise you. I guess I did that all right. What are you up to? Another masterpiece?" He walked around to face the easel. Mia saw his jaw drop, then he turned to her. "Robin?"

"I think so."

"But why the red hair?"

"Well, I was actually doing a picture of a woman I saw—a redhead—who seemed to have your sister's eyes. Your eyes."

"You saw her?" he asked incredulously. "Where?"

"She was at the office. I mean she was a new client, but slow down. Let's not jump to conclusions." Mia feared she was getting his hopes up and couldn't risk the heartbreak he'd feel if she was wrong. "Her name wasn't Robin."

"What do you mean? What did she say her name was? Why was she there?" Ron fired the questions at her.

"I don't know why she was there other than she was a new client... and I couldn't really tell you why the woman was there if I did know. Besides, I didn't talk to her. She saw my mother and that's who told me it wasn't Robin. I snuck a peek at her appointment book—don't tell—and the name was Rachel Long." Mia pointed to the image on her computer screen. "But these two drawings really do look like the same person."

Ron looked from one to the other. "For sure. And they both look so sad... or scared. Why did you draw her like that?"

Mia looked into those same eyes and understood Ron was desperate to know... to find answers.

"I'm not sure, Ron. I guess it's just what I saw." And it was. To Mia it was a familiar expression. The woman with the auburn hair and blue eyes looked desperate for help.

Chapter Twenty-six

Haunted by the image of a woman he thought could be his sister, Ron's inner dialogue was chaotic. He stared into the darkness of his new surroundings. He vacillated between the absolute conviction that he'd finally found his sister and the inevitability that it was all wishful thinking. *But she's got to be alive.*

After a few years of getting no answers, Ron had given up asking God for help in finding his sister, at times doubting His very existence, yet lying in the darkness on this night, Ron wanted to pray. He didn't know what else to do.

God, I don't know if you're listening... I don't even know for sure that you exist anymore... but if you're there, I need your help. Ron searched for words, unsure what to say... how to ask for help after all these years. *I'm sorry I don't have the kind of faith Mia has, but it's kind of hard to believe you care after...*

He waited in the darkness. In the silence of the dead of night. But there was no answer. He thought about Mia next and wondered where she got her faith. Then he wondered something else. *Okay God, so how come you listen to her, you answer her prayers, and you leave me here without a word? Why?* Tears filled his eyes, and he was overwhelmed by loss and emptiness. Nothing seemed to make sense anymore. Nothing was familiar. *What the hell am I doing?*

Sleep finally came, but it was a restless sleep filled with dreams. In that early morning hour just before waking, he saw Robin, fifteen-year-old Robin, but he couldn't get to her. She was calling him, crying, begging him to help her. He ran, and when he got close, she disappeared, only to appear somewhere else. Just before he awakened, he got close. Really close. But when he reached for her, he hit a wall. A wall made of glass. He pounded on the glass, but it wouldn't break, so he stood with his nose against the barrier, tears streaming down his face, and watched as rain began to fall on her. She looked back at him and the rain turned red. With her hair soaked in red rain, the woman cried. For now, he was no longer looking at his fifteen-year-old sister. He was looking at the woman with tortured eyes and auburn hair.

The next two days flew by for Ron. Friday was filled with paperwork, getting acclimated to his new small-town police station, and reviewing cases—active as well as cold ones—but mostly paperwork. Before heading back to his apartment, Ron decided to make one quick stop.

Even though his new partner had already talked to the doctor, Ron wanted to visit the vet's office and talk with anybody else who knew Treva Wolf. You never knew who might mention a detail that could be the link to solving a crime. Unfortunately, he didn't learn anything new, and even the pretentious guy who worked with the vet and seemed to want to impress him with how much he knew about her, didn't really add any new or relevant information.

At the end of an exhausting day, Ron was ready to spend time with his girl but he'd forgotten she and Julie were going to a bachelorette party for a good friend. So instead, he settled for a fast-food dinner while watching the local news and weather—tomorrow promised to be sunny and pleasant—then pouring over his notes about the "ring murders" as they had decided to call them.

In need of a distraction, he turned the TV back on and started watching *The African Queen*, one of his favorite old movies, but he didn't see much of it.

Oh damn, ten o'clock. Ron had fallen asleep and woken to a John Wayne flick. Although he was a fan of the Duke, he decided to call it a day and hit the sack early. He hoped to make up for the rest he'd lost the night before.

Sleep came quickly in spite of his long nap in front of the TV, but it was another restless sleep filled with shadows and murders and women's lifeless bodies. He had finally had enough when he dreamed of a woman falling from the sky. A woman with red hair. He could hear her screaming, and he started running forward. He had to catch her. He ran and ran until suddenly he was the one falling. He awoke with that falling sensation, soaked in sweat, and sat straight up in bed.

Two large cups of coffee later, Ron showered and got ready for his day with Mia. By then he'd shaken off the last of the nightmares and was ready for the respite of a day in the sun. They were to meet for breakfast in the café downstairs. Mia had suggested she pick him up, and they'd take her car to do some much-needed shopping. Before heading down to the coffee shop, Ron looked around his barren apartment through her eyes and knew she was right. It definitely needed... something.

Mia was right on time, and Ron's day brightened just seeing her. He loved the little bounce in her walk and the way her eyes crinkled with her smile... the smile she was wearing as she came toward him.

"Good morning, handsome," Mia said. "Before we get breakfast, could you help me get a few things out of the car?"

"Sure. We'll be back in a few, Emmitt," Ron called over his shoulder to the barista.

Moments later the two of them returned, each carrying several framed pieces of art. Another early customer had grabbed the door for them, and they headed straight up to Ron's apartment to unload the treasures.

"These are fantastic, Mia." Ron was especially impressed by the 16" x 20" oil painting of a sunset over the sea with a sailboat silhouetted against the sun. "I love this one. It's so peaceful... but couldn't you sell this and make a lot of money?"

Mia laughed. "Well no, I don't think a lot of money... maybe a little. But it's worth more to me to see how much you like it. I saw this one summer when we were vacationing by the sea in Delaware. I took a picture of it, but then I knew I had to paint it someday." She pointed over the ugly plaid sofa. "I thought it might look good there."

"Perfect. Should I go ahead and hang it now?"

"Oh, gosh no. That can wait. I'm hungry!"

After a quick breakfast, the two did a whirlwind of shopping for lamps, new curtains, and other things to make Ron's place a little homier. "And maybe one of these days you can replace that living room furniture," Mia said.

"You mean just because it's hideous?"

"You said it, I didn't. But I don't want to have you spending all your money. That can wait, right?"

"No, let's go look at some furniture."

"Are you sure?"

"Yes, love, I'm sure. And don't worry, I can afford it." Ron and Mia had never really discussed finances, and he realized she had no way of knowing how much money he had, especially since he basically lived off what he made as a detective. Somehow it had never felt right spending money he wished he'd never inherited.

The rest of the day flew by, but by dinnertime Ron felt their mission was completed. "I've never in my life done that much shopping in one day. I don't know about you, but I'm exhausted."

"Yeah," Mia said, "that was a bit of a marathon. Sorry. I know you guys hate shopping."

"Yeah, typically true, but you know what? I didn't hate it." They both laughed. "Seriously, it was kind of fun shopping with you and thinking about making this place a little nicer." Ron looked around at his bleak surroundings. "I've always lived in furnished apartments and really never thought about or cared how they looked. It was just a place to eat and sleep when I wasn't working." He grinned and put his arm over Mia's shoulders. "But now I plan on having company."

"And would that company happen to be me?"

"It better be!" Ron put his hands on his hips and scanned the living room. "Maybe tomorrow I can pick up some paint for these dingy walls."

"Oh good, yes! What color were you thinking?"

"White, I guess. That goes with everything." He saw Mia roll her eyes. "What's that look? Am I wrong?" he asked with raised eyebrows.

"Well no, not wrong exactly, but seriously... white?"

"Oh, I forgot, I'm talking to an *arteest*. What would you recommend? Pink? Purple?"

Mia gave him a gentle swipe upside his head. "No, wise guy. But maybe at least something like Champagne Ivory, Coventry Gray, or Toasted Almond..."

"Well, how 'bout you come with me tomorrow and help pick it out? Color is your thing, and I'm not sure what you're even talking about." Mia laughed, and Ron loved the way her whole face lit up. "I could maybe meet you after church, grab something to eat, and then hit the paint store."

"Or you could come to church with me, maybe the eight o'clock service, then breakfast, then paint?" The way Ron was feeling about God right now, he thought he might be struck by lightning just entering His house. But how could he resist Mia when she slid her arms around his waist and looked at him with those beautiful eyes? "Don't forget we're having dinner at Mom and Dad's later, around three, so you can meet my brother Bobby."

"Church again, huh? Is this what it's going to be like when we're married?" The words had slipped out, and seeing the startled look on Mia's face, he wished he could suck them back in.

"Wait, what?"

"Just kidding," Ron laughed nervously. "I mean, someday. I mean who knows—"

Mia interrupted with more laughter. "Calm down. It's okay. Let's go get some dinner."

"Good idea," he said guiding her toward the door before he could get in any deeper. *But, yes, someday... maybe...*

CHAPTER TWENTY-SEVEN

I guess I oughta cool it for a while since all of a sudden, the cops seem to think my flyers didn't fly on their own. But they don't really know a thing. And that cop that was here the other day doesn't have a clue. He was nosin' around asking questions about Treva so I gave him some answers... led him on a merry chase.

I almost busted when he asked me about her ring. Did I ever notice if she was wearing a wedding ring? And I'm playin' with it in my pocket the whole time. Ha! My little memento right there and he didn't have a clue.

So, maybe just this one more... then I disappear.

Damn, it's hot already this morning! I was out there with this humidity, sweatin' my ass off, and that little chippie didn't show up on the trail yesterday or this morning. Well, I wasn't gonna waste all day waiting for her, so I decided maybe I might have better luck checkin' up on the other one. I thought she might be out riding around on her little mower again, but no luck. Guess it's too early.

Maybe because it's Sunday. Yeah, I don't guess I ever caught her mowing on a Sunday morning. Probably a church goer. Humph! Maybe I'll come back later.

Then I figured maybe I'd go have a closer look. Yeah... the whole neighborhood was pretty much dead—quiet as a graveyard. I strolled on up through the yard to see what I could see, and the blinds weren't even closed. There was nothing to see in there but a bunch of paintings and stuff. I thought about going up to the deck, but I was afraid that might be pushin' my luck. So I was gonna sneak around to the front, but halfway along the side of the house, I heard voices. They were laughing.

It was that artist chick, Mia, and I could hardly believe my eyes... she was with that damned cop. Well, that was a little too close for comfort, so I got the hell outta there. I'm thinking I might be pushing my luck going for that fish. I'd better stick with the writer. She already took the bait anyway. Only one more week...

CHAPTER TWENTY-EIGHT

Mia snuck a quick look at Ron and tried to read his expression. He looked almost pained, and she wondered if the minister's words were hitting too close to home.

Mia always felt a sense of calm when seated in her usual spot in the fifth pew from the front. The familiar wooden bench with the red hymnals in the rack in front of her, the red kneelers which had been added when she was an early teen, the candles glowing, and the beautiful stained-glass windows depicting precious scenes from the Bible all combined to say "welcome, be at peace." But it was obvious Ron was not at peace, and most certainly not comfortable as he squirmed in his seat.

It was the Old Testament reading that first appeared to cause his discomfort. *After these things the word of the LORD came unto Abram in a vision, saying, Fear not, Abram: I am thy shield, and thy exceeding great reward.* Genesis 15:1.

"Is everything all right?" she whispered.

Ron's only reply was a nod and a two-second smile Mia didn't believe, but with the preacher beginning his sermon, she didn't have time to pursue it any further.

Mia was, of course, quite familiar with the story of Abraham and Sarah and their longing for a child. There was little hope of them bearing a child at their advanced ages, but God made Sarah the unbelievable promise that she would be the mother of nations.

Abraham was seventy-five when God made this promise and many, many years passed, but God kept his promise. Sarah gave birth to Isaac when she was ninety and Abraham was one hundred years old. The preacher implored the congregation not to give up hope, and he assured them God would not forsake them. He ended by saying, "It may look like your situation, whatever it is, is never going to change, but in a split second... in the blink of an eye, God can completely resolve it."

Following the sermon, the congregation stood to say the Apostles' Creed. That's when, out of the corner of her eye, Mia saw Ron brush his finger under each eye. She passed him a tissue, and a look of understanding—though she wasn't sure she understood at all—and he looked down at the floor avoiding her gaze.

They didn't speak until they were back in the car, and Mia struggled with whether to ask him what was going on or leave it alone. She decided to follow his lead.

"Where do you want to go for breakfast?" she asked.

"We've got to go to the Sweet Glen Diner," he said looking straight ahead and pulling out of the church parking lot.

"Okay, sure. That's fine with me." Mia waited a moment and added, "But what do you mean by *we have to*?"

"Call me crazy, but you know that redhead you saw and drew the portrait of?" Mia nodded. She could hardly forget it. "Well, I had to follow-up and find out more about her. I know it's silly, but when you said it wasn't Robin—but you gave me a name, Rachel Long—I had to find out more about her."

"But Ron, I shouldn't have even told you her name. I mean, I wasn't thinking about confidentiality." Mia felt a wave of nausea. What had she done?

"Hey, don't worry. I didn't go into anything too personal. I just googled the name... and guess what?" Mia wasn't sure she wanted to know, but he told her anyway. "Her husband owns the diner. Coincidence? I don't know."

Now Mia's arms were covered in goosebumps. Maybe there was a reason she'd been stirred to draw the diner. Could Rachel actually be Robin? "Ron, are you thinking what I'm thinking?"

He still hadn't looked at her since they left the church... until now. "I don't want to get ahead of myself, yet. I mean, what if it's her? But why would she change her name? And why wouldn't she let me know she was alive?"

Mia saw the anguish on his face and searched for something to say but came up blank.

"She's my sister, Mia—my twin sister. It doesn't make sense."

"Ron, we don't know for sure that it's her. They say everybody's got somebody out there that looks just like them." She saw the crease between his eyes deepen but had to keep going. "And think about it. You haven't seen her in fifteen years."

"Yeah, I know," he muttered.

When they got to the diner and slid into the booth, Mia's favorite waitress came right over, coffee pot in hand. "Good morning, folks. Tea for you, right?" Connie asked. She poured Ron's coffee then said she'd be right back to get their order.

"Now what?" Mia asked when they were alone again.

"I'm not sure. But I felt like I needed to come here. Who knows, maybe we'll run into her and settle this once and for all."

It wasn't too long before Mia realized how prophetic his words had been. Connie came back with Mia's tea, took their order, and started to walk away, then turned back.

"Oh, I think the owner is coming in shortly, and I know she wanted to thank you for the picture. She and her husband both really liked it. Did you see it up there?" She pointed to where it hung. "I hope she gets here before you leave."

"I hope so, too," Ron said after Connie walked away.

When their food came, Mia ate with gusto—waiting until after church had given her quite an appetite—but she noticed Ron pushing his eggs around the plate rather than digging in as usual.

"Are you okay?" she asked, and when he nodded, she added, "Then can I have a piece of that bacon you haven't touched?"

He pushed the plate toward her without a word.

"Ron, we're not in a hurry. We can hang out until she gets here, okay? The paint can wait."

About the time Mia finished her Belgian waffle, Connie came back with the coffee pot... and news. "The owner just came in, and I told her you were here. She should be out in a minute."

Mia couldn't read the expression on Ron's face, but it looked like a mix of hope and fear. When the kitchen door swung open, they didn't see the woman with auburn hair. Instead a little blond-haired toddler came running out.

"Ronnie, wait," came a voice from behind him, and then there she was. "I'm sorry," she said catching up with the little boy. "He got away from me."

She had a lovely very familiar, shy smile and the bluest eyes. *It's like my picture has come to life.*

"You must be the artist," she said. "I wanted to thank you, and..." She glanced across the booth at Ron and abruptly stopped. Mia looked from her puzzled face to Ron's. He looked at the diner's owner and uttered one word.

"Robin?"

Mia looked from one to the other in those next few seconds—seconds she was certain must have felt an eternity to Ron—and she was sure the woman blanched, but when she finally spoke, they weren't the words Mia had expected.

"No, no, my name is Rachel Long. Thanks for the painting," she said scooping up the toddler and quickly vanishing into the kitchen.

"It's her," Ron said. "That voice... I mean those eyes, the voice, and a little boy named Ronnie? We've found my sister." Mia saw the tears filling his eyes and reached across the table to take his hand. "But why..." He stared at the door. Then without another word, he grabbed the check and headed to the register.

Once outside, he opened the passenger side door for Mia who stood looking at him. Both hands leaning against the roof of the car, Ron's head drooped. "Get in," he finally said brusquely.

Mia could tell his emotions were in turmoil so she quietly slid into the car, but before he could close the door, they heard someone calling, "Wait!"

Chapter Twenty-nine

Present day

"Dawn, could you keep an eye on Ronnie for a few minutes?" Robin asked the girl who'd been busy bussing tables. "He'll be fine eating his Cheerios. I just have to run outside for a minute." Her three-year-old was in his highchair in a corner of the kitchen where he appeared content until she headed for the side door. His face puckered up as he prepared to object, but Dawn handled it.

"Sure, Mrs. Long. He's my little buddy. Aren't cha, Ronnie?" Dawn seemed to adore the little boy she sometimes babysat. She grabbed a powdered doughnut out of the open box the staff had been sharing.

By then, Robin was out the door. She had to catch them. She had to find out.

"Wait," she called to the man leaning against his car.

He spun around, and Robin searched his face. It looked like her Ronnie—the one she'd lost all those years ago—only not. Besides, it couldn't be him... yet he'd called her Robin. *But he's dead. They said they killed him.* The man's face blurred as her eyes filled with tears.

"Who are you?" she asked barely above a whisper.

"You know who I am," he said moving closer.

"No... That's impossible—"

"It's me... your brother. And I know it's you... but Robin, or Rachel, or whatever you want to call yourself, I don't understand— "

"Shh," she interrupted. "I can't talk here. But... but, oh my God. It really *is* you. They said they killed you. I thought..."

Robin saw the look of disbelief on his face. *Those bastards!* She was nearly paralyzed by the gamut of emotions flooding over her. Rage—relief—joy—fear.

"Ronnie, oh Ronnie, it really is you..." Robin looked back over her shoulder, still stunned, but also aware the world she had created for herself might be about to come crumbling down. "I'm so sorry, but I... I have to talk to my husband. I mean, I have to explain..." Reaching out she touched his face to be sure he was real. Glancing over at Mia then back to her brother, her breath caught.

"It's okay, Robin." Ron was half laughing now, half crying, and Robin could see he was experiencing the same kind of crazy, shocked emotions, only without the fear. Her brother's voice reached her as though from a distance. "It doesn't matter. Whatever you have to do. Just so I know I won't lose you again."

"Never," she answered quickly, again looking toward the diner's side door. "Can I meet you later after I have a chance to take care of some things?"

"Of course," he said reaching into his pocket. "Look, here's my card. Call me anytime. Whenever you're ready. But don't make it too long—I've been searching for you for fifteen years."

Robin was looking at the card. "You're a detective," she said. "Wow." Unable to resist for one more minute, and no longer caring about having to explain to anyone, she tossed caution to the wind and threw her arms around her twin and cried openly. "It's a miracle." When she managed to pull herself away, she finally looked at Mia, the young woman whose artwork had seemed to bring them together. "Is this your wife?"

"No, we're not married," he answered smiling. Robin noticed the color flowing from his neck up into his cheeks.

"Oh, I see, but you'd like her to be, wouldn't you?" she whispered with a reminiscent feeling of the fifteen-year-old she'd once been. As Ron's blush deepened, Robin laughed through her tears.

Mia, who Robin could see had obviously been entranced by this whole dramatic scene, finally got out of the car and approached her. "It's nice to meet you, Robin."

"Thank you, and thank you for your wonderful picture of our diner. I—" The lump in her throat kept Robin from completing her thought. She swallowed hard, turned back to Ron and said, "I've really got to get back. My little boy, oh that's right, you have a nephew." She loved the way her brother's face lit up.

"I kind of thought so when I heard his name."

"I had to name him after you because... because I thought—"

Ron embraced his sister once again. "I am honored."

Going back inside after a tearful goodbye, Robin found her toddler covered in powdered sugar.

"Are you okay, Mrs. Long?" Dawn asked.

"Yes, yes, I'm fine," Robin said, grabbing a tissue to wipe away the lingering tears and runny nose. "I just had a bit of a tearful reunion with someone I hadn't seen in years."

Connie returned to the kitchen with an empty coffeepot, and Robin didn't miss the curious look she shot her way. "Who was that guy?" she asked in a half-whisper.

"I'll tell you all about it later, but don't worry. It's a good thing." *A really, really good thing. But Kevin...* "Are you ready to go, little buddy?" And though Ronnie fussed a bit at having the powdered sugar washed from his face, his usual good disposition returned, and he raised his arms to his momma. Robin thanked Dawn for watching him, and once she had him outside and strapped into his car seat, she started the engine and hit the voice command. "Call Kevin on cell," she said.

He answered on the second ring. "Hey, what's up? Everything okay at the diner?"

"Yes. What time do you think you'll be home?"

"We just finished the first nine, and we're making the turn. Why, do you need me to come home sooner?"

"No, enjoy the back nine. Hit 'em hard but not too often, and I'll see you in a couple hours."

"Are you sure nothing's wrong?"

Robin could hear the concern in his voice—which was understandable since she almost never called him on the golf course—so she rushed to reassure him. "Nope, nothing is wrong." In her mind it wasn't a lie. It couldn't be wrong that her brother was alive. "I just want to talk to you about something, and by the time you get back, Ronnie will be napping. It's all good."

After saying goodbye to her husband, Robin realized she would need every bit of the next couple of hours to figure out how she was going to explain to her husband that she was never Rachel Cooper. She wondered if he could possibly understand or ever forgive the lie.

Still in shock, with her mind spinning, Robin rehearsed a hundred ways to begin telling her husband the long, complicated story behind the lie, and yet two and a half hours later, when she stood facing him, she was at a complete loss. The words she'd prepared would not come out.

"Is Ronnie down for his nap?" Kevin asked.

Robin said he was and watched as her husband washed his hands, grabbed a beer out of the fridge, and came to sit on the other end of the sofa from her. Although she hated the smell of beer and the ugly memories it often summoned, she welcomed the extra seconds it gave her.

"So, what did you want to talk to me about?"

Gripped by panic, Robin heard the words coming out of her mouth and realized it was *not* going to be now. "It's actually no big deal," she lied, "but I ran into an old friend at the diner this morning."

"Oh yeah? Who's that?"

"Just a guy I knew from way back in high school."

"Not your first love, I hope—"

"No," Robin laughed nervously. "He was more of a buddy... like a brother." She wondered if a little truth mixed with the lie made it any better. Any less deceitful.

"Okay, so did you invite him for dinner or something? Is that the big thing we had to talk about... because you know I'm fine with having company. You're the one who never wants to socialize, Miss Homebody."

"No, I didn't think to do that—I probably should have—but he suggested getting together for lunch to talk about old times." Seeing a puzzled, possibly suspicious look on her husband's face, Robin realized he might, in fact, believe it was an old flame. She quickly added, "I think it was actually the woman's idea. I don't know if they're married or dating or what, but she said lunch sometime tomorrow would be fun. You don't mind, do you?"

"No, why should I mind? But you know I can't come along. I'll be at the diner most of the day tomorrow."

Yes, I know.

As soon as Kevin finished his beer and went out in the garage to clean his clubs—because they had to be ready for Wednesday's game—Robin pulled out her brother's card and with butterflies of excitement and a bit of vertigo, quickly punched in his number.

Ron answered on the first ring like he must have had the phone in his hand.

"Hi Ronnie, it's me." She heard the shakiness in her own voice, and when he returned her greeting, Robin thought he sounded a bit nervous too. "I... I wondered if maybe we could get together for lunch or coffee tomorrow."

"Yes, of course," he answered immediately. "Do you want me to come there?"

"No! I mean, how about I meet you somewhere away from where I work?"

"Sure, anywhere at all. I have an idea. How about the Hav-A-Cuppa Café? My apartment is right upstairs, so we could take as much time as we need to talk. After all, we've got a lot of catching up to do."

Ron said he'd let his partner know he needed an extended lunch, they decided on a time, and said goodbye.

"Okay, great. I'll see you tomorrow, Ronnie." Robin spun around at the sound of her husband's voice behind her.

"Ronnie?"

CHAPTER THIRTY

"Are you sure you're all right? We don't have to get the paint today, you know." Mia was certain Ron was in a state of shock yet he was acting as though nothing monumental had just occurred. "And Mom and Dad would understand if we skipped going over for dinner."

"No, I want to do both." Ron reached for Mia's hand and the reassuring squeeze helped put her mind at rest even more than his words. The fact that he held on to her was somehow comforting. "I'm anxious to brighten up the apartment and even more anxious to finally meet Bobby."

"But what about Robin?"

"I told you, I can't really do anything more until she calls, and I doubt she'll get back to me today. And even if she does call while we're at your mom's, I doubt if she'll want me to drop everything and go rushing back over there."

"Well, obviously if that happens, we would understand a jump and run. I mean, it's not every day you find your missing sister." Mia couldn't imagine the thoughts and feelings Ron must be having. "I couldn't hear everything you and Robin were saying, and I thought you two needed your privacy, but did she say anything about why she changed her name?"

"We didn't get that far, but I know she must have been through a lot."

Mia saw his jaw clench and the vein in his temple pulsed. "But why did she never get in touch with you?"

"She thought I was dead, Mia. Apparently, the bastards who killed our parents told her they'd killed me too."

Mia winced from his tightened grip on her hand which he quickly released, and the anger on Ron's face was almost frightening. She had never seen him look so furious. "I'm so sorry." The words felt inadequate but it was all she could think to say.

"Hey, the important thing here is, I found her. She's alive and well, and it's hard to believe, but I have my sister again." He sat silently. His white knuckles on the steering wheel regained their normal color. As the seconds passed, a smile slowly crept over his face smoothing out the deep creases on his forehead. "And I guess I have two people to thank," he said with a look her way.

"Really? Who?"

"Well, obviously you led me to her. If I hadn't met you, fallen in love with you," he said glancing over at her again, "and followed you here... and then there were your drawings. I mean, wow!"

Mia smiled, grateful to have been a part of it all but then wrinkled her brow. "So, who's the second person?"

"I thought you'd guess. What was it your preacher said this morning? Something about *you might think your situation isn't gonna change, but in a split second or the blink of an eye...*" He cast another sidelong glance her way, added a wink, and pointed upward.

"Oh," Mia silently gave thanks.

"It's crazy, really. Last night I prayed about it—and I'd given up on that and God a long time ago—and I was angry because I didn't get an answer. Same as always." Ron blew out a breath and shook his head. "And then this morning... that whole thing about Abraham and Sarah—not that I necessarily believed it, but—well, I somehow *knew* we had to come to the diner, and boom!"

***

Mia took the lead when they got to the paint store. It wasn't long before they were unloading rollers, paint pans, tape, and gallons of paint at Ron's apartment. "Maybe we can have a paint party next weekend and get it all done at once," Mia suggested. "And you can stay a night at our place if the fumes are too much."

"Do you think anybody else is gonna want to waste their weekend painting my place?"

"Sure. We'll throw the idea out there at dinner tonight and see if anybody bites."

"All right, if you're sure. But I don't want to put anybody in an awkward position where they feel trapped into helping."

"Leave it up to me..."

Mia didn't hear Ron's phone—he almost always had the ringer off—but she saw him jump and grab his cell from his pocket.

"She's coming over here tomorrow," he said after ending the call. "I don't think there will be much sleep tonight." He had barely uttered the last word before he was squinting at the phone he still held in his hand. "Now what? Sorry Mia, I'd better take this." He moved into his bedroom saying, "Yeah, Jason. What's up?"

Not wanting to eavesdrop, Mia wandered into the kitchen and opened the refrigerator. There wasn't much inside. A dozen eggs, butter, ketchup, mustard, lunch meat, four beers, spring water, and a 12-pack of Diet Pepsi. The final item put a smile on Mia's face. Since Ron never drank diet sodas, she knew this, along with the K-cups of English breakfast tea, were there for her. She was popping the top of one of the Pepsi's when Ron caught up with her.

"Everything okay?" Mia asked noticing the frown line between his brows.

"Huh? Oh, yeah. Grab me a water, would you? We might have a lead on the killer from the last murder. Nothing definitive, but we've got a possible witness who saw the victim having dinner at The Black Angus the night before we found her." Ron took a big swig of water. "We're gonna check it out tomorrow afternoon."

"Sounds like you're going to have a busy day tomorrow," Mia said moving close. "Let's just enjoy today, huh?"

When they got to the family home, they found there was already a house full. Mia ran to hug her little brother, Bobby, who was lounging on the couch with his arm around the very attractive girl she'd heard so much about. Mia warmly greeted her when introduced. "Hi Megan, I'm glad to finally meet you."

"Yeah, we're not sure what you see in this guy," Destiny said. Being the youngest sibling, she took a lot of teasing, but she had learned to dish it out as well. "But it's cool he finally found somebody who can put up with him."

"Now you know why I haven't brought you around before," Bobby said lunging at his little sister who was too quick for him. "Shouldn't you be helping Mom in the kitchen?"

"I was just kidding," she called over her shoulder making a quick exit.

It was a full house—even for a big place like the Reeds'—and Sarah had decided to serve dinner buffet style, so everyone filled their plates to overflowing but still gathered around the huge dining table. Halfway through the meal, when Mia mentioned the prospect of painting Ron's apartment the following weekend, the family responded exactly as she had predicted. Even Mia's parents jumped on the bandwagon, but when Ron said they'd have more helpers than paint brushes, Sarah said she'd provide the snacks and Craig said he'd stop in and check their work after a round of golf.

Destiny had scheduled a fun practice round with one of her team members and Bobby and Megan would be attending a friend's wedding, so they wound up with a hardy work force of four with Julie, Cody, Ron, and Mia meeting at nine o'clock, Sarah bringing lunch at noon, and Craig joining the fun around two. Mia knew it was going to be a fun day with all the family working together and had a great idea for how to end it.

"How about when we're all done, we go back to our place for pizza?"

"No," Sarah jumped in. "Not pizza. That's no fit food for people who have worked all day. Why don't I make us a good homecooked meal?"

"No sense in you cooking, Mom. If pizza isn't enough, how about we throw some stuff on the grill? What d'ya think, Julie?"

"Sounds like fun." Julie lowered her head then peeked up through long lashes and whispered, "But sorry... I have a date."

CHAPTER THIRTY-ONE

R on sat on the edge of his seat leaning in toward his sister. He still couldn't believe she was alive and well and sitting right in front of him in his apartment. "Yeah, the red hair probably would have thrown me off if Mia hadn't painted this picture," he said jumping up and finding it among the artwork Mia had left with him.

"Wow, that's unbelievable. But how? I mean, we'd never met, so..."

"I can't really explain it, but she had actually seen you somewhere." Ron hesitated to say where. Everything was too new between them to know if he dared mention his knowledge that she'd seen a therapist. He wanted to respect her privacy, and he didn't want to risk upsetting her.

"Is she in the habit of drawing every stranger she sees?" The edge in her voice made Ron nervous.

"No, but... wait. There's another picture I have to show you. Mia has a special gift," he said over his shoulder dashing into his bedroom.

"What do you mean? What kind of gift?"

Ron came back holding the first picture Mia had done of Robin—the one with blonde hair. The one that had shocked him back when he'd first met Mia while investigating another murder. He handed it to Robin and watched her eyes widen as she took it in. She looked from the picture to Ron's face and back to the picture.

"But, but how? I, I don't understand."

Ron explained as much as he knew about Mia's strange ability to draw people or places she'd never seen, and how she had once even helped police find a lost child using her gift.

"I've heard about people like that, but I never really believed they were legit," Robin said. "But you believe her?"

"Yeah, I do. Actually, I'm starting to believe a lot of things lately that I'd given up believing in." A huge smile spread across his face and he added, "I'm sitting here looking at some of the proof." He watched his sister's face relax and recognized the smile he hadn't seen since they were a couple of teenagers celebrating their birthday together. In that moment, he saw his fifteen-year-old sister and all the years and distance seemed to disappear.

He didn't want to let go of that moment, but his mind was bombarded with questions, and he finally pushed himself to speak. "I'm almost afraid to ask, but I have to... and you don't have to answer, but I hope you can... Robin, what happened?" He waited and hated the change he saw cross her face, and the way she lowered her head before she spoke.

Her smile had faded, and she continued to stare at the floor. As the seconds passed, Ron believed she might not answer—might not be able to answer—but then she began.

"It was like a terrible nightmare." She spoke so softly that Ron leaned in closer to hear her. "But I couldn't awaken from it." Robin explained how Charlie and Buddy drove through the night, how they drugged her for days, and how she found herself a prisoner in their basement for years.

Ron's heart pounded and he broke out in a sweat. As he listened to his sister's story, he imagined the hell she'd endured and was sickened by it.

He could tell she was sparing him by leaving out details, especially when she said, "They did things... I, I can't talk about it... I'm sorry."

"Don't apologize, Robin. You have nothing to be sorry for. If only I'd found you."

"How could you? You were only a kid. And you lost Mom and Dad too." Robin's final words seemed to break through the dam she'd built to protect herself, and a flood of grief poured out. Ron and Robin embraced each other and finally mourned the loss of their parents together.

Sometime later, after Robin had given Ron a brief description of her escape and the life she'd created for herself since then, Ron asked about his nephew.

"I knew when he was born," she said, "that I had to name him after you, and now when I look at him, I swear he looks just like you did as a little kid… at least from what I remember of pictures we had back home. Wait! Do you have any pictures? Pictures of Mom and Dad and us?"

"Yes! I didn't keep much from the old house, but I kept Mom's photo albums. They're in one of those boxes I haven't unpacked yet," he said pointing to the small stack of boxes in the corner of the room. "Maybe I can find 'em quick," he said checking the time.

"You have somewhere you have to be?" Robin asked.

"I do, but a few more minutes won't hurt." Ron saw that Robin also checked the time on her phone.

"Oh gosh, we have so much to talk about, but I really have to get going too. Ronnie's with a sitter, and I told her I'd be back by about two, and it's nearly that now. We've got to do this again soon."

Ron saw the pleading look in her eyes. "Of course we will. Are you kidding? Now that I've found my little sister, do you think I'm gonna let her go?" Having been the first one out of the birth canal, Ron had always kidded about being her older brother, and he liked the familiar laugh the teasing brought from Robin. As she got to her feet, Ron saw the amusement gradually fade to be replaced with worry lines.

"I have to have a difficult conversation with my husband, but hopefully it will be all right once I've explained. Then maybe we can have you and Mia over for dinner. And you can get to know your nephew."

Ron didn't think she looked as confident as she sounded, and he still wondered why she hadn't told her husband the truth, but those were questions that could wait. "Let me know if there's anything I can do to help."

After a long embrace that neither sibling seemed to want to end, he said goodbye to his sister and watched her walk out the door, knowing this time, he would see her again. And in time he would learn more about those lost years, but he already knew enough for his hatred of the men who had caused his family so much harm to be multiplied. The need to find them and make them pay was growing, but Ron shook it off to focus on the more immediate problem.

There was another bad guy—a serial killer—he needed to stop. Unless they could figure out who was killing these young women, the murders would continue, and knowing there was another innocent woman out there who could become his next victim made his stomach burn with a sense of urgency.

Ron locked up, grabbed a coffee-to-go on his way through the café downstairs, and headed to The Black Angus where he planned to talk to the hostess.

Fortunately, she was able to identify the victim, Treva Wolf, and remembered her because of her high-pitched, girlish giggle. Unfortunately, she didn't remember much about the woman's dinner date.

"I think he was about average height and weight... but kinda well built—you know like he works out—and I think maybe his hair was dark. Jill might remember him better. I'm sure she was their server because I remember her spending a lot of time at their table." The hostess rolled her eyes. "While other customers were waiting..."

"Okay, can I talk to this Jill?"

"Oh, she's not here."

"Well is she coming in later or do I have to come back tomorrow?"

"It wouldn't do you any good. She's using vacation days to go help her grandma up in New York state." Putting her finger by the corner of her mouth, she added, "But I'm pretty sure she said she'd be back to help with the Friday night crowd."

Through gritted teeth, Ron asked, "Can you give me her phone number? I'll try calling her."

"Yeah sure, you can try, but good luck! She told me the cell reception up there in the mountains is spotty at best."

Ron took down the number and went out to his vehicle and gave it a shot, but the hostess had it right. It looked like he might have to wait until the end of the week to talk to this waitress who may or may not be able to give them a clue to the man's identity. *Whoever he is, he's our murderer.*

CHAPTER THIRTY-TWO

Robin cherished her nighttime ritual with her little boy, and Ronnie loved playing in the tub when he got his bath. He liked it so much, his willingness to get out of the tub usually depended on Mommy's promise to read him a bedtime story, which she loved as much as he did, maybe more. Snuggle time with her son was Robin's very favorite time of day, and tonight, she didn't want their snuggle time to end.

"Read it again, Mommy," Ronnie begged, and although it was tempting, Robin decided twice was enough.

"We'll read it again tomorrow night, sweetie. Now it's time to go to sleep." Robin stroked his brow, and watched his eyes get heavier and heavier until he couldn't fight it any longer. Before long he was fast asleep, yet Robin lingered, not wanting to do what she knew she must do.

Finally returning to the living room where her husband sat on the couch watching the golf channel on TV, she curled up on the other end facing him. "Kevin," she said softly, "can I talk to you about something?"

"Sure, what is it?" he asked looking her way.

"I'm not sure exactly where to begin, but well, it's a long story, and it starts way back when I was fifteen." She saw Kevin's sudden interest when he grabbed the remote, turned the TV off, and repositioned himself so he was fully facing her.

"Are you okay?" he asked.

"There's so much I've never told you about my life... about who I am." She saw her husband's eyebrows draw together and forced herself to go on. "First of all, my real name was Robin Bishop."

Kevin's jaw dropped. "What the hell are you talking about?"

"I'm sorry. I'm so sorry. Let me explain."

"Yeah, good idea."

The most difficult part for her to talk about was the murder of her parents, and as she told her story, she read the gamut of emotions that crossed her husband's face. Anger. Sorrow. Compassion. Confusion.

"But why didn't you tell me?" he asked. "I mean, I get why you changed your name, but I don't understand why you didn't trust me enough to tell me."

Robin hated the look she couldn't read when he said those last words. She guessed it was a mix of anguish and frustration. She wondered if he would ever trust her again. Or forgive her.

The next couple of hours were filled with intermittent conversation and long silences. At one point Kevin said, "I guess that explains a lot."

"What do you mean?"

"I mean why you push me away when I want to make love to you. Are you thinking of those two animals? Do you think I'm like them?"

"No! I mean, you're nothing like them." Robin slid closer and took his hand. "I love you... but, I... sometimes I..." She wanted to explain, but couldn't find the words, and her eyes filled with tears.

"Oh God, Rachel, it's okay," Kevin said gently pulling her into his arms. "It's okay. We're okay."

Robin wasn't sure how long they sat that way, but it was long enough for years of tension to drain from her body. And she loved it when her husband said, "So when do I get to meet this brother of yours?"

CHAPTER THIRTY-THREE

I'm counting the hours. Yeah, in another twenty-four hours she'll be mine... and I thought I'd have to wait until Saturday. Haha, I love it when a plan comes together. Those first three were good—better than good—they were great, but this is gonna be the best one yet. Yeah, maybe after this one, I can get outta this small town and hit the big city. Maybe New York. They've got some real killer buildings there. But first I've gotta finish up here.

My little Trixie thought she could put me off for another week, but nope, that's not happenin'. She called this morning all apologetic and making excuses.

"I'm so sorry, but a bunch of us are helping a friend paint Saturday, and I'm not sure when we'll get done, and the family wants to come back here after. Can we maybe postpone our dinner until next weekend?"

I couldn't believe it. It's all about *her family* and *her friends*. And did she ask if I wanted to join them? No, of course not.

She was gonna put me off for another week. And she calls me on Thursday to cancel? Two days' notice? I don't think so. And I can't wait another week! Who does she think she is? She's just like all the rest of them. Just like those girls in high school. They don't appreciate me... they never appreciated me... none of them.

Not even Karen. Tried to give her my heart... and I would'a been good to her. But no, I slip the ring on her finger, and she takes it off and throws it back at me... and laughs! That bitch! Well, screw that, and her and all the rest of them. I'm not the sucker I used to be.

Wait another week, my ass! Yeah, so I just turned on the charm. "Oh luv," I said, "another whole week? But I've been so looking forward to this Saturday after having to put it off once already. And I'm not sure I can manage to move things around next weekend." I paused for effect, then I said, "But here's another possibility. My calendar is free tomorrow night..." She didn't need to know my calendar's free every night.

There was a long pause, and I wasn't sure she'd bite, but I waited... gave her time to think about it. Finally, she said, "You know what, yeah. I could do that. Can you pick me up around six?"

"I was thinking a little later," I said.

But then she comes back with, "If you don't mind, I don't want to make it a late night since I have to get an early start Saturday morning."

So, I told her sure, that would be fine. Man, I hung up and my hands were shakin' and I was sweatin' like a pig. After another hot shower though, I looked in the mirror and started feeling a lot better. This isn't Harold the Pillsbury Doughboy geek. This is Hardbody Harry, and any broad is gonna feel lucky going out with this guy.

Getting dressed, I thought about this Julie again and held my hands out in front of me. Steady as a rock—no more shaking. It's all working out, and she thinks she'll get home early, but I have a surprise for that little chick. She won't be getting home early, and she won't be doing any painting on Saturday. Not after her Friday night flight!

CHAPTER THIRTY-FOUR

When Mia arrived home, she went straight to the crockpot to see what was filling the kitchen with such an enticing aroma. She was delighted to find her sister's special pulled pork, and since it had been many hours since early lunch between clients, it was calling her name. *I can't wait!*

"Oh, there you are, Simmie. Are you hungry too?" Mia normally waited to have dinner with her sister, but since Julie's car wasn't in the garage, and she was starving, she quickly grabbed one of the rolls from the pack Julie had left next to the slow cooker. That's when she noticed the note.

Picking up and cuddling Simeon, Mia read the message and discovered she would be eating alone tonight. Julie had eaten early and gone to meet with her critique group at the local library.

"Looks like it's just you and me, boy," she said. "At least she left dinner for us... well, for me. But I'll take care of yours... or did Julie already feed you when she fed Willie?" Simeon gazed at her, but he wasn't talking. "I do wish she would've said." Mia pulled out her phone and shot her sister a quick text. *Did you feed the kitties?*

Before she could put the phone down the answer swished in: *Fed Willie not Sim. Sorry. Was running late.*

"All right, fuzzy butt. I'll feed you," Mia said shaking her head. "Your Auntie Julie is home all day and doesn't have time to feed you. Bad Auntie." She couldn't quite understand how her sister always seemed to be "running late" other than her habit of procrastinating. Mia was beginning to remember how annoying some of her sister's habits could be and hoped moving in together hadn't been a mistake.

After feeding her feline, Mia changed into a pair of shorts and tank top, made herself a pulled pork sandwich, grabbed a water, and headed down to her studio. It had been a full day, and though she knew she'd chosen the right profession and felt blessed to be doing what she loved, it often left her emotionally depleted by the time she finished her final client notes. Mia hit her playlist for relaxation, took a bite out of the sandwich, and looked around at her surroundings.

Her studio was her happy place. Even when bone-weary, all the color and creative tools energized her. Joined by Simeon who had apparently satisfied his hunger, Mia put her sandwich down and picked up her sketch pad. Within minutes she was looking at a portrait of her pretty little gray fluffball. "I like it," she said holding it at arm's length. "Oh, you like it too, huh?" she said in response to Simmie's purrs.

By the time she finished her dinner, Mia had let go of the day's stress and was ready to paint, but as she reached for her brushes, she got a call from her favorite detective.

"Hello there," she said. "I thought you were working tonight."

"I am. I'm in the car heading north to meet up with that waitress from The Black Angus. I finally got through to her this afternoon, and she was driving back from her grandmother's. She agreed to meet me at her place at seven-thirty. So how was your day?"

"Long... but good. I miss you. We're still on for tomorrow night, right?"

"You better believe it. We have lots to catch up on over dinner. Did I tell you I talked to Robin again?"

"No. How's she doing?"

"She sounded pretty good. I'm meeting her for lunch tomorrow. How about that... two dates and with two of my favorite people on the same day. Listen, I'm getting close to this Jill's address, so maybe I'll give you a call later, okay?"

"Sure. I'll talk to you later," Mia said. Then before ending the call she remembered something. "Wait! Are you still there?"

"Yes. What's wrong?"

"Nothing's wrong. It's just that Gabby mentioned something today about Nancy Owens, that first victim. Maybe you already knew this, but I wasn't sure."

"What is it?"

"Well, Gabby said she thinks she remembers Nancy saying something about a guy with a British accent."

"Does she think this is the guy we're looking for?"

"She said she doesn't really know, but when she and Mom were talking about Nan over lunch, it just came to her."

"Okay, thanks. Well, I just pulled up to the address this waitress gave me so... gotta go."

"All right. Love you," Mia said.

"Love you too, bye."

Ron ended the call, and Mia smiled at the phone. "That was our boyfriend, Simmie," she said. "All right, let's try this again." She picked up one brush, then another, then put them both down and went for the charcoal pencil.

This wasn't what she had planned. Her idea of doing another watercolor of the lake was replaced by the need to follow a compulsion to do something in charcoal.

What began to emerge before her eyes was dark... a dark silhouette of a man and a woman. There wasn't much detail. Simply the two forms and a feeling of familiarity. Mia's earlier calm and relaxation faded as the image emerged along with a mood of darkness and something more. Something sinister and evil.

CHAPTER THIRTY-FIVE

When Ron rang the doorbell there was an immediate loud response from inside. Jill Martin obviously did not live alone, and when she answered the door, she had a tight grip on her four-legged companion's collar and appeared to be using every bit of her strength to hold the shepherd back. Ron held up his ID which may have reassured Jill but had absolutely no effect on the dog.

"Hold on. Let me put Heidi in the other room," the curly-haired blonde called through the storm door. "Stop it! Hush!" she told the dog to no avail. "Sorry about that." Jill opened the door when she returned. "She wouldn't really hurt you. C'mon in. Heidi's a good dog but she hasn't learned not to jump up on people and try to lick them to death. She's still a puppy, actually."

"That's a pretty big puppy," Ron said.

"Yeah, but she's only nine months old." Jill stubbed out the half-smoked cigarette that was about to fall off the ashtray. "My dad gave her to me when my ex and I split up. He doesn't think it's safe for a woman to live alone, you know."

"Your father is a wise man, and German shepherds are usually great watchdogs."

"Oh, he really is—my dad I mean—he's one of the good guys.. But he's a worrier... and I know he's right. As friendly as Heidi is, she scares the bejesus out of anybody coming to the door. I'm sorry. I'm rambling. You wanted to ask me about that poor girl."

"That's okay, Ms. Martin."

"Oh, you can call me Jill." She reached for the pack of Marlboros on the coffee table, thought better of it, and put them down.

"Thank you, Jill," Ron said pulling out his notepad and pen. "I was told you were the server for her and her date. Is that correct?"

"Yes, and I couldn't believe it when I saw her on the news. I'd just been talking to her. And she was so friendly and nice. And he—the guy with her—left a good tip too." The dog's intermittent barks, whines, and scratching on the door didn't stop. "Heidi, hush!"

"Do you remember anything in particular about Ms. Wolf's dinner companion?" Ron wanted to complete the interview for Heidi's sake, but also to escape the stench of stale cigarettes.

"Not much, really..." Jill appeared to be searching the ceiling for answers. "Oh, except he was kind of good looking... sort of looked like a jock. You know, like he works out maybe. I remember his arms," she said smiling and closing her eyes for several seconds. "He was wearing a short-sleeved shirt—a nice one—and you could tell he had some good muscles."

"Was there anything at all that might have stood out?" Responding to Jill's puzzled expression, Ron clarified, "Like was he particularly tall or short, or did he have any scars, tattoos?"

"Hmm, no. No, I didn't see any. I mean he might've had tats where they didn't show, but I remember he was well built. You know, muscular."

Ron decided he probably wasn't going to get anything new from this waitress who was simply going to keep repeating herself with no real help. *Time to wind this up.* "Well, I appreciate your time, Jill. I'll get out of your way so you can let poor Heidi out. But if you think of anything else," Ron handed her one of his cards, "please give me a call."

"Sure. But I don't think I will," Jill said grabbing her Marlboros and walking him to the door. He had one foot out the door when she said, "Oh, there is one thing. I mean it's probably not important, but he did talk funny... with some kind of an accent."

Stopping in his tracks, Ron asked, "Can you tell me what kind of accent, Jill?"

"It was one of those like from England or Australia or someplace. It was *real* sexy," she said with a wink.

Back in the car, Ron scribbled in his notepad. Mia had learned from Gabby that the first victim was seeing someone with a British accent. *Finally, a lead. Someone with an accent...*

Ron pulled away from the curb and called his partner. "Hey, Jason. We may actually have a lead."

"Oh yeah? Lay it on me."

"So, two out of our three so-called suicides—Owens and Wolf—were seeing someone with an accent, probably British. Maybe Australian. My guess is it's the same guy."

"Sounds like a good guess to me. How about I poke around and see if anybody ever saw the Dawson woman with somebody like that?"

"Yeah, good idea. No wait, let me," Ron said thinking of his sister. "It turns out I know the owner of the diner where she worked."

"Oh yeah?"

"Yeah, long story. I'll fill you in sometime, but I can follow up on this one tomorrow. I'll let you know what I find out."

When Ron finally crawled into his bed later that night, he tossed and turned, pondering the possibilities of their few leads being enough to catch a killer. It might not be a lot to go on, but it could be enough. He sensed they were close... so close. Maybe Robin would be the key. Maybe she could unlock the mystery and he could catch this murderer and prevent another innocent woman from being killed.

CHAPTER THIRTY-SIX

Promptly at noon Robin saw her brother hop out of his Land Rover and stride toward the entrance to the diner. She felt the smile spontaneously spread across her face mirroring the joy in her heart. She still couldn't believe he was really alive and that somehow, they'd found each other.

Being married to Kevin she had created a family—their family—yet she'd still carried the loss of her parents and brother, that hole inside since her birth family had been taken in one horror-filled night.

But she shook off the terrible memory when Ron stepped through the door, and she saw the familiar smile that until days earlier she thought she'd never see again in this lifetime.

After a quick greeting, which included a bear hug, Ron asked where she wanted to sit. She directed him to a big booth in the back where her husband and son were already settled.

"Ronnie, I'd like you to meet my husband, Kevin, and of course you know who this little guy is," she said ruffling her toddler's hair.

Ron shook Kevin's hand then quickly turned his attention to his nephew who was busily chewing French fries and stuffing pieces of hotdog in his mouth. "Hi there, Ronnie. He's a good-looking young man," he said to the parents. "And maybe you'd better try calling me Ron now, huh sis?"

"I can try. Two Ronnie's could get a bit confusing." She turned to her three-year-old. "Ronnie, guess what. This is your uncle. Can you say hello to Uncle Ron?"

The little one looked puzzled, then hid his face behind his hands. Robin signaled Connie who had been standing by, and she came over carrying a tray with water, coffee and iced tea. "This is

Connie, our manager and my best friend. She'll take good care of us."

"I remember you usually get coffee, but Rachel said you might want an iced tea." Connie smiled and left both on the table.

Robin didn't miss her brother's probing look when Connie left. "I legally changed my name years ago, and... well, everybody knows me as Rachel. It's strange. I totally think of myself as Rachel now." She looked at her husband, took his hand, and added, "I am Rachel Long. I left Robin Bishop behind to start a new life. I didn't want to remember her life... but now, now that you're here, all of a sudden I'm Robin too... your sister." Looking back and forth at the two men, her throat tightened and she felt the sting of tears in her eyes.

Kevin's reassuring smile and the way he squeezed her hand helped her swallow the lump in her throat.

"Hey, don't worry," Ron said. "Rachel is a good name, and I'll get used to it. And now you're my sister, Rachel. It suits you. Besides, Robin was a silly, pimple-faced, boy crazy teenager." He gave Kevin a wink. "But Rachel is a not-so-bad-looking, happily married mother of one handsome little slugger."

This was the brother she remembered—the one who teased and tormented her growing up—the brother she'd missed. And mourned. Alive and teasing her again.

"Are you okay?" Kevin leaned in.

"I'm good," she said sniffing and wiping her eyes. "These are happy tears. It's all a bit overwhelming." Looking at her brother, she added, "It's still hard to believe you're alive and sitting across from me, Ronnie."

"Me Wonnie!" the three-year-old said indignantly, then hid his face when everyone laughed.

"Yes, you are. And this is Uncle Ronnie." Still obviously feeling bashful, the little one stole quick glances at his uncle then looked away and giggled each time.

Robin thanked Connie who appeared with a tray full of food despite the fact no one had placed an order. "I hope you don't mind," Robin said to her brother, "but I had them fix one of your favorites. You do still like mac and cheese, don't you?"

Ron rubbed his hands together gleefully. "I sure do. Especially when it's crunchy on top like this... just like Mom used to make."

"It took quite a bit of experimentation to duplicate her recipe, but I think this comes pretty close."

After trying a bite, Ron said, "It's perfect. I... um..." He cleared his throat and seemed unable to go on. Robin recognized her twin's unexpected show of emotion. She knew how that feeling could sneak up on you when you least expect it and make the loss as fresh as if it had happened yesterday. She pushed the memory back where it belonged. It was obvious Ron did the same.

For the next fifteen minutes he and Kevin dug into their lunches, exchanged pleasantries, and spent time getting to know each other while Robin's focus was primarily on little Ronnie. Before long, the toddler got restless. A small dish of ice cream bought them a little more time, but with the final spoonful and his mother wiping his face, the child had had enough.

"I think someone is ready for his nap," Kevin said. "Why don't I take grumpy-pants home? Then you two take as long as you want catching up."

"Thanks, Kev." Robin slid out of the booth to let him get up and free Ronnie from his highchair. Still amazed and grateful for her husband's eventual understanding and acceptance, she put a hand on his cheek as she kissed him and the baby goodbye.

"Bye-bye, Unca Wonnie," her son called back to them just before they disappeared into the kitchen. It made her heart swell.

A look of delight appeared on her brother's face. "So, everything really is good with you two now?"

"Better than good, actually. I should have told him long ago, you know? It was stupid of me, but I was just scared. Damaged goods and all." Robin stared at her plate and pushed the food around. "And then, the more time went by, the harder it was to bring it up... until I decided that part of my life could simply stay buried."

"Until I showed up. Sorry if I—"

"No!" Robin chuckled. "It's good. It's all good. How could I ever be sorry about that? But, like I told you on the phone, when I told Kevin you were my brother and all the rest of it, we talked well into the night. I told him everything—I mean everything—and it's crazy, but he seemed to love me even more after... after he had time to absorb it all."

"It's not crazy at all, Robin, oops, sorry... Rachel."

"No, stop it. You can call me Robin. People have childhood nicknames, right?" She saw his whole demeanor change as he sighed with relief.

"You sure?"

"Yeah. If anybody who doesn't know the whole story asks, I'll tell them it was my nickname growing up. 'Cuz I hopped around like a little bird!" They both chuckled at the idea.

They talked through two more cups of coffee before Robin saw her brother look at his phone for the second time. "Is everything all right?" she asked.

"Yeah, just keeping an eye on the time. I've got to check in with my partner by two o'clock. We're working on a lead for these murders. Which brings me to something I'm hoping you might be able to help me with."

"Me? Is it about Dana?"

"Yes."

"I doubt if I can be much help, but if she was actually killed, I'd do anything to catch whoever did it. What did you want to know?"

"Just this... do you know if she was seeing anyone with some kind of accent?"

"Oh gosh, I have no idea. I never really got to know Dana that well, but Connie worked with her a lot. She might know."

Robin caught Connie's eye and waved her over to ask.

"No," Connie replied, "but there was this one guy—I never waited on him because he always asked to be in her section. Good looking guy with a British accent." The description she gave was about as helpful as the one Ron had gotten from Jill Martin. "Do you think he...?"

"Do you remember his name?" Ron asked.

"What? No, I, I don't think so." Connie lowered her eyes, cupped her chin, and shook her head. "I'm not sure... wait, I almost have it... Yeah, Larry maybe... Yes, that's it. I'm pretty sure his name was Larry."

"Listen, if we get our forensic artist down here, could you work with him and see if we can get an image of this guy?" A quick phone call and Ron was able to arrange for them to meet just two hours later. Connie looked to her boss for approval.

"Of course," Robin said. "You've got this place working like clockwork, and either Kevin or I can run in if they need anything. We're only ten minutes away."

Ron thanked Robin for her help before he left, and as she lingered over coffee, she hoped he would catch this sicko killer. And then she wondered if it was possible... could he solve a really cold case and finally catch two other killers and punish them for their heinous crimes?

CHAPTER THIRTY-SEVEN

"A last name would be a lot more helpful, but there can't be that many Brits named Larry in the area, right?" Having shared this latest clue with Jason, Ron added, "And in a few hours we might have an idea what he looks like. We're gonna nail this guy, Jason... and we've gotta do it soon." *Yeah, Larry, whoever you are, we're gonna stop you.*

Splitting the list of names of people they wanted to go back and question, Ron jumped back in his Land Rover and headed for his first stop, the Reed Mental Health Center. He had never met Gabriella Ortiz, but he'd carefully read the notes from Jason Evans's interview. Though it hadn't been a whole lot of help, Mia had given him an important tidbit—the accent. *Maybe she'll remember more.*

Unfortunately, she didn't. Gabby was waiting at the front desk when Ron arrived and escorted him back to her office. "I think I told the other detective everything," she said. "Except like I told Sarah the other day, I remember Nan said he had a sexy accent."

"Do you remember if Ms. Owens mentioned where this man was taking her for dinner?" Ron asked.

"No, I would have said it if she had. I cannot believe it."

"What's that, Ms. Ortiz?"

"I cannot believe anyone could hurt her. Nancy was a good person. We all loved her so much." Gabby reached for the tissues on her desk and crossed herself.

"I'm sorry, ma'am." Ron paused to give her time to blow her nose. "Just one more thing. Did Ms. Owens ever mention someone named Larry?"

"No, no, I am sorry. Do you think this Larry is the one who killed our Nancy?"

"We don't know for sure, but we're following every lead. I appreciate your time, Ms. Ortiz, and if you think of anything else, will you call me?" Ron stood to leave. "Say, do you know if Mia is still here?"

"*Si*, yes, I think she is with her last client." Gabby checked the time. "She should be out soon... about five minutes."

Ron thanked her and made his way out to the waiting room, grabbed a magazine and a seat, then leafed through the pages mindlessly. Moments later, Mia emerged holding a little curly-haired girl by the hand. The child let go and ran to her mother holding up a drawing. "Look Mommy, it's a bumblebee!" she said excitedly.

As soon as Mia finished speaking to the little one's mother, she turned and said, "Det. Bishop?"

Ron leapt to his feet and followed her back to her office. She stepped aside for him to come in, then closed the door behind her and walked into his arms. "Not that I mind, but what are you doing here? I thought you were going to pick me up at the house," she said. "Change your mind?"

Ron wanted nothing more than to spend the rest of the evening with Mia, but that was going to have to wait. "I'm sorry, sweetie. Change of plans. I've gotta work." He watched Mia's smile fade and apologized again. "We're getting closer to finding the man who killed those three women."

"Thank God. Did what Gabby said about a guy with an accent help?"

"Definitely. The waitress at the diner confirmed it. Apparently, there was a customer with an accent there who always wanted to sit in the second victim's section—Dana Dawson."

"Oh Ron, is that enough to go on?"

"Well, it's more than we had," he said, "and we finally have a name."

"What? So you know who it is?"

"Not exactly. It's just a first name, but that's something. We finally know we're looking for a guy named Larry who all the women describe as good-looking, well built, and with an accent. Probably British. Oh, and the manager from the Sweet Glen is meeting with our forensic artist to see if we can get a sketch of the guy."

"So now what?"

"Now Jason and I go back and question everyone again, hoping somebody can identify this Larry. That's why we've got to get on it tonight. Every day that goes by is another opportunity for him to strike again. We can't let that happen."

"Of course not. I understand, but will you call me later?"

"Absolutely! And tomorrow is all us... and a whole bunch of other people... and paint." Pulling his girl close, Ron kissed her and wanted more, but managed to drag himself away. "Wish me luck, sweetie. Talk to you later."

Back in his vehicle, he pushed his longing to spend time with Mia out of his mind and focused on the next name on his list. Nancy Owens ex-fiancé, Garrett. *Where are you, Larry? It's time to put an end to your murder spree.*

CHAPTER THIRTY-EIGHT

Mia's final client of the day demanded her full attention, but somewhere, lurking in the back of her mind, she sensed something else was waiting for her attention. The paranoia of the woman she was working with combined with the fact that there was truly a killer out there, and it complicated matters.

"I know he was staring at me," the woman said. "When I got back to my car with my coffee, I saw him leaving the Starbucks. I'm sure he was following me, and I reported it to the police, but I don't think they believe me."

"What makes you say that?"

"You can tell. Their tone of voice, you know? And the cop said, 'What did *this one* look like?'" Wringing her hands, Samantha began to cry. "You believe me, don't you?"

"I don't believe you would lie about what you thought was happening, but—"

"He *was* following me! I know he was. What if he's that guy they say killed those women? I could be next."

Mia moved her chair closer, leaned in, and placed her hand on Samantha's. "It's okay, Sam. I know the police are getting closer to catching the killer. Can you tell me a little bit more about this man from the coffee shop? Can you tell me what he looked like? Did he say anything to you?"

"He was big and kind of scary looking. He had real dark hair, looked like maybe he was Italian or Spanish or something, and he had tattoos all over his arms. Oh yeah, and he had a little beard. But no, he didn't say anything to me."

"So, you didn't hear him speak at all?"

"No. I mean, yes, but not to me."

"But did you hear him say anything?"

"Well, yes. I heard him order a cappuccino."

Mia thought for a minute. "Did he tell the barista his name to put on his cup?"

"Yes, it was John or Jim or something. Why?"

"Was there anything different about this man's voice? Anything at all?"

"I don't know," Samantha said. "It was kind of rough maybe. Why are you asking me all these questions?"

"Well, I happen to know some things about this case—some things the police haven't disclosed to the public—and I can assure you the man they're after doesn't fit the description you gave me."

Mia spent the rest of Samantha's session reassuring her, guiding her through relaxation exercises and scheduling an appointment with their staff psychiatrist for a med check. Happy this was her final client, Mia scheduled her for the following week, saw her out, and wrapped it up for the day.

Although Samantha had been resistant to the idea, on the drive home Mia considered making another attempt to introduce art therapy into her patient's treatment plan. She knew from her own experience as well as many of her clients' how much it could help people to relax. Just thinking about it made Mia anxious to spend time in her own little studio. But first she needed dinner.

The original plan had been Ron taking her out to one of her favorite places, The Moonlight Café, and although she preferred not to dine there alone, her taste buds were definitely set on enjoying their Italian cuisine. She phoned in her carry-out order, made a quick stop to pick it up, and headed for her haven and some much-needed relaxation. That niggling feeling still hadn't let go.

"There's my little fuzzy-butt," Mia said when she found Simeon waiting for her. "And they say felines don't greet their humans. What do they know?" Picking up her furry friend, she nuzzled him and laughed in response to one of his rare meows.

"No, Simmie, I know it smells good, but what's in this bag is not for you. Besides, Julie probably already fed you," she said. "Where is she anyway? Hey, Jules!" She'd seen her sister's car in the garage so she checked upstairs only to find an empty room. *Must be out for a run.*

It wasn't until Mia sat down to eat that she spotted the note.

Changed my date to tonight so I won't have to cut out early tomorrow. Simmie and Willie have been fed. Don't let them tell you otherwise.

Mia was pleased that her sister wouldn't be rushing off when their paint party came back to the house, and she didn't mind having the quiet home all to herself either. She transferred part of her shrimp scampi and salad onto her own dishes—the rest would be saved for another meal—then poured herself a glass of white wine and pulled up her playlist for relaxation to dine by.

With her appetite sated and her few dishes placed in the dishwasher, Mia poured herself a little more wine and carried it down to her studio to settle in for an evening of creativity. Simeon immediately hopped up to his favorite spot, practically posing for another portrait. *Why not?*

Mia thought to use her favorite medium, watercolors, but her hand was somehow drawn to the charcoals instead. After not too many strokes, it was obvious Simmie could relax. What was emerging was not a Persian cat. It was not a cat at all.

Working feverishly, Mia became lost in her creation. As she added layers and continued to define the image, a man's face emerged. It became more and more familiar until—covered in perspiration in spite of central air—she sat back and viewed a portrait not of her doing.

It's him... oh dear God... a British accent... Julie...

Mia grabbed her cell phone and punched in the top name in her favorites. Ron was obviously busy questioning someone because the call went straight to voicemail.

"Ron," Mia said into the phone. "The guy with the British accent—the killer—it's not Larry. It's *Harry*!"

CHAPTER THIRTY-NINE

"You're looking quite lovely tonight," Harry told Julie from across the table. He rarely handed out compliments, but when he did, he expected the recipient to hand one right back to him. They were, after all, lucky to be seen with him.

However, Julie did not reciprocate as she should. All she did was thank him.

"You've changed your hair again, haven't you?" he asked.

"Yeah, I've heard blondes have more fun, so I thought I'd see for myself. And I made it lighter this time so the pink would work."

Harry laughed with her, knowing her fun would be short-lived. Besides, how much fun would a writer have anyway? Most of them were nerdy geeks... introverts who lived in their own little fantasy worlds. They didn't usually have much to offer in the real world with real people.

But this one seemed a little different. More animated and yeah, maybe fun. He could probably even like her. *Maybe... No!*

Harry thought for a minute maybe she could be a keeper. For a real girlfriend. But he knew better. It wouldn't take long before she'd decide she was too good for him. Just like all the other yuppy puppies. No, he wouldn't let this one throw a ring in his face and put him down. She'd be the one going down.

"What?" Julie said.

"Excuse me?" Harry had no idea why she said that.

"You were smiling, like you thought of something. What were you thinking about?"

"Was I? Forgive me, luv. I suppose I was simply enjoying your company so much," Harry lied. "Tell me more about your writing. What exactly is it that you write?"

Julie prattled on about the magazine articles and essays she wrote for publication—for which Harry feigned interest—but his curiosity was actually piqued when she told him about the novel she was working on. "So, it's a mystery, you say?"

"Yes. Kind of a whodunit," Julie said. "I haven't worked out all the plot twists and red herrings... you know, how to leave enough clues for my readers to think they know who it is and yet surprise them in the end. But I'm working on it, and it's fun. So different from the nonfiction stuff I'm freelancing."

"Fascinating." Harry looked into her eyes while thinking no one would ever know whodunit. Not in the book and not in real life.

"May I get these out of your way?" their waitress asked, reaching for the dishes. "And will you be having dessert this evening?"

Harry smiled and nodded, looking at his dinner partner. "Of course. What would you like, luv?"

"I probably shouldn't but... I'll have the peach cobbler."

"And I'll just have coffee," Harry said. It was going to be a long night. After his fun with Julie, he planned to hop in his Jeep—already packed with all his personal belongings—and head north. By the time they found the girl, he'd be long gone. *A new name, a new place, and lots of new friends to be made.*

"More wine, luv?"

"No, thanks. I think I'd like coffee. Decaf, please," she told the waitress.

When Julie's coffee was placed in front of her, she reached for the sweetener, but before she added it, Harry tapped his front teeth and said, "I think you've got a little something there."

Julie immediately put her hand in front of her mouth, ran her tongue over her teeth and asked, "Did I get it?" Harry smiled and shook his head. After another unsuccessful try, she excused herself to "powder her nose" and get rid of the evasive piece of broccoli.

"I'll go ahead and sweeten your coffee and by the time you get back your dessert should be here. Do you take two?"

Julie nodded as Harry pulled her cup to his side of the table selecting several blue packets. As soon as she was out of sight, he dumped the sweetener and, since she wasn't getting tipsy, added a little something extra into her cup that he'd brought just in case. This would make the next step so much easier.

When Julie returned, she wolfed down her cobbler then apologized for being such a pig. "I love peaches and I haven't had peach cobbler in so long, I couldn't help myself."

Harry didn't mind. He actually kind of liked watching her gobble it down. She didn't seem as phony as some of the bimbos he'd watched nibble at their food like rabbits. *I wonder if... no.* He fought off the second thoughts he was having. *Don't get your hopes up, stupid. You know what would happen.*

Julie stifled a yawn. "Oh, I'm so sorry." Face red, she added, "I guess I should have gone for some caffeine after all. I don't know why I'm feeling so sleepy. It's not the company, I assure you."

Harry smiled. Her cup was empty, and its effects were becoming obvious. He knew they'd better soon be on their way, or they'd be drawing too much attention. "This has been lovely," he said placing enough cash to cover the bill plus a generous twenty percent tip on the check—no need to be remembered for over tipping—and led Julie out.

By the time they reached his Jeep, the drugs were definitely doing their job. He helped his date into the vehicle, quickly went around and hopped in himself, and took off.

"I'm sorry, Harry. I didn't think I drank that much wine, but I'm so—"

"No worries. You just relax." He checked frequently, and he thought she was sleeping until she sat up straighter and pulled her phone out of her purse.

"Wait, uh-oh. I think you made a wrong turn, Harry," she said groggily.

"Really? That's okay. I know another way. Besides, it's a nice evening for a ride."

"Oh my goodness," Julie said after turning her phone back on. "I missed three texts... three texts from my sister..."

Harry took his eyes off the road long enough to watch as she tried to read the messages. She shook her head and rubbed her eyes. Harry knew this one was in the bag.

"Here, let me get that for you," he said taking the phone easily from her hand with its loose grip. "You just rest."

"But, but I think... it said... Harry..."

"It's okay. Relax, kid. We'll be there soon." *That's it. Go to sleep... Yeah, she's ready.*

Harry slipped the phone into his pocket. That would go over the edge with her... all in good time. But that wasn't the first thing on his agenda. *A man has needs, and you, my little Trixie, can help with that... and then you can fly.*

CHAPTER FORTY

Harry struggled to sit tight, knowing he should probably wait for it to get a little darker, yet feeling the urge to get on with it. He almost succumbed to his desire when another car slowly rolled off the main road and onto the trail leading up to where he was parked.

"Damn sunset watchers!" he muttered. The other driver parked not too far from him and got out, camera in hand, set up his tripod and waited. Harry saw the man glance his way, but with his arm around Julie, the photographer must have decided to give them some privacy.

Though it was only a matter of about fifteen to twenty minutes, the wait seemed endless to Harry who had broken into a cold sweat by the time the sun set and the guy loaded his equipment back in his car and took off.

As soon as the other vehicle's taillights disappeared onto the highway far below, Harry jumped out of the car, pulled Julie out of the passenger's side, and tossed her roughly across the backseat. She barely stirred when he unbuckled his belt and started to pull down his pants.

"Shit!" Harry saw another set of headlights coming toward them, so he pulled up his trousers and jumped back in the driver's seat. *Nobody hardly ever comes up this damn road. Why now?*

Then he remembered Julie said she'd received text messages from her sister. *Sonofabitch!* Considering it could be that Mia—or worse yet her cop boyfriend—all Harry's bravado began slipping away. *No! This isn't happening. Not now.*

The car didn't turn toward the west like the photographer had. Besides, in the near total darkness, there was nothing there to see. The headlights were getting closer... blinding him. *Damn it to hell!*

He leapt back out of the front and into the backseat, pulling Julie into a sitting position next to him, and put his arm around her like they were two kids making out. *Maybe it's some other guy looking for a place to do his girl.*

Julie moaned and made an effort to sit up on her own. "What... I can't..." She struggled feebly then surrendered to the drug.

"Shh," Harry said. "Just relax." He grew angry at the sweat now soaking his armpits, and gripped his captive more tightly. The headlights came straight toward them, and when the car stopped no more than twenty yards away leaving the headlights on, he knew it was the cop.

"Harry Tate, get out of the car!" a loud voice commanded through a bullhorn. Harry didn't move. "We know it's you, Harry, and we know you've got the girl with you. You need to let her go!"

Harry put his hand up, trying to block the light and see the guy behind the voice, but it was impossible because the cop had positioned himself behind the driver's side door. Harry couldn't see a thing, but he wasn't giving up. He was too close. Too close to finishing up in this town and moving on. Minutes passed seeming like hours, then he had an idea. *I'm not gonna let this sonofabitch ruin everything.* He was parked just a few yards from the edge of the drop-off and calculated the risk.

Grabbing Julie, who was about as limp as a ragdoll, he pulled her half on his lap and slid one leg out the door. He was glad she didn't weigh much as he got out of the car dragging her with him. He moved slowly toward to the edge.

"Harry, stop!" the voice commanded. "Don't do this. There's no way out. Come on. Let me help you," Det. Bishop said.

Harry heard sirens getting closer. *The sonofabitch called for backup.* "No, you listen to me, Mr. Bigshot Detective. You better call off your buddies. They ain't gonna help you or her," he said with no hint of an accent. "You think you're the boss. You think you're gonna make a fool outta me, but I ain't nobody's fool anymore." Harry felt his sweat-soaked shirt sticking to him.

Gripped by panic he shouted, "You'd better get outta here, or she's going over!" He inched slightly closer to the drop-off.

"Now you don't want to do that, Harry. If you hurt her, I won't be able to help you."

***

Mia watched in horror as Harry slid out of the back of his car holding her sister like a shield. She knew Ron was poised to take a shot, but he couldn't possibly get Harry without the risk of hitting Julie.

"Save her!" Without thinking, Mia quietly opened her door and quickly, silently crept around the perimeter. She had no plan except to somehow rescue her sister. With no weapon and no way to stop this serial killer, she was about to just lunge with all of her force when something caught her eye.

***

Hearing a noise somewhere behind him, Harry jumped, heart pounding. He gripped the girl tighter, and looked over his shoulder scanning the darkness. *Get a grip. Probably a damn squirrel.* "Turn those damn lights off so I can see you, damn it!"

"Let her go, and I'll turn them off. C'mon, Harry. Let's talk about this."

"Yeah, right! You think I'm stupid, don't cha? Well, I ain't stupid!" Harry took another small step in the direction of the drop-off. "I had you all fooled. And all these stupid bimbos too... they all fall for my accent." His burst of maniacal laughter sounded strange even to him. "Get it? They *fall* for it!" His crazed laughter erupted again as he finally grasped that nothing he said was going to get this cop to leave.

"Maybe I'll just fly away with you, kid," he murmured into Julie's ear. He took another step toward the edge still holding her tight. He heard the cop holler something and come running toward him. *Maybe we'll take this flight together.*

That would be Harold Muncy Tate's last thought before leaving this world forever.

***

Mia heard the warning again—like a silent whisper. It said, *"Save her,"* and urged her forward. She crept unnoticed behind the killer, painfully close to the edge of the overlook.

"Maybe I'll just fly away with you, kid," Mia heard Harry mumble.

Mia started to wonder whether all those times she'd seen him on her morning runs had been just as manufactured as his fake British accent. That sure would explain why he never seemed to have worked up a sweat.

Had he been stalking her as a potential target? Mia wasn't engaged, but she certainly was in a committed relationship. But there was no ring on her finger... yet.

Seeing Julie slack in this man's arms, Mia flashed back to Adam Grant describing when he saw Nancy Owens lying dead on the sidewalk. *"I'm sure someone pushed her from that rooftop,"* he had said. In that instant images flashed through her mind of Dana Dawson—dead—and Dr. Curtain's sweet receptionist found lying dead at the bottom of this very cliff... and now Julie... as helpless as Mia had been in her own kidnapper's cage long ago...

Something inside her roared at the injustice of one sick human using their strength and power to control another... and to take everything from them. Even their life.

No!

Ron's headlights shed enough light for her to spy the rock, and without another thought, she stood and lifted it with both hands, heaving it up and into the back of the malicious murderer's head.

She heard a sickening sound of the rock splintering bone.

Harry's hold on Julie loosened... Mia caught her sister's arm and with every ounce of her strength she yanked her back just in time. The once cocky charmer now staggered sideways toward the edge of the cliff.

Mia focused all her attention on Julie as the force of wrenching her away from the killer made them both fall. Luckily Julie's fall was cushioned by Mia who hit the ground first. The surge of adrenaline began to subside as Julie's dead weight pressed her into the hard ground. *But she's not dead!* Mia felt her sister's breath on her cheek. Mia hadn't seen him fall, but when she looked up, Harry was gone.

Then she saw Ron, gun drawn, sprinting to the edge of the cliff. He turned back and hastened to her side. He was breathless and she saw a mix of fear and anger on his face.

Chapter Forty-one

Mia sat up and held her sister's limp body in her arms. She couldn't control the trembles shaking her as she stroked Julie's hair and looked up at Ron standing over them both.

"What were you thinking, Mia? You could've been killed!" Ron's voice cracked, and Mia was shocked by his angry tone. There hadn't been time to consider the danger to herself, after all. When you see a madman about to kill someone you love, you just act.

"Is she...?" Ron stooped down and took Julie's wrist to check for a pulse.

"She's breathing," Mia said. Ron quickly called for an ambulance and had them dispatch the police. When he ended the call, Mia asked, "Do you think she's hurt?"

"We'll get her checked out, but it doesn't look like she's been injured."

"Ron," Mia couldn't continue. Choked by tears, she could do nothing but let him hold her. The three of them huddled there together until the police and ambulance arrived. Julie stirred from time to time, but seemed unable to wake.

"The bastard must have drugged her, sweetheart, but don't worry. I'm sure she's going to be okay."

While the EMTs were checking Julie out in the back of the ambulance, Ron and Mia walked to the edge and looked down at Harry's crumpled body far below. Mia gazed in disbelief and—thinking it could have been Julie's body they were looking at—she turned and buried her head in Ron's chest.

"You saved her life, you know," Ron murmured. "It all happened so fast. I didn't even hear you get out of the car. When I saw you behind him with that rock, I... God, you scared me so bad."

"I'm sorry. But I couldn't let him... I mean I thought he was going to push her over. I... I couldn't let that happen." The tears filled Mia's eyes again and poured down her face.

Playing it all back in her mind, Mia shuddered.

"Hey, are you okay?" Ron lifted her chin as if searching her face.

"I, I killed him."

"No. Stop... What you did was save your sister's life. You had no other choice."

Ron's reassuring words helped, but Mia feared she would never stop hearing the sound of that rock crushing a man's skull.

After answering a few questions for Det. Evans who was now on the scene, he told her she could go in the ambulance with Julie while he got the rest of what he needed from Ron.

"Are you sure you'll be all right?" Ron asked as she climbed into the back with her sister. Mia managed a nod and quick smile. "Hang in there, and I'll join you as soon as I can."

It was more than an hour later that Ron made it to Madison General where he found Mia sitting by her sister's side. Julie was awake. Well, sort of. Still groggy, she faded in and out of the drug-induced sleep, but she'd been lucid enough to grasp that it was over. Mia hadn't gone into detail, but Julie understood that Harry had drugged her and he was now dead and no longer a threat to her or anyone else.

"Where's my phone?" Julie asked sleepily.

Mia looked to Ron who answered, "We found it on the floor of Harry's car. Why? Do you need it?"

"Just wanted to check the time. I don't want to be late."

Mia tilted her head and smiled. "Late for what?"

"Painting."

Mia chuckled. "Don't worry..." She started to explain but decided not to waste her breath. Her sister was already sleeping again. At least her eyes were closed.

But then Julie said quietly, "And he was so charming and had that sexy accent." Seconds later her even breathing indicated she was sleeping peacefully.

"Funny how that sexy accent disappeared tonight," Ron said.

As soon as Ron and Mia got back to her place, they collapsed onto the couch and were holding on to each other when Mia sat straight up. Checking the time, she said, "Mom and Dad should still be up. I'd better give them a call. If this hits the news, they'll freak. I should have called them from the ambulance... or at least when we got to the hospital."

"C'mon, Mia. After all you've been through tonight, no one could expect you to be thinking clearly."

Ron never left her side while she made the call, and the feel of his arm around her shoulders eased the tension still lurking there.

"They're already on their way to the hospital to see Julie," Mia told Ron when she hung up the phone. "And instead of postponing our paint party, everyone agreed to simply adjust the starting time back to noon. And get this... Mom even agreed that in light of all that's happened, we can skip the cookout afterward and just order pizza!"

By the time Mia and Ron grudgingly said goodnight, it was nearly midnight. "Are you sure you don't want me to stay with you tonight?" Ron asked.

Mia assured him, as tempting as that idea was, she would be fine. But as she closed the door behind him, she wondered if she'd ever be fine again. I killed someone. The thought followed her to bed and she feared it would follow her into her dreams.

Mia reached for her Bible, opened to a random page, and read six words that blurred before her eyes. "Forgive, and you will be forgiven."

Am I to forgive Harry Tate? He killed those women. He was going to kill Julie. You can't possibly want me to do that.

But she knew somewhere deep inside that she was indeed to forgive him.

What happened to you, Harry? Why? What made you do such horrible things?

And then she realized, it was not for her to comprehend. She was simply to forgive and be forgiven. "All right, Lord. If you say so," she reluctantly said aloud. "I forgive you, Harry Tate, and may God have mercy on your soul."

Reaching over to return her Bible to the nightstand and turn off the bedside lamp, Mia felt a calm come over her like a warm caress. She whispered, "Thank you for helping me save my sister, Lord. Thank you, Momma," and peacefully drifted off to sleep.

CHAPTER FORTY-TWO

Sitting on the edge of her bed, Robin picked up the glass of water she kept on the bedside table. She kept it there for all the times she awakened in the middle of the night. Holding the glass with both hands to keep from spilling, she took a few sips, returned it to the nightstand, and took several deep breaths... just the way her new therapist had taught her. It helped. A little. But the nightmares were getting worse, and she often found herself more tired in the morning than when she'd gone to bed the night before.

"Are you okay, hon?" Kevin's voice was groggy, and Robin knew he had to get up early to meet with the accountant, so she assured him she was fine and merely had to pee.

He apparently took her at her word and was snoring again by the time she came out of the bathroom. She crawled back in bed and looked at the clock. Four-thirty. Too early to get up. Kevin would worry if he woke up and she wasn't there. Two and a half hours until the alarm would go off. Two and a half hours to lie there, wide awake and haunted by ugly memories.

When will it ever end?

CHAPTER FORTY-THREE

"What's so funny?" Mia asked when she saw Ron chuckling across the room.

Ron pointed to his nose and said, "The paint's supposed to go on the walls, sweetheart." Mia reflexively rubbed her nose which apparently didn't have the hoped-for result.

"Good job, sis," Cody said. "Your boyfriend's right. I think you're getting more on you than on the wall. And you're supposed to be the *painter*," he said throwing up air quotes.

"Ha-ha. I paint people, not walls." Mia moved toward her brother with what she hoped was a menacing look. Unfortunately, Cody held up his roller in defense—which was a lot bigger than Mia's trim brush.

It was a standoff that ended in laughter when Sarah said, "Children, behave!"

"Yeah, Mom, you tell 'em," Julie piped in.

From out of nowhere, Mia found herself batting back tears that threatened again. Amidst the laughter, no one seemed to notice except Ron who covered the space between them in less than two seconds and put his arm around her.

"Are you okay?" he asked. "They're just kidding, you know."

"Of course I know. Don't be silly. I don't know why I'm such a hot mess today."

"Hmm, do you think it might have something to do with everything that happened last night? I mean, you've never... Uh, that is, you've never witnessed anything like that, I'm sure."

Mia was certain he'd almost said *you've never killed anyone before* but checked himself. She appreciated his effort not to hurt her. "It's not that. At least I don't think so." Mia scanned the room and saw that the others were still busy at work while Julie and Cody exchanged playful banter. "It's Julie. Seeing her here...

laughing. Ron, we... we almost lost her." This time there was no holding back the tears as she hid her face in Ron's chest.

"All right, you two. Quit fooling around and get back to work," Julie said.

As discreetly as she could, Mia excused herself and made a beeline to the bathroom—the one room not crawling with roller-wielding painters—and allowed herself a few moments alone to blow her nose and pull herself together before returning to the action. *Get a grip.* Mia suddenly recalled how Julie had been there to support her a decade ago after she'd been kidnapped and held prisoner in a cage for three days. She remembered how important her sister's support had been in the days and weeks that followed, and she vowed to be there for her now.

When she opened the door, she found Sarah waiting. "Are you okay?" she asked placing her hands on Mia's shoulders.

"Yes, but I'm not the one that madman tried to kill. It's your daughter you should be checking on."

"That's exactly what I'm doing," Sarah said pulling Mia into her arms and holding her tight. Then she held Mia at arm's length and said, "You do know I couldn't love you more if I had given birth to you, don't you?"

And Mia knew it was true.

Back in the living room she found Ron and Julie deep in conversation, and the way the exchange ended as soon as they saw her made it obvious to Mia that she was the object of discussion. Heat rose in her cheeks. She swayed slightly.

Before she could think or react, Julie rushed over and gave her a hug. "Thank you," Julie said softly. Such an embrace between sisters would have normally been met with some kind of wisecrack from Cody, but the room was oddly quiet. Everyone busied themselves with the task at hand.

"Holy macaroni, sis," Julie said in a stage whisper. "You could have been killed."

Hearing Julie's usual funny exclamation made Mia laugh. "But I wasn't." She looked around the room and added, "But I think we might be in danger if we don't get back to work."

There wasn't much left to be done, though, so Mia and Julie were assigned cleanup, and before long everyone was admiring their work and saying what a difference the new paint colors made in the apartment.

"If I remember correctly," Craig Reed said changing the subject, "someone promised to feed us when we were done."

"Yeah, I don't know about late arrivals like you, Dad," Cody said, "but I do remember something like that too, Mia. When do we eat? Where's the food?"

"Well, we're certainly not eating here," Mia said. "Our food would taste like paint."

Everyone agreed to meet back at Mia and Julie's place, and Ron called the pizza order in to Marcello's, despite Sarah trying to fight over the bill.

"Damn, bro," Cody said when the pies arrived. "Do you have a few more families joining us?"

"Nope," Ron said. "Just a bunch of hungry Reeds! And I can't help it if you all have different pizza needs. There are wings, too. So, choose your poison... meat-lovers, pepperoni, mushroom, or veggie." He rolled his eyes. "Oh, and I asked my sister to stop by if she could."

Mia pulled out the red Solo cups, filled them with ice, and set out the diet soda, iced tea, and Mountain Dew. "There's also some Budweiser and plenty of water in the fridge," Mia said grabbing a bottle of water for her dad. Though he would've had a beer a few years ago, Craig rarely drank since he'd noticed the beginnings of a middle-aged spread in the mirror.

About the time everyone had their fill of pizza and wings, and that full-belly quiet overtook the room, the doorbell rang. Mia had almost given up hope Robin would get there in time to meet the family. She wasn't sure why that was important to her... but it was.

Ron introduced his sister, *Rachel*, to everyone and persuaded her to partake in the pizza feast. "As you can see, we've still got plenty."

Before long, exhausted but happy, most of the members of the paint party headed home. Ron thanked each of them as they left, and when the only ones remaining were Mia, Julie, Ron, and Robin, they gathered around the table. They chatted about the day's fun-filled workday for a while, but when the conversation lulled, Mia noticed a troubled look on Robin's face.

Unsure whether it was her place to ask, the psychologist in Mia won out. "Are you okay?" she asked.

"What? Me?" Robin asked. "I'm fine. You're the one who... I mean, I heard the news about that guy, Harry Tate, and Ron told me..." she paused and looked at her brother.

"It's okay," he said.

"He told me what happened. Everything. I mean, you all act like nothing happened!"

"Oh, trust me, that's not how it feels," Mia said wringing her hands until Ron put one of his hands on hers, and Julie stroked her arm. "I'm okay," she added quickly. I'm not the one he—"

"I know," Robin said turning her attention to Julie. "But Julie, how are you... really?"

"When I stop and think what could have... you know... that's kind of scary. But it didn't! So what's the point of dwelling on it?"

Mia saw the shadow of disbelief on Robin's face and put two and two together. There had to be a reason she'd seen Robin at the Reed Center. "Robin, it was nothing like what happened to you."

"No," she said. "I guess not."

Julie, who didn't know all the details of Robin's captivity, looked curiously from her to Mia then decided she should say something. "Yeah, honestly, I pretty much slept through the whole ordeal. I'm sure it didn't compare to what you went through."

Following an uncomfortable silence, Mia turned to Ron and exchanged an unspoken message, then turned back to Julie. "Jules, why don't we go down to the studio for a few minutes. I have something I wanted to show you anyway." Julie got up to follow her, and Mia called over her shoulder, "The Reed sisters are going to give the Bishop twins some private time."

"I know what you told everybody this morning, but how did you sleep last night really?" Julie asked, picking up Willie who had followed them downstairs.

"I wasn't lying. I honestly didn't think I would, but I prayed about it. Believe it or not, I actually found peace after I prayed for forgiveness for him."

Julie's jaw dropped. "Forgiveness? For Harry? Are you kidding me?"

"No... I know it sounds crazy, and I'm sorry if that upsets you, but—"

"Jeeze, Mia! He was going to kill me! I almost wound up like those other women."

"I, I know. And I would never have forgiven him for that. But the Bible says—"

"Stop it! I don't care what the Bible says. What are you some kind of s-s-saint?" Finally, Julie's bravado broke, and she was racked with tears.

Mia put her arms around her sister, hating to see her fall apart, but knowing it was something she had to go through before she could begin to let it go. Mia knew Julie wasn't as tough as she pretended to be—and that they both might need to spend some time talking it through with a professional. But she also knew she would always be there for her sister.

Just like Ron would always be there for Robin.

CHAPTER FORTY-FOUR

Robin looked at her brother and it struck her—although they were twins and the bond was as strong as it had ever been, in some ways they were now complete strangers. She wanted to tell Ron about her fears. She wanted to close the distance she felt between them. But she didn't know where to begin.

"Robin, what's going on?" Ron asked. "Are you feeling okay?"

"Honestly, no, not really. I haven't been sleeping too well lately," she said. "I'm sorry if I put a damper on things tonight. I probably shouldn't have come."

"Don't be ridiculous," Ron said. "I really wanted you here. After all, this was a family gathering… and you're all the family I've got."

"Yeah," Robin smiled. "I have Kevin and little Ronnie, but for all these years, I didn't think I had any other family left at all. At least none that I knew anything about."

Robin and Ron's maternal grandparents had died in a small plane crash on the way to their vacation home when the twins were ten, they'd lost their paternal grandmother to cancer, and their paternal grandfather had walked out on her and disappeared from their lives years before. All they'd had left were their parents. Even their mother's sister, Aunt Patty, had been taken from them at an early age by breast cancer.

"I felt so alone I even considered trying to find Grandfather Bishop."

"Don't waste your time, we don't need that man in our lives. And anyway, you're not alone anymore. You've got me," Ron said. "We've got each other, and if I have my way, all those crazy people you met here tonight are going to be family someday too."

"Oh my gosh, are you going to propose?"

"What do you think?" Ron asked giving his sister a wink. "But never mind about that. Let's get back to you. Do you want to talk about what's keeping you up at night?"

Robin looked down at her hands unsure how much she wanted to share, then finally said, "It's bad dreams. Really bad. It's... it's about *them*..." She finally looked up and into her brother's eyes, eyes she knew she could trust. "The ones who..." Robin swallowed hard and felt the sting in her eyes, "...who killed Mom and Dad... and took me and h-held me."

She saw the fury in her brother's eyes.

"And sometimes... I know it sounds crazy, but I see them. I mean I think I really see them." She couldn't bring herself to tell him that she even smelled their sweaty bodies and beer breath. Robin checked her brother's face to look for signs of disbelief, but what she saw in his wrinkled brow and searching eyes looked like he wanted to understand. To help. "I know they couldn't be here—they couldn't possibly find me—only, I mean, what if..."

Ron pulled his chair closer. "My God, I hate what they did to you," he said. "And I get that you were too scared and ashamed—even though none of it was your fault—so you never went to the police, but now, Robin, now it's time. We need to find them," he said through gritted teeth. "They need to pay for what they've done."

"I know you're right." Robin's cheeks burned and with a too familiar cold sweat. The light-headedness returned. "I should have—"

"No, I'm not saying that. I don't blame you. Here, let me get you some water." Ron quickly filled a glass and brought it back to her. "What I'm trying to say is, it's time, sis. And you're not alone."

Robin nodded, took several sips of water, and wiped her palms on her jeans. "But it's been so long. And I don't remember... I don't know where they are. How could we possibly find them?"

"Hey," Ron said with a wink, "did you forget your brother is a detective?"

Robin appreciated his smile, and the lighthearted way he said it, but she also knew it was true. Maybe they really could find the monsters, and she could stop being afraid. Maybe, with Ron's help, the fiends would finally pay.

CHAPTER FORTY-FIVE

During Mia's years studying and working in Pittsburgh, she had missed the time-honored tradition of Sunday dinner at the Reed's, with anywhere from four or five up to a dozen or more people gathered around the extended table. The cacophony of voices and laughter was music to her ears, and having Ron by her side completed the melody.

Today Sarah and Craig were surrounded by all five of their children plus Bobby's girlfriend, Megan—who Mia thought looked like might be the real thing for Bobby—and of course, Ron.

"Jeeze, look at all this food. Really, Mom?" Julie said. "It looks like Thanksgiving. What's the occasion?"

"Do you need to ask?" Sarah handed her the scalloped potatoes to carry to the dining room table. "I'm feeling pretty thankful, aren't you?"

Mia saw the way her mother bit her lower lip and turned back to the stove. She swallowed hard realizing what Sarah must be thinking. *We could have been planning a funeral instead of having a celebration.*

Normally, Craig would ask who'd like to say the blessing, but on this particular Sunday, once the food was on the table, the head of the household simply said, "Let's have the blessing." Silence replaced all the chatter, they took each other's hands, and he prayed aloud giving thanks for the food they were about to receive, the hands that had prepared it, and that all of their family was safe and able to gather and share it together. Julie, who was sitting to Mia's left, squeezed her hand.

A soft chorus of amens and several more seconds of quiet followed the short prayer before Julie broke the stillness with, "Holy manicotti, let's eat!"

"What happened to the macaroni?" Mia asked amidst the laughter.

Since they'd been hearing "holy macaroni" for years, the whole family waited for Julie's answer. She smiled, looked at her parents then her sister and said, "It's time to change it up. After all, it's a new day."

The somber moment of reflection and gratitude quickly returned to joyful chaos of a typical Reed family dinner, but Mia knew the bond with her sister had grown stronger, and their petty differences would never break it.

After enjoying dinner and lingering over the scrumptious peach cobbler Sarah had prepared, they made quick work of cleaning off the table and loading the two dishwashers in Sarah's big kitchen. Then, cold drinks in hand, they all headed out to the deck to appreciate the perfect weather. With sunshine and unusually low humidity, it was a perfect day for throwing horseshoes, one of their favorite pastimes.

"C'mon, you two," Cody said to Mia and Ron.

"No, you guys go first," Ron said as Mia had started to get up. "I need to let all that food digest a little more before I whoop you."

Once Cody and Bobby challenged Julie and Megan and the four headed across the lawn, Ron whispered, "Let's take a walk."

That idea suited Mia perfectly. "We'll be back," she said to her parents and Destiny, who was getting up to go watch the game. Mia saw her father take her mother's hand and knew they wouldn't mind some quiet time.

Ron led her to a secluded section of the Reed property and into the white gazebo Sarah and Craig had placed there as a romantic getaway. When they married and two families of three became one big family of six, it was the perfect little hideaway. As an adolescent, Mia had come upon her parents sharing a passionate embrace and silently crept away. Since then she had often dreamed of recreating that scene with the man of her dreams, and she and Ron had recently done just that.

Sitting on the bench in this quiet spot from which they could see and hear the water rippling over the rocks in the nearby stream with Ron by her side, Mia sighed. "This is nice. Someday I'd like to have a quiet spot of my own like this to sit and read. Or paint."

"Then maybe we'd better build you one."

"Oh, I don't mean now. I don't think it would be the same at the cottage."

"I didn't mean at the cottage." Ron took her hand. "I was thinking when we get a place of our own." He had Mia's complete attention now. Mia couldn't recall him ever talking about them having "a place of their own" before. Her jaw dropped when Ron got down on one knee.

"I think this is how it's supposed to be done," he said reaching into his pocket and pulling out a little box. "Don't look so surprised, sweetheart. I'm sure you know how much I love you, and I can't imagine not having you in my life. So..." He opened the little box, took out a beautiful diamond ring, and asked, "Mia Reed, will you marry me?"

Mia had hoped and dreamed of this moment yet was taken completely by surprise. So many thoughts raced through her head. She'd known him for less than a year, and he was a cop. Was it too soon?

Then she looked into his blue eyes... the bluest eyes she'd ever seen. "Yes, of course I'll marry you." She laughed, bouncing up and down with joy as he slipped the ring on her finger, and she threw her arms around his neck. "I love you," she whispered.

Neither of them wanted to end the kiss that sealed the deal, but when they finally came up for air, Mia looked at her ring and grinned. "Shall we go tell everybody?"

"Sure... but not just yet. Can I please keep my fiancée to myself a little while longer?"

Mia didn't need words to answer. She looked into the eyes that had captured her heart, and when he gently pulled her close and their lips met again, she knew she would be his forever, and her heart whispered, *Thank you.*

WAITING FOR THE WHISPER

SNEAK PEEK

Small town life was exactly what Mia Reed had remembered and expected it to be—well, except for a serial killer and a marriage proposal—and her work at the Reed Mental Health Center had settled into a normal routine... or so she thought.

"I'll be with you in just a minute, Samantha," Mia said to her next client. She motioned to the man sitting next to her. "Detective Bishop, would you come this way, please?"

Mia guided the detective into her office, closed the door behind her, and walked into her fiancé's arms. "What are you doing here, Ron?" She snuggled into the warmth of his embrace. "I have two more clients to see before I'm done."

"Ah, but I'm not here to see you."

"What? Now I'm hurt," Mia teased, pulling far enough away to look up into those blue eyes she loved so much.

"I'm here to interview Dr. Block about the assault and theft last night."

"Oh, yes. Of course. I didn't think he'd even be in today." The staff psychiatrist seemed too shaken after what he'd been through. Her grandfather's practice, The Reed Mental Health Center, had seemed like the safest place in the world... until now. "Why didn't you talk to him last night?"

Ron explained that his partner had been the one on the scene. "But Jason said the doctor was pretty rattled. I'm here to follow up, and as much as I'd like to stay here with you, I believe you have a client of your own to see."

Mia reluctantly withdrew her hands from around his neck, but Ron pulled her in to steal one more quick kiss before heading back to the waiting room. Alone again, she looked at the beautiful marquis-cut one-carat diamond on the third finger of her left hand. Mia still found it hard to believe that the man she'd fallen in love with all those months ago had never bothered to mention he had such a large amount of money that he never touched.

Right now though, it was time to meet with Samantha Collins, and since this particular client had paranoid tendencies, it wasn't a good idea to keep her waiting.

"Who was that man?" Samantha asked as soon as the door closed behind her. She took her usual seat next to Mia's desk, preferring not to have her back to the door. Then she looked at her phone for the second time since entering Mia's office.

"Is something wrong? Were you expecting an important call?" Mia asked, ignoring her client's question about Ron.

"What? Oh no. I was just checking the time. Was he another client?" Samantha Collins was not one to be ignored. "I've seen him before. Was he talking about me?"

"No, of course not." Though Mia was tempted to tell Samantha how ridiculous that sounded, she bit her tongue. "That was Detective Bishop. He's here on official business, but I know him personally and needed to speak with him for a moment." Noticing that her client once again glanced at her phone, Mia added, "I believe we began your session a few minutes late, and I apologize, but we'll make up the time at the end. So how was your week?"

"It was okay, I guess, but that neighbor I was telling you about, he's still watching me. I'm sure of it. I think he was peeking from behind his curtain when I got home last night." Samantha's foot was bouncing rapidly, and Mia could see the rise in her anxiety level.

"I know this feeling of being watched is upsetting to you. Have you been taking your meds?"

"Yes! Well, maybe not every day. I get so sleepy, you know?"

"I understand." Mia watched as her client's foot bounced faster, and she knew the woman's paranoia would only get worse without her medication. "Have you told Dr. Block about the side effects?"

"Yes, but he just said it's something I have to get used to. That my body has to adjust to it or something."

"Well, in the meantime, have you been practicing your relaxation exercises?"

"Sort of... but I've been so busy. I don't always remember."

"I understand, but how's that working? Do you feel better when you practice your relaxation or when you don't?" Mia wondered if the woman had even practiced enough to know the difference.

"I guess when I do it, but I get distracted sometimes."

"Okay, sure. I know we have lots of distractions around us. So let's talk about what you might be able to do to lessen them." Mia spoke to her client about setting up her environment to eliminate some of the distractions like turning off the TV, turning off the ringer on her phone, closing the curtains, and possibly using earbuds to listen to the relaxation exercise Mia had recorded for her.

"Now, what about your drawing? Have you played around with that anymore?" Mia had witnessed the positive effect art therapy had for Samantha and encouraged her to pursue the hobby at home as well as behind the easel during their sessions.

"I did!" Samantha suddenly became more animated. She smiled for the first time since coming into the office and leaned forward in her seat. "I got a sketchpad and a book on drawing animals. I think I can learn to draw after all."

"That's great, Sam. I'm sure you can." Mia had seen her client's actual potential. "But remember, how good the drawing turns out isn't as important as how you feel while you're doing it. How about if we use the rest of our session for your art?"

Once actively involved in creating, Samantha's shoulders relaxed, her foot stopped bouncing, and her brow smoothed.

When Mia told her how impressed she was with the relaxing scene of a lake surrounded by weeping willows, Samantha beamed. But when told their time was about up, she quickly checked her phone again.

"Yes, we ran over a little bit, but I wanted you to have time to finish your drawing." Mia knew her client would have been upset if she didn't have her full session length. Better to go over a little than have Sam believe she'd been cheated out of even one minute.

Mia now had no time to write detailed notes before bringing her last client back, nor did she have much time to change gears to meet the next person's needs, but fortunately she was seeing her favorite lady to end the day.

Miss Edna, as Mia addressed ninety-three-year-old Edna Schmidt, had first sought counseling to deal with the grief of losing her husband several years earlier. After a sixty-five-year marriage, the grief was understandable, but her depression had not lifted in the three years since she'd been widowed.

Edna lived in the same senior community as Mia's "Aunt Bonnie"—who was actually a friend of the family—and who had finally persuaded her to seek counseling. Mia quickly fell in love with this lovely lady and her kind heart, and she was reminded of a special Alzheimer's patient she'd had back in Pittsburgh. But Edna didn't suffer from any noticeable form of dementia. She was sharp as a tack.

Losing her husband had been compounded by giving up their family home a year later—it was too much for Edna to handle on her own—and then losing her ability to drive. There were simply too many losses. Her children lived out of state and worried about her being alone even in a senior living community. They had tried to convince her she should come live with one of them or go to a nursing home. Edna, however, was not ready to give up her independence. She was a sweet but feisty lady who simply suffered from the depression all the losses in her life had forced upon her. Fortunately, she was improving, and Mia always felt good when she got her weekly hug at the end of their sessions.

Today was no different. And she got a second hug from Aunt Bonnie who was waiting to drive her friend and neighbor home.

Normally at the end of the day Mia was anxious to head home, take a walk, have dinner, and relax in her art studio. She had claimed the large walk-out basement as her studio in the house she shared with her sister, Julie, and her sister got the biggest bedroom with a sitting area where she did her writing.

Knowing this was Julie's night to fix dinner and seeing that the rain hadn't let up, Mia had no need to hurry home, so she wrote up her client notes and decided to hang out a while longer to get more details about the previous night's attack on Dr. Block.

"What are you doing still here?" Sarah Reed asked, sticking her head in the door. "I thought you were done almost an hour ago." When Mia explained why she was hanging around, her mother came the rest of the way into her office and took a seat. "What did you want to know? I might be able to fill you in."

"A lot of things. Like do they have any idea who did it?"

"Not really. Douglas said all he knew was that it was a male—young, he thought—and that he didn't hear him come in. He said he was reading over someone's file, heard a noise, and that quick, whoever it was knocked him out cold. I can't believe he wouldn't go to the hospital to get checked out." Sarah shook her head. "Unbelievable, isn't it?"

"Yes, and scary," Mia added. "But why? I mean, the guy just hit him on the head and left? Do they think it was a patient? Maybe somebody didn't like something he said, or what?" The idea that a patient could turn on their therapist was hard for Mia to imagine since the bond she had with her clients was so positive, but she did know Dr. Douglas Block wasn't known for his gentle bed-side manner.

"I don't know, hon. Your fiancé might be able to tell you more. I saw him leaving here earlier. Okay, I'm heading home. Your dad's in charge of dinner tonight so between him and your little sister, I'm guessing it's going to be pizza or subs." Sarah walked around the desk and kissed her daughter on the forehead. "Will you and Ron be coming to dinner on Sunday?"

"Absolutely. See you then." Mia hoped it was true. Ron said he would be free, but what if he got another case? She was beginning to think the only ones who could be sure her detective boyfriend would show up were the murder victims. Or what if he got another clue in the cold case he'd become totally obsessed by since reuniting with his sister? Not that Mia blamed him for wanting to find his parents' killers, but it could be hard sitting on the back burner.

Shaking off her doubts, Mia focused on the work before her, and it wasn't until she had completed her newest client's treatment plan that she noticed the time and the deafening quiet beyond her door. Grabbing her coat, shoulder bag, and umbrella, Mia strode to the doorway but hesitated and scanned the hall before heading toward the waiting room. Never before had she felt uneasy leaving her office in the evening, but then no one had ever been assaulted there until last night.

The rain had stopped, but Mia pulled her coat tightly around her, dashed to her Civic, and locked the door before finally feeling safe. *This is ridiculous*, she thought. *Or is it?*

ABOUT THE AUTHOR

Gloria Bostic is a retired special education teacher from York, Pennsylvania. As a Masters level clinical psychologist, she also worked with women and children to help them overcome abuse. She lives in Dover, PA, with her husband, Lee, and enjoys spending time with her three sons and all her grandchildren.

Also by Gloria Bostic...

Deception Bridge (Book 1)

Valerie Reed is plagued by migraines, insomnia, and a growing anxiety that her happily-ever-after is about to come crumbling down. Tormented by the fear of losing her husband of nearly thirty years, she hangs onto the one thing she knows she can count on – her friendship with the women in her bridge group. They provide a safe-haven with warmth, laughter, and trust... until that trust is broken.

As Val searches for a way to save her marriage and learn to trust again, her life and her bridge group go through unanticipated transformations. Their lives will never be the same, and Val wonders if the power of prayer will be enough to save them all.

Broken Contracts (Book 2)

Through faith and forgiveness Valerie and Andy Reed's marriage has survived and grown stronger in spite of Andy's brief affair five years ago. However, the consequences of his tryst with Susan Walters, a former member of Val's bridge group, may now turn their world upside-down once again.

As Susan's marriage falls apart, all she wants is to be a good mother to the child she had always longed for... yet her life is becoming unmanageable as she continually succumbs to the need for her next drink.

When Valerie, Bonnie, Sarah, and Kathy gather around the bridge table, they share more than the game. Only time will tell what's in the cards.

Premonition Bridge (Book 3)

A threat... A former client warns that her husband is wildly angry that she left him and blames her therapist, Sarah Reed, for ruining his life. He vows to get even.

A disappearance... A member of the Reed family mysteriously disappears without a trace. The only clues to the victim's whereabouts may come from mystifying messages in drawings and dreams.

A reuniting... Family members separated, relationships lost, friendships dissolved... Will prayer and forgiveness be enough for the bridge club ladies to find resolution from the chaos that has invaded their lives?

Out of the Storm

Greta Friedman travels from victim to victory in this story of a young woman's search for the life she's been denied. A childhood filled with loss and abuse leaves her desperate to find love and normalcy, but as a young adult Greta is frustrated by unanswered prayers and a pattern of relationships that end badly... until she meets someone special. When Gabe Engel mysteriously comes into her life, Greta begins the journey that will give her the strength to escape impending danger and finally make her dreams a reality.

Watercolor Whispers (Book 1)

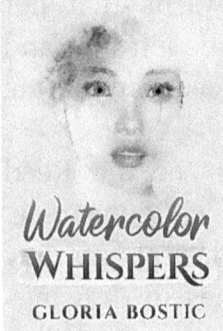

Watercolor
WHISPERS
GLORIA BOSTIC

Art therapist Mia Reed has a calling to help her patients as well as a special gift... paintings that unlock mysteries and help solve crimes. However, Freddie Alessi—an assault victim whose wife has gone missing—leaves every session more disturbed than when he arrived... almost as disturbed as Mia feels about his charming and attractive older brother Anthony. Her brain says run, but his fervent kisses keep drawing her back.

Detective Ron Bishop is intrigued by Mia's gift as he struggles to solve missing persons and murder cases. But when Mia's hand is guided by an outside force, can the clues in her drawings lead to the killer and answer the questions in time?

The
Greatest Aunt

Gloria Bostic
Illustrated by Vicki Friedman

The Greatest Aunt

It's a scary time for Flora when she learns her parents must go away. She will have to go live with her great-aunt, but can't understand why they call her great. Flora happily discovers why and agrees!

www.ingramcontent.com/pod-product-compliance
Lightning Source LLC
Chambersburg PA
CBHW072235170626
46813CB00003B/1231

When Is Enough Enough

LESH

<u>ONE</u>

Summer couldn't believe he had punched her in the face the way he did. Then, he picked her up and threw her against the wall.

Damn, she thought to herself.

At that moment, it felt like every bone in her body had been broken, and she couldn't move. All she could do was just lie there in complete shock. She remembered that he was staring at her as she helplessly lay on the floor and cried out, "I'm sorry. I'm sorry!" – but he didn't want to hear it. He had punched her in the face so hard that she knew she was bleeding, but she didn't know where she was bleeding from. She even seen the blood running down her clothes and onto the floor. There was literally blood everywhere!

He ran over to her and began to pull at her clothes to try to take them off.

"Stop!!" she mumbled, "What are you doing?" She yelled as she tried to fight back, but she felt weak.

"Shut the fuck up!" he yelled. "I'm going to show you what happens when you snitch!"

She tried and tried to put up a fight, but she just couldn't. Every time she moved, it was so painful, and she felt herself getting weaker. The last thing she could remember was him pulling down his pants and forcibly entering her. Then, she blacked out completely.

When she awoke from being unconscious, she couldn't move at all. She was only able to turn her head slightly and glance around the house to notice it was a total mess. The couches were slit, papers and pictures were everywhere, and the furniture was in a disarray.

"Help...please –" she mumbled, but it was so low that she knew no one could hear her. "Reef? Are you there??" she murmured a couple of times, but there was no answer.

A few minutes later, she heard a knock at the door before it slowly crept open. Apparently, someone heard all the commotion and called the police.

"Ma'am, are you ok? Can you tell me what happened here?" the cop asked as he ran over to her. "Is there anyone else here with you?"

She was so exhausted that she couldn't even speak. Almost every bone in her body felt like it was broken.

"Ma'am, can you tell us what happened to you?" they asked again, but she couldn't speak.

Then, several EMTs entered the apartment, began to take her vital signs, and told her that she would be going to the hospital. She didn't have the strength, but she managed to shake her,

head because she was really scared and didn't want to go anywhere.

⌘

"Girl please, you know Reef is not having that, and he would kill you if he found out."

"Yes, he would definitely be mad. Trust me, he would never find out, and I put that on my grave."

The girls laughed it off and continued to sip on the drinks a random man brought them in the club. They may not have spoken to each other every day, but every now and then, the

2

girls would go out just to catch up on things and have a good time.

"OHHHH GIRL!! That's my song! Let's go dance!"

Nakima, Sheree, and Ebony all made their way to the dance floor as "Get it Sexy" by Sexyy Red bumped through the speakers. Some of the men in the club came over and stood by them to try and get a dance, but they weren't beat to talk to any of them.

Nakima, Sheree, and Ebony were all childhood friends with very different lifestyles. What bonded them together was the fact that they were like sisters and had been through very similar situations in life. So, they learned from each other.

Nakima was 25 years old and very attractive. She was brown-skinned, 5'7, with shoulder-length dreads, and hazel eyes. Her body was curvaceous and toned because she used to run track in high school. Surprisingly, she kept the same physique. She was a track star on her high school team and was offered a full scholarship to college, but she didn't go due to various reasons dealing with family. Nakima grew up in Brooklyn with her aunt because her mom passed away from breast cancer when she was fifteen, and it tore her to pieces. She wasn't able to function because she felt like she had lost her best friend. Her father, on the other hand, was always in and out of jail, so they never had a close relationship.

Nakima's aunt tried to do her best to raise her, but she just got out of control. She began running the streets, being disrespectful, dating random guys, and staying out all night. Even though she was young, she was very mature for her age and carried herself as if she were older. Unfortunately, it had gotten to a point where her aunt couldn't handle her anymore and kicked her out. With nowhere to go, she had no other choice but to stay at the shelter. She didn't like the rules they had. There were perverted men always staring and saying nasty things to lure her places for money. Eventually, she left the shelter and stayed with friends here and there, although she had gotten to the point where she didn't care much about her life. All she knew was that she had to make money in order to take care of

3

herself and she would do anything for that. Luckily, Nakima later met Sheree and Ebony, who both changed her life, and they were inseparable ever since.

Sheree was 23 years old. She was 5'7, light-skinned with grey eyes, very curly brown hair down her back, and she had an athletic build as well. She grew up with both parents and was the only child. Because of this, she always had to sneak out and lie to her parents about where she would go because they never let her do anything. Her parent's main focus was to keep her out of the streets and retain her innocence. All she wanted to do was to become a model, but her parents had other plans and didn't want her to, "waste her time," in their opinion. She argued with her parents all the time, but she enjoyed the spotlight and being a part of fashion shows with hopes of being recognized.

After she graduated high school, she went to New York to try and live out her dreams, but was turned down by a major company that felt her work wasn't good enough. She didn't care what they thought and decided to start making clothes for her friends. Eventually, she started working with a low-key company who said they would help her start a business and clothing line. Little did she know, they ended up stealing her designs and moving the business to California. She was so furious and it set her back heavy, so she just stopped all together. What made it worse was that she couldn't fight it because she never signed any paperwork.

On the other hand, Ebony was a 25-year-old, biracial – well at least that's what she was told – but considered herself black. She had big bold eyes and nice full lips. She was about 5'5 with long, brown, flowing hair. Her childhood was wonderful until she was about fifteen. That's when she learned she was adopted. She tried to reach out to her birth parents, but had no luck. Her adoptive parents never gave her any problems about it, and they were very supportive of everything she did.

She had two brothers who were pretty much around her age, but after she found out she was adopted, she shut down and didn't talk to them. She was sexually abused from age thirteen to nineteen and constantly had flashbacks of the man's voice over and over again. She questioned herself all the time, *if only I hadn't been so stupid to think he just wanted to buy me sneakers and take me out to eat.* This day changed her life forever. Her attitude changed. It was now, her against everyone.

No one knew what was going on with her, and they were kind of scared for her. Most people didn't like her because she was very blunt and would curse you out in a minute if you even looked at her the wrong way. Her parents tried to get her some help once they noticed a change in her, but she never went. She became so disrespectful to them and began to run the streets. She became sexually active and craved the attention of men constantly.

When she met Mac Daddy Diamonds, he was like the father she never had. Although he put his hands on her a couple of times, she didn't know how to be treated any other way. She liked what she was doing because it made her lots of money. She also loved the attention she would get from the abundance of men. The compliments she would get made her feel very special. She ended up bringing Ebony into it, and together, they became unstoppable. Mac Daddy Diamonds became crazy and would tell her things like, "If you ever leave me, I will kill you!" You know how it goes... or at least heard stories.

She knew it was time to get out once the physical abuse started. She didn't know any better, but she didn't want this to be the rest of her life either.

⌘

It was Friday night, so you know it was party time!. Ebony and Nakima were going out as usual, they never really stayed home.

"Damn! What am I going to wear tonight?" Ebony says, looking in her closet, while thinking aloud.

"All those damn clothes, and you mean to tell me you can't find anything?" Nakima asks.

"I think I'm wearing a dress to show off my sexy ass. I'ma have all the men on my ass tonight," she said laughing.

She stopped, looked at her, and they both started to laugh. The only thing on Nakima's mind was who she was going to take home tonight.

Before they left, they made sure Sheree didn't want to go. She didn't really go out too much because she was the one who always stayed home and had some company over. Nakima decided to wear a tight dress, and *OH BOY* it was a freak 'um dress. She just knew she was the shit and no one could tell her otherwise. Ebony kept it simple with a one-piece short set to show off her legs.

When they got to NY, they decided to go to the Keybar, and yes, the line was long as hell. As they walked up to the line, everyone turned to stare at them, including the females. They felt like superstars, but they knew that they were staring because they were all so beautiful. This was normal to them, so they just smiled, looked on, and blew kisses at different men. After about twenty minutes, they finally made it inside and headed straight for the bar. Two shots in, they headed to the bathroom to make sure everything was intact. Other girls in the bathroom were rolling their eyes and whispering, but they didn't step up and say anything. Lord knows they didn't want hands, especially with Ebony.

When they exited the bathroom, Nakima locked eyes with this sexy light-skinned dude who had alluring green eyes and tri-brown colored dreads. Her heart immediately began to race as he licked his lips and watched her walk past. He tried to grab at her, but she pulled away and smiled while continuing to walk to the bar and bumping to the music. Somehow, he found his way over to her and came up real close, whispering in her ear and touching her ear lobe with his lips.

"What's ya' name, sexy?"
Chills went through her body as his lips touched her ear by accident. Nakima turned around, put her hand on his chest, and asked, "What is your name?"

Biting his lips, he responds, "Troy."

"Troy?" Nakima questioned as she began to laugh.

"What's so funny?" he asked, looking puzzled.

"Nothing, I just thought your name would be something different."

"Oh ok!" he says and smiles. "Who you here with?" Troy asked. Nakima turned and pointed to Ebony who was on the dance floor. "What's your plans for the night?" Troy asked.

Nakima licked her lips because she knew deep down what she came there for, but she managed to say, "Nothing."

Troy somewhat got the hint and asked if she wanted to chill after the club let out. Nakima nodded her head, ordered another drink, and told him to meet her in the parking lot. With their plans being set, Troy walked away and Nakima continued drinking. She had planned on getting tipsy because, for some reason, she felt like the sex was going to be great. Eventually, Nakima walked over to Ebony to let her know what her plans were going to be afterwards and they continued to dance. Periodically, she made sure she made eye contact with Troy to let him know she was serious, and every time their eyes met, he was staring at her. You could see the lust in his eyes.

When the club let out, Nakima walked with Ebony to Troy's car so she could see she was good and that this is what she really wanted to do. She didn't realize how drunk she was until she sat down in the car, but she knew she had to pull herself together. There was silence in the car at first as they drove off, and then he asked her where she wanted to go. Nakima said nothing at first and just looked at him.

"Oh ok, baby girl, say no more," he said and smiled.

He stepped on the gas and sped to the nearest hotel trying not to give her a chance to change her mind. As they reached the hotel, Nakima stumbled a little when getting out of the car, but tried her hardest to get it together before he could notice. Troy did see it and asked if she was good. Then, he grabbed her hand and walked her to the door.

As they got to the door of the hotel room, Nakima looked at Troy and started kissing him. Troy grabbed her ass and squeezed it. "Damn shorty, ya' ass fat as hell!"

They both laughed and stumbled into the room. Troy started running the jacuzzi as Nakima lay on the bed completely wasted. Troy started getting undressed and begged her to join. Eventually, she gave in, and they both ended up in the jacuzzi, face-to-face, staring into each other's eyes. He didn't know how to go about making his first move, so he grabbed her legs and started massaging them while sucking her toes one by one. Nekima's eyes rolled in the back of her head as she let out small, subtle moans. He made sure to take his time because he could see she was enjoying it. Her body began to tingle as she thought about fucking the shit out of him. She was about to change his life.

She grabbed his hand and they got out of the jacuzzi and headed to the bed. Staring at each other she begins to run her fingers through his hair not thinking in her mind that this man was just too damn sexy. She knew she had him from this point on, so she leaned in towards his neck and kissed him softly. She could feel his heart beating and his dick was now rock hard through his pants. Without hesitation she made him take off his pants as she dropped to her knees and began to lick around the head of his dick. Looking up at his face, she noticed his eyes were closed and he was biting his bottom lip. In her mind, she wanted to drive him crazy, so she began to suck slowly in a circular motion, making sure to keep her eyes on him while palming his balls.

After about fifteen minutes, he nutted all over her face in ecstasy. She couldn't do anything but laugh as he picked her up, threw her across his shoulders, and lay her on the back. Then, he spread her legs and began to lick between her thighs. Once he finally found her clit, he went crazy and started licking, he couldn't believe how good she tasted, After about ten minutes and what felt like five nuts, Nakima made him stop because she wanted to be in control. Out of nowhere, she pulled him up and threw him on the bed. Then, she climbed up on top of him and forced his dick inside of her. She began to ride him slowly, picking up speed periodically to make him plead for her. Both of them filled the room with their moans and grunts.

Eventually, Troy flipped her over and started hitting it from the back. He loved to see her ass jiggle each time he pulled

8

her towards him. After he released, he pushed her away and made sure it went all over the sheets. Both still drunk, they jumped up and got dressed. They had both lost track of time and were amazed at what just happened. Neither one of them had ever had a sexual experience like that before. It was a little silent in the car on the ride home, but Nakima kept getting flashbacks and her pussy kept throbbing. She knew this couldn't have been good for her because she had never felt something like this before. Something in her soul told her that she needed to run far away from what she was feeling.

Immediately, she decided it was best to let Troy know that she had a good time, but wasn't looking for anything serious. Troy couldn't help but look puzzled because he was low-key disappointed. He actually thought that they could have something special, but she shut down the thought of it before it began. That thought plagued his mind as they reached her house. Before getting out of the car, Nakima gave Troy a kiss on the lips and quickly jumped out of the car before he could even attempt to let her out and walk her to the door. All he could do was smile and pull off.

TWO

"Come on man! You know I'll never settle down with no bitch!" Shareef yells as he makes his way to sit down on the couch. "Y'all always have this same convo and my answer never changes. I would fuck a bitch up for real if she ever disrespect me in any way!"

"Yea, ok nigga," Lateef replied, looking at Shareef.

"That shit ain't cute man and a lot of stupid shit happens with bullshit like that," Micah said, shaking his head.

"I ain't worried bout shit 'cause the shit ain't gone happen to me – ever!" Shareef says while looking at them. "I put that on everything!"

Micah laughed as he sipped his beer with a smirk on his face. "What the fuck you looking at bitch?" Shareef asked from across the room.

"Man, the way I feel – it's my way or the highway."

They all laughed and continued to play the game.

Shareef, Lateef, and Micah had been best friends for years, growing up in New Jersey. Shareef was 27 years old and stood at 5'9" with brown skin and brown eyes. He always kept a low haircut with waves and he had a very muscular build. He had the sexiest lips that complemented his perfect smile, which all the ladies loved. Shareef chose to coach young children after school because of his passion for basketball. One day, he lost one of his students due to an accidental shooting, which devastated him. Because of this, he always tried to talk to the kids in the community to ensure that they stayed out of the streets.

He was raised by his father after his parents divorced when he was very young. Shareef never had much of a relationship with his mother because she just chose to stay away. Living with his father, he witnessed all sorts of wild shit and women coming in and out of the house. Seeing how his father lived, he picked up similar habits and felt no pressure to settle down with just any woman. Shareef was single and lived in a one-bedroom apartment.

Lateef had long braids, brown-skinned, 5 ′8" and very skinny. He was 26 years old and unemployed at the moment, so he had to live with his mother. Lateef hated the fact that he lived with his mother, but he didn′t have a choice. However, he and his mom had an amazing relationship, and he cherished it. His mother loved for him to help out around the house and she wanted to actually keep him there, she felt secure and she knew that nothing would happen to her as long as he was there.

Unfortunately, he was clowned all the time by his boys because he didn′t have the privacy he needed. His mom didn′t play with him having all types of females in and out of her house, but he knew he would have his own soon, so he didn′t sweat it. She taught him everything he knew, especially how to treat and respect women. Therefore, he felt as though he understood them very well and thought he knew all about them

Micah, "Pretty boy," was 27 years old. He was light-skinned, had long, thick dreads, green eyes, and was very muscular because he was heavily in the gym. He was a personal trainer, but he had goals to open his own gym. Micah grew up with both his parents in the home. It was just him because his mother had lost a baby.

When he was younger, he remembered his mother and father getting into an argument, his mother being rushed out of the house, and when she returned, she no longer had a big belly. As a young kid, he was so excited to be an older brother and his mother had told him that she was having a girl. Even though he

11

was young, he fully understood that he was no longer going to have a sibling. He would often talk to his mother about what it would've been like if his sister was here. His father, on the other hand, said nothing and would blame his mom, often.

However, when he was growing up, he felt like he had "cool parents." They had him when they were young, so they were able to relate to him more. The boys would always go over to his house to chill because his parents were cool. Right now, Micah lived by himself and didn't have any kids and felt he wasn't ready to settle down. He loved to run games on a lot of women. That's how he got the name, "Pretty Boy".

"Man, what's good for the night?" Micah asked.

They both look at him. "You already knooooow ..."

They had this game they played every time they went out to see who could bag the baddest female. Poor Lateef. He couldn't do much unless he planned on going to a telly. Micah would always win, but lately the girls were feeling Shareef.

⌘

The girls were sitting on the couch talking about all the silly stuff they used to do back in the day.

"I need a real man. I'm tired of niggas out here claiming to be this and claiming to be that and they end up not being shit!". They all laughed, but knew it was the truth.

"I'm going out with you guys next Friday to find Mr. Right!" Sheree said. "I've been cooped up in this house and it's time for me to get out."

"Mr. Right!?! Well, let me tell you about the other night I had." Nakima giggled. " – or at least what I can remember. OH MY GOD!! I remember he was cute as fuck and had green eyes, which I felt like I could look into all night. Girl, he sucked my pussy so good – I almost died. I really can't remember what happened, but the sex was amazing. I did some dumb shit and I told him I didn't want to get into anything. Now, I'm sitting here thinking that was STUPID!!"

Sheree and Ebony had a shocked look on their faces.

"What?!? " Sheree and Ebony said in unison.

"You're crazy – " Sheree automatically went into mother mode and started preaching like she always did.

Nakima shrugged her shoulders and just rolled her eyes.

⌘

"How about what you have going on in your life right now?" Sheree questioned.

They all knew she was serious because she didn't let anyone else talk, just so she could get her point across. "I really care about y'all and don't want anything to happen because, lord knows, I will kill somebody. You guys gotta grow up! You can't keep living like this and I'm dead ass serious."

They both hated it when she got into this mode, but they knew she was telling the truth.

"Shhittttt, ain't nothing happening to me!" Ebony blurted out.

Nakima agreed and just nodded her head. Sheree just looked away in disgust because she didn't understand how they could be so naive about shit going on around them. "Ok, you will definitely learn the hard way. Just watch."

Sheree changed the subject and brought up their potential plans for Friday night.

"Girl, maybe we will do Harbor Rooftop Lounge or The Vault."

"I just have one request. If I go with y'all, can you please not get me into any trouble or try to give these dudes the wrong impression of me?"

They all started laughing and falling to the ground. "Girl bye, don't you know birds of a feather flock together?" Ebony replied.

Sheree sucked her teeth and said with a giggle, " I ain't no hoe."

⌘

Micah woke up the next morning feeling fucked up. He was mad at himself for not giving Shorty his real name. *I mean, everything was perfect,* at least that's what he thought. In a way he felt relieved, but he knew she would remember his face. *God forbid they run into each other again.* All he could think about was how he had never been played by a girl before. He was usually the one to never call back. He called Reef just to tell him the story because he knew he had to be tripping.

"Man, I had the best night. Shorty's ass was so fat I got lost in it and she sucked a mean one, man. I ain't gonna front – I ate her pussy and licked her toes. Then, she played my son. She told me she didn't want to continue and this was just a one-night stand.

Reef immediately started cracking up on the other end of the phone.

"I'm saying, tho. You would've went all out if you seen her too, my nigga. I'm not knocking you, if that's what you felt like doing. It's cool because if I see her again, I'ma act like I don't know her. You know how I do!"

THREE

As Nakima, Sheree and Ebony got ready for their night out, they smoked and got high as hell. See, Sheree used to party with them all the time, but she got tired of doing the same things. Yeah, clubbing and going out every day was fun in her early teens because she was the one who always got all the attention. Now, she was over it. She was tired of always being the center of attention and girls always hating on her made her not want to go out.

"Sometimes loooooveee coooomes around and it knocks you down, just get back up, when it knocks you down...knocks you down." Sheree sang while getting dressed. "That's my shit! I hope they play it tonight!" she exclaimed, winding her hips and glancing at herself in the mirror as "Knock You Down" by Keri Hilson played loudly behind her.

They all burst out laughing as they walked out the door and jumped in the car.

"Fuck! It's mad people out here tonight," Nakima said looking at all the cuties walking past.

"I guess everyone wanted to party tonight!" Sheree said as they parked and decided which club they wanted to go to.

The girls hopped out of the car, and Nakima instantly spotted a club with lights on the rooftop, so they made their way over. Heads were turning and men were mumbling stuff under their breath as they walked past everyone. All they could do was smile and keep it moving.

Tonight was the right night, but Ebony kept complaining about her shoes, which was starting to irritate everyone. "What's the club called," Ebony asked.

Sheree nodded her head. "We don't know because there are not any signs. Do you see one?" she asked in an aggravated tone.

All they could do was just hope they wouldn't be in line for too long. After about a half hour, they finally got into the club and headed straight for the bar. They ordered some shots just to get going and feel out the scene. There was nothing but busted men in the club, and if they weren't busted, they were old as hell. None of them caught their attention, although all eyes were on them. They weren't feeling it at all and decided it was best for them all to leave. Besides, there was a pizza spot right across the street whose pizza was always good.

⌘

"Numba one hustler getting money. Why y'all
        wanna take that from me ah, ah, ah." Reef and Micah nodded as they came out of the tunnel vibing to Akon's, "I'm So Paid."

"Man, that shit goes hard right there!!" Lateef screamed as he pulled up beside them.

After the guys parked, they noticed a club called Pink Elephant. The line was long, but the club looked like it was jumpin'. When they finally got inside, they couldn't help but notice it was packed as hell. People were all over the place and basically shoulder to shoulder. They decided they couldn't handle it anymore and left.

"Damn! What the fuck is going on tonight?" Reef asked in utter confusion as they all spotted a pizza store across the street.

Surprisingly, it wasn't too crowded and a lot of people were sitting at the outside tables. As they got in front of the pizza spot, Micah stopped dead in his tracks. Both, Lateef and Reef, were confused as to why he stopped so abruptly.

"Yo, "Micah says, "isn't that shorty from the other night?"

Reef couldn't remember, and Lateef had no idea.

"OH SHIT!! I think it might be!"

As he stared through the window, Nakima turned around and glared out the window, but she didn't see him.

"We gotta go... like now!" Micah said panicking.

"Yo, why you trippin' like that?" Reef asked. "Didn't you say you wanted to see her again anyway?" he asked as he was laughing and making his way to the club next door.

Micah shook his head. He couldn't help but think maybe, just maybe, they were drunk as hell that night and she wouldn't even remember him if she saw him. Right then and there, he began to have flashbacks and how he actually wanted to run into her, but his pride was getting the best of him.

⌘

They scoffed down their pizza as quickly as they could to head to the nearest club so Ebony could sit her ass down and stop complaining. They noticed a club beside the pizza store before they walked in, so they went back there.

Once they got into the club, they saw the second floor wasn't as packed as the first floor, so they headed there. Ebony headed straight towards an empty chair she had seen at the bar once they got upstairs. From up here, they could see everything happening on the first floor. Out of nowhere, Ebony spotted a man who looked like the dude she had just met the other night, but she decided to keep quiet. *Damn, that nigga still fine as hell*, she thought to herself! Trying not to cause attention, she motioned for the girls to move downstairs.

As Nakima made her way to the dance floor she noticed a man staring at her. It seemed like she knew him from somewhere, but she wasn't sure. She wasted no time and walked over to him.

"What's up?" she asked as she tapped him on his shoulder.

Nakima was surprised when she realized it was the dude from the other night.

"Yo shorty, what's good?"

Nothing much. Just checkin' you out." Nakima said in a seductive voice.

"Can I buy you a drink?" he asked.

"Of course you may," Nakima responded as they walked over to the bar together.

They both ordered Henny and Coke. While waiting for their drinks, Nakima positioned herself where she could stand directly between his legs. Trying to hold herself together, she licked her lips and started to whisper into his ear. He licked his lips, listening to everything she had to say, while grabbing her waist and pulling her closer.

Lateef, looking from afar, didn't know who shorty was, but he made his way over to see if his man was good. By the looks of things, he was alright. Then, Lateef spotted Ebony and Sheree standing by the bar a few chairs down, so he made his way down to talk to them. He caught them off guard, but immediately grabbed Sheree's hand and pulled her to the floor before she could say anything. This left Reef to go over and talk to Ebony, whom he was already checkin' for.

Meanwhile, on the dancefloor, Lateef and Sheree were inseparable.

"What's ya' name sexy?" Lateef asked.

"I'm Sheree, and you?"

"I'm Lateef. Nice to meet you. I couldn't help myself, but I had to come over and talk to you. You're just the sexiest thing in this club right now."

Sheree smiled and thought to herself, *no he didn't use this wack-ass line on me*. Lateef could tell what she was thinking by her expression, so he changed the conversation and asked what her plans were for the night.

"I don't know, but maybe we can link up after the club. My boys already got my girls hot right now so I'm sure we can all meet up."

Then, Sheree started to grind her hips up against him. "If you know what's good for you, you'd come with us later." She whispered.

Back at the bar, Ebony and Reef were still sitting and getting to know each other. Ordering another drink, Reef asked what her plans were. Ebony smiled and hinted at what she had in mind for both of them.

"You want to head back to my place?" she asked.

"Hell yeah. I'm definitely cool with that shorty."

Over in the corner, Nakima and Micah were tonguing each other down and rubbing all on each other. They were drawing so much attention, but they didn't care.

Everyone knew what they were going to do!!!

Nakima and Micah decided to rent a hotel down the street. They woke up fucking. They had a serious sexual attraction to each other, and it was crazy, but they liked it. This time Nakima was drunk, but she was fully aware of what went on. Micah was drunk too. He slipped up and nutted all inside her; even though she noticed, she didn't pay it any mind.

As he lay holding her, he started thinking why he wanted to avoid her in the first place. He couldn't believe he had run into her again and that this actually happened again. He couldn't help but think if she ever thought about the last time they were together, and if she had changed her mind about their last conversation.

"So...Shorty, what's gonna happen with us now?" he questioned.

Nakima smiled. "I was hoping you would ask. I was thinking about you a lot from our last encounter and didn't know if I would ever see you again. I would like to get to know you better, if that's ok with you?"

Micah laughed and said, "That's funny because I thought about you too, but I felt like you brushed me off. I mean is that the kind of stuff you do? I never had that happen to me before."

"We'll see what happens." Nakima said as she burst out laughing.

"Do you live by yourself? Nakima asked.

"Yes, I do," Micah replied.

Nakima bit her bottom lip to this thought, *finally a man with his own shit.*

"Since we're being honest, there's something I need to tell you. My real name is Micah. I shot you an alias because I don't usually tell chicks my name unless I really want them to know."

"What!!?" Nakima asked as she sat up abruptly. "So, you lied to me, huh? I can't believe you! Why would you do that?

"Chill Shorty! We're good now. There's gonna be no more secrets between us from now on and that's my word."

"Yeah right!" Nakima replied.

What else could he be lying about, she thought to herself.

⌘

The next morning, Ebony woke up not remembering anything. The sun was so bright that she could barely open her eyes. Then, she looked over and remembered leaving the club with Reef, but couldn't begin to remember how she got home. As she rolled over to look for her clothes, Shareef woke up and smiled.

"Babe, I've been looking for someone like you for a while now."

Ebony smiled, but in the back of her mind, she knew she was not ready to take it to the next level and just wanted to be friends.

"What the hell happened? Where did my friends go?"

"Well, my boy and ole' girl who were all into each other dipped off right after we left the club. My homie and your other girl are in the room next to us."

"Are you serious?" Ebony asked, looking in disbelief.

"Sheree brought ya' boy here?"

"Lateef? Yeah. I take it Shorty's name is Sheree. Yeah, they are here with us. You and yo' girl were so fucked up last night I wouldn't expect you to really remember anything."

In the back of his mind, he knew everything that happened and couldn't believe how freaky she was. Eventually,

20

they ended up falling back to sleep, and all Reef could do was think about last night.

When they walked into the house last night, Ebony started stripping and dancing. Then, she began to undress Reef until he was only in his boxers. She pushed him onto the couch and pulled his dick out. Without hesitation, she started sucking and sucking until he exploded all over her face. She wasn't done though. She noticed some whipped cream she had in the corner of her room from making drinks earlier.

He was so hard and even though it felt amazing, he was ready to fuck her so bad, but he also wanted her in his mouth. He couldn't wait; he turned her around and started to hit it from the back. Her pussy was so good to him that he stroked it slowly just so she could feel every bit of him inside her. Then, she climbed on top of him and rode him to finish him off. After it was over, they both passed out.

Meanwhile, Lateef was mad because he and shorty wasn't gettin' it in. He didn't want to take advantage of her so he just held her all night. Sheree woke up in his arms, smiled, and fell right back asleep. If things could stay this way, it would be great

Only time would tell.

FOUR

Six years later

The three girls eventually moved out of the apartment that they shared together and branched on their own. Ebony and Reef were still dealing with each other, but he didn't move in with her. He would just come and stay there from time-to-time to give her space. He did have a set of keys to her apartment, but he would always ring the doorbell to make sure he didn't scare her by just walking into her place.

Outside looking in, the relationship between them was weird, but what was understood didn't have to be explained. They both loved each other so much, but they just couldn't commit to one another. Reef had his own reasoning because he had heard so much about Ebony in the streets. From that alone, it was hard to commit to her because there was no way she could be monogamous. Luckily, she never really pushed the issue because she knew how she felt about her.

Ebony was home cleaning, cooking, and waiting on Reef to come home. While she was putting the food in the oven, she heard a strange knock on the door that almost made her drop everything. Despite the knock scaring the hell out of her, it was weird because she hadn't told anyone where she lived besides her girls and Reef.

Before opening the door, she looked through the peephole, but she was unable to see who it was because they had their hands covering the peep hole. They knocked on the door again, but this time it was louder. All kinds of thoughts ran through her head of who it could be. Finally, she decided to slightly crack the door to see who it was. To her surprise, she couldn't believe who the fuck it was and how he found out where she lived. Immediately, she tried to close the door, but he was way too strong for her. He almost knocked her down to push the door back open.

⌘

When Ebony and Nakima were younger, they needed a way to make easy money so they got involved with a guy named Mac Daddy Diamonds. So that it sounded better to them, they referred to themselves as "escorts," but everyone knew what they really were. Was it really easy money – no and they both hated it because he tried to take all of their money any chance he got.

One night they tried to set him up by making him believe they were going to have a huge orgy. They told him to meet them in the hotel down the street from their usual meet up. Little did they know, he figured out something wasn't right and sent his man to see what was up. The dude ended up pulling out a gun on them and making them do all sorts of things they didn't want to do. He also threatened to kill them if they said anything to Mac Daddy or anyone else. They were so shaken up that they just did whatever he said.

After that day, they knew they weren't going to let it fly, especially not Ebony being the person she was. Ebony took it upon herself to go to Mac Daddy Diamonds, and of course, he acted like he didn't know anything. Ebony got so mad that she ended up pistol whipping him so badly that he was knocked unconscious. She also stole about $100,000 from him. That night they vowed that they would get missing and he would never find them again because they knew he would definitely kill them without hesitation.

To her surprise, he was now at her front door. She couldn't even gather her thoughts because her mind and body just froze. For the past couple of months, she knew she felt like

23

someone was following her, but wasn't too sure. Mac Daddy Diamonds grabbed straight for her neck and held on so tight that she thought she was going to die for sure.

He just kept yelling. " Bitch, I found you! Where the fuck is my money?" all while grabbing her neck tighter and tighter.

Ebony tried so hard to kick and try to get loose, but it wasn't working. Suddenly, she felt the grip loosen from her neck and the breath return back to her body. Next thing she knew, she and Mac Daddy Diamonds were on the floor beside one another.

"Babe!! Babe!! Hurry!!" Reef yelled.

Ebony was trying to gain consciousness, but the words wouldn't flow out of her mouth. Out of one corner of her eye, she could see Reef running frantically around the apartment, but she had no clue what was going on. Out the corner of her other eye, she seen Mac Daddy Diamonds lying on his back.

Reef ran into the kitchen to get her some water, sat behind her, and propped her up against his chest. He immediately tried to get her to drink the glass of water he poured, although she was not fully there in the moment.

After some time passed, Mac Daddy Diamonds woke up thinking neither one of them were paying him attention. Reef gently placed Ebony back onto the floor, and he and Mac Daddy Diamonds started going for blows. As Ebony started to regain consciousness, she stumbled to try to get up and help Reef. Although she never thought this day would come, she had always been prepared for it. She ran to her room and found her safe that she had hidden at the bottom of her closet. She grabbed the revolver she kept in there and ran back into the living room. Reef yoked him up and kicked him out.

"DON'T YOU EVER COME BACK HERE OR I WILL KILL YO ASS!!" Mac Daddy took off running through the front door.

Ebony immediately dropped the gun and ran over to Reef. "Omg baby, are you ok? Thank you, God!" She couldn't help but to hug him tightly. She knew, without him, she would probably be dead right now. "Thank you so much Baby. I don't even know what to say!"

"What the FUCK was that!? What the hell?!"

Ebony kept ignoring Reef's questions and kept hugging and kissing him as if he wasn't asking her a thing. Reef really didn't know what to think, but it brought him back to the things he heard about her. He really didn't want to believe any of it, but after this, it all made sense. He really didn't know what to do at this point, so he made sure she was good and told her he needed some time to himself. He didn't know who the fuck this nigga was or his ties to Ebony, but he made it his mission that he was going to find out.

⌘

"BABE!! BABE!! BABE!! HURRY!! Come in the bathroom, hurry, PLEASE!"

She was freaking out and didn't know what to do. These pains were so bad that she thought she was going to die. Micah rushed to the bathroom and stood there in shock.

"What's wrong? What you need me to do?" he asked.
"Call 9-1-1!!"

Micah immediately grabbed the phone. "Hello...Yes, it's my wife. We need you to hurry! PLEASE!! I don't know what's wrong, but she's in so much pain." Micah rushed back over to Nakima and rubbed her back as she lay on the bathroom floor, crying out hysterically. Neither one of them had a clue what could possibly be happening.

After the ambulance arrived, they were taken to the hospital, and she was rushed to labor and delivery. They both couldn't believe she was really pregnant and didn't know. She was full-term and was now in active labor. Within the hour, they both had a beautiful, healthy baby girl. Micah couldn't wait to call his boys. The first person he called was Lateef.

"Aww man! How the fuck could this happen? I mean I know how it happens." Lateef said with a smirk.

"But I thought shit like this only happens to people on TV." Micah said while trying to gather his emotions.

Still in disbelief, he calls Lateef to give him the news.

"Word! Congratulations!" Lateef replied.

It turned out that Nakima was pregnant and didn't even know. This would be her third child even though they weren't prepared or trying. However, she was beyond happy because she finally got the girl she had been waiting for. They decided to name her Sky and she looked just like her mother with her father's eyes. She was beautiful. Four years ago, she also had twin boys named Saadiq and Jaheim who favored their father very much. Nakima knew her boys were going to be a handful, while Micah was happy. Of course, he was ready to put them in any and every sport he could think of.

A few months after the boys were born, they got married. There was no way he wasn't going to spend the rest of his life without her, especially when she had his children. Nakima was proud to say she was the only Mrs. Brown and he was happy to call her his queen.

⌘

Sheree and Lateef were getting married soon. They had a two-year-old son named Marquis and planned on having more because they had just moved into a huge five-bedroom house. Sheree couldn't believe she was really about to marry the man of her dreams. They had finally finished sending out all the invitations, but the only thing that really bothered her most was the fact that she wanted all her friends to be there to be her bridesmaids. Sheree hadn't spoken to Ebony in a couple of years. It was almost as if she had disappeared off the face of the earth and that was weird. Whenever she would ask Lateef if he heard anything, he would just tell her that Ebony was fine. Nakima also just disappeared. She called every once in a blue moon, but they never hung out with one another. She just couldn't help but wonder why they hadn't been in contact anymore. Anytime she would bring it up to Lateef he would remind her that sometimes you just have to keep your friends at a distance.

Ebony was home thinking about what just happened. She couldn't believe he had the audacity to disrespect her like that.

How the fuck did he find me, she thought to herself.

She tried calling Reef, but there was no answer. She couldn't help but cry because Reef had never ignored her calls for this long before. She had no clue where he was or what he could be doing. So, she just lay in her bed and watched her phone, hoping it would soon ring.

After a few hours had passed, she heard the keys jingling at the door. Ebony immediately tried to hide because she didn't know who it was. Then, she heard Reef call out to her.

"Yo, Ebony!"

She jumped up excitedly and ran straight to him only to get brushed off.

"Explain yourself...NOW!"

She rolled her eyes, took a deep breath, and asked, "Are you sure you really want to know?"

He nodded his head. Tears came rolling down her face as she prepared herself to explain.

"Well...when I was a teenager," she started off and cleared her throat. "I hung out with wrong people and ended up doing things I never really wanted to. I ended up working for a pimp. His name was Mac Daddy Diamonds."

"Wait – "

Ebony cut him off before he could finish. "Before you say anything else, just let me explain." Seeing the expression on his face and body movements made her feel very hesitant to continue, but she knew she had to. "I was young, alone, and trying to follow behind people just to make some extra money."

"What!?" Reef yelled as he stood up. "You mean to tell me you were a hoe!!" he yelled.

Ebony ignored him and continued. "I tried so many times to get out, but he wouldn't let me. That man that came here was him. I didn't know he was still alive. I don't know how he found me. No one knew where I was."

27

"Oh bitch!! You're definitely crazy!! Niggas been telling me crazy shit about you and I tried so hard to believe they weren't true. Now, I know some of them are and that's why I treat you the way I do! In fact, I should fuck you up right now bitch!!". Reef jumped up and grabbed her by the neck.

Somehow, she managed to get loose and screamed, "STOP!! You're acting CRAZY right now!!"

"Me? Crazy? Bitch, you had me believing you were perfect!"

"But babe – "

"Don't babe me!! You lucky I'm not tryna go to jail over you. What the fuck am I gonna do with your ass now?"

Ebony sat there extremely quiet and tried to hold back any tears that were fighting to get out. She was too afraid to say anything. Then, she cleared her throat and began to speak, hoping Reef would hear her out. "I'm sorry Reef. I'm sorry all this had to come back at this time. I thought it was in the past and I would never have to worry about it ever again."

Reef mushed her in the face and started walking towards the door. Ebony tried to run after him, but he pushed her down to the floor and slammed the door behind him. She just sat on the floor crying all night long. All she could do was think about how their relationship had evolved over the years. She had gotten to see half of the person he really was and it was totally different. He made her feel like she was the only woman in the world, but Ebony had caught him plenty of times with several different women. She just continued to believe lie after lie because she actually loved this man. There wasn't anything she wouldn't do for him. She cared for him more than she did herself. She wasn't used to that at all.

Deep inside, she was an emotional wreck, and she felt she needed her friends, but she hadn't spoken to them in years because Reef made her cut them all off. He was tired of them telling her to leave him alone and that he was no good. He had lost all self-control. He felt that if he couldn't have her, then no one could. He was crazy in love with her, but he wanted to do whatever and whomever on the side.

After about 20 minutes, Reef walked back into the house and started yelling for her to get off the floor. Ebony stumbled, but she eventually managed to stand up and look Reef straight in the eyes. Before she could open her mouth, Reef backhanded her across the face and knocked her to the floor. Holding her face, Ebony looked up at him, confused as to why he had just hit her.

Without hesitation, she jumped up and slapped Reef back. From his reaction, she could tell he was not prepared for her to hit him back. Any other female would have seen his face and, most likely, would have taken off running like hell. This time, she told herself she was not running from him. They both stood there in silence, looking at each other. Finally, Reef broke the stare down and went into the room. He slammed the door so hard behind him that some of her paintings fell to the ground

Ebony went to the bathroom to clean herself up. Thankfully, there wasn't any bruising just yet or any marks from him choking her. This wasn't the first time that he put his hands on her. She didn't know what to think at that very moment, but so many times, she wanted to leave him. She just loved him so much. Never would she have ever thought things would end up like this. She had hoped that their relationship and Reef would change. Many times, she wondered what her friends would think if they had any idea of what she was enduring. Honestly, she was scared to tell them or anybody else, so she kept quiet and walked around smiling all the time. She knew it wasn't healthy, but deep down, she knew he could be good if the physical abuse stopped.

⌘

Ebony had her girls on her mind heavy and wanted to just hear their voices to see how they were. She also wanted to warn Nakima about Mac Daddy Diamonds just in case he was coming for her next, but she didn't even know if any of them still had the same number. *Fuck it, I am going to call them*, she thought to herself. *What is the worse that could happen?*

Ring, Ring, Ring...

"Hello...Hello..."

Ebony did what she was known for... she froze. For some reason, all she could do was remain quiet because the words wouldn't leave her mouth. *Shit*, she thought to herself as she quickly hung up the phone. Sitting there, she started thinking to herself. *You idiot. What the fuck is wrong with you? Why didn't you say anything?* She didn't know what to say, but before she could think it through, she decided to call back. This time, she was sent to voicemail. *Ok, this is easier,* she thought to herself. So, she left a message.

After five minutes, her phone rang again. She picked it up so fast, hoping that it would be Nakima, but it wasn't. It was a man who called her back to let her know she had the wrong number. Then, it really hit her that she didn't have anyone. She didn't know how to reach out to any of them and she felt really lonely. How could she not talk to her sisters anymore after all the stuff they had been through? *When I need them the most, how the fuck are they not going to be there for me. Why the hell has neither one of them tried to find me to check on me?* All types of thoughts started to swarm Ebony's mind, but deep down, she knew she couldn't only blame them.

To cool off, Ebony decided she needed to go outside for a moment and walk so she could clear her mind. As frustrated as she was, she just needed to talk to anyone at this point, but she had no one. She walked down the street to a nearby park in her neighborhood and sat for hours on end. She often did this when she needed to get away from Reef as well. Most of the time, it worked, and she loved looking at the scenery, but she couldn't shake how she was feeling at this particular moment.

After about 4 hours, she decided it was best to just go home and face whatever was coming her way. She knew Reef was mad as hell at her. All she could do was hope that he wasn't there. When she opened the door, she noticed Reef sitting on the couch, facing the door as if he were waiting for her to walk through at any moment. He scared the fuck out of her because of the look he was giving her. He had the most serious look on his face. *What the fuck is wrong with him now,* she thought to herself.

"Where the fuck you been?" he yelled.

"What!?" Ebony said, rolling her eyes. "I just went for a walk to the park."

It wasn't like him to question her like that. He hadn't done that before. Any other time he wouldn't have given a fuck.

His eyebrows rose up immediately. "You better not be lying to me! I can't even trust yo' ass no more. You're just a motha fuckin' lying ass hoe!"

She didn't know what to say to his accusations. Over the last few years, she noticed that he had become more verbally abusive and his attitude and behavior was very aggressive, which scared the shit out of her. He would get mad at every little thing she did and then apologize like nothing ever happened. She felt like he was the only one she had in her corner right now, and he was truly there for her. A lot of men would look at her and question why she would even be with him. They claimed they would give her the world if she gave them the opportunity, but she would never cheat on the man she loved. Her self-esteem became so low she didn't know what to do. She barely went out of the house unless she really had to or to go to the park to get fresh air. She often secluded herself from the world.

Before she could respond, Reef grabbed her by her hair, pinned her against the wall, and began choking her. Then, he slammed her onto the floor, straddled her, and started to choke her while he was sitting on top of her. Something was wrong with him today, but she didn't know what it was. He had never gone this hard before and he wouldn't let up. *Could it have been the other day*, she thought to herself. Abruptly, he let go of her neck, jumped up, and walked out the door, making sure to slam it shut behind him.

FIVE

The big day finally arrived! Nakima had always dreamed of this moment and couldn't believe it was finally here. Shit, after waiting for twelve months, she was finally about to tie the knot to the man of her dreams she was so excited that she couldn't sleep. With over 200 guests attending, there was just no room for any mistakes. She was filled with nervousness, anxiety, and nausea all at once. She definitely had the wedding jitters, but she just kept thinking to herself to take deep breaths and everything would be just fine. Of course, that was easier said than done. Out of every thought she had, the only one that was really bothering her was the fact that she hadn't spoken to Ebony.

Of course, they were still best friends because that would never change. Nakima just didn't understand why she ghosted her. At first, she would reach out every once in a blue moon and then all communication just stopped. Nakima tried a few times to reach out to her, but had no luck. Even though she sent an invitation to the last address she had for her, she didn't even know if she would be coming to the wedding. It wasn't like Ebony to be this way, but then again, they hadn't spoken in a couple of years. With something this big, Nakima just knew that Ebony would put all their differences aside and be there for her.

Although she would have the support from her other friends and family, it just wouldn't feel right to her if Ebony weren't there.

Finally, they made it to the church. Things were really moving now and it was time to get hair and nails done. Still, *NO EBONY.* Sheree turned to Nakima, who was on her left side, and asked if she had spoken to her.

"Unfortunately, no." Sheree started to get teary eyed. "It's ok, sis. I'm here and you know if she could be here she would. We can't worry about why she is not here right now. Let's go get your pretty ass married and I promise we will find out what's going on later."

Sheree couldn't hold back her tears any longer. She burst out in tears, messing up all the makeup she just had done.

"I'm sorry y'all. Yes, I'm ok." Sheree managed to mumble through her tears.

Nakima began to pat her make-up to salvage any of it that was left before the make-up artist could touch her up. *This can't be happening to me. I've waited so long for this shit for it not to be right. I should be jumping for joy, not mopping around the damn building. WHAT THE FUCK,* was the only thing going through Sheree's mind was, but she was determined not to let it ruin her perfect day.

Finally, it was time to walk down the aisle. Immediately, she felt her legs begin to give out under her as she heard her aisle music begin playing. She turned and looked at Nakima with the most terrified look on her face. Nakima looked her in the eyes and gave her the softest smile to assure her that everything was going to be okay.

As she and Nakima walked out of her dressing room, she noticed how beautifully the place was decorated. Then, she saw her King. He was standing there smiling at just as he did when they first met. She returned the smile, but immediately, she got butterflies in her tummy. She started to get tingles all over her body. Everyone was staring at her in awe as she walked down the aisle.

After about 30 minutes, the ceremony was over, and it was time for the reception!! The wedding was spectacular and definitely a dream come true! Sheree and Lateef enjoyed seeing everyone smiling, having a good time, and celebrating their love for one another.

The reception was the icing on the cake. They had all the food you can think of, but the biggest hit was their dessert bar. They had a bar with over 100 desserts and two huge 10-foot chocolate fountains. Lateef enjoyed it mainly because he had so much fun spreading the chocolate all over Sheree's face. Besides that, they danced the night away and were all over each other. They didn't even care about anyone else in the room.

⌘

"Hello...Hello..."

Click. The phone hung up. Then, it rang again.

"HELLO!! Who the fuck is this?" Ebony yelled.

All morning, someone had been playing on her phone and she was really starting to get annoyed.

"Hello. Look, I wish you would just stop wasting my time playing games."

Finally, a voice says, "Is this Ebony?"

"Who is this?"

"Well, my name is Summer."

"Summer?" Ebony questioned.

"You don't know me, but I've been sleeping with Reef, and I thought you should know."

All types of things ran through her head, and she didn't know what to say.

"What!? Ebony yelled.

There's complete silence. Then, the girl says, "I think I'm pregnant."

"What!? You're what!? By who!?"

"Reef. That is your man, right?" Summer asked in confusion. "We've been sleeping together for some time now. He comes here all the time and tells me he wants to end things with you, but he does love you."

This girl must be out of her mind. Is this the real reason he didn't come home last night because he never stayed out all night long before, Ebony thought to herself as she took a minute

35

to gather her thoughts. Can't let a bitch see her sweat. Ebony had to really think if Summer was lying to her or not. Before she could comment, Ebony heard a male voice in the background. "Who the fuck you on the phone with? Come back to bed, babe."

Click.

Ebony was an emotional wreck and thought about calling Nakima, but remembered she no way of contacting her. She also realized she really didn't feel comfortable with telling anyone what was going on. What she did know is that she wanted to find this girl and Reef so she could fuck them up. All these years she put into this relationship; there's no way. Then she remembered. Someone once told her," What goes on in the dark, always comes to the light," and that was true right about now.

Thinking of how the last few months had been, Ebony put together a timeline she thought to be true. Apparently, Reef had been cheating for about five months with this girl named Summer, who *apparently* thought she was pregnant. *Summer, huh*, she thought to herself. Where the fuck did he meet her and who was she? She knew he had cheated back in the day, but she thought they had moved past that. Nothing like this had ever happened before, and the girl actually knew who Ebony was. Ebony couldn't help but think there was some truth to this situation.

⌘

"Babe!! I can't believe we're finally married!" Lateef said, holding Sheree in his arms. The Bermuda sunset that woke them both up was beautiful. They couldn't wait to explore it with the time they had left. As much as Sheree wanted to enjoy this moment, she couldn't help but wonder why Ebony nor Reef showed up to their wedding. She knew she had mailed the invitations and they had to have gotten them.

"Do you think everything's ok with Reef and Ebony?" Sheree asked Lateef.

He looked down into his wife's beautiful eyes filled with worry. "I'm sure they are fine. They were supposed to be moving to ATL that last I heard because Ebony was offered a new job. Let's not worry. Let just enjoy our time together."

This was all he knew to tell Sheree because he honestly didn't know what was going on or where they were. He and Micah hadn't heard from Reef in a long ass time, which was weird. Sheree took a deep breath, squeezed him tightly, and silently cried herself to sleep.

⌘

Ebony couldn't sleep all morning. Her mind was racing so fast that she thought it was going to explode. Flashbacks ran through her head every time she closed her eyes. She must've fallen asleep for about two hours because when she woke up, it was noon. She decided to hop in the shower hoping it would clear her mind and relax her body.

As soon as she began to wash her body, the curtain flung open and there stood Reef looking at her.

"Why the fuck was you talking to that bitch for?" he yelled.

"Nigga, she ...she called me saying all this stuff. All I really did was listen. Who is she and how the fuck did this bitch get my number anyway?"

"I swear. I don't even know that bitch!" Reef replied angrily.

"But you weren't here last night so where did you go?" Ebony questioned. "You're making yourself look suspicious, and I have no choice but to believe this here right now. She knew too much info and she knew we were together . How do you explain that? How do you know I was talking to her anyway?"

"I stayed at my mom's house last night. I wasn't with no bitch, especially not her. You stupid if you sit here and believe her and you don't even know her. Babe, you know you're my only girl and that will never change."

"Whatever!" Ebony replied and shut the curtains as smoothly as she could because she could already see him getting upset.

Immediately, he snatched the curtain back open and begin yelling. "You really gonna believe this bitch over me? I'm telling you the truth."

He reached out to grab her, but ended up pulling back because he thought it probably wasn't the best idea at this moment. Reef knew exactly what he was doing. Playing mind games was his specialty, and it always worked. What he didn't know was that Ebony started picking up on it. He knew she wasn't going anywhere, and he wasn't going to let her. There were so many times she could have left, but she never did. He made it so she had no one to talk to and nowhere to go. Bottom line, he fucked up with Summer and he had to do something about it.

Ebony finished up in the shower and went into the room to get dressed. Reef, feeling bad, walked into the room trying to hug her and apologize, while still insisting that he didn't know who "the girl," Summer, is. Just by the look in his eyes, anyone could tell that he was slowly getting upset because Ebony really wasn't trying to hear anything that he was saying.

"Reef, please leave me the fuck alone! You tell me you love me and I'm the only one, but you got this bitch calling my phone talking about she's pregnant! What kind of shit you on? I don't have no one calling my phone talking recklessly so why should I believe you?"

"You know damn well if a dude called your phone right now, I'm a fuck you up!"

"Yeah, ok," Ebony replied aggravatedly.
Trying to turn on the charm, "Can we have a special night tonight, babe?" Reef asked while trying to hug and kiss her again. When she didn't fold, he gave up. "Seriously, I got to make some runs, and I'll be back around 8ish tonight." Before shutting the door, he made sure to add, "You better be here."

Thoughts were going through Ebony's mind. She wasn't going to let some bitch get in her way and take her man. This was just another obstacle in the way that she had to get over, but she needed to know the truth.

All dressed up with nowhere to go or nothing to do, Ebony started thinking about her friends and how much she needed them right now. She truly missed their company. So much had changed and she felt a huge distance had come between them, but she knew it was partially her fault. She is the one who let them get to this point because of Reef.

Now, how would she even begin to reach out to her sisters. She would feel so uncomfortable being around them at this point. Sadly, she knew that their relationship would probably never be the same. Even though she felt this way, she knew she had to do something because she was going to lose her mind if she kept going through this shit with Reef on her own.

Fuck it, I'm going to call Sheree, she thought to herself. She couldn't help but get discouraged when the operator came on the line and let her know that the phone had been disconnected and was no longer in service. *Dammit*, she thought to herself, but who would keep the same number after all these years. She didn't know what she needed to do, but she knew she needed to find Sheree because she was the "motherly" one of the group and she knew she wouldn't judge her about anything.

After hours of searching phone books and thinking what to do, luckily, she found envelope that was addressed to her and Reef from Sheree and Lateef. It was stuffed in the drawer in her room. When she opened it, she noticed it was an invitation to their wedding. Immediately, Ebony started to feel even worse because she realized she never even opened the invitation. When she got the invitation, she remembered putting it down on the dining room table and the next day it was missing. She thought she had misplaced it and asked Reef if he seen it. Of course, he said no. Clearly, he just stuffed the invitation in the drawer and hid it from her. *How could I have missed the most important day of my friend's life? She must really hate me right now.* He did that shit on purpose, she thought. She hated him so much right now for that.

Luckily, the invitation had a phone number on it...

After about five rings, a man picked up the phone.

"Hello." Of course, Ebony froze. "Hello!" the man replied again.

"Who is this?" Ebony whispered.

"Who is this!?" The man's voice got deeper as if he was trying to prove his authority.

"This is Ebony. I found your phone number –"

The man cut her off immediately. "Ebony!! Ebony! We've been worried about you. Where the hell have you been?"

"Well, who is this?" Ebony questioned.

"It's Lateef," he said laughing.

"Oh, Lateef" Ebony replied as she sighed in relief.

"Yeah, what's up?"

"I've been trying to get in contact with Sheree for the longest. Can you please give her this number and tell her to call me. I know she must hate me for everything right now, but I honestly didn't know about this wedding or you know I would have been there."

"I'm sure she'll just be happy to hear from you and know that you're ok."

"Well, why wouldn't I be ok?" she questioned him.

"Oh nah! It's just that we haven't heard from you in a couple of years that's all, but call her. Her number is 862-452-7643."

"I know. I'm sorry. Ok I will call her. Thank you for giving me her number. I'll talk to you later." Ebony quickly hung up the phone, she didn't wait for Lateef to even respond.

Then, Ebony sat there and contemplated whether or not to call Sheree. Deep down, she knew that she would feel better if she did call her. Without hesitation, she dialed the number. It rang one time before Ebony hung up.

Right after she hung up the phone, her phone immediately started to ring... it was Sheree. Ebony sat and stared

at the phone. *What are you doing girl? Pick up the phone,* she thought to herself. She was nervous as hell, but she eventually answered the phone.

"Hello."

"Yes, who is this?" Sheree asked.

Ebony didn't even answer, she just started apologizing. Immediately, Sheree noticed who it was as Ebony continued to talk. How could she ever forget her sister's voice?

Without giving Sheree a moment to respond Ebony asked, "What's your address? It's so much I have to tell you, but I can't do it over the phone. I need to see you asap!"

Once Sheree gave her an address, Ebony let her know that it was about an hour and a half from her and that she was on her way. She hung up immediately and started to get dressed. She didn't have any time to think through her moves because she knew if she did, she wouldn't go. She also had to move fast because she didn't want Reef to follow her. As soon as she was dressed, she ran out of the door.

On the way, Ebony got a bad feeling and wanted to turn around. She didn't know how things would be after seeing Sheree for all these years, but she knew she needed her right now.

When she pulled up to the address, it was a huge, beautiful white house with all black trimmings. It had a huge front lawn with beautiful landscaping. From where she parked, she seen there was a huge swimming pool in the backyard as well. It was the most beautiful house Ebony had ever seen. While she looked on in awe, she noticed Sheree looking out the window at her.

Before she knew it, Sheree was running out the door at full speed towards her. When she jumped on her, it caused them both to fall onto the lawn. Both of them started to tear up and just stare at each other. They missed each other so much. Ebony was just happy to see her face and to know that she was welcoming her with open arms. She was so nervous that she would reject her or be angry with her for disappearing.

Sheree couldn't believe how much Ebony had changed. This wasn't the girl she knew from way back when. She didn't know what had gotten into her. She could see the stress in her face and she noticed she had lost a lot of weight. She also noticed she didn't keep much eye contact when talking which

41

told Sheree that she was keeping something from her. All Sheree could do was keep thinking that she should have been there.

After today, if she never talked to her again, she just hoped she was doing the right thing by showing her she was still there for her regardless. When they walked into the house, Sheree sat them down in her beautifully decorated living room. Sheree always had a taste for the finer things in life.

"So, what's been up? How's life? I see you and Shareef are still together, how's that going?"

Ebony got this creepy feeling within her that felt as though Sheree knew something was wrong deep down inside. Ebony took a deep breath, paused, and started to cry.

"I...I don't know anymore. It's like one minute everything is perfect and the next minute things are all fucked up." Sheree could tell she was holding something back, but she wanted to let her finish talking. "Since I haven't spoken to you guys, I haven't been feeling like myself. In fact, I feel fuckin' lost like I don't know who I am anymore." Ebony shook her head in despair.

"Well, you know you're always welcomed wherever I am. I don't know what drove you away in the first place, but I would like us to be like we were before. Even with marriage and kids, we can still have girl's night. I asked Reef about you when I would see him sometimes. He said that you were doing great and just working. You know I'm here for you, right? I'm telling you right now that I will drop everything for you. You just remember we aren't strangers!" Ebony began to cry harder and gave her the biggest hug.

"I'm so sorry I missed the wedding. I didn't even know there was a wedding because you know I would have been there. I have been the worst friend to you and I need to be better. I promise I will be better. The kids need to know who their auntie Ebony is. You know, I would've thought I'd be getting married and having a baby by now. I'm so sorry to be rambling, it's just that I'm so happy to see you. You know, Reef has changed a lot over the years and I just don't know what to do. I mean, I love him and do think we can make things work, but I'm just ready to take things to the next step."

"Has he ever put his hands on you?" Sheree questioned, cutting Ebony off mid-sentence.

Omg, why would she ask that, Ebony thought to herself. Giving Sheree the evil eye Ebony asked, "What would make you ask something like that? Does it look like I would be with someone that hits me?? she answered with an attitude.

"I'm sorry, I just wanted to know. I didn't mean anything by it," Sheree said.

Sheree could tell it was something she wasn't telling her, but how Ebony responded caused her not to press the issue anymore. She was just so happy to see her and wished they hadn't separated like they did.

"A man is going to be a man no matter what. There's some who choose to settle down and be faithful. Then, there's the others that like to have their cake and eat it too. Right now, Reef is doing just that and it's right in front of my face. I was just blind to it. He tells me that I was making things up in my mind and that nothing was true, but as long as I never found out about it, he was good. Now, one of his bitches slipped up, called me, and told me she is pregnant. Now, he is trying to convince me that it's not true. Despite him cheating on me, I thought I was the one that he truly loved. I'm just so lost, Sheree!" Ebony blurted out as she started crying even harder than before. Sheree and Ebony spoke for hours before Ebony realized what time it was. She promised Sheree she would stay in contact with her and told her she needed to leave. When Ebony left Sheree, she almost felt like her old self again. There were some things she didn't tell her because she didn't really want her in her business just yet. She knew she needed to feel like she could really trust her. She was married to Reef's best friend.

Although she was hesitant, she was happy that Sheree didn't judge her. It was nice to actually be around her again. Things would take time, but Ebony was hopeful that everything would fall into place eventually.

Sheree didn't tell anyone, not even her husband, about the details of the talk she had with Ebony. Hell, she still felt some kind of way about her up and disappearing and her not even going to her wedding. If the shoe was on the other foot, she knew Ebony or Nakima would have been pissed off at her. She knew she couldn't hold on to this because she had to make sure she was there for her now. Yes, she was still mad, but she wanted to make sure her sister knew she was going to support her in whatever she was going through. However, she knew they would never be as tight as what they were before because she personally had too much shit going on. More importantly, she didn't want to get involved in all of Ebony and Reef's shit.

SIX

Knock. Knock. Knock!

"Who is it?" a voice calls out from afar.

"Open the door, NOW!" Reef yelled from the other side.

The door opened slowly, and there stood Summer, shocked to see him standing there.

"Well, are you gonna let me in or not?"

Summer opened the door and tried to hug him, but Reef wasn't going for that and pushed her backward away from him.

"Listen, I don't know how you got my shorty's number, but you better lose it right now. Why would you even call her starting shit? That ain't cool. Loose her fucking number and don't ever call her again!! I promise you, if you don't, I will kill you myself!! You hear me!?" he shouted.

Summer was scared as hell because she knew he was serious by the look on his face. "Oh, and if you're pregnant, you better get rid of it, ya' heard? If you need a ride or need the money, I will be glad to help."

Summer was really confused. They had been hitting things off very well the last few weeks. By her being pregnant, she thought they could potentially be a happy family, but now he was acting like this. A whole 180° change. *What could possibly be going on*, she thought to herself. *Would he really kill me with a baby – his baby – in my stomach?*

45

Reef and Summer had history. They had a crush on each other since elementary school, which lasted up until high school. They used to hang out and flirt all the time before they got serious or tried anything. Summer wanted Reef to be her first back then, but it didn't happen right away. One day, her parents went away for the weekend, so she invited him over. She knew she wasn't ready, but thought now would be the perfect time for it to happen, and so it did. It felt so right to her at the moment.

Right after, she found out he had a girlfriend and she couldn't help but be embarrassed because everyone would stare at her and just laugh. When his girlfriend found out from rumors, he stopped talking to her. From that one time, she ended up being pregnant, but got an abortion immediately before anyone found out.

All these years had passed by, and they still hadn't spoken until they ran into each other at a party one night. Just as the first time, one thing led to the next and they were all over each other for days on end.

This time, she figured she would keep it. Maybe they could finally have the family they weren't ready for as teenagers. She even thought he would want to keep it, but clearly, she was wrong.

Reef was trying to keep it a secret, but Summer was on some bullshit, Now, he had to figure out what to do. One thing he did not play with was his wifey. He may do some fucked up shit, but he knew he loved Ebony and wouldn't let anyone come between them – EVER!

⌘

Ebony got home around 8:30 pm and just so happened to remember that Reef had plans, which was cool because she really didn't feel like going anywhere or dealing with his bullshit right now any way. After the whole Mac Daddy Diamonds thing, who knew what type of shit he would be on now. When she opened the door, it was candles lit everywhere and some delicious smelling food. Sigh. She knew what this was. Every so often, Reef would do this for her when he did something wrong and he knew she loved it. Hell, every woman loves to be pampered.

Reef didn't hear her come into the door because he was busy fixing everything in the kitchen. She walked right into the kitchen and hugged him from behind and gave him a subtle kiss on the nape of his neck.

"Where were you?" he asked automatically.

"I... I went to see... Sheree.... Babe, her house is gorgeous with a huge pool, and the new baby is just so aww. Have you ever been there before?"

"No, I haven't," he answered with a bewildered look. *Since when does she go see Sheree and how the hell she find out how to contact her,* he thought to himself. "I haven't even spoken to Lateef like that."

Ebony could tell he was lying, but she didn't say anything.

"That's funny because she said she asked you about me and you told her I was fine. Why didn't you say anything to me?"

"I have a question. Actually, I..I just thought you didn't want to talk to them. You haven't spoken to her in years. Damn, calm down and get off my back!! It's not that serious."

Ebony changed the subject since she could sense he was getting upset. She didn't want to kill the good mood he was in so she just walked away.

"Go get changed into something else. I have some special things planned for you".

All Ebony could do was roll her eyes and head upstairs. When she opened the room door there were presents all over the bed. Typical. It was way too many for her to open in one night so she chose the prettiest gift bag from the array of presents on the bed. Of course, the bag I chose had lingerie in it, she thought to herself, and she was very annoyed by it.

Without much thought, she hopped in the shower really quickly. When she got out, she let her hair down, threw on some makeup, chose the sexiest heels she had, and made her way back downstairs. Yeah, she was mad at him, but she was feeling herself and knew he would too.

When she got to the bottom of the stairs, she could see Reef taking the garlic bread out of the oven. Before she could get herself fully together to present herself to him, he turned around.

"Damn babe!! You look sexy as hell!!" he said as he licked his lips. "Now, turn around and let me see that ass."

As soon as she turned around, Reef smacked her on the ass and started biting his bottom lip.

"Let's go over to the couch. I got something for you." He walked her over to the couch and sat her down. "I'll be right back."

When he came back, he had a tray of different things. He had whip cream, strawberries, ice cream, chocolate and caramel syrup, and ice cubes.

"What is this, Reef?"

"Forget dinner," he said as he placed the tray on the floor and grabbed both of her hands.

Before she knew it, they were both on the floor of the living room and looking into each other's eyes.

He started to kiss her so softly while trailing his tongue down her body. A shiver ran through her as she closed her eyes and melted into his touch. Everything he did to her made her body tingle.

She felt herself starting to climax. There was something about this man. His dick drove her wild, but just his touch could take her there. Before she could fully reach, he started to undress her using nothing but his teeth. Noticing what he was doing to her, he couldn't help but have the most seductive smirk on his face. He knew he had her *exactly* where he wanted her.

As she lay there naked, he pulled a bandana out from his back pocket and began rubbing it up and down her body. When he got to her lips, he grabbed the banana started to move the banana in and out of her mouth as if she were sucking his dick, which she always did well. This was definitely something different, but freaky, and it captivated her.

As he was doing this, he used his other hand to take spoonfuls of the ice cream he had on the tray and smear it on strategic locations of her body. After this, he put whip cream all over her thighs and made sure to put more than enough in her inner thighs next to her throbbing pussy. He wanted her to want him, so he immediately stopped what he was doing, sat back, and looked at her.

"You want me ?"

Ebony nodded her head while biting on her bottom lip. Then, he carefully took his tongue and trailed every area of her body where he put the ice cream, being sure to leave her breast the way they were. He wanted to save the best for last. If he knew anything, he knew what would send Ebony over. As he made his way to her lips, he kissed her with so much passion that it threw her off. *Why is he being so – so passionate? What's up with him,* she thought to herself.

Finally, he worked his way back down to her nipples – her spot. He slowly twirled his tongue around each nipple making sure to lick every inch of them. All she could do was gasp for air trying to calm down. She didn't want to bust yet so she just lay back, enjoyed every moment, and moaned to every little nibble.

Reef knew she was enjoying every second of what he was doing because her body kept trembling and he could feel her pussy contracting against his leg. As he made his way back down to her belly button, he twirled his tongue in circular motion around her stomach, inching closer and closer to her pussy. Ebony's body was going crazy. She couldn't control how he was making her feel, and all she could do was think about how good it was going to be when he entered her.

"Can I taste it babe?"

"Yes...Reef...please babe!!"

Without hesitation, he lifted her legs up and found his way to her clit, Ebony moaned louder in ecstasy as she gripped his head. Reef didn't stop because he wanted her addicted. He was going to make sure she enjoyed every moment.

49

Teasing her, he stopped and looked at her. Her body was shaking uncontrollably and it hyped him up. Just when she thought she couldn't take any more, he
climbs on top of her holding her legs up starting off slowly making sure I could feel him inside of me.

"You like this dick huh!?"

"YES," Ebony moaned. "I love this dick."

This turned him on and he begin to go faster and faster.

"What my name? Say my name!"

Then goes a little faster and asks again, "What's my name?"

" Re...Reef!!"

"Yeah, say it again!"

Ebony damn near screamed out, "REEF!! REEF!!"

"Now turn around," he replied as he tilted her upper body all the way down.

Holding her waist, he started giving it to her from behind. She didn't know what hit her, but this was better than the first time. She was still moaning and cumming everywhere. Loving every bit of it. She hadn't noticed that he nutted inside of her until he stopped and was just sitting there.

Ebony didn't say anything because Reef went in for a second round, but in her mind she was thinking, *did this nigga really nut in me? What was that all about? He never did this before. He always makes sure he pulls out every... every time.*

They didn't even get to eat the food he cooked because they ended up fucking all night. This was something they hadn't done in a long time and she was loving every part of it. She knew that Reef was trying to get back on her good side just in case she decided to leave him. All she wanted was for him to get anger management classes, get rid of his bitch, Summer, and all his other hoes he may have had. Then, just maybe, things could be perfect.

Ebony went to sleep with a lot on her mind and woke up with even more on her mind. Finally, she had a new start, new life, and a new home! As hard as it was to leave, she left everything behind and those "so-called" friends who said they would always be there for her. They lied! They didn't like the fact that she moved to Atlanta with Reef, but if they were real friends, they would understand why. He was the one who was really by her side, and he was the one who understood her as a person.

So many thoughts were going through her mind, but she knew everyone goes through problems. At the time, she felt he was her rock, her everything, her better half, and she still had hopes that they would get married one day – not that things had gotten better. Yes, he had things he needed to work on, but he wasn't hitting her as much, he needed to learn how to be more patient, and he needed to work on his anger management. She also wanted him to put a tile on their relationship. It bothered her that she couldn't tell people if she was his girlfriend or his wife.

⌘

Reef had been gone for a week now. He said he needed to go on an important business trip and expand his company, so Ebony was going to be home by herself. She really didn't mind it because it gave her time to relax, clear her head, and get the feel of Atlanta life. Her only problem was meeting new people, wondering who knew who, and watching out for anything that looked suspicious.

While lying deep in thought, Ebony's phone started ringing. She decided not to answer, and they called back. She knew it wasn't Reef because he was never able to talk whenever he was on a "business trip," and he would mostly call her at night. *Who the fuck is this,* she thought to herself.

For some reason, the number looked familiar, but she wasn't really sure. All she knew was that it couldn't have been anyone that important because she had changed her number.

"Hello?"

The person on the other end said nothing. All she could hear was the person breathing and she could hear air blowing.

"Hello...hello –"

Then, they hung up. For some reason, Ebony felt scared and what made it worse was the fact that she was all alone.

Immediately, she got up and went to every window and every door to make sure they were all tightly shut and locked. Just as she was locking the lock on the last window, her phone began to ring again. When she answered this time, she decided not to say anything. Neither did the other person on the other end of the line once again!

"HELLO!!" Ebony yelled. "Why the fuck you keep playing on my phone?"

"Ebony?"

"Who the fuck is this and what the fuck do you want?"

"You probably don't remember me, but I talked to you a long time ago. This Summer."

Ebony almost fell to the floor. *What the hell could she be calling me for now,* she thought.

"Well, remember when I told you I was pregnant? I had a girl."

"Hold up!" Ebony said in disbelief. "I thought you had an abortion... or at least you were supposed to."

"Well, I didn't say I was. Anyway, I just moved to another town and called Reef when I was in labor. He didn't know I was still carrying the baby, but I got in touch with him. At the last minute, he came to the hospital and signed the birth certificate."

Ebony's face turned so red and she was filled with so much hurt and anger. This was the last thing she needed to hear when things were finally starting to look up for her and Reef. *The nerve of these mothafucka's. How could they? Was this true? How could they have kept this a secret?* She knew she had some words for Reef when he came home or maybe she should act like she didn't know anything just to see if he would tell her.

"Now, he's actually visiting us here."

"WHAT!? SON OF A BITCH!!" Ebony screamed and hung up the phone.

She was furious and pacing back and forth. She didn't know what to do, what to believe, or what to even think. Then, she decided to call Summer back.

"Since you had this baby, send me a pic! NOW!" she demanded. "Tell Reef I said to get his ass home. RIGHT NOW,!"

She hung up and paced through her living room. After an hour passed, Summer still hadn't sent a pic. *How the fuck did she get my number again?* I didn't get a call from Reef that night and she found it very funny. Usually, he would call. She fell asleep mad as hell. When she woke up, he didn't even text her that he loved her, which was even funnier to her.

This couldn't be happening again. Ebony felt like the world was crumbling down on her, but she knew she had come too far to let anything break her. She was too strong of a person to let that happen. She decided it was just best that she waited until Reef come home to tell her what the fuck was going on and where he had been all this time. *Business trip my ass,* she thought to herself, but she knew it was something she couldn't stress about because she couldn't prove it right now.

Fuck it, I'm going out tonight!

SEVEN

He was right out of a magazine. She was undressing him with her eyes, and he definitely peeped her noticing him. He had a nice brown skin tone, low hair cut with the most beautiful curly hair, and the nicest smile that captivated the room, not to mention how sexy he was. Just her type!

She had run into him earlier in the night when he stopped some aggressive drunk ass man that kept bothering her throughout the night. Little did he know, that turned her on. He didn't know, but she was so happy that he was there and had stood up for her because the guy was giving her creepy vibes, and she was scared he would be waiting for her outside of the club later.

Ebony kept her eyes on him the entire night, but she made sure she enjoyed herself. Shit, she felt like that was the least she deserved. When she finally decided to call it a night, she walked out of the club and mentally prepared herself to go home. She didn't even notice the man she had been admiring all night standing outside a few steps from the front door. When he eyed her walking out, he immediately grabbed her and pulled her away.

Ebony couldn't even scream or pull away from him because she was so mesmerized. There was something about this man. She was just stuck, amazed, and wondered why this man would even be interested in someone like her at this very moment. Yes, she was bad as hell, but she was going through some shit and she always wore her emotions on her face.

"You want to take a ride with me?"

"I mean... I guess I could," Ebony replied with a quickness.

He smiled at her and it almost made her cum in her panties. *Damn, he is fucking fine*, she thought to herself. *He can take me anywhere he wants to.*

"Come on then," he said as he grabbed her hand and brought her to his car that was parked across the street.

Ebony hopped in his car, and they drove off into the night. At the moment, she wasn't thinking of anything else. For some reason, the way he kept licking his lips and the vibration she was feeling from the car ride was making her so horny. She couldn't help it, and she got the urge to start touching herself.

Completely thrown off, he looked at her out the side of his eye while biting his bottom lip. Once she started moaning, he looked over at her and then back to the road. She couldn't resist everything her body was feeling. What was he doing to her? Without thought, she reached over and grabbed his dick. She tried hard to get it out of his pants, but she was struggling."

"Hold on baby. Let me pull over," he said in the sexiest voice she had ever heard as he pulled over on the shoulder of the road.

He looked at her with his sexy brown eyes and started kissing her on her neck. His lips were so fucking soft. She had never felt anything like them before. Everything he was doing was sending chills all over her body. *Damn.*

"Wait," Ebony replied as she backed up. "I'm not ready for this. I –"

Without letting her finish her sentence, he leaned in and kissed her, while grabbing her hand at the same time and placing it between his legs, where she could feel the bulge.

"Let's go to the back," he said as he crawled over his middle console and Ebony followed suit.

As they started kissing again, his hands reached down to her panties, "I want to taste you so bad."

She knew what he was about to do. Quickly, he pushed her back, pulled her panties to the side, and started eating her pussy. Ebony let out a subtle moan. Her moaning increasingly became louder as he went up and down her clit with his tongue.

Then, he whispered, "Cum for me baby. This pussy so wet and so fucking good." He said before going back down on her.

"Scream my name," he said

Hell, she didn't even know his name. "Daddy!! D-D-Daddy," Ebony screamed louder and louder as he continued.

She came all over his face. Then, he wiped it off with his shirt, and she got on top of him. She wanted it so bad. She wanted to feel every part of him inside of her, but he must have had other plans. When she tried to pull his dick out of his pants, he moved her hands and gave her the most seductive smile.

Was this some type of joke or something? He must be crazy, she thought. *Like, how could he play with me like that?* She fixed herself up and got back into the passenger seat as he drove her back to her car. When they got to her car, he gave her a hug, kissed her cheek, walked her to her car, and they exchanged numbers. Before she could pierce her lips to ask him if he was actually going to call her, he sped off.

Damn.

She looked into her phone, "Haneef," she whispered to herself.

When she got back home, there was still no Reef. Ebony couldn't help but to start getting mad, but then she thought about what had just happened, and those feelings melted. She wanted to stay in the high she was on.

She decided to draw herself a bubble bath and sat in it for over two hours having flashbacks. She never cheated on Reef and was scared for him to find out because she knew he would lose his mind. Despite thinking about this periodically, thoughts of Haneef flooded her mind. How soft his lips were, his touch, the way he looked at her, and how he touched her. Those flashbacks sent heavy chills through her body and left her pussy wet and tingly.

Every time she thought about him going down on her, her pussy would throb. She couldn't resist it. She had to play with herself to ease the tension she felt within herself. Fantasizing about him and visualizing the essence of him of it all made her explode and her whole body started shaking.

She sat in the tub for about another hour and eventually got out. Then, she walked into the room, sat on the bed, and rubbed lotion all over her body from head to toe, imagining it was Haneef. She just couldn't get Haneef out of her mind. She wanted to feel him inside of her. She needed to feel him inside of her.

When she got to her breast, she began to squeeze her nipples, which sent a crazy sensation to her pussy. It made her jump a little bit because it felt so good. *If only I could have his lips all over my body,* she thought to herself. *What was it about this man that I can't get him off my mind?* Maybe it was the fact that she hadn't been with anyone else in so many years and this feeling was something different. This time when she was playing with herself, she imagined she was riding his dick.

Shit.

She let out the biggest nut. Eventually, she was able to fall asleep, but she tossed and turned all night long because thoughts of Reef plagued her mind.

⌘

Three weeks later.

Ebony hadn't heard a word from Reef. No calls, no text, or anything. She just kept wondering what was going on with him and hoped he wasn't in any trouble.

Was he seeing someone else – well, Summer? Did he really have a new baby? Was everything Summer said the truth or was she lying?

She even tried to call Summer's phone again, but it was not in service. She tried calling Reef's phone, but it was going straight to voicemail. Come on now, leaving for three weeks was a lot of time to be away. A million and one questions ran through her mind. She kept going from feeling angry, sad, very depressed, and alone. Part of her wanted to shut down, but then she remembered that feeling and didn't want to feel that way.

Focus!! Focus!!

She had a new job in a new city and there was no reason for her to be sitting around feeling like this over a man who didn't love her or treat her the way she should be treated. Hell, there were plenty of men everywhere. She just had to find one...or two.

Fuck it, I'm going out, she thought to herself.

There was a new club in the area that her coworkers were talking about, so she decided to give it a try. The only thing she felt like she was missing right now was her friends and how they used to party. Boy, did they have some of the best times ever!

She put on her knee-high boots and the shortest off-the-shoulder dress she could find and headed out the door. It only took her about forty-five minutes to get to the club, which wasn't bad at all. Luckily, the line wasn't long at all, and she was able to walk right in. As soon as she walked in, she noticed a girl staring at her and watching her every move, but she paid no attention to her because she was used to the attention. Maybe she was just one of those jealous people.

Surprisingly, the club was a reggae club, which Ebony had no idea about. Hell, she didn't care though. She just needed to get out of that house. Plus, if what everybody said about Jamaicans was true, she knew they partied hard all night and the men were very freaky.

Within an hour, the club started to get really packed and she made my way to the dance floor. As she was grinding by herself she felt a man come up behind her and grab her waist. She didn't care who it was, she continued to grind until she felt a huge bulge in his pants. It turned her on a little bit, so she had to turn around to get a glimpse of his face.

Damn, she was shocked when she saw who it was. She leaned in and gave him a kiss as he grabbed her ass and pulled her in closer. Honestly, it looked like they were fucking on the dance floor, but the club was too packed for anyone to notice anything. He was making her so horny, so she grabbed his hand and led him to one of the couches they had in the back.

When they got to the back, she pushed him down on the couch, straddled him, and began to grind slowly. He slid his fingers between her legs and began to rub her clit. He was turning her all the way on. As they were caught in the moment, he kissed her neck and whispered in her ear, "Cum for me."

An immediate tingle went through her entire body and she let out a moan while still grinding on him. Her body began to shake and he pulled his hands out from between her legs. Giving her complete eye contact, he licked his fingers and gave her a kiss. Smirking, she hopped off of him to see if anyone had been looking, but everyone was too busy dancing.

She didn't know her next moves, but she knew she needed to find the bathroom to straighten herself up. She walked into the bathroom, wiped herself off, and went to the mirror to fix her hair and clothes.

When she looked up, the girl from before was staring at her.

Aggravated, Ebony asked, "You know me from somewhere?"

The girl shook her head and nodded.

"Oh okay! I'm just trying to figure out why you keep looking at me."

The girl put her head down and walked out of the bathroom as if they never communicated with one another. *That's strange*, she thought to herself. This was the second time she caught this chick staring at her.

Is she stalking me?

What the fuck is wrong with this bitch?

She just hurried out of the bathroom to see if Haneef was still there. She wanted to take him home tonight. She began to search, but the spot was way too crowded for her to be able to find him. With everybody dancing on the dance floor, there was no way possible she could find him. So, Ebony decided to leave, hoping he would be outside waiting for her, but he wasn't.

Damn! If I had one night with that man...the things I would do.

As she pulled up to her house, she noticed her lights were on, and she knew that she didn't leave them on. Afraid to go in, she got out of the car slowly looking around to make sure she wasn't being followed. Hell, maybe she did leave them on. Opening the door very slowly, she peeked around just to make sure she didn't hear any noises. As soon as she shut the door, two hands grabbed her, and hands went over her mouth.

Her first instinct was to start punching and kicking. She needed to do whatever she needed to do to get loose.

Is this really happening?

Eventually, the person let go and yelled out a big, "SURPRISE!"

She placed her hand over her heart. "Reef, you scared the shit out of me. What are you doing here? Why didn't you tell me you were coming?" she yelled.

"What the fuck I need to tell you when I'm coming home for? Who have you been having in this house since I was gone?"

"Nobody, babe." Ebony responded as she backed up just in case he was angry.

He just looked at her with the sternest look. "I just wanted to surprise you because I missed you so much," he replied as he opened his arms to hug her. "Give me a kiss."

Reef didn't notice it right away until Ebony walked into his embrace. "Where the fuck you coming from with this shit on? What? You was out fucking or something?" Ebony didn't respond. "Ebony, you hear me?" Reef yelled as he got directly in her face.

"Why are you questioning me? Where the fuck have you been all this time without any phone calls or anything, Now, all of a sudden, you just show up talking about surprise. Shit, you got to be kidding me. Who were you with? That bitch, Summer?" Reef got mad and went to grab her by the neck, but she moved out of the way. "Don't get mad at me because you're out here doing shit!!"

Reef raised his voice. "BITCH, you better not be out here doing shit behind my back or I'm a kill your ass! You hear me!?"

Ebony rolled her eyes and mumbled under my breath. Reef grabbed her by the neck and proceeded to say, "If you think I'm playing, try me!"

Ebony grabbed his hands to try to pry them from her neck, but his grip was too tight. When he saw that she was turning bright red, he finally let go. She fell to the floor and started crying.

"What the fuck is your stupid ass crying for? Get the fuck up!" he yelled.

Ebony just sat there, still crying, with her head down.

"Did you hear what I said, bitch!?" This time Reef grabbed her hair and tried to pull her up.

"GET OFF ME!! I can get up by myself!!"

Quickly, Ebony stood up and walked over to the couch to sit down. Reef was right on her heels and glaring at her suspiciously. There were so many questions she wanted to ask, but she didn't want to upset him more than he already was.

How could he possibly be mad at me when he was the one that disappeared?

Whenever he was wrong or knew he was caught out there slipping, he always tried to flip back on her as if it were her fault. This always ended up in a very dangerous situation and left her feeling stuck and not being able to defend herself. The funny thing was, this was the only love Ebony knew. She really loved him so much and she hoped things would get better. All her life, the only thing she wanted was to feel loved.

Being adopted and not knowing her parents had her so damaged. She had hope she would find a man to give her the love she never got.. She always felt like she didn't know who she was as a person and all the lies and running around Reef was doing was too much for her to handle. She just wanted to be loved and build a family of her own, but love couldn't possibly feel like this. There was just so much time invested in him, and she

61

couldn't let go. She knew he cared about her, but didn't know why he did the things he did.

Reef spent the night, but they didn't do anything, which was a total shock to her. When the morning came, he quickly got dressed and left, saying he would be back later. He told her to make sure she was home. At this point, she definitely could tell something was up with him.

Why was he being so sneaky all of a sudden?

He left her confused and speechless.

Why did he run out of the house so quickly?

What was he up to?

A few minutes later, there was a knock at the door. *Who could this be,* she thought. As she opened the door – WTF! It was the bitch from the club.

"Bitch, what the fuck you doing on my doorstep!?" she yelled, getting ready to drag her by her hair. I knew you were fucking creepy. I knew you were following me!!" she said, stepping into the girls face.

"Wait!! Wait!!" the girl replied, trying to get Ebony to lower her voice. "I'm Summer. Reef brought me up here. I didn't know why, but now I see he wanted to check up on you."

Ebony's whole facial expression changed. Her eyebrows got all scrunched up and her face turned blood shot red. She was ready to whoop this girl's ass.

"Well, how the fuck you now where I live?"

"I followed him last night to see where he was going."

"Wait, I'm confused," Ebony replied.

"Can I come inside for a minute?" Summer asked.

Bitch, you must be crazy, Ebony thought in her head, but she nodded her head because curiosity killed the cat. She wanted to know what the fuck Summer wanted to talk about.

"Come in and have a seat."

Summer proceeded with caution and looked around to make sure the coast was clear.

"Well, what do you want?" Ebony asked again.

"I...I just came to tell you that me Reef have been living together and raising the baby."

"WHAT! I thought you had an abortion... at least that's what he told me."

Summer shook her head. "It was too late to get one, and Reef told me he would help me. He came to the hospital for my delivery, and he has been there since helping me raise our child."

A piece of Ebony's heart ripped out of her chest just hearing those words, especially since they'd been trying to have a baby. Feeling so hurt, she just began to cry.

How could he do this to me and claim he loves me and wants to marry me?

I thought he wanted a family with me.

Summer continued speaking. "I suspected it was something he wasn't telling me and I got suspicious. I started to do my own investigating. In the beginning, I never even knew you existed. I would've never broken up a happy home, but I needed to tell you this. It's only right. Now, you can believe me or not. That part is up to you."

Just as she was finishing up her story, we heard the doorknob turn. *OMG,* she thought. *I can't take too much more of this.* Reef walked in. *Maybe he will FINALLY tell me his side of the story. Hell, maybe they planned out this little meeting so he could tell me he was leaving me,* Ebony thought to herself.

By the looks on his face when he opened the door, Ebony knew things weren't going to go nice.

"What the fuck you doing here, bitch?" Reef yelled out to Summer.

Immediately, he ran up on her and went straight for her neck. Summer started crying and tried to block herself. In the back of Summer's mind, she knew she was wrong, but she needed to get the story out and see what was going on.

"Why didn't you tell me y'all were still together?" Summer asked Reef while she was trying to get him to loosen his grip on her neck.

Then, he looked over at Ebony's face and saw the tears rolling down. All he could say was that she was lying and Ebony didn't need to believe a word that came out of her mouth. "She's just mad that I don't want her ass," said Reef.

"So, why the fuck she come here with you?" Ebony questioned. "She's here in our home. for what? She's sitting up here telling me about a baby that you said was gone."

"I don't know what's going on. I'm telling you she's lying and don't believe shit she says."

Summer just sat there with a look of confusion because she couldn't believe what she was hearing. She only came to tell her what had been going on was because she felt like Reef was lying to both of them. She really thought that they were going to be a family and raise their child.

Then, Reef walked over to Ebony, got in her face, and screamed, "DON'T BELIEVE THIS BITCH. I'M TELLING YOU!!"

Ebony tried to walk away, but before she could get far, he grabbed a fist full of her hair and dragged her outside.

"Let me go!" Ebony screamed.

Reef dragged her into the car, ran to the other side, and quickly locked the doors.

"Reef, what the hell you doing? You're acting crazy!"

Reef ignored her, started the car, and drove off.

"Shut the fuck up before I slap the shit out of you!"

At this point, she was scared for her life. He was driving like a mad man. She had never been in this situation with him before and she just wanted to know where he was taking her.

"I love you Ebony and I don't want to lose you. Look bitch, if you want to be stupid and believe this other bitch, I will kill both of us. RIGHT NOW!!"

"NOOO!!" she screamed. "Just stop the car so we can talk about all of this."

"Talk about what!?" he screamed. "There's nothing to talk about when this bitch is trying to ruin my life with you and I'm not having that. I love you and I'm sorry if I gave you any doubt about that for one minute. I would never choose anybody over you."

Trying to look at me and look at the road at the same time, Reef started swerving.

"Reef, watch out, please. I love you so much, Reef. You have no idea. I want us to be together forever."

"Bitch you're just lying. Shut the fuck up!!"

He swerved so much this time that he couldn't dodge the car coming straight towards them.

BOOM.

Ebony woke up in the hospital bed with IVs in her arm and her face hurt so bad. She felt like she had gotten hit in her face. Not knowing what was going on, she began to panic, but the nurse calmed her down.

"Where's Reef? Where is he?" Ebony yelled, but no one said a thing.

She began to cry and call out for him. She prayed that he was still alive. The nurse told her she had to calm down and stop yelling or else they would have to give her a shot to calm her down. Once she calmed down, the doctor came into the room and explained she had been in a car accident and could have almost lost her life. Then, began to ask her a series of questions. She was able to answer most of them. Then, he asked the most important question. "Ma'am, who do you believe you were in the car with?"

"My boyfriend! Is he alive? Please tell me he is alive!"

He looked at her as if she were crazy. "Ma'am, there was no one in the car with you when we found you."

Ebony's heart began to pound faster and faster as she shook her head no.

"What do you mean I was the only one in the car?" she yelled.

The police walked in as she was yelling about Reef. They began questioning her as well as if she had committed some type of crime. Again, she explained that her boyfriend was in the car and he was the one driving when a car ran into them. They asked her again and she told them the same thing,

"Ma'am, do you know Summer Wright? "

"No, not at all. Why do you ask that question."

"The car you were in was registered to her."

"I don't know who the hell Summer is!! Can you tell me where my boyfriend is and if he's still alive, please!!"

Again, the police just say they don't know anything about him and that she was the only one found in the car.

That bitch!! I know he didn't leave me alone in the car and didn't even make sure I was alive. Most importantly, why was his fuckin car in her name? He is definitely a liar and boy he going to hear my mouth when I see him, she thought to herself.

EIGHT

"Imagining a life without you is something that is impossible, you make me complete, and I want you to know you mean everything to me."

It had been three days since Ebony was checked into the hospital, and she still, no visits from Reef – not even a call. Today was finally the day she was being discharged. The swelling had gone down a lot, although her body was still in pain, but she only had one thing on her mind. *If this man said he loved me like he did, where the fuck was he? Why hasn't he come to visit? What happened to him on the day of the accident? Clearly, he doesn't care about me,* Ebony thought to herself. She didn't even know if he was alive. She also didn't know anything about his situation or what he had going on. When it came to Reef, Ebony was completely clueless. All she could think about was how she was going to kill Reef if he had Summer up in her house.

When she got home, everything in the house was still in the same way she left it – or at least from what she could remember. There were no signs that Reef or Summer had even been here. She pulled out her phone to call him, but it went to voicemail. She called again, and it went to voicemail again. She even called Summer's phone, and it wasn't in service. Scrolling

67

through her phone, she came across Haneef's name and decided to call him. No answer either.

Damn, she thought.

Five minutes later the phone rang and it was Haneef calling back.

"Hello?"

"What's up with you? How have you been?" he asked.

Ebony explained to him how she had just gotten out of the hospital. She also told him that she needed some fresh air and to clear her mind of everything that had been going on. He suggested that he come pick her up to help her clear her mind. She agreed.

When he pulled up, he called her to let her know he was outside. She came outside looking around as if she were being followed to make sure the coast was clear. Haneef noticed a little swelling on her face, but didn't say anything because he didn't want to make her feel self- conscious or anything. In the back of his mind, he just wondered what happened to her.

"You ok?" was the first thing that came out of his mouth as he gave her a hug and a kiss on the forehead.

She felt a little embarrassed about the way that she looked and hoped he wasn't judging her. She just shook her head yes and told him to drive away. He pulled up to some type of gate and he had to enter a code to get in. All you could see was this community of big houses with beautiful landscaping.

"Where are we?"

"This is where I live baby girl," he answered.

Ebony couldn't do anything, but be quiet as they made their way into the driveway of this huge, beautiful, Victorian-style home. When they got out of the car, they walked up to this huge house with a huge door to match.

"Do you live by yourself?" I asked.

"Yes, I do. My kids usually come on the weekends."

"Kids? How many kids do you have?"

He smiled and responded, "Two. I just got a divorce a few months ago. My wife and I have joint custody of the kids. I

68

usually get them Thursday – Monday and some holidays. Is that a problem?"

"No, not at all. I'm just amazed."

As they entered the house, Haneef made sure to let Ebony know to make herself at home. She did just that and chose to sit on the huge plush sectional in the living room area.

Haneef smiled. "I'm going to run upstairs and run you a bath, if that's ok?"

"Yes, that would be amazing."

"Cool," he said as he ran upstairs.

After some time had passed, Ebony started to get worried because reality sat in. She realized she was sitting in a stranger's home.

"Where are you?" she called out to Haneef as she walked up the stairs and tried to make her way to him.

When she got to the top of the stairs, he told her to take her clothes off and change into the robe that he had laid out for her. She did so without hesitation and walked into the bathroom where there was a nice bubble bath waiting for her.

"You didn't have to do this," she said.

He just looked at her and said, "Get in."

She did just that. The water felt so good on her bruised and banged up body because it relaxed her muscles. He got a washcloth, began to lather it up, and started to wash her body. It had been a long time since anyone did anything like this for her and she was enjoying all of it. Then, he reached down towards her clit and began to play with it. She let out moan after moan because it felt so good.

He whispered in her ear, "Cum for me."

Again, she did just that! This time her legs were shaking uncontrollably. After she finished, he gave her a towel, picked her up, and laid her on his bed. He dried her off and opened her legs wide.

"OMG!!" she mumbled as his tongue rubbed against her clit. "Haneef!" she called out as she felt herself about to cum, yet again.

She buried the back of her head into the pillow and rose her hips up to cum into his mouth. Haneef got up, licked his lips, and said, "MMMmmmm."

She laughed and just lay there trying to catch her breath. He pushed her legs back open, climbed in between them, and asked, "Are you ready?"

She shook her head yes as she tried to prepare herself for what was about to happen. As he entered her, she moved back a little because his dick was big as shit, but she told him to go ahead anyway. She was finally about to feel all that she had been fantasizing about for the last few weeks. Just a couple of pumps had her going crazy because he was just so big. Something that hurt so bad, felt so good and she took it like a champ. She moaned louder and louder as he went deeper. She felt every inch of him in her stomach.

"HANEEF!!" she screamed out and grabbed his face to kiss him.

He kissed her back just the same and she felt like she was in heaven. He kept asking her if she liked it while stroking deeper and deeper. All she could do was bite her lip because she was speechless and he was really going all in.

After about forty-five minutes, he came, but he came inside of her. Crazy thoughts ran through Ebony's head, but she didn't even care. She felt like she was on cloud 9. When he lay beside her, he had the biggest grin on his face. She smirked because she knew she had put it on him just as he had put it on her. Then, she got up and went to the bathroom to try and push out any cum that she could as if it would make a difference. When she went back to lay down with Haneef, she told him everything that she had been through.

It all began to hit her all at once, and she broke down. She tried to stop herself, but all she could do was cry hysterically. Haneef grabbed her and held her tight, letting her know everything was going to be alright until they drifted off to sleep.

The next morning, her phone rang, scaring the shit out of her and almost caused her to fall off the bed. She didn't get to answer it in time, but once she seen who was calling, her heart felt like it was going to jump out of her chest. *Oh shit,* she thought as she looked at the time, It was 9:30 am. She didn't mean to sleep this late, and she didn't mean to spend the night. All she was thinking about was how she needed to get home and she needed to get home *NOW. I have to get home. Reef is going to kill me,* she thought.

She rolled over, but Haneef wasn't in bed with her. She called out to him, but there was no answer.

Shit!

She hopped out of bed, putting her clothes and shoes on almost at the same time. Then, she ran downstairs to see if he was in the house. She ran to the living room, but nothing. She ran to the dining room, but nothing. She ended up finding him in the kitchen. He had just finished making breakfast and putting the food on the table. Breathing heavily, her hair all over the place, she said, " I needed to go home, it's an emergency!"

"What's wrong? Is everything ok? You mean to tell me I made this nice breakfast for you, and you are not going to stay and eat it with me? I thought you wanted to get away. Now, you're in a rush to get back home?" he asked as he looked at her suspiciously trying to figure out what was *really* going on. "What's this emergency? Is it really that bad?"

She looked down, looked at him, and thought to herself, *Shit, it can wait. Why would I be rushing home anyway when I don't even know if Reef is home or not. He waited this long to call me, and for what? He didn't even make sure I was good after the accident he caused. He didn't even know if I was still alive or not. Right now, all I wanted to do was make sure everything was alright with him, and I wasn't even able to do that. If he found out I wasn't home, he would be wondering where I went and I didn't want him to start acting crazy again. At the end of the day, I am enjoying myself with a man that is showing me something different – showing me lots of affection that I have been missing out on. It feels great to be pampered.*

Fuck it, I am going to stay right where I am and keep Reef's ass off my mind.

"It's nothing." She looked him in the eyes. "It was just my best friend. She needed help with something, but it can wait." She gave him a halfway smile and sat at the table.

Ebony noticed that Haneef was staring at her every move and it was making her a little nervous.

"I wanted to do something special for you," he said. "I love making you feel special. I love the look on your face when I do."

"What!? You're crazy," she said shyly, but she honestly loved the attention she was getting.

They both laughed and started to eat. Damn, this man seemed to be the total package, but what was his real situation? What was really wrong with this picture? This just seemed too good to be true, she thought to herself.

"So, tell me about yourself?" Haneef said.

Are you serious? "What is it specifically you would want to know?"

"Just about you. I mean I really don't know much about you, that's all. If we were going to be seeing each other ,I would like to know a little more about you than just your name."

"What!?" Ebony replied almost spitting her juice out her mouth. "Excuse me, you caught me off guard." She said, wiping her face. "Well to start off, I didn't know my parents – I was adopted. What I do know is that I'm mixed. I'm half black and half white. I never got to meet my parents and I don't have any children. Now, I recently moved to Atlanta for a new job position." Ebony stopped and looked at Haneef as if to say, *that's all.*

He laughed and replied, "Well, that was short and simple. So, are you seeing anyone?" he asked while looking dead in her eyes.

"No, I actually just got out of a relationship a while ago."

"Oh, sorry to hear that," he said as he took a sip of his juice. "What happened?"

Oh boy, Ebony thought to herself. *I really don't want to go all into that right now.* "Well, we weren't seeing eye to eye anymore and I had to end it."

"Well, how long were you guys together?"

"About seven years and now we're done. Please don't ask any more questions about this. I'm trying to leave this in the past."

Ebony's phone started ringing again and she just looked at it. Haneef noticed she was a little tense, but didn't want to bring much attention to it. Out of nowhere, Ebony got up from the table and told Haneef she was going to help him wash and clean off the table.

"So, what do we have planned today?" she asked while standing at the sink.

Haneef walked up behind her, puts his hands around her waist, and kissed her on the neck. "Whatever you want to do."

His kiss sent chills up her spine and she quickly turned around and kissed him. "Sounds good to me, but I don't have any clothes or anything and my hair is a mess."

"Don't worry about it," he says. "I think I have something to fit you upstairs. Let's go take a look."

"What is it...some of your ex's old clothing?" she asked jokingly as they made their way upstairs.

He took her into his room and opened the closet. They both looked through the clothes together. Finally, she found a nice little sweatshirt, and it was so warm. She grabbed the sweatshirt, headed straight to the bathroom, and got undressed. When she turned around, Haneef was standing right behind her, admiring her. She was kind of startled because she didn't know he was directly behind her.

"I didn't notice how beautiful you were and your body is very nice!"

She blushed and hopped into the shower. A few minutes later, he hopped in too. They switched positions so that he could get his body wet and soap up his washcloth. The water looked so good trickling down his body. Then, he turned around to face her and began to soap up her body. He made her turn around, face the wall, and spread her legs open.

"Turn around," he said in the sexiest voice.

She did and kissed him. What started out as just a peck had her yearning for more. Haneef threw his washcloth to the shower floor and gripped his arms around her tightly as he pinned her against the shower wall. Turned on, Ebony sucked on his bottom lip and he let out a low moan. She felt his dick get hard as he pressed his body up against hers.

"We have to get out this shower or we'll never make it anywhere," he said as he bent down and begin to suck her breast while he gripped her ass. Immediately, Ebony grabbed his head and rubbed it seductively, as he knelt down and opened her legs so he could reach her pussy. All he did was kiss it, and she already started moaning. It felt so good that she could barely control her body. She didn't want him to stop, but he did. She looked at him confused as her pussy continued to throb.

He stood up and she couldn't take her eyes off his dick. Then, she knelt down as he just looked at her.

"I really want to get out of here. The water is getting cold anyways," he said.

She ignored what he said because his dick was saying something totally different. His dick wanted her and she wanted it. Before he could say another word, she took all of his dick into her mouth. He couldn't keep himself composed as he let out all types of moans. She took his dick deeper and deeper as he started to grab her head. She gagged as her eyes watered, but she didn't care. After everything he had done for her, she wanted to put in some work.

"Suck this dick baby!" he yelled out as Ebony went to work. His legs got weak and he let out a loud, "FUCK," and pushed her head back so he could cum. Then, he released all over the shower floor.

Ebony got up off her knees and replied, " Now, we can get out."

They both washed one last time, grabbed their towels, and dried off. Haneef tried to start with her one more time, but

Ebony felt like being a tease. She told him no and started to get dressed.

Haneef looked disappointed and started pouting, but he started to get dress as well. After they were both dressed, they headed out the door and jumped into his car.

"So, where are we going, pretty lady?" he asked as he looked over at Ebony.

"Ummmmmm, let's go see a movie. I haven't been in a long time and I actually want some popcorn."

He looked over at her. "Is that really what you want to do?"

Giggling, Ebony replied, "Yes!"

"Well, ok then."

Haneef pulled out his phone to check what movies were playing and the times. They agreed on one that started in about forty-five minutes. It was just enough time for them to make it.

When they pulled up to the mall, Ebony realized she had never been there before.

"Is this where the theatre is?"

Haneef parked the car, and they headed towards the entrance. For some reason, something didn't seem right. *What the hell am I doing out with this man like I don't have a man at home? If Reef were to see me right now who knows what the fuck would happen. I must be really crazy,* Ebony thought to herself. *Fuck it!*

She grabbed his arm as they continued to walk, but something deep within told her to turn around. As she did, she thought she seen someone who looked just like Reef and she pulled back immediately. As she turned her head back around, Haneef was looking at her trying to figure out what was wrong.

"You ok?"

"Yes, I'm fine. I thought I dropped something and I was making sure I didn't."

Haneef didn't say anything else about it and continued to walk into the theatre. While in line, they ordered a large popcorn and two medium drinks. The whole time they were in the line Ebony kept acting nervous and turning around every few minutes.

"You alright?" he questioned as they made their way to their seats.

"I'm fine," Ebony answered and gave him the biggest smile.

She really wasn't, though. In fact, she was so nervous that she didn't know if she could actually enjoy the movie. As they found their seats and sat down, Ebony's phone began to ring again. She didn't look at it, but she told Haneef she needed to excuse herself and go to the bathroom. When she got into the bathroom, she pulled her phone out, and there were two messages waiting. One of them said where the fuck are you and the other said I will kill you if I find out you out here cheating! As she read them, her eyes began to fill up with tears. Standing there looking in the mirror at her face, Ebony quickly wiped her eyes, washed her face, and told herself that everything was going to be fine.

Nervously, she walked back to her seat and noticed that Haneef wasn't sitting there. She didn't think anything of it because she figured maybe he had to use the bathroom too. As the previews began to play, Ebony started to eat her popcorn and be as close to normal as she could. She didn't want Haneef to notice that she had been crying. Every time someone came into the theatre, she tried to get a glimpse of their faces the best she could.

After some time had passed, she decided to stop being paranoid and just try her best to enjoy herself. She knew she would have to face the consequences later though. As Ebony was lost in her thoughts, Haneef had slipped back into the theater and sat down.

I've got to get it together over here, Ebony though to herself.

"Everything ok?" he asked as he put his arm around her neck and gave her a kiss.

She shook her head and smiled.

I can get used to this, she thought to herself.

76

NINE

I was having so much fun with Haneef, I began to forget about Reef and the whole situation, he had been blowing up my phone and I was choosing to ignore it but I knew things would end up bad for me anyways. Three weeks had passed so I decided it was time for me to take a break. I really like Haneef, but I also didn't want to get too attached, I still had these feelings for Reef. Three weeks had seemed like a long time, but it really wasn't, I got comfortable, but I knew I had no business being with this man and wanted to go back home.

Ebony was woken up by a nurse taking her blood pressure. "Where am I?"

The nurse looked at her and replied, "Ma'am, you are in the hospital. You came in last night. When you got here, you were very dehydrated. That's why we have the IV in your arm."

"Wow, I must've been really exhausted."

"Yes, it looked like you had been through a lot, so we let you sleep."

"Did anyone come here with me?"

"No, you came by yourself."

"Well ok, I'm just going to continue to rest. I still feel out of it. Can you please tell everyone to not bother me for a couple of hours?"

A couple of hours turned into the next morning. First thing I did was check for my phone, but it wasn't there. She wondered where it could have been. The pain in my ribs was so bad that I couldn't even sit up. As I kept trying to I felt some cramping and pushed the button for the nurse to come in.

"Nurse, I need some pain meds and I need help going to the bathroom."

"Ok, I'll get the meds first. Then, I'll help you to the bathroom."

After the nurse came back with the medication, she assisted Ebony out of bed and into the bathroom. Ebony noticed there was some pink spotting in her underwear, but didn't think anything of it. As she began to pee, she noticed that the toilet quickly filled up with blood. Then, she heard a plop as if something had fallen into the toilet.

"Nurse!! Nurse!!" she yelled out.

The nurse ran in and looked into the toilet. "Ma'am, is it possible that you may have been pregnant?"

"I don't think so...well, it could have been possible."

Immediately, the nurse helped her off the toilet and onto the bed. Then, she called the doctor.

"What's going on?" Ebony asked the nurse, but she informed her that the doctor would be in to speak with her shortly.

When the doctor came in, he explained to Ebony that she was about twelve weeks pregnant when she came in, but they didn't want to tell her right away because they didn't want to stress her out.

"I – I was? Are you sure? "

"Yes, and by the looks of things, you just had a miscarriage. I would like you to get some rest. If you need anything else, just press the call button."

It took her a minute to process what the doctor had just told her and what had just happened. Ebony just sat on the bed feeling numb and emotionless. She had just lost a baby and she had always wanted one. Even through her pain, all she could think about was Reef and wished he was there to comfort her. She wished he knew what she was going through right now even if he was the reason she was in the situation in the first place.

Unfortunately, what happened had happened and there was nothing she could do about it to make it go away. She didn't deserve this – not this of all things. She just put her head back and cried. She cried for all the things she had been through the past couple of years, cried for all the times Reef had put her in a hospital, and cried because she didn't have anyone to talk to about what was going on. She used to be this independent, happy, strong, and confident person. Then, she began to doubt herself and feel really guilty as if everything was her fault. Even though she didn't do anything wrong, she blamed herself.

She was just so used to this and he had her believing she was imagining things and that she made up stories in her head. When she first met him, he seemed like the perfect man. Although he never really got the full story of her upbringing, he understood her more than anything. He made her feel a way that she never felt with anyone else and that's what made her fall in love. Right now, she was one emotional wreck. She was all over the place and there was nothing she could do at this time because she was in a place where a man that she loved put her in.

She was crying so bad that she didn't hear the knock on the door, but when she heard the footsteps of boots, she looked up and was surprised. She felt a feeling of fear come over her, but she tried not to let it show.

What was he doing here? Was he here to really kill me this time?

Even though he did this to her, she still loved him and had to let him know what was going on. Oddly enough, she was relieved he had come to see her this time. He walked towards her and tried to give her a hug and kiss, but stopped when he saw that she had been crying.

"Baby, what's wrong? Are you ok?"

"I'm fine," Ebony replied as she wiped her tears.

If he only knew how much damage he had caused me, she thought in her head.

"I lost a fuckin baby today!" she blurted out.

"Baby, I didn't know you were pregnant?" he asked

"I can't believe this!!"

"I can't believe this either and I'm so upset right now!" he added.

Then, he reached in to give her a hug and she let him. It had been a long time since she felt his arms around her like that and feeling it felt sincere.

"How?" he questioned with a grin on his face.

Ebony looked up at him, "I think you know exactly what happened and I don't want to go there with you right now."

Just as she was starting to get upset, she heard another knock on the door. "Who is it?" she called out, peeking at the person on the other side.

When she seen who it was, her heart almost jumped out of her chest. *How the fuck did he know I was in the hospital? Did he know what had happened to me? Who told him that I was here?*

As he walked towards her, Reef turned around and dapped him up. "What's up, man?"

"What's up, my boy" he said and smiled.

What!?. They know each other, she thought. *I should just end my life right now.*

Ebony had no idea of what was going on. She didn't even know if she should say anything at all. Haneef walked up to her and gave her a forehead kiss. "You alright."

Tears came down Ebony's face and she just looked at Reef, who was looking dead at her. "I'm fine."

"Are you sure?"

Ebony shook her head.

Then, he handed her cell phone to her saying that she had left it at his house.. Reef stepped in when he heard that and asked, "What's up? You fuckin him?" He tried not to raise his voice.

"No! I love you, baby. You know that I would never cheat on you. You know I just want us to be happy and be together. This whole Summer thing has me very upset. It threw me by a big surprise and you really broke my heart. I just want to know the truth, that's all. This baby was supposed to be ours. This is what I wanted to complete our family and now look," she said as her eyes filled with tears.

Haneef just stood there looking confused. He had no idea she had been pregnant and even thought in his mind if it could be his. Then, he felt bad because if it wasn't his, he was fucking her while she was pregnant with another man's baby and that wasn't cool. Listening to the conversation, he turned around and started to walk away.

"Wait!" Ebony yelled after him.

"What the fuck you calling his name for?" Reef asked. "You see this man right here? I've known him for years and I set your stupid ass up. Now, Imma ask you again because I don't know why you are stopping him from leaving right now. ARE YOU FUCKING HIM?" he said while gritting his teeth.

Ebony just looked down and then looked up, making eye contact with Haneef. Then, she looked at Reef and she could see that he was really angry at this point.

"NO!"

Reef bent down and tried to whisper, but he was too upset and couldn't. "You're so smart, but stupid at the same time to believe anything that came out of this man's mouth. I wanted to see how far you would take this with him. I know all about everything." He stood straight up and Haneef faced them as they kept talking. "I know you. I know you all too well and

81

you have been fucking this man. I can look at you and tell. It's all in your body language. You ain't nothin' but a hoe and always will be one. That's why I put your ass in this hospital twice. You gonna learn not to fuck with me!!"

Haneef caught the last sentence and slowly started walking towards them. He had no idea Reef was the one who put her in the hospital – that was the part she failed to mention.

"Did you think I was gone for good? Did you think by you dealing with someone else I was going to go away? HELL NO! Bitch you're mine and you are not going anywhere. So, for that, I'll handle your ass when you get out of here. You see what I did to you already, and I can easily end your whole life."

Haneef walked up to Reef and said, "Yo man chill!"

At this point, he had heard everything being said and he didn't like it.

"I'm not even talking to you. This is between me and my lady," Reef said, stepping in his face. "Your job is done here. What the fuck you still doing here?"

"Cool, but you not going to be putting your hands on her while I'm around. I'm sure of that." Haneef replied as he stepped towards Reef

"I'll do whatever the fuck I want when I want and you ain't gonna do shit about it," he said as he pushed Haneef. "Fuck you thought?"

They both began to wrestle with each other and bump into the walls, making loud noises. Ebony had no choice but to push the call bell for help. They were already aware of the commotion going on and she didn't want to see anyone get hurt. Two security guards walked in and tried to break it up. They were so busy tussling and exchanging words that they didn't see them come into the room. Once the guards broke it up ,Reef yelled, " I'ma get you, bitch! You better believe it!" Then, he was escorted out of the room.

Haneef just looked up at me as if he were saying, "I'm here if you need me," with his eyes and he walked out of the room.

⌘

82

It had been a couple of months and Ebony still hadn't heard from Reef. *Maybe he forgot about me. Maybe he was using this time to stay away and cool down because he was really upset. Maybe his feelings really were hurt this time because he noticed I didn't sit around and be miserable waiting for him to come around. Maybe he went to get the help he needed so that we could make this work.* So many thoughts swarmed her mind. She had no clue, but she just wanted to make sure he was alright and missed him so much. She missed the way things used to be.

Never in a million years did she think things would ever get like this. She loved him for the person he was, and he wasn't always this abusive. She truly believed that they could get the help they needed together to make their relationship work and get married after all. Ebony thought she was crazy for feeling this way, but the love she felt for him was before all the incidents even started. Another thing Ebony knew deep down was that she would rather go through this than end up alone.

She didn't know how to feel about Haneef, and she didn't know if she should be upset with him or not.

Who in their right mind would be so cruel to play a game on somebody like that? Why would you want to play with someone's feelings and emotions? Who even knew if he would ever speak to me again, she thought to herself.

She liked him, he was cool, and his vibe was great. He was a gentleman and the perfect package with potential. She knew that if she was actually looking for someone else to be with, she would definitely choose him. The thought of starting over again and getting to know anyone all over again made her sick to her stomach. All she knew was that everything about him was just right, but when something seems so real, it's too good to be true. She did still feel as though she really didn't get a chance to really see what he was about though.

She had been staying in a hotel for the last couple of months just to be on the safe side. Her landlord had told her that she had to move out of her apartment because of the loud noise complaints. They complained about the yelling and said they had been disturbing everyone. The good thing was it was the beginning of the month, so she had a few weeks to find out what she was going to do.

In the meantime, she was still going to work every day. She needed to occupy her time and keep her mind off of those two men., but work became a task to her. Often times, she would black out and snap out of it when she noticed someone was trying to get her attention. She would almost jump out of her skin when she came back to her senses.

She had trouble concentrating on things and people began to notice and question if she was ok. No one knew what she had been through or what she was dealing with. Her boss even offered her some time-off and she thought that was the best thing for her right now just to get herself back together.

TEN

Out of nowhere, Ebony's phone began ringing, but when she would answer, the person on the other end would hang up. She had a feeling of who it was because no one really called her other than one person.

"Reef, I know it's you! Why don't you come home so we can talk? Babe, I really love you and miss you a lot."

Sometimes he would listen and hang up as soon as he heard her finish a sentence. She knew it was him. She just didn't know why he wasn't saying anything because this wasn't like him at all. He started to call more and more each day, but one time the person on the other end said, "This isn't over. I'm going to kill you!"

It was very clear to her that he didn't let this situation go so easily. She really didn't know why he was so upset when he had a side chick and a baby to think about. He was the one who made this situation go the way it did, but he was mad at her.

Then, he began to harass her over the phone and it started to make her feel uncomfortable with his threats. She paid them no mind because she didn't think he would ever in his life try and kill her – not the person that says he loves her so much. She talked to him and told him that she didn't like what he was saying and that she would like him to stop if he wanted them to be together again.

He did just that, and they were able to have great conversations and it felt like it did when they first met all over again. He told her that he loved her so much and that he was happy she never left his side. He also apologized for everything he had done to her and said he didn't mean to do any of it. Surprisingly, he said that he was away because he was currently in a program getting the help he needed in order for them to move forward.

If he was really getting help, Ebony was so happy because this was a huge step for him. However, he would still have his moments when he still said little slick things, but she didn't take whatever he said seriously. She knew he only wanted to make her scared. He would tell her that no one would ever want her because of what she had been through and that he was the only one for her. She began to believe that for some reason. Whenever she would go out, she would feel as though people were staring at her and it made her very nervous. So, she knew she needed to talk to someone before she fell all the way apart. She just didn't know who.

Some days when they would talk, he would be calm and other days he would seem angry. Ebony thought that it was just part of a stage that he was going through because he still called her all times of the night just to make sure he told her he loved her with all his heart. Despite everything they had gone through, Ebony wanted and needed him right now. No matter how scared she was, she just wanted to feel his touch again. She didn't know exactly what this program would do to him and if it would even make him a better person, but she was ready to see the work he had done for herself.

For a couple of weeks, the phone calls stopped and she hadn't heard anything from him. Then, all of a sudden, he started popping up in different places. It shocked the shit out of her because he hadn't told her he was finished with his program–but secretly, Ebony liked it. When she would see him, he would have an evil look on his face, and it made her freeze as if she had seen a ghost. She would only see him twice out of the week the most, but he never said anything to her. He would just blow kisses and smile. She didn't take his stalking seriously because he had not physically touched her or harmed her in any way. So, she just decided to wait until he was ready to talk.

One day, she was coming out of the store, and someone crept up behind her and put their hands around her eyes. It shocked the hell out of her and she damn near dropped her bags and had a heart attack. When she turned around, she realized it was Reef. He grabbed her and gave her the biggest kiss and hug. She felt tingling all over her body because she truly missed him.

They ended up going out to grab something to eat, and they talked for hours about a lot of different things. She told him about the eviction, and he got extremely upset. He wanted to go beat up the landlord, but she told him it wasn't a need for that. She let him know that she wasn't sure what she was going to do, but she needed to find something quickly because time was moving really fast. He apologized so much and said things had gotten out of control. He wanted her to understand that he was just really mad and took it out on her instead of dealing with it. He told her that his plans were for them to start fresh anyway. Then, he informed her that he had an apartment already set up for them, but was waiting on the right moment to tell her.

She had absolutely no idea he was doing all of this for her – for them. Then, she couldn't help but think to herself, *Summer must have got this apartment for him. Knowing Reef, she probably stayed there, too. Was this some type of hideout spot?* She didn't want to upset him by asking questions so she just kept her mouth shut.

"I will move in with you baby, but you know I want to buy a house, get married, and have children."

He smiled. " I see that is never going to change with you."

Within three weeks, he called and told her that the apartment was ready for them to move in. She thought it was awfully fast, and then her mind started wandering. What if he kicked Summer out and was now moving me in? What if this was some type of trap that I would regret? Do I try and run? I'm sure if I did, he would find me. Even if I did try and run, where would I go when I didn't talk to anybody? Although I was happy, in the back of my mind, I was still a bit unsure of all of this and if I should really believe that he had changed for the better.

Ebony was still going to work and staying at the hotel because she had this strong feeling that she might be making the wrong choice. She would just go to the old apartment, grab little things, and give them to Reef to take to the new apartment. She kept the other things in storage. She had been doing this because, God forbid, if anything happened between her and Reef, she needed to make sure she was good.

Things quickly started to become stressful at work, and she was no longer able to function. She didn't know what was happening to her or her body, but it was affecting everything. She kept having these horrible flashbacks, and she didn't know what was going on. Her boss tried to get through to her, and her

87

coworkers would pull her to the side and try to talk to her. Nothing was working. She didn't open up to anyone, and her body was beginning to shut down. She started feeling depressed all over again.

Unable to complete her job, she was eventually let go. This hurt her so much because she really felt stuck. It was as if she was happy Reef was back in her life, but something was off about her all of a sudden. She wanted to talk to Reef, but she knew he would say that was just her making up things, so she just kept to herself. Eventually, she couldn't afford the hotel anymore, so she decided to move in with Reef.

The apartment was so nice because it was almost like the one they had together, but it felt a lot more homier. She loved it. Of course, they broke it in on the same night, and it was just so magical. She felt like Reef really took his time with her and made it all about her. Things were starting to look as if they were returning to normal again, but she still felt depressed. Even though she felt this on the inside, she tried not to let it show on the outside.

One day, she decided to grab a few more things out of the old apartment. When she just so happened to peek out the window, Reef was standing there looking directly at her. She got so scared that she closed the curtain with the quickness. When she went to open it again, he was gone.

Is my mind playing tricks on me now? What the fuck! Is he really back to following me again? This is the last thing I need right now, she thought to herself. She didn't know what to think, but she knew she needed to be aware of her surroundings more often. She grabbed everything she needed and rushed to her car. When she got halfway down the street, she noticed that she left her purse, so she had to go back.

When she got back to the house, she noticed the door was slightly open.

"Fuck! Did I close it all the way?" she murmured to herself.

She really couldn't remember what she had done. She just wanted to hurry up and get out of there. She ended up finding her purse in the bedroom, grabbed it, ran down the stairs, and headed straight to the car.

When she finally made it home, Reef was sitting on the couch waiting for her.

"Where are you coming from?" he questioned.

Not wanting him to get mad, Ebony replied, "I had to go back to the old apartment and pick up some things."

She made sure not to bring up the fact that she seen him standing outside the window because she didn't want to stir up trouble.

Then, Reef replied, "You think I didn't see you earlier? You've been moving stuff for the past week."

She just looked at him with a puzzled stare. "Babe, what do you mean? The things I left have to be out by a certain time, and I was making sure I got them out."]

"So, what did you do with the rest of the furniture and all the other things?" he asked.

"I sold them because I didn't have anywhere to put them, and I didn't know what was going to happen with us."

He looked at her with a smirk and just let the conversation go. In her head, she was happy that she was able to think on her feet because he looked like he was about to go off.

"Now, get over here and give me some head!" he said with a serious face.

Ebony laughed because that was different of him. He never just asked so, it kind of turned her on. She made her way over to him dancing and biting her lip. He looked at her while biting his bottom lip. She grabbed his face and gave him a kiss making sure to put her tongue in his mouth and ended it with sucking his bottom lip. Then, she lifted up his shirt and kissed his chest as she worked her way down to his pants. Unbuckling his belt, she could tell he was ready so she pulled his dick through his boxers and started teasing it with her tongue.

When she looked up at him, his head was tilted back with his eyes closed. Then, she stopped to tease him.

"What the fuck you doing?" he asked in between his heavy breathing.

She smiled, opened her mouth, and put his dick as far down her throat as she could. When she started gagging, she came back up to the top.

"Shit!" he moaned.

She did it again, but this time she went slower and grabbed his balls at the same time. She made sure it was nice and wet so she could suck it like it was a juicy lollipop. When she felt he was about to cum, she pulled her pants down and hopped right on top of him.

"Baby, wait for me." She whispered into his ear.

Here she was, straddled on top of him and his hands grasping her ass. She bounced up and down. Within five minutes, she came and could feel herself dripping all over him. She could also tell he was into it and loving it because he began to nibble on her ear. Faster and faster, she went as he whispered to her. "Baby, I'm about to cum," and he did.

They did it together.

After, she just lay on top of his chest until they caught their breath. Looking into his eyes, she gave him a long kiss and told him that she loved him. Of course, he said it back. Then they jumped up so that they could shower together. In the shower, they couldn't keep their hands off of each other. Once they got out, they finished in the bedroom. Reef's phone kept ringing the whole time so, Ebony decided to try to pick it up.

He lunged towards her, grabbed the phone, and hurried to answer it. "Hello? Ok. I'll be there in a few."

When he hung up, she questioned who he was actually talking to and where he needed to go.

"Babe, I have to handle something really quick," he said. "I'll be back as soon as possible."

Then he put on his clothes and quickly ran out the door. She couldn't help but wonder what he was up to and where he was going, but she just lay down and eventually fell asleep. She woke up to the sound of Reef yelling at her a few hours later.

"Who the fuck you been talking to bitch!?"

"What are you talking about?" she said, jumping up from the bed.

Apparently, he had picked up her phone and seen she had three missed calls. There was no name stored, so she had no idea who was calling her

"Call the number back right now and see who the fuck it is!" he demanded angrily.

Ebony did exactly what she was told because she had nothing to hide. No one answered the first time and he demanded she call again. This time, a male voice picked up the phone and replied, "Hey, I was calling to see if you were alright."

Fuck! It was Haneef. She could recognize his voice anywhere.

"Who the fuck is it?" Reef yelled in the background.

"I – I don't know. They said they had the wrong number and I just hung up the phone."

The number called right back as soon as I hung up, but she didn't answer.

"Bitch, you playing games with me again? You out here creeping?"

"No! What the fuck you talking about?" Ebony yelled. This time, she had enough of his insecure, jealous ass accusing her of things she didn't do. "I haven't been doing anything and you know it, so don't start this shit. You said you changed and it looks like to me you haven't."

"Who the fuck you talking to?" he said as he walked towards her to get in her face. "Bitch, don't you know I will literally fuck you up if you get smart with me one more time."

"I'm just saying, you're not going to try and say I did something when I was asleep this whole time."

This time, his phone started to ring. When she went to reach for it, he tried to snatch it from her, but she had a grip on it. The name that popped up on the phone was none other than Summer.

"What the fuck is she doing calling you at this time of night Reef? Here we go again with the bullshit! You know what, I knew you were lying. I knew you didn't change and I'm out of this bitch!"

He grabbed her, picked her up, and threw her against the wall. Then, he started to punch and kick her in her face.

"Stop!! Stop!!" she screamed, but he didn't.

Then, he picked her up, put his arm around her neck, and dragged her into the bathroom to the mirror. "Look what you made me do. I don't like hurting you, but you make me mad sometimes and I just can't help it. We could've been together, but you want to be a dumb bitch. You deserve everything that happened to you for cheating on me. You thought this was over? You thought I forgot about that?"

Ebony really couldn't say much because he had a tight grip around her neck and she didn't want him to do anything stupid. Then, he pulled both of them into the tub and she heard a click. She couldn't believe that he really pulled out a gun.

"OMG!!" she screamed. "You don't have to do this."

"Bitch," he yelled. "You fucked up any future we had together, so I'm going to kill both of us right now in this fucking house."

She tried to turn around, but she couldn't.

BOOM!!

The grip around her neck loosened and she turned around and screamed. She got up so fast and was in complete disbelief. She didn't know if she had been shot or if Reef shot himself, but her instincts told her to run, grab her phone, and call 9-1-1. She was shaking so much because she was scared and she didn't want things to end like this. Reef was her everything and all she had was him. *He can't die. Not this way*, she thought to herself. The operator told her that the ambulance was on the way.

When she went back into the bathroom, she seen that his eyes were still open, but he wasn't gone because she could see his chest rising. She just kneeled beside the tub and held his hand. He kept squeezing her hand to let her know he was still with her. Ebony was so scared that all she could do was pray and pray that everything would be alright.

After about fifteen minutes, the ambulance came and took both of them to the hospital, but they were put in separate rooms. Ebony couldn't sit still not knowing anything about him. She had to know if he was still alive. She just couldn't lose him – not like this. She needed answers and she kept demanding somebody tell her something.

"Please, please, you don't understand. I need to make sure he is alive!"

"Ma'am, calm down. Calm down!! You need to relax and take some deep breaths. We don't want you to overwork yourself."

Eventually, Ebony did calm down and she was able to lay back on the bed so they could bandage her up. She was really bruised up this time. She had three broken ribs and a huge bandage on her eye. The doctor actually told her she was really lucky that she was able to see out of it due to the damage Reef caused. *Wow!! He really got me good this time*, she thought to herself.

As she started to drift off to sleep, she heard a knock at the door, She thought she was dreaming until she heard it again. "Come in."

OH FUCK, Ebony thought to herself, *this is just what I need right now. What the hell do they want?*

"Ma'am, my name is Detective Johnson, and I would like to ask you some questions – if that's ok with you?"

"Sure, you can, but what is this in regard to?" she asked as she looked at the detective and raised her eyebrows.

"Well first, I would like to know how you know Shareef Smith?"

"Well, he's my boyfriend and we've been together for about six years. Is he ok? Is he alive?" she asked, panicking all over again.

"Calm down, ma'am. He's fine and he's alive. In fact, as soon as he recovers, he will be going to jail."

Ebony looked at him, teary-eyed, and asked, "Why?"

"We've gotten several calls about domestic abuse that's been going on for some time now, and the young lady would like to press charges against Mr. Smith."

"A young lady? Who the fuck could that be because it sure wasn't me."

"There was also some information given to us that he may be doing the same thing to you, and that's another reason we were here asking questions. Clearly, we can see you didn't do this to yourself, and this was no accident."

Ebony just laughed and replied, "You have no idea what's going on here. I am absolutely fine. We just had a little misunderstanding and that was all."

"So, the question here that we want to know is, how did Mr. Smith end up with a bullet in his head? Could you tell me? Were you the one who shot him? You do know that if you are found guilty of anything, you will be going to jail."

Ebony just looked at him like he was crazy and laughed. "I would never do that to my boyfriend. There's no reason for me to want to kill him. I love this man with all my heart and I don't think you really understand. Now, if you're done questioning me, you can leave, Detective Johnson."

"Ok, if you don't want to give me any information, I will gladly leave. Just remember what I told you," he said as he walked away. "In fact, take my card in case you need to call me for anything." Then, he walked out the door.

Ebony felt as if the detective was messing with her. She didn't know of anyone who would give any information to the police at all. She never knew of Reef doing anything like this to anyone else, not even when they first met. *This detective was just doing his job and trying to use his reverse psychology. There was no way I wanted my man to be locked up. I just want to be with my man,* Ebony thought to herself.

She felt like she had to talk to him because this was getting way out of control. She had to make sure he was okay and she was determined to do just that. It was very hard for her to get up because her ribs hurt so bad, but she managed to maneuver her way out of the bed and into the hallway. She looked to the left and saw no one. Then, she looked to the right. At the end of the hallway, she saw what appeared to be a cop sitting outside the door. She walked up to the cop and asked, "Is this Mr. Smith's room"

"Yes, ma'am."

"I would like to see him, if that's ok. I'm his girlfriend and I need to see him."

"Sure," the cop replied and opened the door for me.

As she walked into the room, she saw someone standing at his bedside, but she didn't pay the person attention because she was focused on Reef. He didn't look up at all when she walked in. He was just lying there with his eyes closed. I couldn't believe who it was.

It was that bitch Summer. She became furious very fast, but she continued to walk up to the bed. When she heard Ebony's footsteps, she turned around and looked like she had just seen a ghost.

"Are you ok?" she asked, looking very worried.

Ebony just looked at her, frowned, and rolled her eyes. "What the fuck does it look like, bitch?

She stood at the bed and stared at Reef. Surprisingly, he didn't look as bad as she thought he would, but he was bruised up. She to grabbed his hand to let him know she was there, and just stared at him. "Whatever I did to get you upset, it won't happen again, baby."

"OH PLEASE!!" Summer mumbled under her breath.

Ebony paid her no mind and continued. "I don't know what triggered it, but don't ever put us in this situation ever again. Reef, I hate to say it, but you really need to go get some help because I can't live like this. I will be there to help you every step of the way. I promise." Then, she leaned in, kissed him, and he kissed her back."

"I will do whatever it takes to make things right. I don't know what's going on, but I've been tripping out a lot lately and that's not me."

"I'm just glad you're ok," Ebony replied. "I was worried about you and I couldn't sleep or think all night."

"I'm ok, babe," he whispered. "I just never meant to really hurt you like this. I mean, look at you. I'm honestly truly sorry!"

Summer chuckled.

'Bitch, you shouldn't even be in this room. This is my man and WE are having a conversation if you can't tell."

"Y'all talking about some bullshit!" Summer yelled. "How do you still want to be with this man and he's hospitalized you several times? When the fuck you going to learn, honey. This isn't love!" she laughed.

"You know what, mind your fucking business. You wouldn't even know what love is. No one wants your ugly ass."

Then, Ebony and Summer started to yell back and forth. It got pretty loud and they ended up being in each other's face. The cop walked in and asked if things were ok, and we nodded.

Reef then told us that we needed to calm down.

"Calm down?" Ebony screamed. "If your stupid ass would've never messed with her, we wouldn't even be arguing right now! You put me through a lot and I sat here and took every obstacle thrown my way. I did nothing, but stand by your side and love you more than I loved myself. You tore me down. Tore me to pieces and you know how much I love you and would do anything for you. You mean the world to me, and I want us to have a future, but how could we like this?"

"Babe, just calm down!" Ebony started crying. "We're good now, trust me," he said as he tried to sit up.

Ebony stormed out of the room because she didn't want to talk to him anymore, yet alone be in the room with him and his bitch. Her head was spinning and she started to feel extremely dizzy. She really wanted him to feel every hit and every bruise he ever caused her. She started to hate him right now for having to deal with Summer. This was all his fault. She felt like Summer ruined their lives and was in the way of their happiness.

As she walked down the hall, she realized her vision was starting to get blurry, and she collapsed outside of her room. The cop noticed Ebony had collapsed and yelled for help. She woke up questioning what had happened to her. The nurse replied, "Oh honey, don't get up just yet. Just relax. You fainted in the hallway and right now you need as much rest as you can. You seem like you have been through a lot and right now is not the time for you to stress. Your body is very weak and needs fluids, so just stay calm. Please sleep, clear your mind, and we'll talk in the morning!"

The nurse tucked her back into bed, and Ebony took the nurses advice. She tried to relax and get some sleep. All night long, she tossed and turned because of the nightmares she was having of her past. She broke out into several cold sweats before she gave up because she just couldn't sleep anymore. She decided to turn over and stare out of the window. That allowed her mind to wander even more, so she just turned on the television.

Of course, there was nothing on at this time of night, so she ended up dozing off. What felt like the best sleep was interrupted by the tech coming in to take her vitals. She also mentioned that she had good news that I would be leaving in two days.

Oh great, Ebony thought, but the nurse could tell by the look on her face that she wasn't happy at all.

"What's the matter sugar?"

"Oh nothing, ma'am," Ebony replied as she put her head down.

"You sure? Most people would be happy when I tell them they are going home, but you seem disappointed."

"Well, me and my boyfriend had an argument, and if I get discharged, I would like him to be home with me, that's all."

"Oh, I see. Well, maybe he is already at home waiting for you. You never know!" she said, trying to cheer her up.

"I hope so!" Ebony replied with a fake smile.

That was almost the best news she had heard and she was ready to get the hell out of the hospital. As the nurse began to head out of the room, Ebony had to ask if Reef was still in his room.

"Honey, I can't release information about another patient but I can tell you that he is not in his room anymore."

97

Ebony put her head down. *Why hasn't he called me to tell me anything? I can't believe he just left like that,* Ebony thought to herself.

She started to feel depressed all over again, but she remembered she was leaving soon and that was the best thing she heard since this hospital stay.

Ebony grabbed her phone because she needed a ride and she needed to set up some type of living arrangements. She had the keys to the apartment that she and Reef shared, but she didn't want to stay there if Reef wasn't there with her. All she really wanted to do was grab some clothes for a couple of days, take a hot shower, and sleep all day long. She didn't feel like talking or seeing anyone right now. The first thing she decided to do was call Reef's phone, but he didn't answer.

Where the fuck is he? I hope he is not with that bitch, Ebony thought to herself. She checked her voicemails to see if he left anything, but there was nothing. She only had a message from Sheree telling her to call her back ASAP. There were also some text messages and missed calls from Haneef asking if she was alright and that he wanted to talk to her.

What the fuck could he possibly want to talk about? What could he possibly say to me to make up for anything he did to me? Why were they just both calling me out of the blue like that? That's weird, Ebony thought to herself.

In desperate need, Ebony decided to call Sheree back and she picked up on the second ring.

"Hey girl! What's up with you?"

Ebony thought before she actually responded. "Oh nothing, I'm just getting ready to be discharged from the hospital in a couple of days. I was in a really bad car accident the other week, but I'm ok. Just thank god I'm still alive. You know it could've been worse."

"OMG!! Why didn't you call me? I told you don't you ever be a stranger to me. Remember, we are sisters! We can talk about anything and I'm dead serious."

Ebony took a deep breath and just started crying. Sheree didn't understand what she was crying for, but she didn't want to pressure her about anything.

"I just can't talk about it right now. I will talk to you later when I get settled" Ebony replied and hung up.

Sheree was very concerned for her friend by the way she sounded and wished there was something she could do to help, but she decided to wait until she called her back.

For a minute, Ebony sat there and cried. She didn't know how her life ended up in shambles.

"How could I ever live a normal life after all of this?" Ebony whispered to herself.

She looked at her phone and decided to text Haneef. She explained that she needed his help and she needed somewhere to stay. She knew that he would help her because she could tell he was concerned about her. Just as she thought, he agreed to help her without hesitation.

On discharge day, he picked her up from the hospital and put her up in a hotel. He told her that he had paid for two weeks in advance until she could figure out what she was going to do. If she needed more time, he told her to reach out to him asap.

"What is going on?"

Ebony looked down at the floor and looked back at him. "What do you mean?"

" I think you know exactly what I'm talking about and I'm sorry you are going through what you're going through."

Ebony tried not to say anything. "This was the first time something like this happened."

Haneef looked at her as if he wasn't believing a word she said. "I just did something that he didn't like and he overreacted. Honestly, it's nothing. I'm sure we'll be back together once we get another apartment."

He looked at her like she was crazy – maybe she was. "I think you really need to leave my boy alone. From the outside looking in, you better be careful before he ends up killing you. This is not healthy at all and I think you deserve better. I also

99

wanted to apologize for the set-up, but I thought about it and I really did fall in love with you over some time. Come with me. Let me show you how love is supposed to be. Babe, listen to me. I don't want anything to happen to you!" he said as he leaned in to give Ebony a kiss on her forehead.

She slipped up, lifted her head, and kissed him on the mouth. They shared the most passionate and intimate kiss like Ebony never had before.

"I wouldn't be able to live with myself if I sat here and let you go back knowing I could have done something to save you."

"Trust me, I'm fine."

"I – " she stopped him before he could say anything else.

"Thank you for your help and thank you for everything. If I need anything, I will make sure you are the first person I call, but I really need to get some rest, right now."

"Would you like me to stay with you just until you fall asleep?"

"Sure, that would be very nice."

He went into the bathroom to run her a warm bath and she turned her phone off for the night. She got undressed and hopped right into the tub.

He came in, smiled, and asked, "Do you need some help?"

She laughed and replied, "Ok."

The minute he went to go wash her with the washcloth, she caught a flashback and almost jumped out the water.

"Babe, you ok? It's just me! I'm not going to do anything to hurt you. Just relax."

"I'm sorry. My nerves are really bad. I haven't been myself lately."

Ebony couldn't help it and burst into tears. She could tell by the look in his eyes that he felt so bad.

ELEVEN

"Miss, what happened? Did someone break into your home?"

Summer said nothing and just closed her eyes as they were putting her on the stretcher. She could hear her baby crying. She was still out of it, but managed to open her eyes and ask to see her child.

"Ma'am, you know we are not allowed to do that, and you know we have to take the baby until we find out what's going on here. It seems as though this isn't a safe environment for any child to be in."

The past couple of weeks, the cops had been getting calls to her address, and nothing would happen. They always thought it was a false alarm because they didn't "see anything" whenever they got to her apartment. She thought she had seen someone standing outside her home, and she thought someone was trying to break in. She was just extremely terrified.

She began to cry hysterically as she watched them take her baby away. She knew she would be able to really get the help she needed because the cops actually believed her this time, but she needed her baby. They searched her apartment fully, told her they would be in contact with her, and let her know it was best that she go stay somewhere else. What she couldn't understand is why it took so long for them to act on the situation when she had already called several times, made so many complaints, and filed a safety notice. He completely violated it and Summer knew she was going to pay for what he did to her.

Finally!

"It was him!" She yelled out. "He did this to me! The guy I've been complaining about for the past couple of weeks. Please find him and lock him up forever. He has to be taken away. I fear for my life and my child's life. I just want my daughter back." She said as she cried hysterically.

"We understand and we are going to make sure we get him," the cop replied, trying to reassure her that things were under control.

"Please, officer, you have to. I'm really scared that he will come after me and kill me."

Summer kept thinking about them catching Reef because she never thought she would ever end up like this! He had never put his hands on her before because he would just yell and threaten her. Half of the time, she never took him seriously because they were not in any committed relationship and he showed her plenty of times he was never going to leave that bitch Ebony. When she finally realized that, she told him that she was going to leave him and that she wasn't going to be competing with someone. She also told him that he could see his daughter anytime, but that didn't sit too well with him. He went crazy. Now, look what happened.

⌘

Ebony woke up feeling refreshed and noticed Haneef had left. She rolled over and stared at the ceiling. When she rolled over again, she found a note and a credit card. The note said:

Hey babe,

> **I hope you had a great sleep. I didn't want to wake you up so I tucked you in quietly. Please**

**call me when you get up to let me know you're
ok and here's my card in case you get hungry!
Help yourself.**

I love you!

Wow, she thought. She was so confused and didn't
know what to think. *This man is just so nice and sweet to me,* she
thought to herself. She reached for her phone to turn it on and
she had so many missed calls. She immediately called Haneef to
thank him again and let him know she was fine. Of course, he
asked if he could stop by when he got off. As much as she
wanted to see him too , she knew that needed to rest, so she told
him to come by the following day. He was ok with her decision
and told her to call him later.

She checked her messages after hanging up and listened
to a message where the person on the other end mumbled, "Be
careful, bitch?

This particular message sent chills through her body for
some reason. Something told her to get up and look out the
window. Luckily, this time, no one was standing there looking
back at her. After all that had happen, she was a little shaken up
and she was constantly scared because she felt as if something
was going to happen to her.

⌘

Overwhelmed in her thoughts, Summer climbed back
into bed, put the covers over her head, and hoped she would fall
back asleep. No matter what she did, she just couldn't.. Instead,
she sat up in bed and wondered what she did to deserve
everything she was going through. She saw many signs of anger,
but never thought he would put his hands on her.

Now she was alone. The man she once wanted a family
with disrespected her and she missed her daughter so much that
it hurt. The thought that she couldn't be with her was killing
her. It literally felt like her heart had been ripped out of her
chest. She had never been away from her since the day she had
been born.

The more and more she sat in the hospital, the more and
more she became panicked by everyone's movement and every

103

sound of footsteps. There was no way she would be able to get any sleep. She didn't feel safe at all! She was so fidgety that she couldn't even lay still in her bed. Eventually, she got up and started to pace back and forth in her room.

She had been in the hospital for four days, but she was starting to feel much better. Plus, they were able to give her some meds to calm her down and the medicine helped her get some sleep, finally. Just as she was going to make some calls to get any updates on the situation with her baby, two officers came into the room.

"We need to ask you some questions."

"Questions? What kind of questions would you like to ask me?"

The first officer looked at her and replied, "We had some complaints that were made a couple weeks ago, but when our officers came out, we didn't find anything."

"Okay...but he was there. He was stalking me and he told me he was going to hurt me. You have to believe me. I'm not crazy! You see what happened to me this time right! What do you think? I did to myself?" she questioned.

"Ma'am, just calm down and tell us, word for word, what happened that day."

Summer began to explain the story and one officer told her to slow down. "Ok sir! I'm sorry. I just want to get this over with so I can get out of here and get back to my normal life."

"We understand, ma'am, but we need to make sure we get the story correctly and get all the details."

Summer started again and spoke in a steady pace. " Well, he called me in the morning and said he wanted to come see his daughter. I said ok and that I would be home around one o'clock because I was running some errands. He didn't like that and thought I was out doing something else. He got mad and hung up. Mind you, this is just my baby father so I don't owe him anything or access to me. He got there around two o'clock and began to pick another argument with me when I told him I was going to move. I told him I wasn't taking his daughter away, but I needed to start my life over again. He didn't like that either. What he did next, shocked the hell out of me because our daughter was in the next room sleeping."

"So, ma'am, it's clear what happened next. There's no need for you to explain, but what we want to know and make sure that you really want to press charges against Mr. Smith."

"Absolutely! I know he will come after me again and I can't have that!"

"Well, we also wanted to let you know that we have him in custody right now. He will be held in the cell unit until it's time for his court date. so, you don't have anything to worry about. We just needed your statement so that we could make sure this is what you wanted to do."

"Officer, before you go, there's something else I need to tell you that I think will be helpful with this case as well. There's someone else I would like to call as a witness. It's his girlfriend. You see, not too long ago, he put her in the hospital as well, and I witnessed the whole thing. I know she will testify against him if she knows what's right for her."

Then, Summer gave up Ebony's name and address. The cops said they would look into the situation.

"If there is nothing else you need to say, I think we've got enough and we will be going now. Keep an eye out for the notice in the mail about the court date and have a good day."

The two cops walked out of the room. Summer was so happy that Reef was off the streets, but she knew this was far from over. Maybe, just maybe, she would get the justice she needed with the help of Ebony. She wanted to call her and let her know what was going but she decided not to because she knew there was a chance that they would argue. So, she decided to lay back in the bed and eventually fell asleep.

A few days later, Summer was finally discharged out of the hospital and immediately placed in a domestic violence shelter. The thought of living there upset her so much. For one, she had no idea what she would be walking into and she didn't like the thought of having to actually stay there. This wasn't her type of lifestyle at all and she just didn't want to be there.

Looking at these women, they were really traumatized compared to her. Some of these women looked like they had been through some serious shit. They were all covered up and walking around looking like zombies. Some of them were very antisocial and wouldn't even look you in the eyes when you spoke. Most of them stayed in bed all day, depressed.

After this case was over, she wanted to move out of town where no one would be able to find her. She wanted to live a normal life with her daughter, and that was it.

⌘

The next day came so fast that Ebony didn't realize she had slept so long. She picked up her phone and there were no messages or missed calls. So, she decided to text Haneef and let him know that she had just woken up and was going to get something to eat. He replied that he would come by to see her later on, but he was a little busy at that moment. Ebony assured him that it was fine and that she would be looking forward to seeing him later.

After she showered and got dressed, she decided to take a Lyft to the old house to see if she had any mail. She was also going to grab something to eat and go right back to the hotel. She used Haneef's card to book the Lyft and when they arrived, she sent Haneef a text letting him know where she would be.

> **Hey Baby.**
> **I am going to my old apartment to grab a few things and get something to eat. My old address is 255 Richards St NW just in case you need it.**
> **Looking forward to seeing you later!**

For some reason, she was hesitant doing this because she didn't like the feeling of having to let someone know her whereabouts, but she knew Haneef was different. So, she took this time in the Lyft to lay back and just relax.

It took her about an hour to get there. When she pulled up to the apartment, she sunk down into the backseat and her heart started beating fast.

"You can do this!" she whispered to herself as she looked up at the apartment door.

As she got closer to the door, she could see that there were no curtains or anything up. "What the hell is going on?" she said out loud.

Before the driver could pull off, she noticed a familiar face.

"What the fuck you doing here?"

The girl looked up and was shocked to see her. "I....I was looking for you," she replied.

Ebony found that strange because she never told her where she lived, ever . "What?" she questioned. "You didn't call me and let me know you were coming. How the fuck you know where I live anyway?

"I was looking for you. Since you aren't happy to see me, I guess I'll be leaving. She tried to walk away, but Ebony grabbed her arm. Of course, she pulled away from her.

"Wait! How the fuck did you get inside?" She turned around and began to walk away. "Bitch!! Bitch!! I know you hear me talking to you right? "

"Who the fuck you calling a bitch? You better watch your mouth."

"What the fuck you mean by that ? I'm good!!"

"Yeah, ok! That's what you think!" she said before she got in her car and drove off.

Ebony was pissed and she wanted to know what the fuck this bitch was doing at her old place. She hopped right back into the Lyft and went straight to the hotel. On the way, she texted Haneef to meet her there and bring some food because she wasn't able to. She also let him know that she needed to talk to him, immediately.

When she arrived back at the hotel, she sat on the bed, and started to look through the mail she grabbed at her old place. One piece stood out to her the most because it had her name on it and it was from the Atlanta Court House.

"What the fuck is this? she whispered as she opened up the envelope. "No way!! Who the fuck!!??? she yelled.

It was a subpoena for her to show up in court for Shareef Smith. Before she could fully process what she was reading, Haneef pulled up to the hotel with the food and knocked on the door. She peeked through the peephole to make sure it was him. When she confirmed it was him, she flung the door open and gave him a hug. He didn't even get a chance to put the food down because she was already all over him . He just smiled and kissed her on the forehead. Just as she was about to show him the letter, her phone rang with a number she didn't recognize. They both looked at each other.

"Answer it, baby."

" You have a prepaid call from an inmate at Georgia State Prison..."

Her entire facial expression changed, but she accepted the call. "Reef....OMG... are you ok? "

"Where the fuck you at?"

"Well, I've been staying at a shelter because you left me with nowhere to go. Reef ,why the fuck didn't you tell me what was going on with you?"

"Babe, just listen. Some shit happened that wasn't supposed to happen and now I have to see what's going on."

"What do you mean some shit happened – other than the fact that you're locked up and you could have told me that I wasn't going to have a place to stay? Is it something more important than that," she asked sarcastically. "Tell me what the fuck could be more important than that. I'm listening."

"I can't talk right now. It's not the time nor place, but I need you to come see me. I would be able to explain it more in person."

"I will fuckin think about it being as though you had no problem leaving me stranded."

"Just come see me like I said!" he demanded. "You better not be fucking with nobody or you know what will happen!" He hung up.

Ebony blacked out as soon as she hung up the phone and dropped to the floor. Those words just didn't sound right to her and brought back so many memories. Just hearing his voice say those things scared the fuck out of her Haneef didn't know what happened. Ebony snapped back to reality because he actually started to shake her.

"That was Reef. He's locked up, but he said he couldn't really talk about why. He also wants me to come see him."

"Well, what you gonna do?" Haneef asked, looking worried. "I don't think it's a good idea at all. You don't know what he may have under his sleeve, and I don't want anything to happen to you."

Ebony went into deep thought, and before she knew it, she blurted out, "But why the fuck do you care what happens?"

Haneef looked and mouthed, "Really?"

"I'm sorry. It's just weird to me how, all of a sudden, you're here and helping me when you were just in some type of plan with my boyfriend. How do I know this isn't another plan to kill me? How do I know you aren't going to kidnap me and torture me?" Ebony started to panic and began to cry. "HOW DO I KNOW!?

He put his hand out and motioned for her to come and take a seat next to him.

"Babe, please just calm down and come sit next to me."

She grabbed his hand, sat on his lap, and hugged him tightly. She cried and cried. Then, she began to tell him everything, especially how broken she was inside.

"The hitting and the verbal abuse had been going on for years. When I first met him, he was the perfect man. He was the only one who really knew everything about me, and he understood me so well. I just fell in love. No one had ever loved me or cared for me in that way. He would do nice things for me and spoil me so much. My feelings kept growing and growing. I felt this was true love. I felt we belonged together, and nobody could tell me differently. He made me feel a way that I had never felt before. He also comforted me like no one ever had. That was the reason why I loved him so much. When the abuse started, I didn't think anything of it at first, but then it became physical. The more and more I questioned, it just didn't make sense to me. I felt like I was safer in the relationship than out."

"Wooow!!" Haneef replied.

He didn't realize she had been through all of this, but he couldn't help but think how she could just sit there and let this happen. He admired her so much in such a short time. She was too pretty to take this type of abuse from any man and if he could do anything to change it he was going to make it happen.

"I never knew he was like that, honestly! I wish I would have found you first and things would've been so much better for you. I would've given you the world." he squeezed her tight and kissed her.

She kissed him back so passionately. There were actually some tingles she felt and she just had to have him in that moment. She put everything behind her for a moment and just let things happen. His touch was so soft and when he kissed her body, his lips were the softest she had ever felt. She couldn't handle it. Before she knew it, she nutted all in her underwear and they were soaked. He lifted his head up and whispered into her ear, "Come for me!!"

That put things over the top and she said, "I will."

His hands began to move a little faster against her clit and her legs began to shake.

"I'm about to cuu–uuuu–mmmmm," she said as he continued to rub on her clit.

She could feel that she was right there. It was building up and she was about to explode. After about 30 seconds, she was cumin all over his hands. Then, she leaned in for a kiss. As she was cumin', he stuck his fingers inside her and made sure to hit her spot. She nutted again. Then, he pulled his hands out of her pussy and his fingers were dripping wet. He licked his fingers again. She smiled and just lay back on the bed so she could try to catch her breath.

As soon as he stood up, she looked at the bulge in his pants because she wanted it so bad. He pulled his pants down, took her underwear off, and went straight for her clit. His tongue game was serious, and she loved every bit of it. He licked between her pussy lips, making sure he could taste all of her juices. Then he brought his tongue back up to her clit, making

110

circular motions. She was trying her hardest to stay still, but it was impossible.

"Fuck, babe!!" she yelled as she gripped the top of his head. Right there!! Right there!! Don't stop. I'm about to cum all in your mouth."

He felt her grab his head tighter and she started to grind all over his face, while moaning very loud. He knew she was enjoying it and he wasn't going to stop. She was about to lose her mind as her legs and body were shaking uncontrollably.

"Stop...," she tried to push him off of her, but he wouldn't move.

Finally, when she really couldn't take it anymore, he got up, flipped her over, and slid himself inside of her so fast she didn't get a chance to say a word. In and out, he pumped and she couldn't help, but to moan with every pump.

"Damn, I miss this shit," he moaned.

Ebony smiled. "Fuck me!!" she yelled out. "I want to feel all this dick!" He grabbed her hair, arched her back, and went in. "This dick is so good!"

She must have cum like five times in three minutes, throwing it back hard. He couldn't keep up with her as she fucked him. He liked to hear her moans. It drove him crazy. As he was about to cum, he took control arched her back lower, grabbed her hips, and pulled her closer with every pump.

"Shiiittttt!!" she screamed.

She was on the verge of having a huge orgasm and she didn't want him to stop. She could tell he was about to cum because he started going faster and making grunting noises. She came first and he came after her, but didn't pull out. Then, they laid down on the bed together and he held her tight as they fell asleep.

They woke up the next morning in each other's arms. When Ebony opened her eyes, she noticed Haneef was still sleep. So, she went back to sleep, but woke up to her phone ringing.

"You have a collect call from..." Ebony hung up immediately.

Her heart began to beat so fast and she began to break into a sweat.

"What's the matter?" Haneef asked as he sat up.

"I just got another call from him, but I hung up."

"Ok....so, what's the problem?" he asked.

Ebony got up out of the bed and replied, "See, I got this letter the other day and I don't know." She picked up the envelope she received from the courthouse. "All the furniture and the curtains from the window were gone."

"So..." he replied, trying not to sound mad.

"I mean, you have to understand where I'm coming from. There's just a lot of unanswered questions that I need to know."

Haneef just shook his head and said nothing.

"Oh shit!!" Ebony blurted out. "Could you open it for me?"

He grabbed the envelope and opened it. "Well, it looks like a subpoena for you to appear in court against him. Do you have any idea why?" he questioned, making sure to look into her eyes.

"No, not at all. That's why I need to make sure he's not in any serious trouble. I need to make sure that I'm not either. You know I love this man with all my heart and I'm not trying to lose him for nothing. This right here, isn't right," she said, crossing her arms and giving him a sad face.

"What isn't right?" he questioned, trying to figure out what she was talking about.

"This – this isn't supposed to be like this. We were supposed to be living our life together, married, and with children. I know...I know this is just some nightmare that I need to wake up from. Haneef, after everything that's been going on with me and everything I've went through, I'm just thankful that you were here to help me. I honestly don't know what I would have done without you."

Haneef couldn't help the look on his face as he tried to grasp what she had just said. It was like she had been brainwashed and couldn't see what was in front of her face. He just kept quiet because he didn't want to start any arguments. He kind of had her where he wanted her to be and it was just a matter of time before she really realized it. He knew that by staying by her side, he would end up with her. He could see all the hurt and pain and wanted to give her the best, but she couldn't even notice that. What he did was very wrong, but he had no idea what kind of person she was. She was gorgeous and filled with so much potential. He could see why Reef wasn't trying to let her go. Haneef didn't care about him and he knew he was wrong for everything he did, so he wasn't fucking with him anymore.

He was determined that Ebony was going to be his.

TWELVE

The next morning, they woke up in each other's arms. Haneef had spent the night to keep her company and put his plan into action. When she woke up, he had his arms around her and was holding her so close. She loved the feeling and didn't want to get up. He made her feel secure, and he made her feel like a woman. Despite everything that happened, she really liked him and she feltlike she was falling in love with him. That feeling scared her because she had only been in love with Reef and felt as if she still was in love with him.

She did feel like she was somewhat confused and him being around her and taking care of her made her feel different. He just seemed like the perfect man, but there was something that was too good to be true about him. Whatever it was, she needed to find out before she could trust him fully.
She tapped his arm and told him that she needed to get up and get in the shower. He kissed her on the forehead and asked how she slept. Then, they both got up and showered together. What a better way to start the day off right.

Haneef had to go to work, so he asked was there anything she needed from him before he headed out.

"No babe. I'm fine." She leaned in and kissed him. *What is this man doing to me. This was supposed to be just a fling and he has me all in my feelings. Pull yourself together,*

Ebony thought to herself. One thing was for sure and that was she needed to get it together if she was going to go see Reef.

She pulled up to the jail and was scared shitless. She was shaking like crazy and hoped nobody was watching her. She had gotten up to the door and was talking herself through what to do next. Because she was in her head, she didn't hear the guard asking how she could help her.

She was a nervous wreck and it was hard for her to focus on what she was doing. Then, she started dropping things out of her bag. She felt like a damn fool. Part of her wanted to turn around and come back another day, but she was already there.

As she approached the front desk, she managed to get out, "I'm here to visit Shareef Smith."

The guard pointed in the direction she needed to go for visitation and told her to have a seat. Sitting in the room made her feel extremely uncomfortable. She hadn't been around this many people, and she didn't know how to act. Because she felt on edge, she basically started to play musical chairs, which had everyone looking at her as if she were crazy.

In her mind, she felt like she needed to be guarded and not make any eye contact with anyone. Then, the cop called like five names, but she didn't hear Reef's name. Another twenty minutes went by, and the cop called another five names. This time she called Reef's name. Ebony got up and walked over to enter the hallway to the area. When she reached the cop, she gave her the name of who she was there to visit.

"Hold on, honey, he has another visitor," the cop said.

Her face dropped.

She went over to the door and tapped on it to let him know he had another visitor.

Who the fuck is visiting my man?

The door opened. Ebony stood there and made sure she was standing in clear view to see who it was. When the girl came out into the hallway she screamed, "Oh hell no, bitch! What the hell you doing visiting my man?" The girl looked at her and rolled her eyes. "NAKIMA!! I know you hear me talking to you

115

bitch!! What the fuck you doing visiting my man!?" Ebony continued to scream, but the girl did not turn around.

At this point, the guard kept telling her she was going to have to calm down if she wanted to visit anybody. She had caused such a scene that everyone in the hallway was staring at her, which she didn't understand because she knew shit like this happened often.

"Well, what the fuck y'all looking at?"

They all turned their heads and kept moving. When she got into the room, Reef smiled at her as if nothing had happened. She walked in with a face full of disgust because she was so mad.

"What's up, babe? It's so good to see you. You lookin' so good. What you been up to?" he asked with a smirk on his face.

She wished he wasn't behind the glass, so she could slap the shit out of him. "What the fuck was Nakima doing visiting you and how does she know you're here? What? Y'all fucking too?"

"Calm down, babe! First off, what are you talking about Nakima for and why you coming at me so angry? That wasn't Nakima, that was my public defender. Laura."

"Oh, so now you think I'm some dumb bitch, huh!? I know who the fuck I saw and you can't tell me different. That's been my friend for years. You think I don't know what the fuck she looks like? I even went to the old house – which you failed to mention you took everything out of. Funny thing is, she was leaving out of the apartment. Let me guess, you know nothing about that either?" She started to laugh. "You have some explaining to do and you better start now."

"Look, I'm telling you that's not who you saw, so just calm down."

"Why the fuck didn't you tell me you moved everything out? Where was I supposed to stay or you just didn't give a fuck about me because you're fucking this bitch? I'm telling you now, if I find out anything about you and her, I'm gone for good! I'm tired of this shit. Now, all of a sudden, it seems you're acting

116

funny. Reef, I thought it was supposed to be me and you against the world. What happened to that? Just fuck me, right?" She began to cry. "Leave me out for dead. Do what you want to me and I'm still here by your mutha fuckin side. Do you know how many people I could've had that would've treated me way better than you? DO YOU?"

"Babe, calm down. I don't want you to get kicked out."

She took deep breaths and calmed down enough for her to be able to sit down.

"Talk fast because I really don't want to hear anything that's going to come out of your mouth. It's probably all lies anyway!"

"Did you even know I was locked up?"

"I had no clue."

"Well, I think I'm in here for that bitch, Summer. I think she pressed charges against me."

"HMMMM, how the fuck did she press charges against you Reef if you wasn't messing with her? If you weren't around her, how could she just magically get you locked up?"

Reef just sat there and looked at her. He could tell she really didn't care too much. She knew he didn't want to lose her, but the way things were going, it wasn't looking too good.

"You know why I'm leaving you. You playing too many games for me right now and you can't even explain anything to me that makes sense. I thought you was different. What happened to the man, I fell in love with years ago? You turned out to be like everyone else and you're just a fuckin liar! I should've never dealt with you! Now, look at us. Look at you and look at our future. It's all messed up! You do know that nothing will ever be the same between us. It'll never go back to the way it used to be, especially if you keep telling lies. I can't take this shit anymore, Reef! What the fuck do you think I'm supposed to do?"

"Babe, I know this shit is very complicated, but I really can't get into it right now."

"Exactly my point! I think you should be telling me everything that's going on right now. Why did you even want

117

me to come visit you? What? You wanted to see if I still looked the same?"

"Who the fuck you think you talking to?" he said as he stood up. "You real slick with your mouth. You better remember who I am and watch it. Check this out, I have a great chance of beating this case and I wanted to tell you that I love you. I don't know what's gotten into you lately, but I do understand things have been all fucked up. I promise, when I get out of here, we gonna get real right." He blew a kiss and touched the glass. "No more bullshit. I'm going to do right by you and I'ma love you the like I was supposed to a long time ago."

She gave him a little smirk and gave him a phony smile. She was so mad that he had wasted her time and that she even came to visit him anyway. She still didn't get any of the answers she wanted. Her mind began to wander off because she was no longer interested in what he had to say and she almost forgot where she was for a minute.

"Babe!?" Reef yelled, trying to get her attention.

She jumped. "What did you say? I'm sorry. I was just thinking about something and didn't hear you."

"You sure you alright? Is somebody messing with you?" he asked.

"No! I'm ok. I'm just really tired and feeling sick. I think I'm just gonna go home and lay down."

"Where the fuck you going? Who the fuck you staying with?"

"Oh, now you want to know my whereabouts, but didn't want to know them enough for you to give me a place to stay. It's none of your business. Just know that I'm safe and that's all that matters."

"You staying with a nigga? Bitch, don't make me fuck you up, for real. You know I love you. When I get out, I just need you to believe that."

She nodded, hung up the phone, and headed straight to the door. She heard him yell that he was going to call her and to make sure she answered the phone. She damn near ran out the lobby. In her mind, she kept thinking it was a close situation. She became very panicky about him finding out anything that she was doing while he was locked up. She couldn't catch her breath and noticed a group of girls staring, laughing, and pointing at her. That made her anxiety worse as she fumbled to dig in her bag and grab her phone.

She didn't know who they were or why they were laughing, but she didn't like the feeling of being laughed at. She almost tripped and fell, but was able to grab her phone and call Haneef. She was breathing so fast. She knew she sounded crazy, but felt unsafe and wanted him to come get her. She didn't feel like she could do anything at this point and it was scary.. He didn't like how she sounded either. Very concerned, he told her to stay where she was at and he would get to her as soon as he could.

She sat at the bus stop for a minute, but still felt that people were looking at her, so she decided to move and walk down the street. She was in such a daze that she hadn't noticed Haneef beeping the horn at her. He hopped out of the car and called her name, but she didn't hear him. Then, he ran up to her and tried to tap her on her shoulder. She still didn't turn around. He managed to stand in front of her and call her name.

She snapped out of it. "Haneef? How long have you been standing there?"

It seemed like she had blacked out or had been completely out of it.

"You ok, babe? You're not looking so good. Let me take you back home."

Ebony just shook her head and got into the car.

THIRTEEN

Ebony didn't know what happened to her over the past couple of months, but she felt as if her life was falling apart. . She cooped herself up in the house and didn't move out of the bed. She didn't even want to answer the phone because it would ring several times a day. For some reason, she just felt like isolating herself. She felt fear.....estranged from the world.

Haneef had taken her out of the hotel and moved her into one of the empty rooms in his house. He would come check on her periodically, but she was out of it. Some days, she wouldn't even answer the door when he would knock, but he made sure she had food.

When she was a teen, she used to have the same feelings, but she didn't know what she was feeling exactly. She didn't know how to describe the feeling if anyone asked her. Sometimes, after time would pass, the feelings would go away, but they would always come back. What she did know was that events from her past were very traumatizing and it would cause her to black out .

Now, she would wake up from her sleep screaming out and begging for help. Haneef was very concerned and he would offer to stay with her to make her feel better, but she always turned him away. It was a huge disappointment to him because he didn't know how to handle the situation, but he did want her to go get checked by a doctor.

120

Ebony knew that was not going to happen. She couldn't even get herself up and out of the house. Hell, she couldn't even walk to the front door. She just felt like someone was out to get her and trying to kidnap her. She knew she needed to shake this feeling and get herself together because she knew the court date was coming up. She needed to have a clear head. She knew she had to talk to someone or at least let Haneef know about her past for him to actually understand.

Haneef knocked on the door. She didn't say anything, but this time, he opened the door slowly. When he walked in, she looked at him, gave him eye contact, but didn't say a word.

"Babe, I have something to eat for you. I need you to sit up and eat. I'm very worried about you, and I just want you to let me help you." He walked over to the bed and put the tray down. Then, he went over to the curtains and opened them to let some light in the room. "Look at you. You have to get up!"

She just looked at him and nodded her head. He had some soup and a sandwich, which was her favorite. He sat down and placed the spoon up to her mouth so she could sip the soup he cooked. He fed it all to her, kissed her on the forehead, and wiped her mouth with the napkin. Then, he got up, walked into the bathroom ran her water for a bath, and walked back to her to get her prepared for a bath. He helped her stand up, took off all of her clothes, and led her to the bathtub.

Although Ebony didn't feel like doing anything, she knew his bath would be so soothing and she loved them, so she didn't put up a fight. He took her hair out of the ponytail and ran his fingers through her tangled hair. His touch sent tingles all down her body and she bit her bottom lip. Then, he poured water on her hair with a cup he had brought to the bathroom with him.

"Babe, I'll be right back. I forgot something in the other room."

Ebony didn't respond. Weird thoughts came to her mind, and she blacked out. She woke up to Haneef holding her head above the water and asking if she was ok. He grabbed the towel, picked her up, and brought her into the room. He had changed the sheets on the bed and made it up for her. He didn't want to leave her side, but somehow she managed to ask for a minute so she could get dressed.

What the fuck am I doing? What the fuck is Haneef thinking about me? Why am I questioning so much. Ebony, girl, get it together, she thought to herself. She grabbed her phone and looked at it. There were over a hundred missed calls and messages, but she didn't want to hear anything because she already knew who it was.

She didn't want that same feeling she felt before of feeling as if he was controlling her life. She had to remind herself that she was safe and she felt secure deep down inside. That's what mattered the most. That was what was going to help her get over whatever it was she was going through at that very moment. She dialed a number, but hung up really fast. She dialed the number again and the phone started to ring.

"Hello..."

"Hello..." Ebony replied.

"Are you ok? You don't sound too good," Sheree said.

"I – I need help!. I don't know what's happening to me and I feel like I'm losing my mind. Sheree, please. I really need to talk to someone and I don't need you to judge me right now."

"Cut it out. I'm not a little kid and I would never do that. Like I told you before...you're my sister!"

Ebony began to cry just from the thought of how they were back in the day. "I just miss us and I miss the way thing used to be. I can't believe I let a man come between us like this – a man that wasn't shit at the end of the day. A man who I thought was the one for me and turned out to be the opposite. I was just so happy for you guys that I wanted to have the things you had! Don't get me wrong, I love this man with all my heart and that will never change. I still see a future with him. It's just some things need to be worked out and I believe we would be fine. The things he put me through... I believe they were all worth it."

Sheree began to get confused with what she was saying because she was rambling in and out of her feelings, but she still let her vent.

"And fuck that bitch, Nakima, too. Can you believe this bitch came out here and she didn't even tell me? I found her coming out of my man's apartment when I went over there to grab some stuff and the bitch had an attitude. She lied too and said she was looking for me, but I didn't tell her where I lived. If I found out what I think is going on, I'm gonna kill that bitch!"

"Wait. What's going on?" Sheree questioned. "What is this about Nakima? What in the hell is she doing there? Hmmmmm, something seems strange about that."

"It does. I also saw her coming out of the visiting room in the jail. So, you tell me if you think something is going on?

"Wait – now this is too much for me to process right now. Reef is locked up? Why? What the fuck is really going on over there?" Sheree was concerned.

"I know it's a lot. I just been dealing with it all right now by myself. Reef and his baby mother. Reef putting his hands on me. Him being in jail right now, which left me with having nowhere to live."

"Why didn't you tell me all of this before!" she questioned.

"Let me ask you something. Do you know anything about Nakima and Reef that you aren't telling me?"

"Well, what I do know is that her and Micah were having problems and he left her. That's about it. I may have to ask Lateef because this is some crazy shit and I really don't want to believe that she would do something like this to you."

Ebony got quiet and just hung up. She texted her the address and told her that if she was a real friend, she would come see her.

Oh shit, I told her the whole story and I didn't want her to really know that. What the fuck did I just do? What the fuck!!

Ebony began to bang her head against the wall, but stopped when she noticed Haneef standing there looking at her.

"What the fuck is happening to me? What the fuck!?" Ebony yelled and began to break down.

Haneef ran over to her and hugged her tightly. He whispered in her ear that everything was going to be alright and that he would never leave her side. He also told her that his love was real and that he loved her and wanted to be with her.

She just looked at him. She was confused because she truly didn't understand why he loved her so much, but she felt that she loved him too. She leaned in for a kiss, but it was interrupted by Sheree calling her back.

She didn't answer. She felt as though she had told her more than enough. Plus, she would be able to tell if she was a real friend or not in a couple of days. She knew she had to tell Haneef that she had given his address out. When she told him, he assured her that he was ok with it. He was happy that she was actually talking and snapped out of the dark place she had gone to.

Ebony wanted to believe that she was back to normal. She wanted to believe that she didn't need any help, but once Sheree came, she insisted that I be evaluated. Haneef felt the same way, and there was no talking them out of it. It felt so good to have a support system to help her through this difficult time. She couldn't have asked for anything better at this moment, and she knew she needed to get better to face this monster once and for all. She had to get strong enough so she would be able to walk in that court room.

Just staring at the front of this place brought back so many memories. She hadn't stepped foot in the door and she was already crying and shaking uncontrollably. She kept thinking about the times she was admitted into the hospital and almost died.

"I can't do this. Guys. I can't do this." They had to practically drag her into the waiting room. "Guys, I'm serious. I can't do this." Ebony started to breath heavy and hyperventilate.

"Nurse!! Nurse!!" Sheree called out. "We need help over here. Please, somebody help! She can't breathe!" she screamed.

They all came running over to Ebony just as she was about to pass out. They hooked her up to an oxygen machine and got an IV started. Haneef didn't leave her side. He stood right there and rubbed her head.

"Baby, I'm here. I'm not going anywhere. I will be here every step of the way!"

She ended up being admitted. She never would have thought she'd be sitting here staring at these four walls – again. This wasn't any way to treat a person or help anyone get better. She knew she had to get out of there.

Am I really that bad that I needed to see a psychiatrist? If I stay in this place, I'm definitely going to go insane.

She knew she needed to pull it together and get out of there right away. She knew how to trick the system. She knew how to act as if she was fine because she grew up doing it every day of her life.

Believe it or not, Ebony had spent four days in the hospital and had slept really well. She had started to feel like herself again. Her doctor came in to talk to her and she told him she was ready to go home. He agreed that she was ready to be discharged and informed her that he would put in the request to have her discharged tomorrow. That was music to Ebony's ears and she couldn't wait to call Haneef.

"Guess what? I'm coming home tomorrow. So, I need you to pick me up first thing in the morning."

"That's good news because I have missed you like crazy. You kind of scared the shit out of me. Like, I never seen anything like that in my life before. I'm really happy. I can tell by your voice that you feel much better."

"I had a lot of time to think while I was in here and I really miss you, too."

They hung up the phone.

She decided that she wouldn't call Sheree right now.

The next morning Haneef was there waiting for her like he said he would. They hugged and kissed each other like it was the first time, all over again.

Wow, Ebony thought to herself.

They got into the car, went to get some food, and went straight home. After they fucked in every room in the house, they just laid in each other's arms. She never knew that she would ever feel this way about another man so fast. However, there was still a little part of her that still thought about Reef. She couldn't shake the feeling that this was supposed to be her and Reer and that she still loved him some type of way, but she wouldn't dare tell Haneef that.

"So, you ready for this court date tomorrow?" he asked.

"Ummm, I think so. I'm just a little scared because I haven't been communicating with him, and I don't have any idea as to what's going on. I haven't seen this man in a couple of months. To be honest, I really don't think I want to." In the back of her mind, she really did want to see his face. "You know that you can't go in there with me. He would kill us both if he found out we were together."

Haneef looked at her with a serious face. "Why do you care if he knows that you're with me?

"I – I don't really care. It's just that we've been doing a good job keeping us low-key, and I want to keep it that way. I don't want anyone snooping around and giving us any problems. Remember how I told you about the girl named Nakima? I don't trust her and I need to find out what she is up to."

"Ok, fine. You want me to wait for you outside. No problem," he said, looking disappointed.

She gave him the biggest kiss. "Thanks, babe," she said as she laid her head on his chest.

FOURTEEN

"I can do this!! I can do this!!" Ebony said to herself as she stared into the bathroom mirror. "I can face this mothafucka."

She walked out the bathroom, put on her shoes, and headed to the car.

"You ready, babe?" Haneef asked as he held her hand.

"Yes!" she said with so much confidence, but she was really shaking and trying to hold herself together.

When she walked into the building, she tried to stop herself from hyperventilating. *Just chill. Everything is going to be alright,* she told herself.

She found an officer at the front desk and asked her where she was supposed to be going. The officer was able to point her in the right direction and told her to head up the elevator. When Ebony got off the elevator on the 7th floor, it was very quiet and eerie. Before she could gather her thoughts, a public defender noticed her and immediately ran over to her.

"Is your name Ebony Harris?"

"Yes, sir."

"Good. Come over here and have a seat with me. How are you?" he asked."

"I'm fine. Just a little nervous," she chuckled.

"Well, Ms. Harris, you have been summoned to appear and testify against Shareef Smith. Do you know this man?"

"Yes sir. He's my boyfriend."

"Oh, so you guys are currently dating now?"

"Yes! Why do you ask?"

"Right now, he is being charged with domestic violence. Has he ever put his hands on you?"

"Of course not!" she replied very loudly!!

"Well, ma'am, I'm afraid to say that you have been called to testify because you were a witness to a crime that he committed."

"What crime? What are you talking about?" she questioned.

"Do you know a Summer Johnson?"

"Summer – I do know of someone name Summer, but what does she have to do with Shareef?"

"She is the one who's pressing the charges and had the subpoena sent to you for you to testify."

Ebony began to laugh profusely, and the public defender couldn't understand what was so funny to her.

"This is crazy! Summer is pressing charges against Shareef?" she asked loudly and started laughing again. "This bitch just doesn't know how to stay in her lane for nothing. She done fucked up now and I don't want any parts of what she is about to put herself in. Ok, what is it I have to do?"

"You need to testify, tell everything that you know, and tell everything that's going on."

"Ok...."

"So, you ready? He asked.

"Right now? Holy shit!! I'm not ready right now!!" Ebony's hands began to sweat and she became nervous. She felt as if she were going to pass out. "Just give me a minute!"

Ebony started to take long, deep breaths and count to 10. She stood up and walked into the courtroom. As soon as she walked in, she spotted Reef, and he gave her a look of surprise. She licked her lips because he looked sexy as fuck in his blue suit. He had some weight on him. Ebony started to fall in love all over again.

He blew her a kiss and then he motioned his hand under his neck and moved it from one side to the other. She opened her mouth wide and almost started to cry. Immediately, she turned her head. That's when she noticed Nakima sitting behind Reef to the left of him.

"Bitch, what the fuck you doing here?" Ebony blurted out, completely forgetting where she was. "If you fuckin' my man, you need to tell me right now and we can handle this as soon as we get out of here."

"Miss please!!" the judge yelled out. "If you can't compose yourself, you will be escorted out of the room. Do I make myself clear?"

"Yes," Ebony replied and rolled her eyes.

"The first person I would like to call to the stand is, Ms. Summer Johnson."

Summer stood up, walked to the witness stand, and took a seat. As the lawyer began to ask her questions, she couldn't help but make eye contact with Reef. He gave her the evilest look, but she paid it no mind. Summer was going to make sure she told everything to the tee. She wanted him to pay for what he did and she wasn't going to lie for anyone. When the lawyer was done with his questions, she got up and walked back to her seat.

"Next person I would like to call to the stand is Ms. Ebony Harris."

Ebony walked up quickly and took her seat. The lawyer began to ask her a series of questions and made sure to look her directly in the eyes. She denied him ever putting his hands on her or him being the cause of being admitted into the hospital."

She looked over at Summer, who was shaking her head in disgust. Then, she looked over to Reef, and he had a high smile on his face.

"That's all the questions I have for you."

Ebony stood up and walked out the courtroom into the hallway. She noticed Nakima was standing there and blurted out, "What the fuck you got going on with my man?"

Nakima looked her up and down and said, "That's my man now, bitch. You fucked up and you better stay out of our way. He doesn't want your sorry ass anymore. Just look at you. Who would want you?"

Ebony couldn't believe the words that were coming out of her mouth. It was if they were never friends. *How could she betray me like this? Like how? Why? She could've at least come to me woman to woman,* Ebony thought to herself.

Ebony lost control and punched her in the face. She beat the shit out of her as if she were some random girl on the street. Eventually, she blacked out and woke up in handcuffs.

"What's going on?" she said as she tried to get out of the cuffs. "LET ME THE FUCK OUT OF THESE THINGS RIGHT NOW!" she screamed, but it seemed as if no one was listening. She stood up and peeked through the window inside the cell. "HELP. I SAID LET ME THE FUCK OUT OF HERE!!" She began to panic and started kicking the door.

Several officers came running. They opened the door and told her she needed to calm down and keep quiet.

"I need to know why I'm here. What's going on? Y'all assholes aren't telling me anything."

"Ma'am, first of all, we need you to lower your voice and don't curse."

"WELL, ANSWER MY FUCKIN QUESTIONS AND MAYBE I WONT BE SO UPSET!!"

"Ma'am, we're going to ask you one more time to lower your voice."

She just rolled her eyes because she noticed that yelling wasn't going to get her anywhere. The officer explained that she was being held until they were able to book her.

"WAIT! Book me for what?

"Ma'am, you're being charged with simple assault."

"Simple what?"

"You attacked a young girl in the hallway and you're being charged with simple assault."

Ebony was very confused and couldn't remember what had happened. "No, that can't be right!" She said, shaking her head. "You guys got it all wrong. I think she was the one that attacked me."

"Well, ma'am, that's something you're going to have to take up in court."

"In court? I'm really going to jail?" she asked as she started to get teary-eyed. "I didn't even do anything. You guys can't do that! I'MA NEED YOU TO LET ME OUT OF HERE RIGHT AWAY."

They just looked at her and laughed.

Ebony was out of it. "Can I make a phone call?"

One officer replied, "Yes," and walked her over to the phone.

She sat there for a minute to gather her thoughts.

"Come on, ma'am! You don't have all day."

She rolled her eyes and gave the officer Haneef's number. The phone rang once and then he picked up.

"Hello?"

"Haneef, you have to help me, please! Please! I need you to come pick me up. They are trying to lock me up!"

"You know I love you, babe. If I could, I would be there in a heartbeat, and you know that, but there is nothing I can do for you right now. You lost control – at least that's the story I was told when I realized you didn't come out of the building. I will be there to see you first thing in the morning! Just hang tight, babe. I love you."

Ebony hung up the phone.

"Ms. Harris, let's go. NOW!!" the male officer yelled as Ebony stood there frozen in time. *This isn't really happening to me, is it? It can't be,* she thought to herself.

Ebony was dragging her feet in fear. You know how you always hear stories about jail and watch them on TV, but you never actually wanted to be the one in that situation.

Well, she was.

The officer walked her over to take fingerprints and mugshots. She still couldn't believe this was really happening to her. Then, the officer handed her a pair of sneakers, shower shoes, and a navy-blue jumpsuit. In a snarky tone, he quickly let her know that navy was the color of the jumpsuits for new intakes as she looked on in concern.

Her eyes started to water, but she didn't let out any tears because she didn't want to show weakness. As she stood there, the officer exchanged places with a female officer. She took Ebony into a room and had her strip naked so she could thoroughly search her. The officer smiled at her awkwardly when she turned around, and it made her feel so uncomfortable.

"Would I be able to make another phone call?" Ebony asked.

" I'm afraid, at this point, you'll have to wait until the morning."

Ebony put her head down and began to put on the jumpsuit she was given. She got dressed and, just like that, she was a criminal.

Of course, it was late so most of the inmates were sleeping. *How the fuck did I get myself into this? All I wanted to do was wake up from this bad dream and forget this happened,* she thought to herself. Her mind was totally blank. She was numb. She didn't know what it was, but she was just unable to process all these chains of events in their entirety.

Completely overwhelmed, she made her way inside and followed the officer with her head down. Out of the corner of her eye, she could see some of the inmates blowing kisses and calling out to her.

After what seemed like an eternity, the officer finally arrived at an empty cell. *Thank god it was empty. All I needed was to have a "roommate" and becomes someone's bitch,* she thought to herself.

She walked in, quickly spread her blanket out onto the bunk, and climbed in. Then, she turned her back to the cell, stared at the wall, and the tears began to flow. She was unsure of herself and not able to fully think properly.

How the fuck was I ever going to get any sleep? Ebony felt like her life was over, and there was no one who could help her at this moment. A feeling of helplessness and despair had taken over her because of all that had happened. It was taking a toll on her. She just lay there and cried. She wished this were all a bad dream and that she didn't wake up in the morning.

All she could do was cry herself to sleep.

www.ingramcontent.com/pod-product-compliance
Lightning Source LLC
Chambersburg PA
CBHW071926220626
47052CB00002B/475